D1646389

3 80

THE

LAST

ASTRONAUT

DAVID
WELLINGTON

www.orbitbooks.net

ORBIT

First published in Great Britain in 2019 by Orbit

13 5 7 9 10 8 6 4 2

A CIP catalogue record for this book
is available from the British Library.

ISBN 978-0-356-51229-7

Printed and bound in Great Britain by
Clays Ltd, Elcograf S.p.A.

Papers used by Orbit are from well-managed forests
and other responsible sources.

Orbit
An imprint of
Little, Brown Book Group
Carmelite House
50 Victoria Embankment
London EC4Y 0DZ

An Hachette UK Company
www.hachette.co.uk

www.orbitbooks.net

For Jennifer,
who always brings me home

PERIAREION

I t's a grand old flag, it's a high-flying flag..."

"The crew of *Orion* wish you back on Earth a happy and safe Fourth of July. We may not be able to set off any fireworks out here, for safety reasons, but we want everybody to know we haven't forgotten what this day means to America."

"That's right, Blaine. And here on *Orion*, we have two reasons to celebrate. Today we passed the orbit of the moon. Today we can officially announce that the four of us have now traveled farther than any human beings in history."

"USA! USA!"

"That's Mission Specialist Ali Dinwari holding the flag we're going to plant on Mars in just a few short months. Next to me here is Flight Surgeon Blaine Wilson, who's keeping us all healthy—"

"Keep it up, keep it up, twelve more minutes and then you can have a hot dog!"

"Blaine's a cruel taskmaster, but it's true—you see Science Specialist Julia Obrador back there on the treadmill, she's waving for the camera. We have to exercise for two hours a day each because there's no gravity on *Orion*. We need to keep our bones in good shape so when we get there, we can walk on Mars instead of crawling."

"You forgot to introduce yourself, Sally."

"Right! Good thing you're here to remind me, Blaine. I'm Sally Jansen, mission commander—"

"Gonna be the first woman to walk on Mars, what what!"

"—Ha, yeah—mission commander on *Orion 6*. We're going to finish this exciting special meal of hot dogs and fruit punch, and then we're going to get back to work. But we couldn't let the day go by without letting America—and everyone on Earth—know that we're—"

"...And forever in peace may you wave!"

"—right on course, headed for a historic moment on the red soil of Mars. Happy Fourth, everybody!"

"OK, *Orion*. Returning to normal communications. Great job up there—the media people are all smiling, which is a good sign."

"Thanks, Houston." Commander Jansen looked back at her crew and gave them a thumbs-up.

"You got it," Ground Control said. "Though—I'm getting a message. It looks like Julia has been neglecting her social media. Remember, you all need to post at least three times a day. If people back on Earth don't hear from you regularly, they start to worry about your mental health. It looks bad."

"Obrador?" Jansen asked.

"I'll do better, just...Jesus. Can I get off this thing?"

Blaine Wilson gave Obrador a nasty grin. "Another nine minutes."

Jansen shook her head, though. There was work to be done. "Forget it, you're done—and don't worry about InstaChat, either, we've got things to do. Wilson, I don't want to hear about it. Houston, this is Jansen, this is MC. Have you found an explanation for that anomalous reading I told you about? On my board I still have a red flag for blowthrough pressure in the number six fuel tank on the excursion module."

"*Orion*, we're assuming it's some kind of faulty relay. Those systems are all locked down for this part of the mission. Blowthrough was never requested, so there's no reason for a red flag, or any kind of flag. Everything else looks good, it has to just be a glitch."

"It's been showing red since we finished our orbital transfer burn. I don't like it, Houston. Maybe I'm being paranoid, but—"

"It's your call, MC. You tell me what you want to do."

Jansen glanced around the HabLab at her crew. They were in good shape, a little pumped from having a chance to call home, even if it was just a recorded message. "This is a good time to check it out. I'm asking for authorization for an EVA so I can evaluate the tank with my own eyes. We good?"

"You have authorization for EVA. Just be careful, MC."

"Understood, Houston."

SALLY JANSEN, ASTRONAUT: Are we really doing this? I don't want to talk about that day. I...OK. OK. Back then, NASA had us do pressers and media ops constantly. I mean, all the time. The Orion program cost billions, and they felt they needed to show American taxpayers what they were getting for their money. They wanted us all to be rock stars, to be TV people. I was never comfortable with that. Jesus. Can we take a minute? Just a minute, let me collect myself. The thing you have to understand is that July fourth, 2034, was the worst day of my life.

Wrestling into the extravehicular activity suits was hard enough in the close confines of the HabLab; climbing through the soft lock afterward was enough to leave Jansen breathing heavily. The HabLab module—where the astronauts lived and worked—was a seventeen-meter-long inflated cylinder made of two flexible walls with the ship's water supply circulating between them. The water kept the habitat cool or warm as necessary, and provided shielding from the radiation environment of deep space, but the module bounced and shook every time you shoved against it, like an air mattress, in a way that did not inspire confidence.

The habitat's airlock was a narrow fabric tube that you had to wriggle through in slow motion, every twist and turn careful and premeditated so you didn't snag any of your space suit's hard parts on the thin walls. One tear in the soft lock and they would have to scrub the EVA until it could be repaired.

Somehow she managed to climb out onto the side of the module, where she helped Julia, the mission's science specialist, make the same transition. Obrador's face was white as a sheet behind her polycarbonate faceplate, with sweat beaded across her forehead. She gave Jansen a nervous laugh and clutched the ship as if afraid she would fall off. It was no surprise she was nervous—Obrador had done plenty of EVAs in simulators, but had never actually been outside the ship since it left Earth. Jansen patted her on the arm to reassure her.

Hell, Jansen wasn't exactly frosty herself. Around them the universe stretched off in every direction, empty and dark. Jansen fought down a sensation of vertigo. This time was different, she thought. Different from all the EVAs she'd done on the Deep Space Gateway station while she'd trained for this mission. It took her a second to realize why.

There was nothing below her. Nothing on either side, nothing above her... nothing at all, just nothingness... forever.

In space, in microgravity, there were technically no such things as up and down. Yet human brains were so well adapted to gravity that you couldn't think like that, you couldn't ever accept it. It had been easier on the space station because the Earth was there, enormous and bright. The curve of the planet was down, your brain could accept that. It could learn to accept that you were flying, that the ground wasn't rushing up to meet you, because there was a down to point to. Not anymore.

Fifteen days out and the Earth was behind them, bigger than any star but far enough away that it offered no psychological relief. Jansen's head started to spin as it tried desperately to find a reference frame—and failed.

"There's always something to hold on to," she told Obrador, who nodded gratefully. "You never have to let go, OK? Just grab something and hold tight."

Inside her helmet, Jansen's voice sounded small and tinny, as if she were hearing herself over the radio. As if it were somebody else offering this good advice.

She looked at *Orion*, at the spacecraft, and somehow found her bearings. There were four modules in her ship, each with its own function. At the back was the service module, which housed the ship's main engine and its fuel supply. Forward of that was the conical command module, the only part of the ship that would go back to Earth once they were done on Mars. The long cylinder of the HabLab was wrapped in an insulating shroud of quilted silver fabric, dazzling in the sun, and then at the far end, pointed right at Mars, was the spherical excursion module, with its landing legs sticking out in front of it like the antennae of a bug. The lander that would set down on the red dust and was where she and Ali would live in close quarters for two weeks while they collected rocks and took meteorological readings.

That was still months away. If she couldn't find the source of the fault, if everything looked fine but the red flag persisted, she knew it was going to irritate her for the rest of the mission. Best to get it cleared up now.

"Hand over hand," she told Obrador as she climbed the side of the habitat module, pulling herself along. "Little by little." She had to be careful not to go too fast, or she might launch herself right off the side of the ship. She wouldn't go far—her safety line would catch her—but she had no desire to find out what that felt like.

"Understood," Obrador replied.

Her helmet radio crackled and spit at her. Just noise on the channel, probably cosmic rays, charged particles hitting her transceiver as they blasted through the solar system at nearly the speed of light. If she closed her eyes right now she knew she would see green pinwheels of fire spinning behind her eyelids. They were exposed out here, practically naked to the invisible energies that filled what looked like empty space. But as long as they were back inside within an hour, they should be all right.

"Wilson, I want you to crack open the excursion module," she called. "I need your eyes on the inside to help me trace this problem."

"Understood," the flight surgeon called back.

"Where do you want me?" Dinwari asked.

"You head down to the command module and strap yourself in." He could keep an eye on their suit telemetry from there, and run the entire ship if he needed to. Putting him back there was just a safety measure, but NASA loved safety measures most of all. "I'm not seeing any damage to the exterior of the spacecraft. That's good. Obrador, how are you doing?"

"All good," Obrador called back. "You think this is a wiring problem? The bus that connects the . . . the excursion module and . . . the . . ."

She could hear the fatigue in Obrador's voice. Every move you made in a space suit was exhausting. They might be weightless, but they still had mass, and every movement, every meter forward meant wrestling with the bulky gear. "Don't try to talk. Save your breath for the climb."

"Thought there would be . . . stars," Obrador said, ignoring her.

Jansen looked out at the black sky around them, the empty stretch of black velvet that could feel so close sometimes it was smothering you and at other times made you feel as if you were dangling over a bottomless pit. "You don't see stars out here for the same reason you don't see stars on a clear day back on Earth," she said. "The sun's light drowns them out." A wave of fatigue ran through her muscles, and Jansen stopped for a moment, stopped where she was and just . . . breathed.

When she'd recovered enough she started climbing forward again. She was almost level with the excursion module. "Blaine, do you have the forward lock open yet?"

"Just about," Blaine called back. "I'm equalizing air pressure between the excursion module and the habitat. It's taking a minute."

"No way to rush it," she told him. "OK. I've reached the number six fuel tank. I'm going to start a visual inspection." A broad, flat belt of metal ran around the excursion module where it mated with the HabLab. The fuel tanks hung off that belt like a ring of bells, each of them nestled in a tangle of pipes and wiring.

The tanks on the lander were separate from *Orion*'s main fuel system—they would be tapped only when the crew was ready to return from Mars. The hydrazine propellant inside them would be used to launch the lander back into Mars orbit, where it would reconnect with the HabLab and the command module for the trip home. For this outer leg of the journey those tanks were completely shut down and inert. They shouldn't be showing up on her control panels at all, much less reporting a low-pressure condition. It was a real mystery.

She could see most of the tanks from where she was, and they all looked fine. Some of them were obscured by the shadow of *Orion*'s big solar panels, though, and number six just had to be one of those. She sighed and switched on the lights mounted on her helmet. "Wilson, how are we coming along in there? I'll need you to crack open the FPI inspection panel."

"Uh," Wilson said, "FPI?"

"Fuel pressure indicator," Jansen said. NASA loved its acronyms, and there were a lot of them to remember. "The sensors are indicating that this fuel tank has lost pressure, which doesn't make any sense. I want you to open up the FPI panel and check the wiring in there, to make sure it isn't the sensor that's broken. There should be a diagram inside the panel showing how things are supposed to look. Just make sure the wires all match the diagram."

"I'm in the excursion module now," he told her. "I'm waving, can you see me?"

She wasn't close enough to any of the lander's tiny viewports to look inside. "Don't worry about me, I've got my own job to do out here. I—"

She stopped speaking. Everything went into slow motion. What she'd seen, what her light revealed—

"Boss?" Obrador asked from behind her.

Jansen licked her suddenly dry lips.

This was bad.

Number six tank was cracked. A big, jagged hole had opened up where it connected to the side of the module. Maybe a micrometeor had struck the tank, or maybe a piece of space debris. Either way it looked as if someone had fired a rifle bullet right through it.

She saw a pool of wetness all around the damaged area, a round, wobbling mass of liquid hydrazine adhering with surface tension to the excursion module's skin.

Then she saw bubbles form and pop in the middle of the glob of fuel. Air bubbles. Air that had to be coming from inside the spaceship. There had to be a leak—the same impact that tore open the tank must have cut right through the hull of the module. Hydrazine was leaking into the crew compartment of the excursion module. The module that they had just filled up with air. With oxygen.

"Wilson," she called. "Blaine, get out of there—"

"There's a funny smell in here," Blaine said, as if he couldn't hear her. As if she were in one of those nightmares where you shouted at someone to stop, to turn around and see the monster right behind them, but they couldn't hear you at all. "Kind of like cleaning fluid, maybe left over from when they sealed this module up. It's an ammonia-y kind of smell."

He was smelling raw hydrazine. Raw rocket fuel, which had aerosolized and filled the tiny module. He was standing in a cloud of flammable gas.

GARTH UDAHL, ORION PROGRAM FUEL TECHNOLO-GIES SUPERVISOR: Hydrazine is very hazardous stuff. It's a simple chemical, but it's incredibly corrosive. The smallest amount, if you breathe it in, can burn the lining of your lungs. It can also self-ignite, given the proper catalyst. Say a patch of rust on the inside of a panel. It's my opinion that once Dr. Wilson entered that module, he never stood a chance.

"Wilson!" she screamed. "Move!"

She pulled herself along the side of the excursion module, pulled herself level with one of the viewports.

"Boss?" Obrador asked again. "What's going on?"

Through the viewport Jansen could see him burning. Hydrazine flames were invisible, but she could see Blaine smashing his arms against the consoles, trying to put out the flames. She could see his hair curl and turn black, could see his mouth open in a horrifying silent scream. He reached toward the viewport, reaching for her. Begging her for help.

Some cosmic mercy had killed his radio. She couldn't hear him, didn't have to listen to him burn. She saw him slam his hand against the viewport, over and over, maybe he was trying to break it, to get out, to get away from the fire—

In a second that fire was going to spread through the hatch. It would spread down into the HabLab. It could spread through the whole spacecraft. It wouldn't stop until it had consumed everything.

Somebody had to get the hatches closed, to contain it. But the only person close enough to do that was Wilson.

There was another way.

Sally Jansen had trained for a million different ways things could go wrong in space. She had drilled endlessly for every possible contingency. She knew exactly what to do in this case. It was right there in her brain, ready to access. All she had to do was open her mouth and say it.

If the two modules separated, their hatches would automatically slam shut. It was a safety feature.

It was the hardest thing she had done in her life. But she was an astronaut.

"Dinwari," she said. "Ali, can you hear me? Jettison the excursion module."

"Commander?" he asked, his voice very small. He might as well be back on Earth, shouting at her through a megaphone.

"Do it!" she said.

"I can't! Wilson's in there!"

Jansen had no time to waste arguing. She scrambled along the side of the excursion module, moving as fast as she dared. She found an access panel between two fuel tanks and tore it open. Inside was a lever painted bright red, marked *CAUTION: EMERGENCY RELEASE*.

She pulled it, hard.

Explosive bolts connecting the excursion module to the HabLab detonated instantly, one of them going off right in her face. Light burst all around her and she was blinded for a second—a very bad second, during which she heard her faceplate start to crack. The explosion threw her bodily away from the module, swinging out into deep space on her tether, out of control and tumbling.

She could barely see anything as she went flying head over heels. She got only a glimpse of her spaceship coming to pieces.

A billowing cloud of condensing water vapor jetted outward from between the two modules, air rushing out of the HabLab. The cloud was cut off instantly as the hatches between the two modules slammed shut.

The excursion module tumbled as it accelerated away from the HabLab. The flexible habitat module sprang back and forth in an obscene motion that Jansen barely saw. She was spinning, spinning out to the end of her safety line, and then it snapped taut and she doubled up, her arms and legs flailing. She grabbed at the line and tried to stabilize herself, tried to get a grip as she looked back over her shoulder.

The excursion module was still moving, still flying away from them, tumbling wildly into empty space, its landing legs whipping around crazily.

Hands grabbed the shoulder joints of her suit, hands that pressed down and pushed her against the side of the HabLab, her cracked faceplate buried in the silver fabric even as ice crystals started growing across her view.

It was Obrador, crouching on top of her, protecting her from the debris that pelted the side of the HabLab all around her.

"Boss! What did you do?" Obrador screamed, but Jansen barely heard her. "What did you *do*?"

There was only one thought in her brain.

Jesus, God, whoever, please. Let Blaine die fast.

SALLY JANSEN: No. No. Stop—that's a lie. That isn't what I was thinking at all. I . . . I'm not proud of this, but if we're doing this, if we're going to be honest . . . my thought at that particular moment was just, you know. This is over. This is it. I'm never going to Mars.

TELEMETRY CHECK

EXCERPT FROM AUTHOR'S FOREWORD TO THE 2057 EDITION OF *THE LAST ASTRONAUT*, BY DAVID WELLINGTON

It's my firm opinion that you can't understand what happened later unless you know what she was thinking, what she was feeling, that day in 2034.

When I was hired to write about the events of October 2055, I was told we needed to get the story on people's streams as soon as humanly possible. The public needed to know what had happened and what it meant. I was able to fulfill at least one of those goals. I did the research and put together a thing that looked like a novel and read like the instruction manual for an X-ray machine. The technical information was there, and the facts that were a matter of public record. Nobody understood what any of it signified, though. I didn't understand, myself. I'm not sure I fully understand it now.

I've been lucky enough to receive a lot of new information since then. Most importantly, I was given exclusive access to interview the people involved. I've included snippets from those interviews in the text of this new edition. I've also included the brief examination of the last day of the Orion 6 mission that you've just read. I think it may be the key that unlocks the true meaning of what happened during the mission of Orion 7.

*But I've gone further than that. This is no longer a piece of jour-
nalism, no longer just a recitation of facts. I've tried to explore the
psychology of the people who were there, even when this is, for various reasons, no longer possible. In many ways Sally Jansen's 2055
mission was not just an exploration of objects in space, but also a
journey into the human mind. I feel the story is better for these intro-
spections. You can judge for yourself.*

*Our story picks up twenty-one years later, when only one man
in the entire world knew what was happening. I've done my best to
examine what he was thinking, that day he jumped out of bed and
onto a train.*

Sunny Stevens pulled at the drawstrings of his hoodie. He wished
he'd thought to change his clothes before he crossed half the country for this meeting. It had all been so last minute... When NASA
actually answered his message, he'd basically just walked out the
door. He'd never actually expected this to happen, and he hadn't
thought to prepare.

Now it was time to make an actual decision. He could still walk
away—say he was sorry, but he'd made a mistake. Take the train
all night to get home and go to bed and pretend he'd never even
thought of this crazy plan. Go back to work tomorrow at the Hive
and hope nobody was monitoring his email.

Or he could go through with this.

He'd been sent through security, taken down a long hallway, and
told to wait. Someone had asked him if he wanted a cup of coffee, and
he'd said yes, because he hadn't actually been listening. Now he was
sitting on a yellow leather sofa that probably dated back to the Gemini
program, deep inside the maze of office complexes at the Jet Propulsion Laboratory. NASA headquarters, ever since 2052, when they'd
shut down the Johnson Space Center in Houston, after the flood.

A place he'd wanted to be since he was five years old. Back
then, he'd wanted to be an astronaut. He'd wanted it so bad he'd
devoured every piece of space news that came across his stream.

When Sunny was ten he'd watched Blaine Wilson burn alive in space, over and over.

By the time he was fifteen America no longer had an astronaut program.

Sunny had been devastated. His dream was shattered. Instead of flying through space he'd studied it through telescopes and become an astrophysicist. He would get out there, among the stars, one way or another. By the time he'd gotten his PhD, he'd accepted the fact that he was never going to pilot his own spaceship, never going to talk to Ground Control from a million kilometers away. He'd learned to live with that, to almost accept it.

And yet…now he was here. In Houston. For real.

He was thirsty, and he was hungry, but mostly he was worried that he wouldn't be good enough. That he wouldn't be able to make his case convincingly enough to even get NASA's attention. But his data was sound. It was good. There had to be someone here who understood its importance.

He'd been waiting for only about fifteen minutes when a man in an old-fashioned suit and a string tie came walking down the corridor toward him. The guy was white, maybe seventy, maybe seventy-five. He was what Sunny's mom would've called bone skinny. He was carrying two cups of coffee.

Here we go, Sunny thought.

"Dr. Stevens? I'm Roy McAllister. Associate administrator of exploration and operations." He handed Stevens one of the coffees.

"It used to be called human exploration and operations," Stevens said. He set the coffee cup down on an end table. He never drank the stuff.

"I beg your pardon?"

Sunny wanted to shake the man's hand, but he was worried his palm would be sweaty. "Your job. It used to be called human exploration and operations. You were in charge of manned spaceflight. Back when NASA did that kind of thing. You ran the Orion program. Now you're in charge of deep space probes."

McAllister's face was sunburned and weathered and hard to read. There was no missing the pinched annoyance there, however. Had Stevens already screwed this up?

"It's my turn to correct you. I'm not quite so old as you may think. By my time we called it 'crewed spaceflight.' Not 'manned.'"

"Right," Stevens said, closing his eyes in shame. "Right."

"At any rate, I believe I'm the person you wanted to talk to. Your message was a bit cryptic," the old man said.

Sunny cleared his throat. "2I/2054 D1," he said.

And that was it. The die was cast. No going back to the Hive, not now.

McAllister's smile faltered a little. "I'm sorry, I don't think I understand."

"That's its name. Its designation, whatever," Sunny said. He knew he was babbling, but he couldn't stop. "I haven't given it a name yet. I'm pretty sure I get to name it. I discovered it, after all."

McAllister nodded and pointed at a door a little way down the hall. "Let's go in my office and talk about this."

SUNNY STEVENS: *After the* Orion *disaster, NASA said they would take a couple of years to study what went wrong. Make sure it couldn't happen again. It took most of a decade, and with every year that passed NASA's budget got slashed, and slashed again. Congress invested, instead, in private sector space programs. After NASA went bankrupt in the forties, they had to break up the second International Space Station and drop its pieces in the Pacific Ocean. After that, commercial spaceflight seemed like the only game in town. So when it was time for me to find a job, I didn't even think of applying at NASA. By 2055, NASA hadn't trained an astronaut in ten years. It was still around; it takes forever for a government agency to die. Their mission had changed, though. No more spacewalks or golf games on the moon. Instead they put all their budget into two things: satellite surveys of the damage caused by climate change and deep space probes to the planets. Robot ships. Nobody declared a national day of mourning if a robot blew up in orbit around Neptune.*

⋆　　⋆　　⋆

McAllister sat down behind a cluttered desk and folded his hands together. He gestured for Stevens to take a seat across from him. "I understand you work for KSpace."

Stevens grinned and plucked at his hoodie. "What gave me away?" The hoodie was bright orange—KSpace's color—and there was a pattern of tessellating hexagons down the left sleeve. KSpace's logo.

It wasn't a logo that was likely to make him a lot of friends in NASA headquarters. KSpace saw NASA as the esteemed competition. NASA saw KSpace as the boogeyman.

"Yeah, I'm on their deep space research team, over in Atlanta." KSpace had its center of operations in Georgia, in a sprawling campus called the Hive. The place where Sunny had lived, played, and worked for the last four years. The Hive had some first-rate telescopes, so he'd liked it there. Until now. "Basically we do cosmology and astrophysics."

McAllister nodded. "The message you sent me contained the orbital elements of an...asteroid? Comet? Something like that. An object passing through the solar system. I had one of our people take a look, and they just about split their skin."

"I have more. More data I can give you," Sunny said.

For more than a year, Sunny had been tracking 2I. He had *terabytes* of data on it. He knew its albedo, its mass—he had spectroscopy and light curve analyses. He'd been building his case for a long time.

When he took his data to his boss at KSpace, he'd been told it seemed interesting. That the company would look into it. That had been three months earlier, and since then he'd heard nothing. Not a peep.

Somebody had to do something. Somebody had to send a ship to go look at this thing. If KSpace wouldn't do it, then Sunny was sure NASA would. It would *have to.*

Except judging by the look on McAllister's face, NASA didn't necessarily agree.

"Dr. Stevens, what you're offering me is proprietary work product," McAllister said. He leaned back in his chair. "I'm not sure exactly how business is done at KSpace, but I imagine that any research you did for them was on a strictly work-for-hire basis."

Sunny nodded and looked down at his hands. He'd known this would be a problem, sure. But the data—

"Meaning that if you turn this data over to me, you could be sued for breach of contract. And NASA would be breaking the law by receiving stolen goods." McAllister frowned and fluttered one hand in the air. "Technically."

"I know," Sunny said.

"So why don't you tell me why you came here? What you want from NASA."

Sunny took a deep breath. "A job."

"A job," McAllister repeated.

Sunny opened his mouth to say more. All that came out was a laugh. It wasn't a fun laugh. It was a laugh of desperation.

"We're always looking for good astronomers, but if you want to apply to work at NASA I'll direct you to our hiring portal—"

"I want to quit KSpace and come work here," Sunny said. "It's . . . kind of complicated, because I'm still under contract in Atlanta. I want to break that contract. To do that, I need to be protected. From, you know, KSpace's legal team." Sunny winced. "It's a pretty good legal team. I want a decent salary, though that's, you know, negotiable, and health insurance, and maybe two weeks' vacation. I have one more demand, too, which is pretty big but—"

"You have a demand." McAllister's face turned very cold. "Dr. Stevens, I don't think you understand. I just said that I can't accept the data you've offered me. Which means I can't, in turn, offer you a job. I'm sorry you had to come all the way down here for this."

He started to rise from his chair.

Sunny had one last chance. Just one chance to save himself here. Time to pull out the big gun.

"It's decelerating," he said. "Spontaneously. It's spontaneously decelerating."

Sunny had taken a pretty big risk, coming to NASA with this. He had hoped to talk to one of its scientists, not an administrator. His only hope now was that this sunburned bureaucrat had enough of a background in orbital mechanics to get the point.

McAllister didn't stand up. His eyes didn't bug out, and he didn't gasp for breath. But he did reach up and scratch the side of his nose, as if he was giving Sunny's outburst a little bit of thought. Finally he said, "All right. Maybe there's something we can do."

Maybe—maybe he did get it. Maybe he understood why this was so important.

McAllister studied Sunny in silence for a while. "Perhaps you should take off that sweatshirt before we go any further."

Sunny grabbed two handfuls of orange hoodie. "Uh, I'm not wearing anything underneath. Today's my day off. When your message said to come here, I just ran for the train. I didn't think about clothes."

McAllister reached up and touched the device clipped to his ear. Presumably he was calling an assistant or somebody. "This is McAllister. Yes. Would you do me a favor and find a man's shirt, somewhere? I know it's an unusual request. Just bring it to my office."

A staffer showed up a few minutes later with the new shirt—a white T-shirt from the JPL gift shop. It showed the old logo, a red swooping curve over a navy blue disk.

"Welcome to NASA," McAllister said.

REENTRY

*G*lide *angle good. Fuel at 2%. Solar panels charging with 81% efficiency.*
The data flickered across the top of Hawkins's conscious-
ness, never quite penetrating the threshold of attention. His pulse
and respiration were slightly elevated, but well within acceptable
parameters. He was hungry for a fight, and he was very close to
getting one.

It wasn't easy, matching velocities with a Russian spy satellite.
The Russians had learned to take up improbable, eccentric orbits
that brought them over their targets only once every forty-seven
days, or orbits that swung so low that to catch them you had to
graze the atmosphere. Even finding his prey had been difficult.
It was wrapped in a Vantablack blanket, blacker than coal, which
absorbed radio waves instead of reflecting them. As if he were hunting a sniper, he'd looked for the glint in his prey's eyes—the lenses
of its cameras.

There was a war going on up there, in the high orbits. A war of
slow calculation and mathematical precision.

*Distance two kilometers and closing. Jamming enemy communications on
Ka-band and millimeter wave. Deploying armament.*

The X-37d, Hawkins's weapon platform, looked like a miniature
space shuttle with no windows. Its cargo bay doors swung open,
and a single jointed robotic arm unfolded itself like the hunting leg
of a praying mantis. The spaceplane had been in orbit for nine hundred days, carrying out a variety of missions. Its micromissiles had
been fired long before. Its high-energy laser couldn't draw enough

power when the X-37d was on the night side of Earth. This time, Hawkins intended to grab his prey with a mechanical hand—and rip it to pieces.

He edged closer, taking his time. If the Tchaika-class satellite caught wind of him, it might run. It had three-axis thrusters that could be used to change its orbit, and if he lost it now he might never find it again. It didn't see him, though, as far as he could tell. Its cameras were pointed downward, toward a military installation in Alaska.

Hawkins reached forward with his robot arm, its grasping claws wide. Just a little farther now. He expended a tiny puff of his remaining fuel to close the distance.

Perhaps the Tchaika felt the exhaust of his engines. Perhaps it had some subtle sense for when a predator was near. Its own thrusters lit up, and it started to speed away from him. Hawkins growled in frustration—then brought his arm back and swung it around, hard, so that the claw smashed against the satellite's hull and sent it spinning out of control. He felt the impact in his hand, felt it reverberate all the way up to the bones of his wrist. The Tchaika tumbled away from him, and he'd poured on more delta-v to catch it when—

Lights came up all around him. The universe vanished.

Hawkins blinked and snorted and sneezed. He was sitting in a trailer in Utah, surrounded by the black boxes and haptic peripherals of a military-grade virtual reality rig.

He'd been on duty for seventeen hours straight. Suddenly he could smell his own body. Feel how his legs had fallen asleep. The X-37d didn't have legs. He'd forgotten his own.

There was a knock on the door behind him. He climbed, carefully, out of his chair and went to answer it. Salt-laden air billowed into his climate-controlled domain, and he squinted into a sunny day out on the Great Salt Lake. "What," he grunted, brain still half lost in orbit.

Then he snapped to attention. "Sir," he said. "I'm sorry, I was—"

"At ease," General Kalitzakis said. "Major, there's someone here to talk to you. I'd like you to give him your full attention."

Standing behind the general was an old guy in a woven straw

cowboy hat and a dusty maroon suit. Thin as a rail. Hawk's eyes still weren't quite focused on the real world, but he knew he'd never seen the man before. Looked like a civilian.

The thin man looked Hawkins over, then turned to the general. "This is the man you recommended to me?"

"He's the best I've got," Kalitzakis said.

Hawkins couldn't help but stand a little taller, push his chest out a little more.

The thin man nodded and held out a hand. "Hello, son. My name's Roy McAllister, and I have a new mission for you. You've been reassigned, effective immediately."

Hawkins was still half up in space, his mind still focused on chasing down the Tchaika-class. He fell back on muscle memory, drilled into him over his twenty-year career in the military. His hand snapped up in a salute.

"Sir, yes sir," he said. "Permission to take a shower before we leave?"

McAllister smiled. "Granted, Major."

MAJOR WINDSOR HAWKINS, THIRTIETH OPERATIONS WING, UNITED STATES SPACE FORCE: The X-37 series of uncrewed drone vehicles are reusable, aerodynamic spacecraft with long loiter times in orbit and multimission capabilities. We launch them out of Vandenberg AFB outside of Lompoc, California, and they are operated remotely from several space force facilities. That's all I can say about them without direct authorization from the Joint Space Operations Center.

Parminder Rao was *livid*.

Administrator McAllister was away from his desk, so there was nothing she could do but pace up and down in the hallway outside his office. Sometimes she stood there with her arms crossed, sometimes she put her hands down at her sides but kept them balled in fists. Occasionally she took the sticky note out of her pocket and glared at it again. It still said the same thing. *Please see me for a new posting ASAP.* That was all.

He'd fired her with a piece of paper. Who even still used sticky notes? There was a human resources portal on the JPL intranet for this kind of communication. There were conflict resolution channels, and appeal forms she could fill out—

When the building's main door opened and she saw McAllister walk in and head toward her, it was all she could do not to run to meet him and start shouting questions. As he passed her he gave her a nod as if he knew why she was there. Well, he'd better.

"Come in," he told her. As he seated himself behind his desk, he asked, "Dr. Rao, how long have you been working for me?"

"Five years," she said. "Five years of my life. All of it on one project, the Titan Express mission."

In truth, though, Rao had spent her entire life building up to Express. She'd worked her way through years of school, ending up with a combined MD and a PhD in astrobiology. Then she'd worked her ass off getting this job at JPL. All so she could build Titan Express, an interplanetary probe mission. If she could secure funding for Express, it would take five years just to build the probe. Then it would still take another three years just to get to Saturn's largest moon, the only place in the solar system other than Earth with liquid lakes on its surface. The probe would drop a tiny boat onto one of those lakes, then sieve through the liquid methane looking for any sign of microbes. If it was successful, it would be the first time life had ever been found outside of Earth's atmosphere. It would be a scientific breakthrough of incredible proportions. It would be the crowning achievement of her career.

Except this morning Titan Express had been canceled.

Without warning. Without discussion. Her life's work just— canceled.

"I came in to find my workstation locked down. All of my data, all my notes, my preliminary blueprints for Express—everything gone." Being angry, Rao thought, was better than breaking down in a crying mess in public from the horror of it all. Those were her two options, as she saw it. She picked angry. "How dare you? Do you know what kind of hoops I've had to jump through, how much paperwork, how many people I've had to schmooze?"

"I do," McAllister told her. "Would you like to sit down?"

"No," she said. "No. I would not like to sit down. I'd *like* to hear an explanation. They tell me you've been out of the building all day. Someone said you went to Utah. Was there a good reason you weren't here to explain this to me eight hours ago?"

"Yes," McAllister said. "Dr. Rao, I understand your frustration. If you would just sit down, I think I can give you something. Maybe not a full explanation, not yet. But I've chosen you for something very special, and I think—"

"You're changing my job? Without asking?"

He smiled. Despite her anger, despite her fierce energy, he looked at her and smiled, and she was certain, absolutely convinced, he was excited.

Parminder Rao had worked in the same building as Roy McAllister for five years, and she had never seen him angry, or red in the face, or even annoyed. She had certainly never seen this little faraway smile, this slightly distant look in his eyes before.

She sat down.

"I have some data here," he told her, reaching up to touch the device clipped to his ear. Her own device, a tiny nose stud her mother had given her, vibrated in response. He had sent her a very large file. She flicked her eyes downward and an overlay came up across her vision, showing her column after column of tiny numbers.

"These are—what? Orbital parameters for something. A rock, or…" There was something wrong with the data. It didn't look right—some of the numbers were way too big. "Why are you showing me this? I'm an astrobiologist, not an astronomer."

"But you see it. Don't you?" McAllister asked.

And then she did.

If those numbers were correct—

"Oh shit," she said.

"You realize now why I took you off Titan Express? Why I have a new job for you that I figured might be right up your alley?"

"Uh-huh," she said. Because that was all she could say. Every bit of brainpower she had was busy checking those numbers, rechecking them.

They kept coming up the same. The data had to be correct.

And they changed... everything.

PARMINDER RAO, NASA ASTROBIOLOGIST: At the time I didn't even know the thing's name, or who had discovered it. I only knew it was decelerating, and that meant everything. Objects in space move unless acted on by a force. That's the basis of Newtonian mechanics. Planets, comets, asteroids all move at the same speed in their orbits, only slowing down or speeding up when gravity pulls on them, when they encounter drag... This object was spontaneously decelerating. Meaning it was slowing down under its own power. It wasn't some dead rock tumbling through the solar system. It was a spaceship.

There was a green smudge on the horizon, a little margin of tortured sunlight under a deck of dark clouds. Storm weather for a storm that had done its worst and now was moving on, the clouds heading up the coast at fourteen kilometers an hour to wreck somebody else's weekend. It was March in Florida, in the second half of the twenty-first century. Hurricane season.

There were twelve divers in the airboat. It had originally been owned by a company that did manatee watching tours, but now it belonged to the City of Titusville. Chuy, the divers' boss, had brought his family with him, his wife Esmee and his kid Hector. Hector was up in the prow, watching the waves break around the boat's sharp nose. His mom kept one hand on the waistband of his pants so he didn't fall out, but the kid had spent most of his four years out on the water, and nobody was really worried.

In the stern Sally Jansen checked her gear. Each diver had brought their own, some of them still relying on big scuba tanks and regulators. Old, well-loved hoses wrapped in tape and scuffed-up regulators. Most, like Jansen, had rebreathers no bigger than a small knapsack. She pressed her mask against her face and tested the seal, then nodded to herself and checked her weight belt to make sure it wasn't too frayed. Then she checked everything a second time. Old habits.

It wasn't a long ride out to the flats, but it was one she dreaded a little. The boat cruised around the northern end of Merritt Island, half of which was permanently flooded and edging over into marshland, crowds of white birds standing on the roofs of drowned houses. If you looked closely you could still make out a rectangular shadow just below the water—the long strip where space shuttles used to land. South of there was nothing but memories. The old assembly building and the tall gantries like the skeletons of proud towers were barely recognizable now, draped in long vines and covered in bird nests. Over the years storms had softened the old structures, rust and rain making them melt like candle wax, but slowly, oh so slowly.

It stung. It still stung, even after all these years, to see Canaveral brought low. *I could have moved away*, Jansen thought. *I had years and years to find some other place, some other hole to hide in.* But that old pain was like a pair of shoes that pinch your feet but you wear them enough and they get broken in and then you convince yourself that's comfort, that's as good as it's going to get.

"OK," Chuy called from the front of the boat. "We're here."

She waved back at him, not wanting to shout over the roar of the engines as they powered down. Eventually they died out and there was no sound but the slap slap slap of water on the hull.

It was the signal she'd been waiting for. Jansen flipped backward into the blood-warm water, felt it surge up all around her in a welter of silver bubbles. She closed her eyes, and for a moment, one perfect, silent moment, it was almost there.

The old, desired feeling—weightlessness. It was almost the same as flying free in infinite space. Almost.

She opened her eyes. The other divers were plunging around her, each like a comet hurtling around the sun with their own trail of bubbles.

Time to get to work.

SALLY JANSEN: When I came home from space they offered me a job at the astronaut office, a desk job with a pension and health care, which sounded great. I lasted two days. I felt like all those eyes, all those people staring at me, were burning holes in the back of my shirt. I was the woman who lost the second space race, right? After the Chinese landed on Mars, after America gave up on space—nah. I couldn't do it. There were a lot of tears and people wanting to shake my hand on the way out the door. Nobody was cruel. But I think they were glad to see me go.

The seafloor off Canaveral sloped gently out toward the abyss. Here the bottom was only about six meters down. The water had been stirred up by the storm, and visibility wasn't great, but as the divers kicked down through rays of wavering sunlight, Jansen could make out the turbines easily enough. There were hundreds of them, round hunched shapes like a herd of buffalo grazing on the mud. Each turbine was three meters wide, its cowl shaggy with sargassum. Inside the cowls knife-thin fans turned sluggishly, moved by warm water streaming northward from the Gulf of Mexico, generating electricity from the current. Good energy, clean as it came, but the generators needed constant maintenance. Anyone with a dive certificate could make a living down here, just keeping those turbines free of debris and spinning.

They'd come out today because after the storm half the turbines were reporting nonfunctional. Jansen saw the problem right away. A piece of old fishing net had fetched up across the turbines, making it look as if they were snared in a giant spider's web. The net must have been drifting for years, skating along the sea floor at the whim of the currents, until it snagged on the machines. It was thick with captured detritus, old bits of wood and fish bones and human trash that it had scooped up along the way.

Clearing it was slow, painstaking work. To avoid damaging the turbines they had to cut the net free strand by strand. The thick plastic cord was designed to stretch rather than tear, and you had to hold it tight with one hand while you sawed away with the other. She gathered up huge bunches of the stuff, tying it up in big knotty clumps that they could easily haul away when they were done.

She tried not to get depressed at the amount of human refuse stuck in the net's coils, the countless old chip bags and dead batteries and just so much plastic, shopping bags and yogurt cups and egg cartons, discarded paint cans that were probably toxic and old smartphones that definitely were. The colors all still bright as they would be for another thousand years.

The trash she pushed away from her, let it be carried away by the current. There was so much of it there was no way to gather it up for proper disposal. She tried not to watch it float away as she cleared the faces of the turbines.

But then she saw something that made her heart skip a beat—and a moment later made her laugh inside her mask. A tiny pair of arms reaching out to her, pleading for help. Tiny brown plastic arms. She cut the owner of those arms free and stared at it for a while, then shoved it in one of her pockets. She could take a better look later. For now, the fishing net required her full attention.

When they were done, as the boat sped back toward shore she teased the salt water out of her short hair and leaned back, getting used to breathing real air again. Somebody handed her a beer and she raised it in thanks. She'd drunk half of it before she thought to look in her pocket.

The thing she'd found was a very old action figure, a little brown creature half-bear and half-ape with a doglike face, its thick fur lovingly sculpted. A bandolier ran across its chest. It had a bad gash across one foot, maybe from hitting the turbine's vane. Its eyes were a bright and staring blue.

She felt as if she was being watched. She looked up and saw Hector staring at the toy in her hand. "You know this guy?" she asked. "He's got your daddy's name, kind of," she said.

"His name is Jesús?" Hector asked.

"Chewbacca," she said. Hector gave her an expression so serious it made her smile. "This is Chewbacca." She held the little figure up and made it dance for him. She tried to imitate the Wookiee's gargling roar.

Hector's eyes narrowed.

"What's that?" Chuy asked, coming over. He hunched down next to her and took the figure, turning it over and over in his hands. Then he whistled. "That's something!" he said. "You know you could sell this online, right? Some of these old toys, they go for big money. *Big money*, OK?" He pulled off his baseball cap and rubbed his forehead, then pulled the cap back on in one quick, practiced motion. "Rich people, they'll buy just about anything, if it's old enough."

Hector was still staring.

"You ever show him a *Star Wars* movie?" Jansen asked.

"Movies? He's got his own stream," Chuy said. "What would he want with that corny old stuff?"

Jansen nodded and handed the figure to Hector. She looked him right in the eye, and he seemed to understand—this was a gift. He frowned in acceptance, then ran off to his mother, who was handing out sandwiches in the bow.

Jansen sat up and let the wind off the water finish drying her hair. Chuy sat down next to her in companionable silence. She handed him her half-finished beer and he polished it off as they watched the waves.

"You want to come for dinner tonight?" he asked. "We're making pad thai. Esmee got some real sticky rice, even, from that new fancy grocery store."

Jansen shook her head. He always asked. About one time in ten, she took him up on the offer. He had a nice little ranch house in Oak Park with a patio out back where she could sit and play with his kids or—more often these days—watch them while they ran VR shows, eyes encased in thick goggles, hands twitching at their sides. She would make sure they didn't wander out of the yard—when they tried she would put a gentle hand on their shoulder and turn them around. Then Esmee would come out and the two women would make small talk, slow, pointless conversations that were mostly about just sharing space. She liked those evenings. Chuy was the closest thing she had to family these days, since her mother died. Close enough.

How much of life was made of *close enough*s and *almost the same*s, she wondered? Most of it, maybe. But tonight she felt like being alone.

"You OK?" Chuy asked. He couldn't make direct eye contact when he said it, but she knew he was genuinely concerned, and she smiled.

"I'm OK."

"OK, you're OK," he said, puffing out his cheeks. He was a good man. "Hey, you know you got a call, right?"

Jansen looked down at the gear bag at her feet. Through the thin nylon she could see a pulse of amber light. It was coming from the bow of a pair of sunglasses in there, an old set of AR sunglasses that she really needed to replace. The light told her she had an urgent unanswered message.

The light had been pulsing for nearly two days now. She'd checked to see where the message was from, and since then she'd just tried to ignore it. She'd figured it would go away eventually. She was more than a little annoyed that it hadn't.

"I'll answer it when I get home," she lied.

Turned out she didn't get a chance.

Long before they reached shore, Esmee stood up in the stern and pointed out over the water, and everybody looked to see some kind of small aircraft gliding toward them, its landing gear almost skimming the chop. It had three ducted props and a glass bubble canopy, though as it got closer they could see there was nobody inside. It pulled up beside them, chewing at the air with three big rotors. Chuy stopped the boat and looked at Jansen with deep concern.

There was a NASA logo on the aircraft's fuselage. No matter how far it had fallen, NASA still had the coolest planes, Jansen thought. A light on its nose flared yellow. "Jansen," the plane said, in a gender-neutral voice. "Message for Sally Jansen."

She felt all those eyes digging into her spine. Everybody staring. She reached in her bag and pulled on the sunglasses.

And saw Roy McAllister standing on the waves, in augmented reality.

"You've been avoiding me," he said.

The computer that generated his image made him bob up and down in time with the boat, so that he seemed to be dipping his toes in the Florida water.

Come on, Roy, she thought. *Take the hint. I just want to be—*

She couldn't even finish that thought. Because he smiled, and all the planes and crevices of his face shifted, and she saw for the first time how old he'd gotten. Damn. He must be seventy now, at least.

"Hi, Roy," she said. Her voice was tiny and weak.

"I need your help with something. In California."

California meant the Jet Propulsion Laboratory. JPL was NASA headquarters these days. This was a job offer.

It wasn't the first. Roy McAllister had tried to do right by her, through the years. When she quit NASA, he'd tried to get her work at Boeing. Then at some science foundation. Those jobs never lasted. What was it going to be now?

"Just do me a favor," Roy said. "Before you say no, come to California. Let me show you some things."

A memory rushed through her, like a chill. The day they brought her to the Capitol Building in Washington. A semicircle of senators staring down at her, asking her questions, so many questions. Asking if there was some way she could have saved *Orion*. Asking her how she could have finished her mission. How she could have saved Blaine Wilson's life.

She'd been sitting at a wooden table, with three microphones stabbing up at her face, and nobody had bothered to bring her so much as a bottle of water. She'd felt exposed, endangered. As if, if she said anything, if she moved or even cleared her throat, vultures would pounce and tear her to pieces.

And underneath the table, Roy McAllister had reached over and held her hand.

She looked back, over her shoulder. Hector was staring at her, his child's face impossible to read. Esmee had one arm across his chest, protecting him.

Jansen smiled. "Chuy," she said, "watch my stuff, OK?"

"OK," he said. His mouth disappeared under his mustache as he sucked in his lips. "Yeah, OK," he said, and put a hand on his baseball cap, maybe expecting that the little plane's prop wash would blow it off.

The plane's canopy swung open. She jumped up and grabbed a handhold and climbed inside.

PREFLIGHT CHECK

Sunny had given this presentation multiple times. The first time, when he'd talked to McAllister's boss—NASA's administrator, the head honcho—it took ninety minutes to get through. When he gave the same talk to NASA's advisory groups, then the mission directorates and the staff offices, he'd gotten down to a tight twenty. Then one day they'd put him in front of a 3-D camera and told him he would be speaking directly to the president of the United States. That time he'd been given five minutes.

Now he was giving the talk one last time. They promised. He was still a ball of nerves as he headed to classroom six at JPL and loaded all his files into the screen on the podium. Whom could they possibly be bringing in this time? The secretary-general of the UN?

The classroom could hold 120 people. Today only four came in and sat down in the big stadium-style chairs. Two of them sat down in the middle rows, a couple of seats apart from each other. A Southeast Asian woman in a cardigan and some military guy with tons of medals on the front of his uniform. He took his hat off and carefully sat it on the seat next to him. Sunny caught the woman's eye and smiled. She gave him back a very fast, tight little smile, then leaned forward and hugged her knees, as if she was very nervous. Maybe she had some idea of what he was going to say.

Two more people came in and sat down in the front row. Roy McAllister and a middle-aged woman wearing a pair of cheap AR sunglasses. It took Sunny a minute to realize whom he was looking at.

"Wait," he said. "Wait—she's—you're—"

"Clearly you recognize Ms. Jansen," McAllister said. "So let me introduce you. Everyone, this is Sunny Stevens. He's an astrophysicist working in our Planetary Science Directorate. He may look young, but don't let that fool you. He's well on his way to his first Nobel. Most likely for the discovery he's going to tell you about today."

Sunny nodded, barely listening. It was her. Sally Jansen, looking right at him.

The woman who'd killed Blaine Wilson. The woman who'd lost the race for Mars. What the hell was she doing here? This was top-secret stuff, not meant for every washed-up astronaut NASA could drag in off the street—

"We're a bit tight on time, Dr. Stevens," McAllister said. "Perhaps we could...?"

Sunny nodded and exhaled deeply. He was a little thrown, but he could do this. He knew it all by heart. He just wished—he wished Jansen would take those sunglasses off. Who still wore AR sunglasses? Everybody in his generation just used an earring or a nose ring as their device. The sunglasses made it impossible to see her eyes. To know what she was thinking.

Still, she was just one more person he needed to convince. Sunny knew what was at stake with these presentations. He tapped the screen on the podium and got started.

Light bloomed above them as an AR image formed, pixels coalescing out of the air.

"This," he said, gesturing at the air above their heads, "is an object called 1I/2017 U1. Also known as 'Oumuamua, which is a Hawaiian word meaning 'first messenger.'"

In augmented reality the object turned lazily on its short axis. It didn't look like much, honestly. It was a cigar-shaped lump of rock, a dull red in color. The image was heavily pixelated. "We never got a really good look at it. It came into the solar system way back, in 2017, long before I was born, and, uh..."

It occurred to him that some of the people listening to him were old enough to remember 2017. They sat there looking like lumps of rock themselves. He brushed off the thought and went on.

"It was just another rock, right, a piece of space debris, not even big enough to worry about." Scale bars appeared around the image, showing that 'Oumuamua was thirty-five meters across and 230 long. "They couldn't even figure out what it was, back then. Whether it was an asteroid or a comet. There was one thing about it, though, that got a lot of attention. It didn't come from our solar system."

The image zoomed out to show the track 'Oumuamua had taken around the sun. It dove out of deep space almost perpendicular to the plane of the ecliptic—the plane around the sun's equator where all the planets orbited. Moving very, very fast it swung around the sun, looping around to shoot off at a new angle that sent it past the inner planets and then, eventually, back out into deep space.

"We still don't know where it came from. Maybe somewhere around the star Vega. But yeah—it came from out there. Out there in the galaxy." As he warmed up, Sunny had to fight the urge to bounce up and down on the stage. This is where it got very interesting. "It passed through interstellar space—it might have been out there for a hundred thousand years or more. Then it very briefly passed through our solar system before heading back out into the dark. Our telescopes weren't great back then, and we barely got a look at it. But it changed—well, a whole lot of things in astronomy. It made us really think, for the first time, about what else was out there."

He tapped the screen, and 'Oumuamua's path traced a white curve around the sun. He tapped the screen again, and a second curve appeared.

"In astronomy, if you see one specimen of a new type of object, you know you'll find more of them if you look. The universe is so big there are very few unique things in it. We had to assume it wasn't the only interstellar rock out there. Back in '17, KSpace was still working on launching their first rocket, but already they had a strong interest in astronomy. They set up a radio telescope survey to look for more I objects. About three years ago I took over that project. Specifically, I created a new search pattern that focused on the part of the sky where 'Oumuamua originated. I figured if one rock came from that direction, maybe more of them would come from the same place. It turns out I was right."

The second white curve traced almost exactly the same arc as the first. "This is 2I/2054 D1." He couldn't help but beam out at his sparse audience. "My baby."

He turned and watched the white curves, entranced as always by the cosmic duet.

"If 'Oumuamua was weird, so was 2I, and in all the same ways. It has the same deep-red color. It's the same basic cigar shape, about eight times as long as it is wide. That was enough to pique my interest. But then I used a light curve analysis to get a better idea of its size."

A graphic representation of 'Oumuamua appeared as a small spindly shape floating in front of the screen. A tiny blur of low-resolution pixels. 2I appeared above it—and dwarfed it.

"2I is about three hundred and fifty times bigger than 'Oumuamua. Identical in almost every single way, except on a massively larger scale. I've estimated it's about ten kilometers across and eighty kilometers long. And it's currently headed toward us, eating up twenty-six kilometers every second."

Sally Jansen coughed for his attention. "That sounds fast," she said. "Too fast."

Sunny gave her a tentative smile. At least she was paying attention. "Oh yeah," he said. "And that's why 2I is super interesting. Both of them, 'Oumuamua and 2I, they came at us about the same speed. Interstellar speed, call it. Most comets, even the really fast ones, top out at about five kilometers per second. The fastest spacecraft ever built—*Voyager 2*—is moving about fifteen kilometers a second. There's one difference, though. Comets and planets and everything natural will keep the same speed pretty much forever, right? We know the laws of physics, and how they apply to big, dumb objects moving through space. 'Oumuamua followed all those rules. It came in super fast. Then it sped up as it swung around the sun, which makes sense; it used the sun's gravity to get the slingshot effect, to speed itself up. Originally," he said, pointing at the white curves above his head, "we thought 2I would do the same thing. Swing around the sun, build up a good head of steam, and head back out for the stars, so fast we would barely get a look at it. That's what I was expecting—what everybody was expecting. Except then it didn't."

He tapped the screen. His heart was pounding in his chest. This was the thing he needed to explain. The reason he kept giving this presentation.

"It slowed down," Stevens announced. "Decelerated. The last time I checked, it was down to about twenty-one kilometers per second, and it's still slowing. It shouldn't be doing that. I mean, there are reasons why an astronomical body might decelerate, sure. Drag or a collision with another object or...whatever, but none of them fit. 2I wasn't acting like a normal space rock, but what did that mean? Then it went and answered the question for us. It changed course."

On the screen the white curve bent inward on itself, moving away from the sun. "With no physical explanation, it started moving in a direction we didn't expect." The white curve made a delicate, graceful arc toward the plane of the ecliptic—and the orbits of the planets. One planet in particular.

"It's headed towards Earth," Stevens said. "If it continues on its present course and deceleration, in about six months it'll pass inside the orbit of the moon. By that point it'll have slowed down to less than eleven kilometers per second. In other words, less than Earth's escape velocity.

"To me," Sunny said, "this looks like a classic Hohmann transfer orbit." He waved at the screen, and the trajectory continued as a dashed line. The view zoomed in so they could see the curve bending around the surface of Earth. "This is just speculation, but I'm thinking it's going to eventually execute another course correction, one using very little delta-v. A minimum expenditure of thrust. With just a little nudge, it could enter a polar orbit of the Earth."

Jansen leaned forward in her seat. The AR simulation was good enough Sunny could see the white curves crisscrossing the black lenses of her sunglasses.

"Comets and asteroids don't act like that," she said. "What you're saying—"

Sunny did bounce up and down a little then. He shoved his hands in his pockets because he didn't know what else to do with them.

"It's not a comet or an asteroid. It's a spaceship. It's a spaceship moving under its own power."

"And if it's coming from deep space—that means it's a starship," McAllister said, softly. "An alien craft."

ROY MCALLISTER, ASSOCIATE ADMINISTRATOR FOR EXPLORATION AND OPERATIONS, NASA: We attempted to make contact with 2I every way we knew how. We had a team from the SETI Institute design a series of radio signals that would indicate our presence, our intelligence, and our desire to communicate. We used the most powerful radio transmitters in the world to send the signals, repeating the message hundreds of times a day. There was no response, not even an acknowledgment that the aliens had got our call. We needed to know—as soon as physically possible— what its intentions were. It wasn't an academic question. It was possible that 2I intended to take up orbit around Earth. It was also possible it was sent to crash right into us. An object that large, moving at that velocity, would wipe out all life on the planet. I took Dr. Stevens's presentation to every government scientific and political body that would listen. I found a lot of doors open to me—it didn't take an astrophysicist to understand how important this was.

Parminder Rao hurried out of the classroom feeling as if she were going to explode with excitement. She was trembling, and she had to put her hand against the wall of the corridor outside. She had to catch her breath.

The soldier or airman or whatever came out next, adjusting the cuffs of his dress uniform as he walked toward her. "I can see why they wanted to bring in the space force," he said. "This is seriously scary." He was about forty, she thought, with close-cut hair turning to steel gray at his temples. He was frowning, and his face looked as if he did a lot of that. He had his hat in his hands, and he was turning it around and around. "I'm sorry," he said, and tucked the hat under his arm so he could stick out a hand for her to shake. "Windsor Hawkins. I'm with the Thirtieth Operations Wing."

She had no idea what that meant. "Parminder Rao," she told him. "Astrobiology. I think it's a little early to think of this as some kind of interstellar invasion."

"That's not what I'm worried about, it's—"

"Excuse me," she interrupted. The door of the classroom had opened again and Sunny Stevens had stepped out. She ran over to him and grabbed both his hands. "You're absolutely sure," she said. "One hundred percent."

Stevens smiled, a big, bright smile that made her want to laugh. Everything seemed brighter just then, the colors more intense. She studied every little gesture Stevens made, every shift of the muscles of his face, because there was still some part of her that thought maybe this wasn't real. That it was going to turn out to be a hoax, or a glitch in some computer model.

"I can't go to a hundred, I guess, but—ninety-nine percent sure?" he said.

Rao couldn't help herself. She grabbed him in a tight hug. "I've spent my whole life looking for aliens," she said. Since the summer in middle school when she'd read Asimov and Clarke and Leckie, it had been the thing she'd dreamed of. "I've been looking for bacteria in Mars rocks and the lakes of Titan, but this . . . If they can build a starship, they have to be intelligent," she said. "They have to be coming here to talk to us."

"They've been silent so far," Stevens pointed out, but she didn't care.

She wanted to press her face into the crook of his shoulder and cry. Happy tears.

But then the door of the classroom opened again and two more people came out, and Rao had to step back, out of the hug. McAllister and Jansen walked past, not even looking at them. Sally Jansen wasn't looking at anything—she seemed lost in thought.

When they were out of earshot, Stevens leaned in close. "What's she doing here?" he asked. "You know who that was, right? The woman who almost went to Mars."

Rao looked up at him in surprise. "That's a little cold."

"She killed Blaine Wilson," Hawkins said.

Rao's eyes narrowed. "And saved two other astronauts," she pointed out.

Stevens shook his head, and then his big smile was back. "Ancient history, guys. Listen. McAllister wants us to meet him this afternoon for another briefing. I'm not sure why, but I assume that we—all three of us," he said, nodding at the space force guy, "are going to be working together. Should we go get lunch? We can talk some more about 2I."

"We shouldn't discuss anything in public," Hawkins said. "We should order in. Ms. Rao, do you have an office here, in the building?"

She didn't bother correcting him—she was Dr. Rao, but at the moment she didn't care what people called her. She was going to talk to aliens...

Hawkins cleared his throat.

She looked down and saw that she still had one hand on Stevens's arm, and that she was gently stroking it. Stevens didn't seem to mind.

Just the excitement, she thought. They were all so excited. "Sure," she said. "Um, down this way," and she started walking toward her office. She spun around as she walked and looked back at the two men.

"Aliens!" she whispered.

She wanted to run up to the roof and shout it at the sky.

McAllister took Jansen deep into the heart of JPL, to a room she'd never actually seen before, though she knew it by reputation.

Together they watched a small army of technicians move a very large packing crate from the JPL loading bays to the antechamber of the Twenty-Five-Foot Space Simulator. Men and women dressed in paper from head to foot, with special nonconductive, lint-repelling shoes, walked the container with excruciating slowness toward the big doors. Careful not to bump or jostle the crate in any way.

The Twenty-Five-Foot Space Simulator—which, in classic government fashion, was actually twenty-seven feet across—was one of NASA's most famous assets. It was a National Historic Landmark, and for good reason. It had been used to test space probes from

Ranger to Voyager and a dozen more since. It was a stainless steel cylinder eighty-five feet high, with doors as thick as a bank vault's. Once a piece of space hardware was put inside and the doors were sealed, the interior of the cylinder could be turned into all kinds of hell. The temperature could be raised to hundreds of degrees, or lowered to well below zero. All the air could be pumped out of the cylinder until it formed a hard vacuum. The contents of the cylinder could be bathed in ionizing radiation for hours or even days. All to prove the hardware in question was safe to take to space.

The technicians moved the big crate right up to the Simulator's doors, then got to work cracking it open.

"Who knows about this?" Jansen asked.

McAllister had told her how top secret his project was. How important it was that the general public not find out about 2I until NASA had some actual information to give them. He still hadn't explained why she'd been brought into the loop.

"For the moment we're limiting exposure. Only a handful of people in Pasadena know. Congress and the president. Of course, KSpace knows, because Stevens was working for them when he found it. The Russians have been informed. So far they're happy to let us take all the risk. The Chinese are getting ready to launch a vehicle as well," McAllister said. "Though they're being tight-lipped as to its specifications. We're not sure if they're sending tai-konauts, or simply a probe. Or a nuclear missile."

She turned and gave him a questioning look.

McAllister shrugged. "Is paranoia such an unreasonable response? This thing could be coming to kill us all. Our space force is getting their own weapons ready for launch, too. If 2I is hostile, we won't have a lot of time to take countermeasures. Better to have weapons up there, ready to fire, than find out too late that we need them."

"This is first contact, Roy," she said.

And suddenly—it hit her. What that meant.

Sally Jansen had been to space. She'd looked back at Earth and seen how fragile it was, and how alone. She'd looked out across empty light-years and felt the incredible distance between stars.

She'd never believed in UFOs, never thought humanity would ever detect so much as a radio signal from another world. Yet here they were.

How could you deal with that? How could anyone come to grips with the size of this? How did you not just shut down, give in to the shock?

She used to be an astronaut, damn it. She knew the answer. You fell back on your training. You considered the problem through the lens of what you knew, what you were sure of. Roy McAllister was thinking of it as a series of problems. A national security problem. An engineering problem. Problems he needed to solve.

She tried to do the same. How did this affect her, personally? What was it going to mean to her? She struggled with even that. She felt dizzy with the size of what they were talking about.

"This could be the biggest event in history. Human history."

"I'm aware," he told her. "That's why, when I went to Congress, I told them we needed a crewed mission of our own. We need to send American astronauts up there, to meet this thing face-to-face."

Jansen stared at him. "A...crewed mission. A NASA crew. On a mission."

"Yes," he said. He was taking her through this slowly, she could tell. Trying to let her fully understand each new revelation. By the way he kept popping his knuckles, though, she could also tell he needed her to catch on fast.

"Congress has been nickel-and-diming NASA for decades. They're the reason we don't have any astronauts anymore, for God's sake. How'd they take this?" Jansen asked.

"They gave me a check. Not as big a check as I asked for. But maybe enough."

Her mouth actually fell open. That—that *never* happened. NASA had been begging and fighting for scraps of money since the last Apollo mission flew. The aborted mission to Mars had taken decades of saving and scrimping on a shoestring budget, and years of meetings and proposals and meetings about writing proposals. Every time a new president or a new Congress got elected, NASA had to start over from scratch. Now—Roy had gone to Washington, given one presentation, and walked away with all the money he needed?

Apparently this was the mission that the money people had been waiting for.

"Of course, all the cash in the world can't make a mission just magically appear," McAllister told her. "We'll need to scrap a bunch of our robotic exploration programs and divert funds, people, and equipment into this thing. We don't have Canaveral or Houston anymore, so we'll need to borrow one of the space force's launch pads and run control from right here at JPL. We're not set up for training astronauts—we'll need to rebuild a bunch of resources we've lost, write code for new training simulators, hire back people we laid off a decade ago, reuse rockets and space suits that have been sitting in warehouses for decades. It's going to take every asset I've got to pull this off in the given time frame. Assets like this one."

Down below them, on the floor of the Simulator, they had finally gotten the crate open. The spacecraft inside had been sealed away for twenty-one years, but a lot of effort had gone into keeping it in good shape. It had been packed with excruciating care into the big steel container, which had then been welded shut to make it airtight. Then it was pumped full of nonreactive helium to protect the contents against rust or corrosion. For decades it had been housed in a high-security warehouse, guarded night and day by armed soldiers.

Technicians with pry bars and power wrenches moved in to take down the walls of the crate while its top was lifted away very carefully by a crane. When it was done, the spacecraft lay revealed, as shiny and new as the last time she'd seen it.

Down to the paint job. Down to the name ORION 7 lovingly stenciled just below the American flag. She didn't say anything, because she knew if she opened her mouth her voice might break. This wasn't Orion 6, it wasn't her ship. But it was so close.

The conical command module was covered in square black protective tiles. The HabLab module was deflated, perched on top of the command module like a big saggy silver doughnut, secured by yellow nylon straps to keep it from flopping around. There was no

Martian lander attached to this spacecraft—that was the big difference between this ship and the one she had almost flown to Mars.

"We had three of these—7, 9, and 15—in storage, so if there's a problem with this one we have two spares we can cannibalize for parts." He took a step forward until he was right by her shoulder. He reached out and touched her arm, but she didn't move. "There's no time to design and build a new spacecraft. We needed to go with what we had in dead stock."

Jansen wasn't surprised. NASA never threw anything away—one of its operating principles was that it never wanted to reinvent the wheel. The *Orion*s were directly based on technology from the old Apollo missions that had put men on the moon almost a hundred years earlier. Proven technology.

They were also the last crewed spacecraft NASA had built. Twenty-one years and it still didn't have any other way to get people into space.

"Honestly," McAllister said, "it's in better shape than I expected. We'll need to replace the batteries and the reaction wheels. Update the star trackers, install new carbon scrubbers...but for the most part, it's ready to go, right out of the box."

She understood how important that was. McAllister's mission was on a deadline and there were realities to face, constraints to work within. She got it.

As the technicians started moving 7 into the big cylinder, she turned around so she wouldn't have to look at it anymore.

She used to be an astronaut. They had given her *Orion 6*—it had been her ship. And then everything had gone wrong. Her whole life had fallen apart. Why was he showing her this? Why tell her about 2I when it was being kept secret from the rest of the world? What the hell did he want from her?

McAllister wasn't a cruel man. He took one look at her face and led her out of the observation room and down a hall to an unused conference room, where they could talk.

ROY MCALLISTER: Sally Jansen knew that ship better than anyone alive. She'd piloted it halfway to Mars and back. I trusted my staff, my scientists, and my engineers, but I needed her eyes on this. A lot of people pushed back against involving her, but I was certain: this couldn't work without her. I still believe that, after everything that happened.

"I wanted to talk to you about my crew," he told her. He touched the device hanging from his ear and an AR window opened in front of her, displaying a series of personnel dossiers.

She reached up and touched the one on top. Photographs and service records blossomed all around her. *HAWKINS, WINDSOR. MAJOR, USSF, THIRTIETH OPERATIONS WING*, she read.

"A military man," Jansen said, a faint smile tugging at the corner of her mouth. "So if the aliens come swarming out of 2I, ray guns blazing, you have somebody to fight them for you."

McAllister grinned. "Hardly. *Orion*'s mission is to make contact, not start a war. There are no weapons on the spacecraft—that might send the wrong message. Though if it turns out the aliens do mean us harm, we'll be ready with a response. Hawkins's job is to serve as a military analyst. If you look here, you'll see his credentials are exemplary. He was handpicked by the Pentagon."

"You didn't choose him yourself?" Jansen asked, surprised.

"One of the conditions Congress attached to my budget was that I had to work directly with the military. Paranoia runs deep. I approve of their choice, though. Hawkins has over a thousand hours working in space, flying an X-37d."

Jansen shot him a look. "You mean that drone spaceplane of theirs?" She knew a little about it. A robot spaceship that looked like a miniature space shuttle with no windows. Supposedly they used it to kill enemy satellites. She didn't know for sure—all its missions were classified. "He flies that thing? It's a lot different flying a spaceship when you're in it, not sitting in a bunker in Nevada playing with a joystick."

"Utah, actually, and it's all done with haptic response VR these days. Don't look at me like that. He's supposed to be an extraordinarily competent man."

"Sure," Jansen said dryly. She swiped Hawkins's file away and went to the next one. *RAO, PARMINDER, MD, PhD*, she read. The picture showed a smiling young woman with short black hair. "Doctorates in medicine and astrobiology. She must like to keep busy. Looks like she's about eighteen."

"Everyone under forty looks like that these days," McAllister said. "Better medicine, better nutrition...Meanwhile, those of us who grew up in the twentieth century all look like desiccated mummies." He smiled to show he was making a joke. He made them so rarely you needed a signal to know it was happening. "Rao works here at JPL, with me. I've known her for years, and she has my complete confidence."

Jansen swiped the file away—then stopped in surprise when she saw who was next.

STEVENS, SUNNY, PhD

"You met him today," McAllister pointed out. "What did you think?"

Jansen had spent half her life training to be an astronaut. She knew the kind of person who was right for the job, and who would wash out early. She'd seen it happen again and again. Stevens wasn't the type to make it.

She gave McAllister a dubious look.

Roy shrugged. "He's brilliant. No, really. No one else even thought to look at 2I, back when it was just one more bright dot in the sky. We might have missed this thing—right up until it parked itself on our doorstep. And he's studied it for more than a year now."

She supposed that counted for something. Still.

McAllister shrugged. "When Stevens came to me originally, bringing his data from KSpace, he had conditions. He wanted a job. Specifically, he wanted to be an astronaut. He said he's wanted to be one since he was five."

"Like every other kid in America," Jansen pointed out. Except that wasn't true anymore, was it? Now they all wanted to be stream celebrities. "Wait. You're saying—he bargained for a seat on this ship?" That wasn't how this was done. Jansen had spent years of her life qualifying for a shot at a mission. She had worked her ass off. This guy came in and just demanded it, and it was handed to him?

"Without his data, there would be no mission."

"He's blackmailing you. No, it's extortion—or something," Jansen said, irritated.

"I've chosen to see it a different way. I get a world-class astrophysicist and the closest thing we have to an expert on alien spacecraft." McAllister shrugged. "Sometimes you don't get to choose your battles in this life. Sometimes you take what's handed to you."

"I think I understand now," she said, "why you brought me here. You've got a crew with no real experience. For all their degrees and qualifications, not one of them can be trusted with a spacecraft."

"We chose the best people in America for the job," McAllister said. "Sadly, these days—we didn't have a class of astronauts to pick from."

"So you want me to train these people, right? Teach them how to be astronauts? We don't have much time."

"Four months."

Jansen shook her head. Astronaut training, back in her day, took two or three years—and that was just for the basics. After that you might spend another year learning about your specific mission. She'd spent eighteen months simply learning how to walk on Mars. To get people ready to work and survive in deep space? Four months was ludicrous. They might as well go untrained. "I'll do what I can, but... Wow. This is a recipe for disaster, and you know it, Roy. You need a team to go talk to aliens—and this is all you could come up with?"

McAllister sighed. She saw, suddenly, what a strain he was under. How hard he'd worked on this. "There are things I just don't have. I don't have time for more training. I don't have the ability to spend months looking for the right people—I need to go with people I have in front of me right now. And I don't have astronauts, not anymore. Which brings me to this. I need someone on *Orion* 7 who can actually fly it. I don't want you as a trainer, Sally. I want you in the fourth seat. As mission commander."

Her whole body turned to stone. There was no other way to describe it. She couldn't move. Her lungs seized up and she couldn't breathe.

For twenty-one years she'd lived with what happened to *Orion* 6. With the fact that she had personally, with her own hands, killed

Blaine Wilson. It didn't matter why she'd done it. It had never mattered why. It had meant the end of her time as an astronaut. It had meant she would never go to Mars. It had meant she would never go to space again—the thing she had loved more than anything in her life.

And now. Just like that. He wanted her back.

What he was asking of her—

How could he ask this of her?

Dear God, she wanted to punch him in the jaw. She wanted to grab him and pull him close and sob into the lapels of his jacket. Damn it, this wasn't fair.

It wasn't fair at all.

"I know it's a big ask."

She snorted in surprise. Talk about understatement.

"If there was anyone else..."

"Julia Obrador. Or Ali Dinwari," she suggested. "They were on *Orion 6*. They have the skills you need, and the training."

"Neither of them ever served as MC on a mission. Besides which—Ali died about four years ago. He was run down by an autonomous car in San Francisco. As for Julia, she's living in Mexico, making high-end pottery. She has three kids and a husband."

Jansen understood what he meant by that. Julia had something to lose. This was going to be a dangerous mission, maybe the most dangerous NASA mission since the moon landings eighty years earlier. If Jansen died up there—who would miss her? Chuy and Esmee?

"You have the qualifications I need. You know this job inside and out. I don't have anyone else who fits that bill. Sally—we thought we were done. We thought we weren't going to get any more crewed missions. Now this happens. We need you. I need you."

Blood surged through her head, making her cheeks burn. She felt as if her skull were tightening, crushing her brain.

"I'm offering you a second chance. How many people get those, in life?"

She let go of the breath trapped in her chest.

She couldn't say what she wanted to say. *I killed Blaine Wilson.* Those words wouldn't come out of her mouth. She knew how Roy would respond anyway. He would say that she had saved three other lives in the process. That had always been his line. So instead she voiced the second-biggest objection she had to his proposal.

"Roy. I'm fifty-six years old."

"And in better shape than any of them," he said, gesturing at the files in front of her. "Plus there's the fact that no one knows *Orion* better than you."

"I don't know. I don't...Look, it was bad enough last time. You picked me to be mission commander of *Orion 6*. A woman. The media had a field day with that. Even before we launched, my social media was just one big hate fest. After we scrubbed the mission, I had to delete every online account I had."

"I remember. I saw some of the posts about woman drivers," McAllister said tightly.

"Did you see the death threats?" she responded.

Which hadn't even been the worst of it. She didn't want to tell him, even now, about the trolls who had told her in loving detail what they planned on doing to her. What they claimed she deserved.

McAllister looked shocked, but he just shook his head. "I don't care about those ignorant fools. And I don't care if you're a woman or a man, black or white—I don't care how old you are. You're still the best astronaut I ever trained."

Jansen rubbed at her face. "Roy! Roy, what the hell are you doing? What are you asking from me?"

"I'm asking if you still have it, Sally. If you're still the astronaut I picked to be the first human being to land on Mars. I think you are, but you *know*. If you say to me right now that you're the wrong person for the job, well, OK. I'll find someone else. Somewhere. Or you can say yes. You can say yes, and you can go back to space."

Her hands were shaking. She couldn't control them.

A second chance. A chance to redeem herself, to show she really was the astronaut he believed she was. Or a chance to screw up again and prove to everyone exactly what she was.

"What's your answer, Sally? I need it right now."

CLOSE APPROACH

*R*OY MCALLISTER: *Orion 7 launched on a beautifully clear day in September, atop an SLS Block 2 rocket out of pad SLC-6 at Vandenberg Air Force Base. For this launch I personally served as FC, flight controller, and CAPCOM, the only voice that the astronauts would hear from the ground. The launch was textbook. First- and second-stage separations went smoothly, and there were no problems with orbital insertion. We needed this one to be perfect. NASA had never had so much riding on a mission. No. Not just NASA. The human race.*

Watching the Earth from space was better than any VR stream Parminder Rao had ever experienced. There was always something changing: Cloud shadows drifting with perfect slowness over the Alps. Rivers and lakes catching the sun in sudden, blinding flashes of light. The glowing spiderwebs of cities on the night side.

She was hovering in the cupola module, a little dome of polycarbonate windows mounted in a metal frame at the front of *Orion 7*. For the moment, while it was still pointed back at home, she was taking in one last view. She caught her breath as a meteor streaked by over Australia, an arrow-straight line of light that flared into nothingness as she watched.

Beautiful, she thought.

Then the view glitched, big blocks of pixels cascading across the surface of the planet, ruining it. Reminding her this wasn't real.

She reached up and touched the twin devices mounted on her cheekbones—two little circles of plastic. She'd been looking at an

AR view of Earth, a telescopic view. When she shut down the over-lay, she saw Earth as it really looked now. Just a bright-blue dot far, far behind them, the only thing breaking up a panorama of black. She couldn't even see the stars. Thirty-three days since they'd launched. She'd thought she would get used to the emptiness, the endless stretch of nothing. She never had. Instead she had kept her eyes locked on that blue dot, the sole point of reference in the universe.

Except—it wasn't the only thing she could see. Her breath caught in her throat as she realized for the first time she could see another dot out there. Tiny, and very dim, a dull red that disappeared if she tried to focus on it.

2I. Their destination.

The aliens.

She could see them with her naked eye. Excitement percolated through her as if her bloodstream had just been carbonated. She should tell the others. She turned around and pushed open the vinyl flap that separated the cupola from the HabLab, the main module of the spacecraft. The others would come running, she knew. While they'd made plenty of telescopic observations over the last month, this was a special moment, an important—

Music burst over her as she stuck her head into the HabLab, the pounding rhythm of Chinese ultrapop, a whirling vortex of guitars and drum machines.

BOOM BOOM BOOM-SHAKA-LAKA. BOOM-SHAKA-LAKA.

"EVERYONE MUST DANCE NOW."

"*Orion*, this is Pasadena," Roy McAllister called. "We're hearing some-thing over your acoustic telemetry feed. Everything OK up there?"

It would take fifty-two seconds to get a reply. McAllister stood up from his seat and paced back and forth in front of his console. He had the big chair, but there were a dozen other people in the control room with him, all of them watching a massive bank of screens at the far end of the room. The biggest of those screens showed *Orion* 7's question mark–shaped trajectory, its path to 2I following a broad curve that would let it match velocities with 2I as it plunged toward Earth. The ship was well into the descending node of the hook, now—only a week or so before it would arrive.

He hadn't been sleeping, the last few nights. He knew he wouldn't be able to relax until they actually got to the alien starship. Of course, he was fooling himself if he thought he would be able to sleep then.

There was so much riding on this mission. Whether *Orion* found friendly aliens up there or a weapon hell-bent on destruction, nothing was ever going to be the same.

"DANCE DANCE DANCE."

"Pasadena, this is *Orion*," Jansen said, making him flinch. He'd almost forgotten that he'd called for a status check. "Everything up here is A-OK. Stevens is just blowing off some steam."

BOOM BOOM BOOM-SHAKA-LAKA. BOOM BOOM.

The entire HabLab was shaking to the beat.

The largest module of *Orion 7* was essentially a big balloon with two walls made of thick, reinforced vinyl. They were basically living inside a bouncy castle. The minimal furniture inside the HabLab—their sleepsacs, the little table where they took their meals, their screens and storage lockers and equipment—all of it was bolted to the soft walls in such a way that when they played music or screened a movie, everything vibrated with a droning hum.

BOOM BOOM BOOM.

Hawkins was on the treadmill, jogging to the beat. He scowled when he saw Rao enter the module, then rolled his eyes to indicate he wasn't mad at her. He grasped the hand bar of the treadmill and squeezed until his knuckles turned white. His hands always scared her a bit. They were rough, gnarled, the knuckles twisted. Rao had been a doctor long enough to know what that meant. Hawkins must have spent his formative years bouncing from one fistfight to another. From the way his nose was slightly off center she knew it must have been broken enough times that it wouldn't set properly anymore. He'd never been anything but immaculately polite to her since she'd met him, but she never felt quite comfortable around him, either.

She touched her devices and saw that he still had thirty-nine minutes left in his scheduled stretch on the machine. "Keep it up," she called, shouting over the thud of the music. As the mission's flight surgeon, she had to make sure they all got two hours a day on the torture device. Living in microgravity for a month could turn your bones to mush if you weren't careful. "Pick up your pace and you might set a new record!" To encourage them all to stick to their exercise schedule, she'd created a log of how much virtual distance each of them covered during their daily run, then challenged them each to beat the others' scores.

The idea had been met with mixed degrees of enthusiasm.

Hawkins just rolled his eyes again and frowned at the back of the module, the walled-off area where they slept and bathed. Sunny—she was supposed to call him Stevens, they were all going by their last names now—must be back there, she thought.

"EVERYONE IS REQUIRED TO DANCE."

"Towel, Major?"

Hawkins flinched as ARCS—their autonomous robotic crew support—approached him on tiny puffs of air. Rao knew he had never liked the robot, and she had to admit it creeped her out sometimes, too. It was made of nothing but plastic arms, three of them connected at a mutual shoulder. Each arm ended in a white hand that was entirely too human for good taste. The hands were modified versions of the prosthetics given to wounded soldiers, which explained why they had simulated fingernails and slightly raised ridges on the knuckles to resemble hair. It used one of its hands to grab and hold on to one of the upright supports of the treadmill. Another held out a white microfiber towel.

Hawkins grabbed the towel and smeared it around his face and neck, soaking up his sweat before it could get loose and float around the module. "Do you happen to know," he asked Rao—she could barely understand him over the music—"how loud music has to be before it damages the human ear?"

"Why don't you tell me?" she asked. She actually did know—eighty-five decibels with prolonged exposure, or a hundred for even a short duration—but she assumed this was one of those times people asked a question so they could tell you the answer.

"I'd say this qualifies," he muttered.

"If it keeps him sane," Commander Jansen said from over their heads, "I'm all for it. Hawkins, nobody complains when it's your pick for movie night and you only want to watch documentaries about World War II."

Rao glanced up and saw Jansen drifting along the ceiling of the cylindrical module like a fish bobbing along the roof of a tunnel. The mission commander was dismantling one of their oxygen generators, taking it apart piece by piece. As she removed and secured each component, she would stab the air with her index finger, probably making notations on a virtual clipboard Rao couldn't see.

If there had been a competition for who was the most fastidious and disciplined on board, Rao knew that Jansen would win every time. The woman never stopped working.

Rao admired this and found it terrifying, in roughly even measures. *BOOM-SHAKA-LAKA. EEK. EEK.*

Rao kicked off one yielding wall and grabbed the flap that partitioned off the dormitory section of the HabLab. Normally she would have cleared her throat or coughed to indicate she was coming in, but there was no way Stevens would hear her over the music, so she just shouldered her way through the flap and into the dim chamber beyond.

This was Stevens's scheduled sleep shift, but he was out of his sleepsac, floating in the middle of the tiny chamber. He was thrusting his arms back and forth and shaking his hips.

At least he was getting some exercise.

She started to reach out, to tap him on the shoulder. Then she jerked her hand away, not wanting to be presumptuous. He must have felt the air moving as she reached for him, though, because he spun around and gave her an incredibly serious look. For a moment he just hung there, slowly floating away from her. His eyes met hers and he raised one eyebrow.

"YOU MUST DANCE." *EEK. EEK.*

Rao felt her cheeks grow hot. Stevens was still looking at her.

"You heard the man," he said.

"I beg your pardon?"

Stevens grabbed her hand and spun her around in the air. She shrieked in surprise, then tried to cover the noise she'd made with a laugh. He put a hand on her hip and they were dancing. Rao looked back over her shoulder, making sure neither Hawkins nor Jansen could see them.

EEK. EEK.

"What the hell is that?" she heard Hawkins shout. Maybe he was trying to be heard over the music, but that was unnecessary—Jansen had switched off the sound system, and the only thing they could hear was the repetitive screech.

EEK. EEK. EEK.

"It's the proximity alarm," Jansen replied.

"What the hell are they thinking?" McAllister demanded, pounding his console with one fist.

No one in the control room bothered to answer him.

Up on the big screen, *Orion*'s trajectory was identified as a blue curve. A second, orange curve had been projected up there as well. A curve that crossed the blue, which had triggered the alarm.

It was KSpace. McAllister had known that the commercial spaceflight group had launched its own mission to 2I. He'd been following its progress closely—often with gritted teeth. It had been a close thing, but he had managed to get *Orion* off the ground a full week before the KSpace rocket. He had assumed, in his planning sessions, that NASA would have a week alone with 2I before the competition arrived.

As he watched the orange curve intersect with the blue, he realized that wasn't going to happen. "They're going like a bat out of hell," he said. He called out for his FDO, his flight dynamics officer. The woman looked up at him with wide eyes. He tried to remember her name, but he was too stressed out. "How are they moving that fast?"

"It looks like they've got some kind of compressed plasma engine, low specific impulse, but they've been running it nonstop since they launched, building up velocity." The FDO shook her head. "It doesn't make sense—it's an incredibly wasteful flight profile. They'll need to burn even harder to brake when they arrive at 2I, to match velocities."

"Fonseca," McAllister said, suddenly remembering her name. At his age you celebrated the small victories. "It makes perfect sense. It means they get there first."

"It's like a shot across our bows," Hawkins said.

The four of them were inside a virtual reality environment, floating in empty space. The trajectories of the two ships swooped around them as Jansen zoomed in on the display.

It was all over before she could even get the display up and running, of course. At the speeds the two ships were traveling, the KSpace ship had passed across their trajectory and was already well on its way back into deep space. "NASA says they were tracking them this whole time, but didn't expect them to come within a thousand kilometers of our position," she said. "They didn't know what was happening until it was too late to give us a warning."

"How close did they get to us?" Rao asked.

"About sixteen kilometers." Jansen shook her head. They'd all had some training in orbital mechanics. At their current velocity, that kind of separation between spacecraft was dangerously close.

"So they intentionally changed their course to buzz us." Hawkins nodded significantly, as if the commercial spaceflight group had just declared war on him personally.

"It's part of the corporate culture over there," Stevens pointed out. "KSpace never settles for second place." He reached out and manipulated the display, extending it forward in time. The digits of a clock spooled upward as he extrapolated KSpace's course. "Looks like they'll arrive at least a day ahead of us."

Rao knew what that meant. It meant that the honor of true first contact—the first meeting between humans and an extraterrestrial species—was going to go to a private company. Not to America or the UN. Not to NASA.

"Well, shit," she said.

* * *

PARMINDER RAO: I'd spent my whole adult career studying poten-
tial aliens, hypothetical aliens. I'd done experiments to see whether life was
possible in the methane lakes of Titan, or in caves deep under the surface of
Mars. None of it mattered anymore. I was going to meet real extraterrestri-
als, see them with my own eyes. The fact that KSpace was going to get there
first was something we had to accept, but I'll admit—it hurt our morale. We
would just have to settle for being the second group of people ever to meet the
aliens.*

---

* AUTHOR'S NOTE: Due to the historic nature of the *Orion* 7 mission,
NASA requested that the four astronauts take time out of their busy schedules
to record intermittent "confessionals" concerning their emotional state and
their reflections on the mission. Whenever they had a moment to themselves
they were supposed to contribute to this oral history. Some of them contrib-
uted more than others. I've placed them in the narrative as close as possible to
the moment in the mission's time line when, I believe, they were recorded.

STAY/NO STAY

L ADELLE NOONAN, FLIGHT ACTIVITIES OFFICER: Much sooner than anyone would like, 2I was on target to reach Earth orbit. It had still failed to respond to any signal we could think to throw at it. We were concerned about having competition from KSpace—of course—but it didn't change anything. Orion had a mission itinerary to stick to, a flight profile that couldn't be changed. The work had to go on.

"Everybody hold on. We're going to have gravity again—just a little of it," Jansen said, "and just for a second." She grabbed a handrail mounted on the wall of the cupola.

ARCS grasped the handrail right next to her with one of its robotic hands. "I am ready for acceleration, Commander Jansen," it said.

"Thrilled to hear it," she said, and then she opened a screen to display *Orion*'s engine controls.

Another week had passed—a week of bad freeze-dried food and minimal contact with Earth. No one was complaining now, however. They had finally arrived.

The cupola was just big enough for the four of them to squeeze into at the same time. The air in the module got very thick and humid, but the polycarbonate windows were designed to resist condensation, so at least they didn't fog it up with their breath.

They were still a hundred kilometers away from 2I, and closing that distance very slowly. The mission profile suggested they approach in the most nonaggressive way possible. For the last day they'd been edging forward.

Now there was just this little distance to cover. She tapped a touchscreen, and the service module at the back of *Orion* came to life, the engines belching flame—just for a moment. The spacecraft surged forward until the mass of 2I filled her entire view. She felt a gentle tug pulling her back toward the HabLab, but nothing her muscles couldn't counteract.

2I had been visible with the naked eye for a while now, and they'd spent plenty of time looking at the red dot as it grew steadily larger. This was the first time they were close enough to see it for real, to make out fine detail.

The first thing Jansen noticed was that 2I was big. Very big. She knew it could be difficult to judge the size of objects in space when you had no points of reference, but when you looked at 2I you *felt* its size. It already looked big enough to swallow *Orion* in one bite—if it had had a mouth.

It was dark red in color, just as Stevens had predicted. It had an albedo of just .09—meaning it reflected only 9 percent of the sun's light that hit it. About as dark as asphalt. That red wasn't original to 2I—it was discoloration, the result of constant bombardment by cosmic rays as the object moved through interstellar space.

In shape it was long and thin, as expected—though rather than "cigar shaped," as Stevens had originally described it, it was spindle shaped, thick in the middle and tapering toward the ends. It was hard to tell, however, because the shape was obscured by profuse superstructures on the hull. Every part of 2I's surface was covered in incredibly convoluted shapes like pyramids or conical towers or... spines? Horns? Thorns? Some of them were fifty meters long, sticking straight out from the surface of 2I—though they covered it so densely that it was impossible to say where they stopped and that surface began. Each of the spiky towers was covered in smaller versions of itself, cone-shaped projections mounted in a spiraling procession over the full surface of the tower. Those smaller towers were in turn covered in miniature versions of themselves. They had examined that surface structure through a telescope at various magnifications and found that the pattern was repeated no matter how deep you went. The shapes, the angles, the spiraling curves were replicated ad infinitum.

"It's a fractal. Those are like Sierpinski pyramids," Rao said after they'd studied it for a while. Jansen and Hawkins looked back at her in incomprehension. She shrugged. She would explain as best she could without giving them a math lecture. "Near-infinite complexity created by elaborating on simple rules. If you wanted to build a shape with as much surface area as physically possible, this is what you would come up with. It's amazing."

"It doesn't look like any spaceship I've ever seen," Jansen said.

"Well, it wouldn't, would it?" Stevens replied. "Humans didn't make this thing. It's not going to look like what you'd expect."

Jansen shook her head. "There are rules, though. Laws of physics, of aerodynamics. You want the hull of your ship sleek. Even if it's only ever going to be exposed to interstellar hydrogen, you want it smooth so debris just bounces off of it rather than catching in those—I don't know. Spikes."

"Unless the whole point *is* to catch stuff. *Specifically* interstellar hydrogen," Stevens said. "You want all that surface area to gather as much hydrogen as possible, so you can use it as fuel."

"Maybe," Jansen said. She wasn't thinking about science just then.

"I don't see any sign of weapons," Hawkins said, as if he'd read her mind. "No gun barrels, no missile racks." He snorted in derision. "Though they could have all kinds of guns and nasty toys and I would have no idea what I was looking at."

No one in the control room at JPL spoke. The silence was broken only by the occasional beep of a telemetry tracker marking time or the crackle of radio static as the first images of 2I were beamed across millions of kilometers of space.

Roy McAllister stood before the big screen, taking in every detail. Watching as the red towers on the hull of the starship slipped by, looking for anything he could get a handle on, anything that might suggest that this was a vehicle built by intelligent beings—beings they could understand, beings they could reason with.

He turned and made eye contact with General Kalitzakis, the man in charge of the military aspect of the mission. Kalitzakis was shorter than McAllister by nearly a foot. He'd been a fighter pilot thirty years earlier, and back then, when the pilots actually had to control their aircraft from inside their cockpits, there had been a maximum height for the specialty. His face was tense as he watched the screen, looking for any sign of aggression.

They both knew there was a chance that 2I would simply attack *Orion* on sight, that the big ship would swat Jansen and her crew out of the sky. No one doubted it had the technology to obliterate them without real effort. If that happened, Kalitzakis would immediately take over, pushing McAllister out of the way. At that point the mission wouldn't be about first contact anymore. It would be about the defense of Earth.

"Pasadena, this is *Orion*." Jansen's voice over the radio made everyone in the control room jump a little. "We're watching 2I closely. So far there's been no change. I'm taking us in a little closer."

Kalitzakis gave McAllister a tiny nod. McAllister touched the device on his ear. "*Orion*, we copy," he said.

They were so far away from *Orion* it would take nearly a minute for his voice to reach the astronauts. Radio signals moved at the speed of light, but over these distances even that was achingly slow. If something did go wrong, it would take that long before anyone on Earth even knew it had happened.

2I grew larger and closer and larger and closer. Jansen started to worry that it might change course while she was approaching and ram right into them. It was an irrational fear, but she had a hard time shaking it. It was very difficult to look at something that big and not imagine it rolling over on you, falling on you—crushing you to a pulp. The idea made Jansen's stomach flutter more than the acceleration.

It wasn't so much the threat of instant death, she thought. The instant part was good—you knew there would be no pain. No, the reason she was afraid of being crushed by 2I came from a different quarter. She was afraid it wouldn't even notice when it killed her. It would smash her to a stain on one of its spikes—and never even know she'd been there.

How the hell were they supposed to get this thing's attention? They were gnats buzzing around the horns of a water buffalo. At the very best they might hope to make it swish its tail in annoyance.

She fired *Orion*'s retros to cut their acceleration. Two plumes of vapor lanced forward across the view from the cupola. She fired some positioning jets for a tiny fraction of a second to cancel any drift, then switched on *Orion*'s reaction wheels to keep them from tumbling.

When she was done, *Orion* seemed to hang motionless in the sky, next to an equally becalmed 2I. It was as if they were locked together, though nothing but Newton's laws kept them so closely paired.

McAllister called to confirm that she'd finished her maneuver. "*Orion*, we need a STAY/NO STAY check."

"Pasadena," she said, "we are STAY."

She took one last look through the cupola and saw nothing but dark red. She'd brought them within two kilometers of the tops of the spikes, about halfway along 2I's length. And there, for the moment at least, they would remain.

"'As idle as a painted ship / Upon a painted ocean,'" Hawkins muttered.

"Hmm?"

"Sorry. I was quoting Coleridge," he told her.

"'Rime of the Ancient Mariner,'" Stevens added.

Jansen knew the poem. The story of a sailor who lost his crewmates. She wondered if, on some level, Hawkins was making a dig at her. She decided to be generous and assume he wasn't. She said nothing. None of them did, for a long time. There was too much to see.

"Huh," Rao said. "There—you see what I see, ma'am?"

Jansen nodded. "You've got good eyes."

For the benefit of the others she pointed out a dot of orangish light hovering near one of 2I's narrow ends. Just a tiny speck of brightness against the dark landscape of red. "I thought it was a star at first, maybe Sirius," Rao said. "But then it passed in front of one of the towers."

Jansen brought up an AR overlay and shared it with the others, a magnified image that filled one pane of the cupola's polycarbonate. The orange dot resolved into an actual shape, a little like a chess pawn, with a large round head atop a cylindrical body. At the back the cylinder flared out in a short skirt.

The entire ship was painted bright orange, with a pattern of tessellating hexagons twisting around the cylindrical section. They could see the corporate name painted on the spherical module, with the name of the ship underneath it in a different font:

KSPACE
wanderer

There was no sign of activity around the KSpace ship. Jansen tried to hail it on the radio but got no response. "They've been here for at least a day already. I'm hoping we can convince them to share their data," she said.

"Unlikely," Stevens told her. He knew his former employers. "KSpace never gives anything away for free."

"If they've learned something useful," Jansen said, "if they've found a way to communicate with 2I—they can name their price."

McAllister felt a touch on his elbow. He was so keyed up he whirled around to face Kalitzakis. The space force general was smiling, though his eyes were still guarded. "Looks like the immediate crisis has passed," he said. "If the aliens didn't open fire on KSpace, I doubt they're going to shoot down our people, either. Copy me on all the data you collect about the surface structures, will you? I need to put a reaction plan together." He picked up his hat from where it lay on a nearby console. "For now, I'm going to assume the mission goes ahead as scheduled. Which means I'll get out of your hair. Though if anything changes, especially if 2I shows any sign of hostility—"

"You'll be the first to know," McAllister told him.

"We have a saying in the space force," Kalitzakis said. "'Trust, but verify.'" He nodded and took one last look around the control room before he headed for the door.

Once he was gone McAllister sank back down into his chair and stared up at the big screen, the one that showed the view from *Orion*'s cameras. 2I filled the view, its weird spiral superstructures glinting as the light caught one peak, then another.

The control room was suddenly full of noise, of people congratulating each other. Someone passed around a bag of peanuts—an old JPL tradition. Eating peanuts was supposed to be good luck. Mostly it was a way to recognize the anxious moments of a mission. They'd certainly reached one of those.

When the peanuts reached McAllister, he took a few, even though his doctor had warned him to cut out all sodium. He made a mental note to order unsalted peanuts—there would be plenty more tense moments to come.

"All right," McAllister said to the alien starship. To its crew, or whatever had steered it here. "You came a long way to get here. You must want to tell us something. So talk."

MERYL NGUYEN, NASA PHYSICIST: Communicating with 2I began with contact, and that was the A-number-one priority for Orion. We needed to send a signal and then have the aliens respond to that signal. That would prove they even knew we were there. And that would be the first step toward finding out what they wanted.

"KSpace *Wanderer*. Come in, please. This is NASA *Orion*. Come in."

Jansen had been trying to reach the KSpace ship since they arrived, and it hadn't answered. The irony wasn't lost on Rao. There were three spacecraft in the local vicinity, and none of them were talking to each other.

She didn't worry about it too much. They had work to do.

Their current task was assembling specialized pieces of equipment designed by NASA for contacting 2I in wavelengths other than radio waves. For months now Earth had been trying to send radio signals to 2I. Enormous networks of radio telescopes had pointed their dishes at it, hoping for an answer—any kind of answer.

There had been none. No response whatsoever, on any radio frequency. So NASA had provided *Orion* with a bunch of experiments in nonradio communication. The gear for these experiments had been packed neatly in special crates, where they had remained, untouched, since launch. To save space they had been packed in pieces that needed to be assembled before they could be used.

The crew spread out, making room wherever they could. The absence of gravity meant they didn't need workbenches or tables, but it also meant that packing materials and empty boxes and loose screws and hardware filled up all the available space. Hawkins and Jansen had claimed the wardroom, the larger forward section of the HabLab. They were putting together a multiwavelength antenna, a big parabolic dish that could broadcast everything from microwaves to gamma rays, in case 2I could hear only longer frequencies.

The antenna had a lot of small parts that needed to be assembled. Hawkins pulled open a plastic bag full of nuts and bolts, and they went flying in every direction, unbound by gravity.

"Son of a bitch!" he growled. Then he looked up, sheepish, and met Rao's gaze.

She forced herself not to so much as smile, much less laugh, as he bounced off the walls, trying to snag all the floating hardware before it could get sucked into their air vents.

She pushed her way back into the dormitory, where Stevens was putting together a tunable laser that looked like a bazooka with a rainbow-sheened lens on one end. He sent her the assembly manual, and it popped up in her augmented reality view. "It's like the world's largest laser pointer," she said as she studied the diagrams and instructions.

"If there's a giant cat inside 2I," Stevens said, "we're golden."

Rao let out the laugh she'd held back before. It came out a little too loud. There'd been a lot of that, lately, people laughing too loud or talking over each other or just staring off into space. The closeness of 2I—the realness of it—had them all on edge.

"What's this thing?" Stevens asked, holding up a big cylinder with a tiny hole on one end.

"It's a neutrino gun," she said. "Maybe don't look *directly* into the aperture?"

Stevens laughed. "Are you kidding? Neutrinos barely interact with matter. Billions of 'em shoot through Earth all the time, and come out the other side without even changing direction."

"Still, now," she said. "I like your face the way it is. Don't go blowing it off just because you got curious."

It was the first time the two of them had been alone since they'd danced in the air, since the day *Wanderer* blew right past them. It was the first time she'd had to think about what being alone with him meant.

So far it had meant watching him, watching him move and float through the HabLab. Then darting her eyes away whenever he caught her looking. It meant laughing too hard whenever they bumped into each other in the close confines of *Orion*. It meant treating each other as professionals. Serious professionals.

Rao knew what she wanted from him. She also knew she was very, very good at controlling her impulses when she needed to focus. Most of the time.

She reached under their collapsible shower unit for a bolt that had floated away from her. When she came back up, Stevens put his hands on her shoulders. He leaned in close to kiss her neck. She'd kind of been expecting that, so she stiffened up.

"Hey," he said. "Was that...OK?"

Rao laughed. "It was...extremely OK. Honestly," she said. "But Sunny—we're working." When he didn't let go immediately, she turned around and pushed him gently away. She tried to think of something to say that would defuse the situation. "You must be as excited to meet the aliens as I am, don't lie."

"I'm excited about a lot of things," he said, with an utterly innocent expression. That made her laugh again.

It had been a long time since they'd left Earth. A long time to spend so close to him, often sleeping right next to him. She'd never even tried to deny the attraction.

He put his mouth very close to her ear. "Are you seriously going to tell me you don't want to be the first person to have sex in space?" he asked.

Her eyes popped open wide and she yanked her head back to see his face. When she saw the big, overly innocent grin there, she exploded in laughter. He'd been joking. He'd only been joking.

"That is so not fair, saying that to an overachiever like me." It had taken a lot of drive to get where she had in life. Telling her she could break a record or get higher marks than someone else or— dear Lord—be the very first person to do something—

He grasped her shoulders—very gently—and pulled her close. She laughed, but it was more of a nervous laugh this time. A long streamer of bubble wrap tried to drift between them, and she batted it away from his face. That made her snort at the absurdity of everything.

He smiled. But he wasn't laughing. He'd been at least a little bit serious.

She took a deep breath. Let the tingles run down into the small of her back. Then she cleared her throat. "I think," she said, "that I'm not thinking very clearly right now. And that maybe as excited as I am by getting to meet our alien friends, I might be a little less able than usual to make good decisions. What I do know is if Commander Jansen found out, we'd both be in hot water."

She reached out and grabbed his hand. Rubbed the back of it with her thumb. He never looked as cute as he did when he was pouting, honestly. "It won't be much longer until we're back on Earth. They say anticipation makes it better, right?"

The expression on his face made her want to melt—to give in— but she stood firm. She turned around and got back to work.

From the command module she could just hear Jansen say, "KSpace vehicle. Please come in. Please acknowledge."

The new equipment was all incredibly sensitive and fragile. It had been stored during their journey because it was too delicate to be mounted on the outside of *Orion* while they were performing high-g maneuvers. None of it was designed to function inside the HabLab's thick walls, though, which meant somebody had to go outside to install it all.

Jansen had chosen to do the EVA alone. As mission commander, she should normally have given the task to somebody else. But she was the only one of them who'd ever completed an EVA before, and she didn't have time to train the others.

She pulled on her liquid cooling and ventilation garment—basically a one-piece romper made of plastic tubes full of water, which would keep her body temperature stable while she was out in space. Then she put on her snoopy cap, a tight-fitting head cover that had headphones and a microphone built into it, so she could communicate with them by radio while she was outside. Then she was ready for the actual suit.

Jansen remembered having to struggle into space suits, back in her day. Wrestling with the hard upper torsos and bonking your head on the inside of the helmet, every time. The long hours of pre-breathing you used to have to do, to avoid getting the bends from the underpressurized suits.

Getting into the suit was a problem NASA had finally solved—by turning the suit into a miniature spacecraft all its own. Their Z-3 suits had suitports, hatches on their backs that could be connected directly to an airlock on the HabLab's wall. Meaning that to get into the suit, Jansen just had to open a door and climb through feetfirst. It still wasn't easy. She had to get her legs situated, then push her arms partway into the sleeves, then squeeze her head down against her chest until she could maneuver it up into the helmet. It was not a comfortable process, but it took a few minutes instead of the better part of an hour. Once she was in she simply sealed the

back of the suit—closing the airlock behind her at the same time—
and then undocked from the HabLab, exactly as a visiting spacecraft
would do.

Except first she had to wait for permission. "Pasadena, this is
Jansen. I am ready to begin my EVA. Please confirm."

The time lag was down to twenty-nine seconds each way,
getting shorter every day as 2I approached Earth. It would still take
a full minute, though, before she got a response. She could only sit
there, her arms and legs dangling in front of her, stuck by her back
to *Orion*. She spent the time trying not to stare at 2I. She failed, of
course. It filled up half the sky in front of her. She felt as if she could
reach out and touch it. Though Stevens had told her that was a bad
idea—if you tried, its fractal surface would scrape your flesh down
to the bone. It would be like running your hand over a belt sander.

She tried to look, instead, at the orange dot that was *Wanderer*,
currently floating near one end of 2I. Forty kilometers away—it
might as well be on the far side of the moon. She had rarely in her
life felt so alone.

When McAllister's voice crackled in her headphones, she had to
fight her natural urge to flinch at the sudden sound.

"Jansen, you are cleared for EVA. Be careful."

"Right," she said, and reached a hand across her chest. The
hard upper torso—the inflexible chest of the suit, which felt like a
cuirass—was covered in equipment and screens and controls. She
found the one she wanted. It was a simple knob, made large enough
that gloved fingers could turn it easily. She had to lift a clear plastic
cover to get to it. Trying to keep her breathing normal and calm,
she twisted it all the way to the left.

The suitport connection behind her gasped as it released. She felt
herself drift forward, just a few centimeters.

She was free of the ship. Floating free, eight million kilometers
above the Earth. Two kilometers away from an alien megastructure.

Very much alone, with nothing at all above or below her, forever.

"Suit is responding as expected," she said. "Internal temperature
is a comfortable twenty-one Celsius." There was a reason astronauts

endlessly reported their status while on EVAs. It wasn't for the sake of NASA, which was too far away to do anything if something went wrong. It was to help them focus on their work. If she kept talking, she wouldn't think to look down.

Down, at this moment, being in the direction of Earth, a crescent of blue so far below her it looked very small and noncomforting. Especially when compared to 2I.

She grabbed a handrail on the side of *Orion* and turned around so she could look at her ship. She did a quick visual inspection—standard practice during an EVA. It looked as if *Orion* had come through its long journey undamaged.

She had worried about this moment. The last time she'd performed an EVA had been twenty-one years before. The day that she killed Blaine Wilson. She'd half expected to have a panic attack. Instead all she saw was the work ahead of her. She could do this.

Piece by piece, the signal equipment was passed through an airlock on the side of the HabLab. She removed each piece from the lock and snapped a tether on it, making sure it wouldn't float away, then went back for another.

In ideal conditions—back on Earth, say, on level ground—installing the equipment would have been child's play. Doing it in a space suit made the work exhausting but not exactly mentally challenging. The new equipment was all designed to slot into sockets on the exterior of the HabLab, standardized connectors that would let her just click the gear into place. The neutrino gun screwed into a round collar near the cupola. It took forever to rotate it until it locked into place. She had a little trouble with the parabolic dish of the multiwavelength antenna, but only because it was so big—nearly a meter wide. Even though it weighed nothing now, it still had mass, and she had to wrestle it into place. Once she had it seated, though, all she had to do was plug in two patch cords, one for signal and one for power.

The tunable laser gave her the least trouble. It had to be mounted to the front of the HabLab, on a complicated universal joint that would allow it to be pointed in any direction. Then she just had to hook it directly into *Orion*'s main power feed—it would pull a lot of current when it was switched on.

Her work was done. She started to say she was ready to come back. She was sore and tired from even this short EVA. It would be good to get back inside, to get all this gear off her back.

Except—

She was already out here. This might be her only chance.

She looked over at *Wanderer*, the KSpace ship. It was about ten kilometers away, just floating there. As enigmatic as 2I, in its way.

Well within her range.

She switched on the high-gain transceiver on her suit's communications package. "KSpace vehicle," she called. "Please come in. I've been trying this frequency for . . . fifteen hours now. Please give me some sign you're listening to this channel."

There was no response.

Nothing. Not a word. Stevens claimed that was just KSpace's way—that the big company didn't play well with others. Jansen had a nagging feeling there was another reason.

Maybe they were in trouble. Maybe they'd had an equipment failure. Maybe—

She didn't even want to think about it. But what if they were dead in there? *Wanderer* looked fine through their telescopes, but plenty of terrible things could have happened to the crew that would leave the ship undamaged. They could have lost pressurization and all asphyxiated. Or maybe 2I didn't like people snooping around. It could have attacked them before *Orion* arrived.

She had lost Blaine Wilson on *Orion 6* because space was inherently dangerous. Because there were so many ways it could kill you faster than you could react. The only thing that kept astronauts alive was that they paid attention. When little mysteries and unexpected readings came up, astronauts jumped on them.

She needed to know. She needed to know why KSpace wasn't answering her calls, because it might make all the difference in keeping her own crew safe. She was not going to let another astronaut die, not now. Not when her second chance depended on it.

"Pasadena," she said. *Don't ask for permission*, she thought. *Beg forgiveness later.* "Pasadena, I'm going to extend my EVA by approximately one hour. I'm also going to go off tether."

YSABEL MELENDEZ, EXTRAVEHICULAR ACTIVITY OFFI-CER: *Astronauts don't unhook their safety lines. Ever. It's just too risky. We experimented with it back in the eighties, during the STS missions. We gave our people MMUs, or Manned Maneuvering Units. They looked like big high-tech armchairs, and they let you fly around like Superman. Astronauts loved them. Looooved them. Astronauts volunteer to sit on top of rockets full of extremely volatile liquid fuel and get shot into space. Astronauts are crazy. We got rid of the MMUs fast—they were ridiculously unsafe. And way too tempting.*

Jansen reached down and unhooked the carabiner that attached her to *Orion*. She took a deep breath, even though space suit protocol advised against that. She was still a human being, and she was frightened half out of her wits. She was also determined to do this.

Her suit could make the trip, of that she was sure, because of the SAFER system: the Simplified Aid for EVA Rescue. There were jets in the shoulders and knees of her suit that would let her fly through open space. They were supposed to be used only in emergencies, in case her tether snapped somehow, but they were rated for heavy use just in case. Every time she breathed out, the suit absorbed her carbon dioxide and stored it in special tanks. The suit jets could use that gas as propellant—and she would make more of it over time, so there was no danger of its running out.

So it was possible. Possible, but ill-advised.

But if she was doing this, she needed to do it now—she was certain if she changed her mind and just headed back inside *Orion*, she wouldn't be given another chance.

She touched her keypad. Jetted CO_2 out of her suit nozzles and accelerated in the direction of the orange spacecraft as fast as she could go.

For a moment—it was perfect.

All her concerns, all her fears were put aside. She was in space again, and it was perfect. The best feeling in the world—ultimate freedom. She closed her eyes and just felt her body moving unhindered through empty space. Diving off the Florida coast had been a pale imitation of this. Even flying a plane couldn't compare to the pure abstract liberation of floating through space. Her breathing calmed, and she thought—she could do this. She was going to be OK. She would go and knock on *Wanderer*'s hatch and the KSpace crew would wave at her through their windows and everybody would have a good laugh. It was going to be OK.

And then her radio crackled and brought her right back to the realization that she was on an unsanctioned EVA, headed to what was probably a ghost ship full of dead people.

She knew exactly what McAllister was going to say, and what tone of voice he would use.

He was calm. Very proper. "Jansen, this is Pasadena. We have you performing an unsanctioned maneuver during your EVA. Can you confirm?"

He knew exactly what she was doing. He had telemetry on everything from the sweat output of her armpits to the amount of propellant in her jets. She was sure he knew why she was doing it, too. He was giving her a chance to tell him he was wrong, that she had some completely different plan in mind.

She wouldn't lie to Roy McAllister.

"I'm going over to the neighbors' house," she said. "The one with all the hexagons. I'm going to knock on their door and ask to borrow a cup of sugar."

It took a full minute before he spoke again. During which time she moved nearly a kilometer and a half away from *Orion*. The construction of her helmet made it impossible for her to turn around and look back and see how far she was from safety. She had a rearview mirror glued to one sleeve of her suit for just that reason. She made a point of not using it.

"Sally," McAllister said, "this wasn't part of your EVA plan. You know we didn't authorize this."

She reached for her keypad, intending to stop herself and turn around and fly home. She was already guilty of insubordination. She wouldn't stoop to mutiny, too. If he told her to turn back, she would. Immediately.

"I don't think this is a good idea," McAllister said.

But he didn't tell her to turn back.

She was five kilometers from *Orion* now. Halfway there. Turning back now wouldn't make this less dangerous. She had plenty of propellant in her tanks. She was breathing so hard—from the fear—that she was probably filling them back up as fast as she was emptying them.

"They've got me worried, Roy," she said. "What if they're sick over there, or injured? If somebody on *Orion* needed help, we would expect them to give it."

Seconds ticked by as she waited for the signal to fly to Earth and back. Before he spoke to her again.

"They haven't sent a distress signal," McAllister replied. "I've been in contact with KSpace headquarters, down here on the ground. They've been polite, but not exactly forthcoming. They wouldn't want you to do this."

"Too bad," Jansen said. She could feel her heart thundering in her chest. The KSpace ship had grown enormous in front of her. Not 2I enormous, but big enough her body didn't like it. Deep parts of her brain were telling her that she was falling, that she was going to smack right into the orange spacecraft, fast enough to break her bones.

She stabbed at her keypad and sent gas jetting from the four nozzles on the front of her suit, pushing back against her forward thrust. Decelerating, hard. Her knees and shoulders lurched backward but her butt kept flying forward, and she had to do some fancy flying to keep herself from spinning out.

She stabilized, then tapped out a few more quick burns to move herself closer to the spacecraft, toward the spherical module at its nose.

"I'm already here," she said.

* * *

SALLY JANSEN: Space is dangerous enough without everybody measuring their dicks all the time. If KSpace was in trouble, I was going to help. That's all I was thinking.

When Sally Jansen first saw the KSpace ship, despite its orange paint job she'd recognized its design immediately. Just as *Orion* was based on old Apollo technology, *Wanderer* was a near copy of the old *Soyuz* spacecraft.

She ought to recognize it. A *Soyuz* had been the first spacecraft she ever flew on. She'd been on board strictly as a passenger, of course. Her very first mission to space had been a quick trip to the second International Space Station, where she'd finished her astronaut training. She'd flown up to ISS-2 in a *Soyuz-MS*, then returned to Earth in its command module. That had been back in 2030. Before the Russian and American space programs had stopped working together. Back when Americans were still allowed aboard Russian spacecraft.

That *Wanderer* was based on the *Soyuz* spacecraft wasn't altogether surprising. They were the most reliable spaceships ever built—in their various permutations they had performed hundreds of missions ferrying astronauts and cosmonauts up and down, to and from low Earth orbit.

It did, however, make her feel sorry for the KSpace crew. Their ship had no HabLab, no special crew modules. Most of its mass was taken up by a big service module, its engine, which contained no crew-accessible space. Ahead of that it had a command module, which was just big enough for three people lying down in crash couches, and the spherical orbital module, which wasn't exactly roomy. The three KSpace astronauts must have spent weeks in those cramped quarters, while the NASA crew had space to stretch out and comfortable places to sleep. The *Wanderer*'s journey to 2I must have been miserable for the crew. They must be going stir-crazy by now.

Assuming they were still alive in there.

Wanderer didn't have handrails like *Orion*, so she pulled herself along the side of the orange ship using whatever handholds she could find, until she reached one of the porthole-like windows in the orbital module.

Moving carefully, she reached up and turned on one of her powerful halogen headlamps so it shone in through the window. She peered inside.

There was nothing to see in there but shadows. All the lights inside had been switched off.

Maybe the KSpace crew was just sleeping. Well, if they were, she was about to wake them up.

She pulled herself around to the nose of the craft, toward the airlock. Jansen knew how to open it. She'd trained in how to do just that almost thirty years before. It was designed to be easy for someone wearing bulky space suit gloves to handle.

She had a moment of panic as she reached for the hatch, wondering if it might be locked—but no, nobody would build an airlock that could be locked from the inside. What if you got stuck outside with no way back in?

The hatch swung back easily.

If this had been a Chinese mission, or a Russian ship, what she was doing might be an act of war. KSpace wasn't a government agency, though, it was a private company. Which meant she was only breaking and entering. She figured it was worth it.

She shouldered her way inside and closed the hatch behind her. She and her suit just fit inside the narrow airlock. She activated the inner door, and there was a roaring rush of sound as air filled up the airlock before the door swung open.

Beyond it was darkness.

She braced herself. If something had gone wrong, if the crew had run into trouble, they would almost certainly be dead by now.

What if there was—something—in there with them? Something that had boarded their ship and torn them to pieces? Maybe 2I's crew had boarded *Wanderer*. Maybe there was some homicidal alien still inside—there was no telling what the aliens looked like, much less how they would react to humans getting so close to their ship. What if they had boarded *Wanderer* and slaughtered all the crew?

She told herself she was being ridiculous.

Still. It was time to call *Orion* and let them know what she was about to do.

"*Orion*, come in," she said. "I'm entering the KSpace ship now. Everything OK over there?"

"This is Hawkins. We're fine. McAllister wants me to pilot *Orion* over to your position, so when you're done you won't have to fly all that way back. You OK with that?"

"Just be careful. If you ding up my spaceship, it's coming out of your allowance," she told him.

It helped to joke around a little. It made her feel less as if she were about to climb headfirst into a crypt full of ghosts.

She pushed her way out of the airlock, into the orbital module. It was hard to see anything by just her suit lights, but she could tell the place was a mess. Tools and empty cartons of equipment floated all around her. A food tube bounced off her faceplate, splattering her view with what looked like spaghetti sauce. There was a patch of soft cloth on the back of her right glove, which she used to wipe the mess away.

She could hear something. That meant there was air in the module—sound didn't travel in a vacuum. She followed her ears and found a bulky equipment box mounted on one wall. Fumes vented from its side, and the whole box juddered back and forth, as if it were trying to rip itself off the wall. She looked through its clear plastic front and saw that it was a 3-D printer, currently sintering together some piece of equipment she didn't immediately recognize. Maybe a replacement for something that had broken.

Why didn't we get a 3-D printer? she wondered. The KSpace ship might be based on an antique spacecraft design, but everything she could see was shiny and high tech, the best equipment private sector money could buy.

There were no bodies in the orbital module. She searched

carefully to make sure. But she did find something weird. The interior walls were covered in thin padding with a white vinyl covering, and back near the airlock leading to the command module, someone had drawn on the padding with a red pen. At first she thought it was a note—maybe left behind by a desperate crew in case anyone ever found their abandoned ship. She steeled herself to read the last words of a dying astronaut.

Then she saw there were no words. Just crude drawings of a woman with exceptionally large breasts, and next to her a giant penis with hairy testicles.

She laughed out loud.

"What's up?" Hawkins asked her. "Did you find them?"

"No," she called back. "Just—well, they must have gotten pretty bored on their way here, that's all. I'm going to check the reentry module now, keep me updated on your maneuver. Let me just—"

She stopped talking. She had been reaching for the hatch between the orbital and reentry modules. It started moving before she could even touch it.

A thing that looked exactly like a human skull poked through the hatch and stared at her with blazing blue eyes.

OK.

OK.

Not *exactly* like a skull. It was made of plastic, for one thing. It didn't have a nasal cavity or any teeth. It was mounted on a spindly neck and it used one very thin arm to push open the hatch. It was a robot designed to look like a human being, but built out of very thin parts, presumably to save on weight and materials. Maybe that was also why it didn't have any legs, just a stubby torso.

"My name is GRAM, for general robotic assistant and medic," the robot told her. "Commander Foster and his crew are away from the spacecraft right now. Can I take a message?"

JOINT ACTIVITY

EXCERPT FROM KSPACE MARKETING MATERIALS

KSpace is a subsidiary concern of CentroCore Corporation. KSpace was founded in 2021 by Kyung Leonard, the man who would become Asia's first trillionaire. KSpace launches satellites for the private sector and the military of every first world nation. KSpace operates three orbital factories that are set up to create drugs and raw materials that can't be produced under the effect of Earth's gravity. KSpace: Working Always, for a Future for All. KSpace: Busy as Little Bees!

McAllister took a maglev train to Atlanta. To visit the Hive.

The American headquarters of CentroCore took up hundreds of acres outside Atlanta. Whole towns had been taken over as housing and office space for the corporation's employees. The actual nerve center was a geodesic dome half a kilometer wide—one of the largest buildings in America, just slightly smaller than the Pentagon. Two more domes were stacked on top of it, giving it a distinct beehive look. The skin of each dome was subdivided into hexagons ten meters wide. These were normally transparent, but they could be individually polarized if the people inside wanted privacy or shade. The whole structure functioned as one giant solar cell, soaking up the Georgia sunshine.

McAllister straightened his bolo tie and walked toward the front door, passing between a double row of giant plastic bees.

There was a woman waiting for him at the front entrance. She was perhaps forty and dressed in a conservative suit, but half of her head had been shaved and then tattooed with the image of a stylized dragon. As McAllister approached, the dragon reared back and breathed fire across her temple. He hadn't been expecting that, and he flinched a little.

Maybe that was the point of the display.

She smiled and offered her hand. "Charlotte Harriwell," she said. "I'm KSpace's vice president of crewed operations." His opposite number, in other words. "Thank you so much for—"

"Is this McAllister?" a man asked, running over to meet them. He wore a blazer over a dark-blue shirt, and sharply pressed trousers—but no shoes. He looked about fifty years old, though he'd clearly had extensive plastic surgery, so it was hard to tell.

NASA had relaxed its dress codes since the days of oxford cloth shirts and pocket protectors, but whatever was happening here was beyond McAllister's experience. He was an old man and he found younger people exhausting, most of the time. "I am," he said. "May I ask—"

"Kyung Leonard. Leonard Kyung, take your pick. In Korea we go surname first, but this is America. Right?"

Charlotte Harriwell confirmed that it was with a nod.

"We want to thank you for coming all the way out here," she said. "We know just how busy you must be. When we invited you, we weren't sure you would come."

McAllister shook the woman's hand. "Professional courtesy demanded it, at the very least," he said.

Kyung Leonard laughed. "Professional courtesy! Damn, I love working with public sector people. They're always so *fucking* helpful!"

He was almost shouting. McAllister looked around and saw dozens of people in the lobby, but not a single one of them even looked up. Maybe they were used to this.

"Sorry, sorry. Sorry," Kyung said. "I had to fly in from Singapore and there was no time for sleep. Thank God that's optional these days. Come on! I have an office here, it's the top dome, right?" Harriwell nodded. "Right. The best view. Come on. Wait—did you want a coffee or something?"

"I'm fine," McAllister said.

"Great." Kyung threw an arm around his neck and nearly dragged him toward an elevator.

EXCERPT FROM WIKIPEDIA ENTRY: "KSPACE," 10/11/2055

KSpace is one of five main subsidiaries of CentroCore, a transnational corporation. It is joined by KMed, KHome, KTelecom, and KLife, the corporation's food and beverage division. While KSpace is the least profitable of the five, Kyung Leonard himself is quoted[by whom?] as saying he considers it his most important contribution to the future. Mr. Kyung is famous for committing millions[how many?] from his own personal fortune to the construction of the KStation in low earth orbit, which was the world's first orbital hotel, operating from 2028 to 2029, when an unexpected system failure caused it to deorbit well before the end of its planned life span.

The office at the top of the Hive did have a spectacular view, though Kyung waved a hand as they entered, and most of the transparent dome turned solid black. "Circadian rhythms. They'll fuck you every time." The trillionaire went to sit behind a desk that was a single slab of wood three meters long. There was nothing on it except a pair of disposable devices—rubber dots that Kyung affixed to the sides of his nose.

This was the man, McAllister remembered, who had convinced the world to stop referring to their smart devices as "phones," mostly by selling billions of wearable computers at reduced prices. He'd destroyed most of his competition within five years. Even McAllister used a KDevice, which clipped on to his ear.

"Funny how things work out, right? If that little thieving piece of shit Stevens hadn't run to you—well. If he hadn't stolen from me, nobody would know about this thing. And you and me wouldn't be talking right now. Funny."

"I suppose that's true," McAllister said, attempting to be diplomatic.

"Charlotte's going to tell you everything, OK? She's got me up to speed, broad-picture-wise, but she knows the whole story. Charlotte's great," Kyung said. He tapped his devices and his eyes glazed over. Clearly he had entered a VR trance. "Don't worry, I can still hear you."

Harriwell smiled. There was nothing strained in that smile. She didn't seem put off by her boss in the least. "I'll give you a quick briefing as to where we are," she said, "and then we'll discuss our options. All right?"

McAllister nodded. No one had offered him a seat. He decided to pick a chair and sit in it. At seventy-five years old, he disliked standing for too long.

Harriwell moved around the dome as she spoke. She would occasionally lift a hand and an image would appear in the air around her, until she was surrounded by translucent panes of light.

First she brought up three photographs. They showed young, smiling people dressed in orange KSpace hoodies—just like the one Sunny Stevens had worn when he first came to NASA. "These are Commander Willem Foster, Mission Specialist Taryn Holmes, and Mission Specialist Sandra Channarong. Our coworkers. As you know, they approached 2I/2055 D1—we call it the Object. I know you've chosen to refer to it by its provisional name, 2I. They arrived near the Object about fifty-two hours ago. The *Wanderer* had made the journey in good condition. All of our telemetry shows ship systems optimal. Commander Foster reported they were in good health and high spirits. They were anxious to get to work. They approached the Object at a minimum distance of one kilometer and started their attempts to make contact immediately. About nineteen hours ago, shortly before *Orion* was due to arrive, they performed an EVA."

"All of them? At the same time?"

Harriwell looked surprised he would ask that. "That was part of their mission profile."

NASA would never have heard of such a thing. "We do things differently. Please continue."

Harriwell nodded. "Foster and his crew proceeded directly to the Object, where they...made contact with the surface. I was going to say they landed on it, but of course its surface gravity is far too low for anyone to stand on it. Commander Foster reported all was well, and that they were going to proceed to examine the airlock at one of the Object's distal points."

An image appeared before her, a simplified view of 2I. McAllister had been studying his own maps of 2I for long enough that he recognized the pattern of the spines that stuck out from its hull.

There were only two spots on 2I's surface that were free of the crystalline spines, and they were at each of its ends—what NASA called its poles. The one on the south pole—the end pointing away from Earth—was a thin seam about ten meters long. The hull around the seam was cracked as if the seam had been open at some point, but now had sealed itself shut. The discontinuity at the north pole—near where they'd found *Wanderer*—was much larger. It took the shape of a dome about fifty meters across, with an irregularly shaped opening at its topmost point.

NASA's imagery analysts believed that the two discontinuities were airlocks. Access points to the interior of 2I. That was only a tentative analysis, however—Jansen and her crew had not yet explored either of them in detail.

The view Charlotte Harriwell shared with McAllister rotated until the north pole was centered. The words *PRIMARY AIR-LOCK* hovered over the image, with an arrow pointing at the dome.

"The *Wanderer*'s crew proceeded to examine this area with their own eyes. They performed some experiments to determine how the airlock worked. It's a completely automatic system—whenever someone enters the dome through this aperture, the whole dome rotates to face the interior. They reported that they were all in good health and ready to explore the Object."

McAllister coughed discreetly. "I'm sorry. Are you saying they just—went inside? They didn't send any probes or drones in first?"

"It was Commander Foster's call to make. Here at KSpace we believe in individual initiative," Charlotte Harriwell said.

He managed to keep from rolling his eyes. "At NASA we're big believers in safety first."

"That's why we're winning this particular space race," Kyung said.

Both McAllister and Harriwell turned to look at the trillionaire. He said nothing more, though, but simply sat there staring into empty space.

Harriwell continued. "Our astronauts went inside the Object to perform an extended reconnaissance. That was our last communication with them. It appears that whatever the Object is made of, radio waves can't penetrate it. There's no way to communicate with anyone inside."

The view expanded until 2I's airlock looked like a giant red eye staring right at McAllister. Gnat-like objects appeared, swarming around the airlock. He blinked and realized what he was looking at—this was video, presumably shot from *Wanderer*. The gnats were people.

He watched the three KSpace astronauts fly into the pupil of the eye until they were swallowed up by its darkness. A few seconds later, the eye started to move. The pupil drifted to the left—and then disappeared as it reached the edge of the clearing.

For about a minute, the dome was unbroken, a dark-red hemisphere in the middle of a forest of complicated dark-red trees. Then the pupil of the eye reappeared—on the right side of the dome this time. It moved steadily until it was back at the center of the eye.

The gnats didn't come back out.

"How long was their EVA supposed to last?"

"Six hours," Harriwell said. She looked down at her hands. "They're more than twelve hours overdue right now."

McAllister nodded. "I see why you wanted to speak with me in person. This is...a delicate situation."

How do you tell someone their people are probably dead?

"Three days of consumables," Kyung said, without otherwise moving. The sudden eruption made McAllister jump.

"I'm sorry?"

"Charlotte, tell him the consumables situation. Tell him they're still alive."

Harriwell nodded. "They took three days' worth of food, water, and oxygen with them. We believe they can survive for another fifty-six hours. It's possible they'll emerge from the airlock anytime now, and be confused why we were so worried." She scratched herself under her chin. "Obviously that's what we're all hoping for."

"At KSpace we don't hope," Kyung said fervently. "We *believe*."

McAllister ignored him.

"We know NASA's mission to the Object is vital," Harriwell said. "Out of everyone on Earth, the three of us here probably understand that better than anyone. We know what could be at stake if your crew suffers a delay to their operations."

McAllister nodded. This was what they'd brought him here for, then. He decided he wouldn't make them beg. That was beneath him—his entire life had been devoted to safe human exploration of space. "We're ready to offer any assistance we can in helping your crew get home," he said.

Charlotte Harriwell bit her lip. She looked as if she wanted to say something but didn't dare.

"He doesn't get it," Kyung said. He tore the devices off his face and jumped up out of his chair. He stalked toward McAllister, his hands in the air. "He doesn't get this at all. Charlotte, tell him. Tell him what we wanted to say."

Harriwell took a deep breath. "We're very grateful that you want to help. But the official position of KSpace is that our astronauts are in no danger."

"No danger," McAllister repeated. The KSpace crew was twelve hours overdue on an EVA. If one of his astronauts were that late, with no communication—dear God. He would be running to anyone he could think of who might be able to help. He would be tearing out what was left of his hair.

"Hell, for all we know," Kyung said, "they could be in there having a tea party with the aliens. Who did we send from market development? Sandy, Sandy Channarong? Ooh, she's good. She's probably in there making deals with the aliens already."

"It's extremely unlikely your people would be able to communicate with 2I's crew, much less make business deals with them," McAllister pointed out.

"You know how you get rich in this world?" Kyung asked. "You ignore everyone when they tell you something is unlikely. Because they didn't say 'impossible,' did they?"

McAllister rose from his chair. "I'm sorry. You had me come all the way out here so you could tell me to leave your people alone? To back off?"

"You are familiar with the laws about exploitation of objects in space?" Kyung asked. "They say we have the rights to whatever we find. Sovereign rights."

McAllister was no legal scholar, but he knew the basics. The United Nations had long held that everything outside the atmosphere of Earth was the common property of all humanity. In the last few decades, though, the United States had taken a different view. For instance, there were laws on the books now that allowed a commercial space agency like KSpace to plunder asteroids for their resources—and keep all the profits.

2I was no asteroid. Kyung's message was clear, however. If NASA tried to intrude on KSpace's salvage rights, it would be running the risk of a long and costly legal battle.

"You could have told me as much in a text message," McAllister said.

Charlotte Harriwell gave him a meaningless smile. "We wanted to discuss this with you face-to-face, as a gesture of goodwill. How did you describe it? Professional courtesy," she said.

Kyung seemed to think that was hilarious. He laughed and laughed.

*   *   *

EXCERPT FROM A BROCHURE CIRCULATED
AT THE PARIS AIR SHOW, 2054

The newly redesigned Wanderer-NX *is the most advanced space-craft in the KSpace fleet. It is partially reusable and meets all industry standards for safety and pilot comfort. Depending on its mission, the* Wanderer *can be launched atop a variety of boosters, including existing American, Russian, and European rockets.*

"Confirmed, Pasadena," Jansen said. She reached up and touched her devices, then turned around to look at the rest of the crew. For a long time she didn't speak.

"Come on, Sally J," Stevens said, drumming on the wall of the HabLab with one hand. He realized he was doing it and stopped. "McAllister said something. You were talking for a long time."

"They went into 2I. They were supposed to come out more than twelve hours ago, but they never did," Jansen said.

"It's not normal to be that late on an EVA, is it?" Hawkins asked.

"No," she replied.

"But it's not—I mean, it's not long enough that we can assume they're dead, either," Hawkins said.

"No."

Stevens launched himself across the HabLab. Headed toward Jansen. "Just because they're KSpace doesn't mean they're bad people," he said, trying to look her in the eye. He was certain he knew what McAllister had said, and he couldn't bear it. "Foster I don't know. Taryn Holmes, I used to call him Terry, he and me worked on a SETI survey a couple years ago, we didn't find anything, but he taught me how to surf. And Sandra—"

He stopped himself.

The portraits of the three KSpace crew members were up on one of the HabLab's screens. Smiling, wearing orange KSpace hoodies. Looking excited to explore the universe. There had been a picture of Stevens in the same pose, in the same sweatshirt, hanging on the wall of an office in the Hive. Before he quit his job and ran away to join NASA.

"Sandra," he said. In the picture she had cut her hair short. She had a mole on her left earlobe. So she'd never had that removed. She used to talk about it . . .

"What is it, Sunny?" Rao asked, putting a hand on his shoulder.

He glanced back at her, not wanting to say it. "She worked in market development, not my area, but we met at a party and for a little while we, you know. Dated. We—" He shook his head. "We're still good friends."

He expected Rao to pull her hand away, and maybe say, "Oh," and look away from him, but she didn't. She squeezed his shoulder and moved until she was floating right behind him. Close.

"We need to go after them," he said. Stevens felt as if a boiler in his head were building up steam. He felt as if his eyes were bugging out of his head. "Jansen—if you don't want to go over there, I will. I'll go right now."

"Hold on," Jansen told him, calm as always. "McAllister had his own thoughts on this. Our original mission didn't include us boarding 2I, at least not this early on. He was very clear about that."

"God damn it! We have to save them!"

Jansen's eyes snapped into focus, as if she'd just come out of virtual reality. She looked straight at him.

He flinched, a little. But he was certain he was in the right. "You can't let them die. You can't just—"

"Stop," she said.

Stevens pushed off the side of the treadmill and moved away from her, getting as far from her as he could. He realized he'd been about to grab her. To shake her, he thought. Which would have been an idiot move.

"Just shut up a second," she told him.

Jansen reached over and touched the nearest screen. Stevens could see what she was doing—she didn't hide it. She had just switched off their radio. No one on Earth would hear what they said next.

"Yes," she said. "Yeah. We're going."

★   ★   ★

SALLY JANSEN: I know what they're going to say. I lost an astronaut once. He died on my watch. I had some kind of deep-seated need for redemption. I wasn't thinking that at the time. All I knew was, the second I saw Wanderer, I felt something was wrong. I had to do something. Say I was compensating if you want. Say I was being paranoid, I don't give a damn.

Stevens whooped and punched the inflatable wall hard enough it rippled. "Yes! Yes!"

"Wait," Hawkins said. "Just—just wait!"

Jansen ignored him. She moved over to the nearest screen and started the warm-up sequence for the EVA suits.

She was the commander of this mission. She wasn't interested in hearing his opinion of what she'd chosen to do. Apparently that didn't sit well with him. He kicked his way across the HabLab and grabbed her arm.

"Are you insane?" he asked. "You can't risk our lives just because—"

"Let go of me," she told him.

He pulled back, lifting both hands as if in surrender. She could see from his face, though, that he hadn't accepted anything.

Rao was still on the far side of the module, touching Stevens's back. Now she moved away from him, just a little. She gave Stevens a complicated look before she spoke, but clearly she intended to be heard, too. "We have our orders," she said. "NASA was pretty clear on this—we're not supposed to *touch* 2I. We're not supposed to get any closer to it than we are right now. Back on Earth they said that could be taken as aggression, and—"

"We're not on Earth now," Jansen said. "McAllister didn't foresee this. He didn't make any plans for astronauts going missing."

Hawkins glared at him. "Am I the only one who's going to say it? Seriously?" He let out a bitter laugh. "They're dead!"

Stevens bristled. "Hey!"

Hawkins didn't look at him. He was too busy trying to stare Jansen down. "They're dead. They broke into an alien spaceship and the aliens killed them. How can you not see that?"

Jansen tried to ignore him, but he wasn't done.

"It's the only explanation that makes sense. But...this isn't about *Wanderer*'s crew. Is it?" She tried to turn away, but he followed, getting right in her face. "It's about you. You want to be a hero. You want to make up for past mistakes."

Maybe, she thought. *Maybe*.

But it was still the right thing to do.

Jansen stared him down. "I'm the commander of this mission," she said. Intending for that to be the last word. "Stevens," she called.

"I won't be a part of this," Hawkins told her. "I refuse to help you get yourself, and maybe all of us, killed."

"Fine," she told him. "Then stay here while I go over. Stevens. Sunny!"

Stevens looked up with a start, as if he'd been lost in thought. "Yeah?"

"I'm going right now. You coming?"

Instead of answering her directly, he looked over at Rao. She was chewing on her lip, clearly agitated. Clearly scared. Her eyes searched Stevens's for a moment. Then they cut away. Rao hugged herself and looked at nobody.

"Yeah," Stevens said. "I'm in."

YSABEL MELENDEZ, EXTRAVEHICULAR ACTIVITY OFFI-CER: So we had a brief loss of communications, which was bad enough. Then I noticed on my board that two of the EVA suits had been undocked from Orion. *Which meant two of our people were out on an unscheduled EVA. That's...that's pretty much my worst nightmare, that my astronauts would just go out for a walk and not even tell me. I called Administrator McAllister, of course, but he was still on his way back from Atlanta. He told me to sit tight. I had no fucking clue what was going on. Sorry for the profanity.*

The second he got back from Atlanta, Roy McAllister raced to retake his chair in the control room. All the screens in front of him displayed the same view—a camera feed from *Orion*'s exterior hull. It showed the backs of two space suits, slowly receding from view.

The top half of every screen was just a blur of dark red, the north pole of 2I out of focus as the camera tracked the astronauts.

"Commander Jansen," McAllister said, "this is Pasadena. Come in, Commander Jansen. Copy, please."

Every eye in the control room was watching McAllister. The ground crew was holding its collective breath. They all wanted to see what he was going to do next.

He was going to wait nearly a minute to get an answer. That was what he was going to do.

He knew what Sally was doing. Up to this point no one had specifically told her not to do it. Just like last time, when she'd gone off tether to investigate *Wanderer*. He'd allowed that to happen. A sin of omission. He wouldn't make that mistake again.

"Copy, Pasadena," Jansen eventually said.

"Commander, your current EVA was not scheduled. You're giving us all a good fright down here. I want you to turn around." He decided not to wait for her reply before he said more. "We discussed this, Sally. We talked about you going over there, and I told you I thought it was a bad idea."

He tried to keep his breathing calm and level as he waited for her reply.

"You didn't specifically order me not to go," she said.

McAllister sat down and rubbed at his forehead, trying to ward off the headache he knew was coming. "Well, I am now. Turn around, Sally. KSpace made it very clear they don't want your help. You're endangering Dr. Stevens by taking him out of the ship."

That last was a bit of dirty pool, McAllister thought. He knew Jansen had been traumatized by Blaine Wilson's death. That she would do anything to protect her people, and that he was being manipulative. Still, she had started this by defying him. He couldn't let that stand.

Thirty seconds ticked by. Sixty. Still there was no response.

"Commander Jansen—" he started, but then she interrupted him.

"Those people in there could still be alive," she said.

McAllister gritted his teeth. "Commander—"

"Sir," someone said. McAllister looked up, ready to bite their head off.

It was the CATO, the communications and tracking officer, who was in charge of all radio communications with *Orion*.

"Sir," CATO said. "Commander Jansen has switched off ground communications. She can't hear you."

Melendez, the EVA officer, was standing up, leaning over her own screen. "I'm still getting telemetry and biodata from both suits," she said. "What do we do?"

McAllister scrubbed at his face with his hands. "Do? There's nothing we can do." Technically that wasn't true. They could remotely switch off power and life support to Jansen's suit. They could let her suffocate in the hope she would take the hint and turn back. Though she was smart enough to figure out how to override their remote commands, he imagined.

They could call *Orion* and speak with Major Hawkins and have him relieve Jansen of command. That might not be enough, either.

Realistically? They could do nothing.

McAllister took his hands away from his face and looked at the sea of expectant faces all around him. "We sit tight and wait for her to come to her senses."

EXCURSION (1)

AMY TARBELIAN, FLIGHT PSYCHOLOGIST: All four Orion astronauts had been screened thoroughly before launch. We wanted to make sure they were up, mentally, for the stresses ahead of them. We knew that Sally Jansen had suffered a traumatic experience in her past, but she was tough as nails—resilient, I guess, is the better clinical term. If anything, we believed the tragic loss of life during her aborted Mars mission would make her more determined to keep her people safe and alive. It didn't surprise us that she would extend that quasimaternal impulse to the Wanderer's crew. We didn't expect, though, that she would defy a direct order.

"Oh shit. Oh shit, oh shit. Oh motherfucking shit."

Jansen didn't bother looking back to see what was happening behind her.

"Keep it together, Stevens," she said. "Come on—tell me what's wrong."

"I'm, uh, tumbling a little," he said.

"We covered this in training. How do you fix a tumble?"

"Jets. Suit jets. Right. Just a touch of... OK, that made it worse. Jansen—Jansen, I'm upside down!"

She touched the keypad on her glove and spun around. Used a little propellant to get closer to him. He was slowly spinning, his legs coming up over his head.

"Remember the first rule," she told him.

"There is no up, there is no down," he said.

"Right. Just because I look upside down to you right now..."

She reached him and grabbed hold of his arms. Got him stabilized. "OK. There."

"Thanks," he said. She could hear him gasping for breath over the radio.

She needed to distract him. "So," she said. "You and Rao, huh?"

It worked—she heard him gasp, and, though it was hard to tell when he was in a space suit, she thought he turned bright red, too. "I have no idea what you're talking about," he said, in an exaggeratedly serious voice.

Jansen laughed. "You do realize that there are cameras all over *Orion*, right? And that Mission Control listens to every word we say?" She knew how easy it was to forget that. "And—I'm not going to name names or anything, but believe me, you wouldn't be the first. Why her, though? If you don't mind me asking, and since we're out here with something approaching privacy."

He touched his jets until they were facing each other directly. Which meant he was flying backward and couldn't see 2I. Probably for the best—she could catch him long before he ran into anything. "You mean other than she's the only woman on the ship who's... age appropriate?"

Jansen laughed. "Son, I would break you in two."

"We're scientists. Parm and me, we speak the same language. I guess it started there. But hell, you don't pick the people you like, do you? Sally J, are you going to tell me you never fell for somebody at the wrong time?"

"That's pretty much the story of my love life, actually," she admitted.

"Oh yeah?"

Jansen sighed. "Back when I was picked for *Orion 6*, well, I was in the news streams a lot. I was with a very nice, very tough guy. Baxter, an air force pilot, but he couldn't handle the fact I was suddenly more famous than him. Yeah. Bad timing. Then after I came back...there was this woman, and that was good. Having somebody to talk to. Maybe, if I'd waited a little longer, it could have worked. I was pretty broken. Mary did her best, but in the end she was more interested in psychoanalyzing me than getting me into bed. And when somebody tries to fix you when you're not ready—" She realized that maybe she was oversharing. "Listen, just—if the two of you make a mess on my spacecraft, just clean it up."

"Wh-what?"

"There are some things nobody wants to clean out of an air filter."

He was looking her right in the eyes. She glanced away—and then he erupted in a howl of laughter.

"Now," she said. "Isn't an EVA easier when you're not hyperventilating?"

"Yeah. Yeah, that helped, talking. Just—there's got to be a name for it. They've got names for all those phobias. Ailurophobia is the irrational fear of cats. Triskaidekaphobia is fear of the number thirteen. Right?"

"Sure."

"What do you call the fear that you're going to go flying off into space, forever?"

"Sanity," she told him.

ROY MCALLISTER: I could have been more forceful with Jansen. I could have threatened her with criminal charges when she refused to return to Orion. God help me, I think I agreed with her, though. That we had a duty to rescue the KSpace astronauts. I made the appropriate protests, followed the rules. Then I let her go. Of course, I reserved the right to have her clapped in irons as soon as she was back on the ground.

As they approached the alien ship, Stevens used his jets to turn himself around, to get his first close-up look at the surface of 2I. Almost immediately he wished he hadn't. The tall spires loomed over them in every direction. Giant, furry pyramids that rose away on every side. Though he knew better, he couldn't help but think they were the buildings of some ancient, cyclopean city. Which would make the giant dome some kind of temple dedicated to elder gods.

Stevens could hardly imagine trespassing on that solemn place, but without so much as a word Jansen passed through the weirdly shaped aperture and was gone, and for a moment he was alone, floating weightless over the brooding landscape. As terrified as he was of what they might find inside 2I, he liked even less the idea of being on his own outside. He touched the keypad on the back of his glove to activate his jets and followed after her, into the shadows.

The darkness inside the airlock was absolute. Jansen's suit lights provided the only illumination. She played them across the inner wall of the airlock, and Stevens saw just how big it was. You could have parked *Orion* and *Wanderer* side by side in there, easy. The interior was smooth and featureless and round, nothing more than a spherical shell, with no visible controls or sensors or—

Something moved through the light, and he yelped in panic. It was just an empty foil packet, though, crimped along one edge. He caught it and saw the hexagon logo of KSpace printed on one side. "Glow sticks," he said. "It's a package of glow sticks." It was empty.

"What do we do now?" he asked.

"We wait," Jansen said. They had both watched the video of *Wanderer*'s crew entering this airlock, but they still had very little idea of how it operated. "McAllister thinks it's set to cycle automatically once anybody's inside. How it knows we're here is anybody's guess. I don't see any sensors."

"You don't like this," he said. He could tell from the way her light moved, jumping from one spot on the featureless inside of the airlock to another, never staying still. Sally Jansen, the old, experienced astronaut, was nervous.

It didn't help him manage his own fear.

"Once we trigger this thing," she said, "2I will know we're here. I don't know. Maybe it's been watching us the whole time, maybe it scanned us the second we arrived, but before it felt like we were invisible. Beneath notice. Now we're scuffing our shoes on the welcome mat. We don't know what we're going to find inside, and—"

She stopped and swung around, her light disappearing as it stabbed out through the aperture behind them. His own lights lit up nothing but her suit.

"What is it?"

She pointed, and he saw the airlock had started to move. The aperture swung to the right. It reached the edge of the clearing and the view of space beyond grew steadily smaller, like a waning moon.

"*Orion*," Jansen called, "we're about to enter radio silence. Give us twelve hours. Not a minute more."

"Acknow—"

Hawkins's voice was cut off instantly as the airlock rotated so the aperture was completely occulted.

"Acknowledged," Hawkins said. He turned to look at Rao. The two of them were inside the cupola, watching 2I as if there were something to see. Hawkins waited until he saw that the airlock had completely cycled.

"They'll be back soon enough," he said. "In the meantime, we still have work to do. We need to keep trying to contact 2I."

Rao didn't look at him. Eventually he left the cupola. He figured she would follow when she was ready.

The airlock stopped rotating without a sound. It came to rest with the aperture 180 degrees from where it had started, facing directly into the interior of 2I. Jansen stared through the hole—

—and saw nothing.

There was no light within. Just darkness, more profound than the depths of space. Her suit lights stretched out ahead of her, reflecting off nothing at all.

As her eyes adjusted she saw what looked like thousands of tiny comets, darting and falling across her light.

"What is that, water vapor or something?" Stevens asked.

She looked down at her suit and saw that the fabric was moving a little. Ruffling as if it was caught in a slight breeze. It stopped almost as soon as she noticed it.

It had been nothing like the sudden blast of air you got when a normal airlock equalized pressures, but she was sure it was the same in principle. When the airlock had been open to space it had been filled with nothing but vacuum. Now that it was facing the interior it was refilling with whatever atmosphere existed inside 2I.

She looked down at the trace gas analyzer mounted on the front of her HUT. A line of green lights extended across its tiny screen, and then a series of symbols and percentages scrolled up. "Argon," she said. "Not much of it, about a fiftieth of an atmosphere. A little water vapor, yeah." She watched the particles of vapor whiz across her vision. "You think anything living could breathe argon?"

Like aliens, she meant, but she was leery of using that word, especially there. *Speak of the devil and he doth appear.*

"I don't know," Stevens said. "That's Rao's specialty, astrobiology. We can ask her when we get back."

"Right," Jansen said.

She was scared. Normally she would have tried to hide that from Stevens—both as his mission commander and because she didn't like people thinking she was weak. Now she couldn't care less. If he wasn't just as terrified as she, he was an idiot.

"This isn't cool," she said. "Is it?"

"I'm about to shit my pants," he said.

"That's why astronauts wear maximum absorbency garments under their space suits," she told him. "OK. This isn't going to get any easier." She kicked off the wall of the airlock, launching herself toward the aperture that now led directly into 2I's interior. She put out her hands to grab the lip of the opening—then yanked them back in a hurry.

Something had gone flashing past her. Something solid.

Well—not flashing past. It was actually moving pretty slowly, though at a steady pace. She followed it with her suit lights and saw what looked like a metal knob moving around the circumference of the aperture. A bright-orange safety line was tied to it, leading out of sight.

The line moved away from her—everything beyond the aperture was moving, revolving around the opening. It took her a second to understand what was going on. She poked her head through the aperture and moved her lights around in a circle. She saw that what lay beyond the aperture was a cone that flared out away from her at a nearly forty-five degree angle, as if she were at the bottom of a rotating bowl with steep sides. The orange safety line marched up the wall of the cone, stretching out of the range of her lights.

She timed the cone's motion and found it made a full rotation every three minutes, maybe a little less. It was easy enough for her to climb up into the cone and grab the rope. It pulled her along as if she'd jumped onto a merry-go-round and grabbed one of the horses' tails.

She looked back and saw Stevens's helmet, his face lost in the glare of his suit lights. He slid away from her, rotating until he was upside down. No, she thought. She was the one rotating. He was standing still, inside the airlock, which didn't rotate.

"Come on," she said. "Looks like we're climbing from here."

SUNNY STEVENS: When I saw that the entrance to 2I was rotating, I had a pretty clear idea what was going on. 2I was much too small to generate gravity like you would get on a planet. The interior of the ship was one big drum centrifuge, rotating to generate centripetal acceleration. We didn't feel any gravity there, at the center of the rotation, but as we descended into 2I, we would feel more and more of it the farther we got from the axis. How much gravity we would eventually experience was impossible to say at that point. I would have needed to know the radius of the drum and how fast it was rotating. We could only speculate.

Once the two of them were out of the airlock, it started to rotate back to its starting position. Soon the aperture rotated away from them, and they were looking at a smooth hemisphere at the end of the cone.

Jansen was no fool. Before they started climbing she tested how they were going to get back. Luckily, that was easy. It turned out even the slightest touch on the back side of the airlock made it cycle again until they could access the aperture. They had a way back, when the time came.

Once they found *Wanderer*'s crew.

*   *   *

At first they had to pull themselves along the rope, hand over hand.

Jansen had no doubt that KSpace had left the rope there for exactly that purpose. It was pencil thin, made of braided Kevlar. Bright orange—the same color she'd seen splashed all over *Wanderer*. KSpace's color. From her perspective the rope didn't hang straight but had a subtle curve. Even the small part of it she could see in her suit lights was distinctly curved to the left. Coriolis force, she figured. It felt strange—what about this place didn't?—but it was just physics. Nice, normal, predictable physics.

The rope was tied off to a piton that Foster and his crew had hammered into the surface of the cone. They had guts, she had to give them that. They would have had no idea how 2I would react to having a spike hammered into its skin. They'd just figured they needed a climbing rope, so they'd installed one.

It was utterly dark inside the cone. The only light came from her suit lamps. She kept them pointed at the rope so she could see where she was going, but that meant she couldn't see anything else. Darkness hovered over her. It crouched on every side. The dancing motes of water in the air meant she could see out to only about twenty meters—beyond that could be anything.

The cone kept expanding, the curve of the floor becoming shallower as they went on. They were like ants climbing down inside the neck of an empty soda bottle, having no idea what they would find ahead of them. The geometry of the place left her feeling disoriented and confused. Soon it didn't feel as if she was in a conical space at all, but merely as if she were pulling herself along a perfectly flat, perfectly vertical wall. It was an illusion, but it was one that was hard to shake.

She wished she could. She felt she was no longer inside an object with a solid hull—instead she felt as if she'd been transported to the surface of some featureless, endless planet. The darkness around her was infinite, stretching out in all directions. Space had never felt that empty. That absolute.

At first she tried calling out, using her suit radio to call for Foster and his people. To try to make contact. There was no response, so eventually she stopped calling. Stopped talking. It was work, hauling herself along like that. She could hear her own breathing, heavy and rough inside her helmet.

Stevens was behind her. Maybe it was easier for him—all he had to do was follow her. Jansen didn't think to ask. She just kept moving, forward into the dark.

Eventually she noticed that the tips of her boots were dragging on the floor. She stopped for a second and tried to stand up. It wasn't easy, but she managed to keep herself stable. She wanted to scuff her boots against the wall—which was now becoming a floor—but she knew that doing so might launch her off into space.

Away from the rope.

She reached into a pocket of her suit and took out two small, complicated devices like carabiners, each with gears and a tiny motor mounted on one end. She'd taken them from *Wanderer*. These were what the 3-D printer had been making when she broke into their orbital module. She'd wondered, at the time, what KSpace wanted with climbing gear. Now she understood.

The carabiners were belaying devices. Motorized ascenders. Designed to keep mountain climbers from falling off their ropes. The motor would help you climb back up, too, making it a lot easier than using only your muscles.

She turned around and showed Stevens how to clip one of the devices to a D ring on his suit, then thread the rope through the gears. If they started to fall, if they moved too fast in any direction, the gears would mesh together and clamp down on the rope, braking them. The motors connected directly to their suits' power supplies, but for the moment she left them unplugged. They would be a lot more useful on the return trip, when they needed to climb all the way back to the airlock.

For now—she took a step forward. Gingerly lowered her boot onto the surface. She wasn't sure what the inner hull was made of, but it was rough enough to give her a little traction. She took another step, holding on tight to the rope.

She looked back at Stevens. She saw his face inside his helmet. His forehead was beaded with sweat. Sweat that was starting to trickle down his cheeks.

She nodded. He nodded back. She turned to face the rope again. Took another step.

Soon they were walking easily. The floor had become a slope. She could feel a gentle tug from below, like a hand grabbing her belt and pulling her forward, into the dark.

That was just gravity. Gravity was OK.

She fought to control her breathing. Took a step. Another.

Her light caught something just ahead. Something that wasn't just more rope. She hurried forward, her feet slipping a little.

The orange rope ran out about five hundred meters down from where they'd started. It was tied off to another piton.

Just beyond that was a third piton. It anchored a second length of rope, falling away into the dark.

SALLY JANSEN: As we descended, through the dark, the slope felt like it was getting steeper and steeper. It wasn't—the gravity was just getting stronger, so it felt like if we let go of the rope we would just fall straight down. There was another consequence of the increasing gravity. I started feeling very nauseous. I knew right away why. For nearly a month I'd been living in microgravity. My internal organs had all climbed up into my rib cage. Now they were racing to get back where they belonged, and my stomach was in last place. I knew I could handle it. I wasn't going to vomit inside my helmet. I was a little worried for Stevens, though.

When they found a third rope below the second, it was bad. When they found the fourth rope, Stevens barely shook his head in disgust.

The fifth rope was probably the hardest.

The gravity increased with every meter they descended. He started feeling heavy, as if his suit were full of rocks. His feet started to slip—if it hadn't been for their belaying devices, they would just slide downward, into the mist, into the dark...

The thought of it kept at him. It kept popping into his mental space, even as he tried to think of other things. He tried working out math in his head, trying to figure out how big the drum could possibly be. He thought about gyroscopic precession and nutation, about the fact that the outer hull of 2I ought to be rotating as well, in the opposite direction from the drum. The universe outside the drum felt very far away, though. The rope in front of him was right there.

If he unclipped his ascender and just let go...

He would slide at first, and then, as his speed increased, he would start to roll. By that point he wouldn't be able to stop himself.

He would keep accelerating. He would fall faster and faster, exponentially so, as the hungry gravity sucked him down into the murk. There wasn't enough air pressure here to provide any significant drag—

He took long shallow breaths and tried to focus on the climbing. When they reached the sixth rope, Jansen insisted on stopping for a minute, both to take a rest and to try calling *Wanderer*'s crew on the radio, again. He supposed he was glad for the rest. His legs ached from the constant stress of walking down the slope, of bracing himself with every footfall. When the break ended, though, he found a new kind of anguish awaiting him.

From this point on, Jansen decided, they were going to go down backward.

The gravity had grown strong enough that they weren't walking down a ramp. They were climbing down a steep hill. They would use their hands and their belaying devices to rappel down the rest of the way.

They got themselves turned around. For a second they had to unclip their ascenders from their D rings, which meant they were holding themselves up by pure muscle power. It took Stevens three tries to get his ascender to clip back on.

Jansen reached up and slapped his boot. Time to go.

Backward. Down into the dark. Hand over hand on the rope. The ascender took most of his weight. Still, within minutes his arms were burning.

That was bad. The dark was worse.

Before, he'd been behind Jansen. He could see her lights ahead of him, could see that the world existed down there. Now all he could see was a patch of the slope behind them, a little double pool of radiance made by his own suit lights. The light shifted and bounced around. Most of the time he could see the rope he was holding on to. Sometimes he couldn't.

He was intimately aware of the vast volume of darkness all around him. Above him, to either side. There could be anything out there. Some enormous monster reaching toward him with silent claws. Aliens watching him with inhuman senses, waiting for the right moment to swoop in and snatch him away from the slope. To drag him upward, always screaming, into nothingness.

They found a seventh rope. And then an eighth.

The mist got thicker as they descended. Their suit lights speared out for maybe ten meters, then five. Beyond the glowing vapor there was...nothing.

He tried thinking about Sandra. She had come this way, climbed down this very same rope. Had she spent the whole time wondering what it would be like to let go?

No, she wasn't like that. He didn't think she'd had a dark thought in her life. Sandra had been bright and chirpy and fun—their dates had been little adventures. She'd taken him on a bicycle tour of wineries in Northern California, once—a long day of riding and drinking until they could barely steer their bikes and she'd fallen off of hers but still she'd been laughing, still she'd thought it was hilarious, and when he ran to help she dragged him down into an avocado field or something and she pulled down her bike shorts and they'd fucked right there, under blue sky and in the smell of growing things—

Sandra was still here, somewhere in the drum. Maybe dead. Maybe badly hurt and unable to get back to the ropes.

He couldn't imagine that, not clearly. It was impossible someone like her could exist in this eternal darkness.

He thought of Parminder. He wondered if he would ever see her again.

The ninth rope was the hardest. He'd been wrong about the fifth rope. Back then, he'd thought maybe this descent could end. That there was a level floor below them, something they were working toward.

As he slid down the ninth rope, a little at a time, bracing himself with his feet against the slick floor, the darkness filled the inside of his head and he stopped thinking rational thoughts at all. His brain was glued to the bottom of his skull, and he could only slide, and stop, and slide, and stop, because that was what he did now.

Slide and stop. Listen for the sound of Jansen sliding down. Wait for the rope to stop shaking. Then it was his turn. Slide, slow down, stop. Wait for Jansen. Kick off the wall. Slide. Slow down. Bring his feet up to catch the wall. Brace himself.

His arms felt as if they were being pulled out of their sockets.

Kick off the wall. Slide. Slow down. Stop.

Nothing but mist...

There was a tenth rope. Of course there was a tenth rope. There couldn't not be a tenth rope.

Kick off the wall. Slide.

He closed his eyes, just for a moment. It didn't matter. The ascender caught him, slowed his fall. It would be faster if he let go. All he had to do was unclip. Gravity would do the rest.

Kick off—slide—slow—stop—legs up—brace—wait—kick off—

When they reached the bottom of the fourteenth rope, Jansen reached up and grabbed his boot. She was saying something, he realized. She'd been talking to him for a long time.

He'd been so lost in his own nonthoughts that her voice seemed to come to him from very, very far away. At first he couldn't make sense of the words.

She shouted, her mouth wide behind her faceplate.

"We're here."

SALLY JANSEN: Fourteen ropes. Climbing down was ... It wasn't much fun, it ... There were fourteen ropes. Seven kilometers total, fourteen ropes of five hundred meters each. Fourteen ropes, and ... fourteen ropes, and we made it to the bottom. Fourteen.

* * *

The slope never really ended. It just became so gentle that Jansen felt as if she were walking on level ground. When she was sure she wouldn't fall, she unclipped from the final rope and stumbled forward a meter or so, then slumped to the ground.

Jesus, her knees hurt. Years of jogging had given her calves of steel but worn out the cartilage in her knees. It felt as if someone had hammered a spike into her left leg. Her shoulders were ridiculously tight, and her back...

She lay there for a while just breathing, just focusing on her own body. Her brain still needed time to catch up. She'd grown disoriented there toward the end, sometimes feeling as if she were climbing up instead of down. Sometimes all too aware that she wasn't standing on a planet's surface but inside a rotating drum. She'd started to feel as if she were upside down, a fly crawling on an inverted surface.

She looked over and saw Stevens had fallen facefirst onto the ground, which he clutched with his hands as if he was afraid he was going to go flying off into space. His eyes were closed, and his mouth was moving, but she couldn't hear him saying anything.

"Are you praying?" she asked him.

"Doing math," he gasped. "Angular momentum. Doesn't make sense. The outer hull should be rotating, too. Conservation of..."

She blocked him out.

She climbed to her feet and used her suit lights to check out the ground around the final piton. It looked as if KSpace had set up a base camp there. She found a stack of oxygen cartridges for their space suits—all of them still fully charged, ready to be used. They weren't compatible with NASA suits, so she left them alone. She found a box of assorted climbing gear: mallets and pitons, more rope, what looked like maybe crampons that would fit over space suit boots. Scattered around the supply cache were a dozen or so glow sticks, presumably left there so *Wanderer*'s crew could find this place again when it returned.

The glow sticks were dull and dead. They were supposed to

work for only twelve hours, and that deadline had long since passed. KSpace must not have been back this way since it entered 2I.

Jansen understood what that was likely to mean. She didn't care. Until she saw bodies, she had to assume that Foster, Holmes, and Channarong were all still alive.

The equipment cache was neatly arranged, and it seemed all the foil bags and plastic cases were untouched. At least that was something—it meant no aliens had been this way. Even friendly extraterrestrials would have examined the gear, right? Out of sheer curiosity they would have opened everything and checked it out. But it looked as if this stuff had been untouched since KSpace left camp. The one exception was an orange flag, just a square piece of vinyl mounted on a wire stand. It lay on the floor a couple of meters away, as if it had been dropped in haste. She picked it up and studied it—and noticed there was something attached to the stand. A tiny memory stick, about two centimeters long.

She plugged it into a port on the side of the communications panel on her HUT. There was only one file on it, a video clip. She blinked twice in rapid succession, and her devices brought the file up in an AR window that seemed to be projected on the inside of her helmet. It made her wince right away—the video was badly degraded, mostly just snarling glitches and artifacts. Likely that was a result of 2I's magnetic field, just like the pops and clicks on her radio. She thought she could make out the shape of a helmeted figure, but then it was gone again. The audio was nearly as bad, but she could hear a few of the words.

VIDEO FILE TRANSCRIPT (1)

Taryn Holmes: ...descent was...we're...

Willem Foster: [indecipherable]

Foster: ...of *Wanderer*. My crew is in good physical shape and... not yet made contact, if indeed there's anyone...no signs. Nothing?

Holmes: They must be...don't want to talk. They've been pretty clear on that so far and...or...

Sandra Channarong: First scans look...not much to...better idea when we're closer to [indecipherable]

Foster: OK. I'll leave this record here, at base camp, in the interest of being thorough. We're going to take an hour's...have a meal, and then...

Foster: I'll make another log entry when we find something. Right now I'll set off a flare, to make sure we don't...

Foster: [indecipherable]

Jansen played the file three times, but couldn't make out any more of what the KSpace astronauts were saying.

It was all so maddening. The file was garbage, almost completely devoid of content. Yet what was there suggested...

No. She couldn't get ahead of herself.

She wasted about ten minutes trying to raise the missing astronauts on her suit radio. It occurred to her that the alien crew of 2I might hear her as well, and for a second she panicked. Then she remembered that that was the reason she was here in the first place. To make contact.

It had sounded like a better idea when she was safe outside, in her own ship.

It didn't matter, anyway. No aliens appeared to seize them. No one at all answered her call.

With the gain turned all the way up on her comm set, all she could hear was static and a ghostly, distant popping. A constant, rhythmic click that rose in volume, then faded away, but never quite disappeared.

"You hear that?" she asked Stevens.

He rolled over on his back and stared at her through the faceplate of his helmet. "Yes," he said, as if he had chosen the simplest possible answer that would make her leave him alone.

She listened to the noise for a long time. Hoping it would resolve into voices, or maybe just a beacon of some kind.

The clicking, popping sound was almost inaudible sometimes. Other times it grew so loud she had to turn the gain down or risk being deafened. She wanted very much for it to mean something. She wanted it to be a signal from *Wanderer*'s crew.

It sounded too basic, though. Too natural, in its way. It wasn't a human sound.

"*Wanderer*, come in," she said into the ambient noise. "This is Jansen, commander of the NASA spacecraft *Orion*. We're here to help. Please acknowledge."

There was no response.

She walked over to where Stevens lay. He hadn't moved since they arrived. Bending only from the waist—her back groaned in complaint, but her knees were all but locked up—she held out a hand. Stevens took it and, grumbling a little himself, let her lever him up to his feet.

She checked the display on the front of her suit. "It took two hours to get here. Let's be conservative and say it's going to take three hours to get back up to the airlock, even using the motorized ascenders."

"Oh, let's," Stevens said.

"That gives us seven hours to find your friends. You ready?"

His face grew serious behind the polycarbonate of his faceplate. "Yeah," he said.

SUNNY STEVENS: I wanted to find Sandra and Taryn and Commander Foster. Yeah. I was very worried for them. After what we'd seen, after failing to get them on the radio, though, I don't know. Maybe I was starting to accept that Hawkins had been right. I was pretty sure at that point we were looking for bodies.

Sally Jansen had wanted to go to Mars. It had been her dream since she was a child, to walk on another world.

This was the closest she was ever going to get. She knew that. She wished she could feel excited. She wanted that thrill to run down her spine, her stomach to clench in knots as she thought of what she would say, the first words spoken by a great explorer.

Instead—there wasn't a lot inside her just then. Mostly fear and worry.

The inner hull of 2I was a dull, nonreflective grayish brown. A noncolor. Jansen kept one of her suit lights pointed down at the ground directly ahead of her so she could see where she was walking. She needn't have bothered. The surface they crossed was perfectly flat and seamless. Slightly rough, enough to provide good traction for walking, but not so rough she had to worry about scraping her gloves on it if she fell onto her hands.

"Porous," Stevens said.

"What?"

"I was wondering why the floor isn't covered in water. The mist ought to stick to it, right? Except it's bone dry. The floor here is porous. It's draining the water away as fast as it can accumulate."

"Noted."

She kept her other light moving back and forth, searching for any sign of the *Wanderer*'s crew. It never showed her anything new. The murky fog that had lain over them like a wet blanket on the way down had thinned out, and visibility had increased to about thirty meters. At least, she thought, they might have some warning if aliens came charging at them out of the dark. If they were looking in the right direction at the time.

With no light, and no landmarks, navigation could have been a problem. Luckily there was an inertial compass built into her suit display. It showed that they were walking straight forward from KSpace's base camp, along a line parallel to 2I's axis. She had no reason to assume that Foster and his crew had headed in that direction, rather than right or left around the curve of the drum, but she had to start somewhere.

She paused every five minutes or so, both so she could try the radio again and because walking was exhausting. If their suits had been heavy and unwieldy in microgravity, they'd certainly never been designed for use at the bottom of a gravity well. They were each carrying an extra thirty kilograms on their back just to keep them alive, and every step sapped some of her energy.

"Seven kilometers down the slope means five kilometers down in elevation," Stevens said, working out a math problem, maybe to fill the silence. "Back at the airlock I didn't think to actually time the rotation of the drum, but it felt like about one rotation every two and a half minutes. So the centripetal acceleration feels like—"

"Point eight g," she said. Beating him to it.

"Yeah," he said. "That's about right. How did you . . . ?"

"I'm an astronaut. You learn what different kinds of gravity feel like. Do me a favor, will you? Save your breath for walking."

But of course he couldn't.

She supposed different people handled fear different ways. For her it was focusing on what she was doing. Paying perfect attention to each step, to maintaining a routine of checking her compass, checking her radio, sweeping her lights back and forth. Repeated actions that rewarded her with exactly the same results every time, which made her feel a kind of security even in the endless dark of 2I.

Stevens was a scientist. Which meant his way of dealing with an uncertain world was to try to understand it. To measure it and draw hypotheses about its terrors. Jansen had known plenty of scientists in her time—she'd seen it before.

"The temperature's gone up a few degrees since we arrived," he said. "This place should have its own weather, sure, assuming the drum is one large continuous space."

"It's getting hotter?" she asked, suddenly interested. "How hot? Dangerously hot?"

"Well, no. It was hovering about five below zero when we came in. Now it's about two above."

"Let me know if it gets much warmer than that," she said. She hadn't felt the temperature before. There were kilometers of water-filled tubing inside her suit to make sure she kept comfortable in freezing cold or boiling heat—in space you could get either one, depending on whether you were standing in sun or shade.

Now that he'd made her think about how cold it was, though, she couldn't stop thinking about it. The misty darkness was cold enough to freeze her solid if her suit lost power. Good to know.

She held up one hand to warn him she was going to stop. She checked her radio again.

Nothing but that clicking that went in and out, fading away and then rising to buzz in her ear, loud enough to make her want to switch off her radio. She didn't. There could be a distress signal hidden in that noise, and she wouldn't be able to hear it. Frustration threatened to overwhelm her. She fought it back and kept listening.

Occasionally there was a brief warbling tone, a kind of wavering ghost voice that she knew meant nothing but was maddeningly close to a human sound. Like a voice sped up to a hundred times its normal speed.

"Static discharge," Stevens told her.

"What?"

"An object this big can build up an electric charge without even trying. The floor material, whatever it is, is probably a good insulator. Just the friction of the air sliding against the floor of the drum builds up a static charge. There's nothing to carry that charge away—no good conductors in here—so the charge just builds and builds. Eventually the floor can't hold any more electricity and it has to discharge somehow."

"Like...lightning? You're saying there are lightning storms in here, and that's what I'm hearing?"

"Doubtful," he told her. "We would see flashes if that was the case, not just hear them over the radio. No, I think there must be some other method for the charge to drain away. Maybe the argon in the air is constantly getting ionized, but then—sorry, Jansen. I don't know. But I don't think we're going to be electrocuted anytime soon."

"I suppose that's something," she told him.

She tried calling out to Foster and his crew again.

There was no response.

"So that explains the squeals. What about the clicking sound?" she asked. "You definitely hear it. It's not just me. So what is it?" she asked.

Stevens lifted his hands and let them drop again. "Some kind of rapidly oscillating electromagnetic field. Your guess is as good as mine."

Jansen nodded. She'd thought of something. "Electromagnetic fields can interfere with radio signals, right?"

"Sure," he said.

"So it's possible that Foster and his crew can't hear me. That my signal is getting drowned out."

"Well... maybe," Stevens said.

Her suit light caught the edge of his faceplate and he blinked and winced and threw up a hand to screen it out.

"Sorry," she told him. She swung her head around and pointed her light out into the dark.

She would take a maybe. Life was full of maybes, and sometimes they turned into yeses, and—

A sudden wave of fatigue ran through her, and she felt a desperate need to sit down. She wasn't as young as she used to be, and her body wasn't used to this level of exertion under the crushing weight of real gravity, not after a month in space. She'd started to sweat inside her liquid cooling and ventilation garment. She laughed. Getting her hopes up took way more energy than she had to spare.

"Listen, we need to take a real rest. Twenty minutes."

"Yeah, sounds good," he said.

Together they sat down on the floor, back to back so they could prop each other up. So nothing could sneak up on them.

Not that it seemed likely. If the aliens inside 2I wanted to approach them, surely they would have done so already.

Right?

Jansen set her lights to sweep back and forth in a regular pattern, sweep all she could survey. All the nothing that was out there.

There was a little tube in her helmet that was full of water. She sucked on it, not having realized how dry her mouth had gotten until just that moment.

She stared out into the dark and the fog.

She couldn't see Stevens. She couldn't see anything but the

nothingness her lights played across, rolling back and forth, back and forth.

For the moment she was all alone in that great, empty space. It didn't feel big to her. Instead she felt tiny. Microscopic.

She called out, called the KSpace astronauts by name. And in that moment she was sure they couldn't hear her. That nobody could, or ever would. She didn't even think the KSpace crew was dead. Instead she thought they'd never been there. That this had all been some cruel prank, that she'd been led here just to feel this alone, this small.

Her imagination was getting to her. In astronaut training one of the things they'd told her was the importance of not seeing shapes in every shadow, not falling prey to the phantoms inside your own head. You had to hold on to what you could prove, the data your own senses provided, and let everything else go.

So when she saw the flicker of light off in the distance, at first she wouldn't let herself believe it was there. It had to be a hallucination. Then her light swept around again and—there. Yes. There was a little glimmer dead ahead of them, a half-seen glow.

"Come on," she said, scrambling to her feet. "Come on!"

Jansen ran forward, toward the light.

She could hear her boots thundering on the hard surface of the interior hull. Her lungs burned with the effort, and her shoulders ached from the weight of her suit pulling down on them. The D rings on her torso jangled and bounced and she heard them ringing like bells—the air in 2I was thick enough to carry sound waves.

She reached up to adjust her suit lights to point straight ahead as she ran. She half expected the gleam of light up there to vanish. For it to have been nothing but a mirage. Instead it grew stronger. Brighter.

It could be the lights of the KSpace crew's suits. It could be some procession of aliens come to meet them. It could be...

A reflection.

Her own lights bouncing back at her.

Her boots slipped a little under her, and she nearly tumbled to the floor. She threw her arms out to her sides for balance and skidded forward another meter or so.

She gasped for breath. She steadied herself. Looked straight ahead. At a wall of ice.

Ice. That was what she'd seen. Her lights reflecting off a surface of frozen water.

The floor she'd skidded on was covered in a thin layer of it, a sheet maybe a centimeter thick. Dead ahead the ice grew thicker and rose around her in phantasmagorical shapes. Humps and piles of it, growlers and bergs, ribbons and arches and caves of ice. Great curving prominences of ice, as if enormous waves of water had flash-frozen in place, overhangs of ice bearded with icicles like dragon's teeth.

Her light caught a million bright surfaces like facets of a titanic diamond. Some of them were bright enough to blind her, some just dull gleams. Meltwater dripped from every spike and curve in the ice, pooling in the depressions and caverns, trickling around her feet. She could hear it falling, the rhythm just slightly off, each drop taking just a fraction of a second too long to fall and splash to the ground.

Ice. Some of it as thin and transparent as glass, in some places grown so thick it looked blue and solid as stone.

She stepped forward, across the thin layer that covered the ground in front of the wall. She had to plant each footfall carefully so she didn't slip. She turned and gestured for Stevens to stay back, on the dry ground. He looked more than ready to comply.

Another step, another, a third, and she was there, at the wall. She reached out and touched a long stalactite of ice, as thick around as her waist where it hung from a ledge over her head. Her glove was well insulated and she couldn't feel its cold, but she could imagine it, imagine the way it would burn to touch that ice with bare fingers.

She looked up and saw that the ledge wasn't level—it sloped down to one side. She made her way to her left and then reached up, looking for handholds. The ice was rough and varied enough that she found purchase. She hauled herself upward, swinging her aching leg up to get over the edge; then with incredible care and slowness she climbed up until she was standing on top of the wall.

Her lights speared out ahead of her. The mist had mostly cleared, and she could see for hundreds of meters. Beyond the wall of ice lay...more ice. As far as she could see. Away from the wall, it settled down into long gentle hills and valleys, with liquid water pooling in the low points. Nothing marred the white surface, no rocks or plants or any sign of life, much less intelligence. She thought of the ice valleys of Antarctica, which had remained untouched for millions of years before they were first seen by human explorers. Great frozen deserts where nothing lived.

She turned and looked back at Stevens, who stood in a little oasis of light a dozen meters behind her. She could barely see his face through his helmet, but she could read his body language just fine. He looked hopeful, expectant. He was waiting to hear what she'd found up there, on top of the wall.

A deep convulsive spasm ran through her chest, made her back shiver. It wasn't a sob, but it was something like it. An upwelling of anguish and emotion. An inescapable, existential feeling.

She kicked at the ice at her feet, sending chips of it flying into the air. She kicked again and nearly tripped, nearly fell backward off the wall, but caught herself in time. She kicked at the ice again, and again.

"Jansen?" he called.

She rose to her full height. She wished she could wipe her mouth, but her helmet was in the way. She gave the ice one last, vicious kick.

"There's nothing here!" she cried.

HANDSHAKE PROTOCOL

ROY MCALLISTER: *We remained in constant contact with* Orion *throughout the period while Jansen and Stevens were inside 2I. As frustrated as I might have been with her refusal to follow my orders, I was desperate to know what she found inside. I know that General Kalitzakis was waiting with as much anticipation as I was. This might be our best chance to find out what 2I's crew wanted with Earth.*

Where the hell were they? Rao checked the time. Jansen and Stevens had been gone only a few hours, but . . . how long was this supposed to take? Every minute that passed with no word from them felt like torture. If something had happened to them—how would anyone ever know? They would just disappear, and there would be nothing they could do about it. She knew Hawkins wouldn't risk going over there to look for them.

It would have been easy for Rao to spend the entire time in the cupola, watching 2I and waiting for them to come back. It was very much what she wanted to do. So she forced herself not to do that. Instead she headed back to the dormitory section of the HabLab, where she would be less tempted to stare out the windows.

She tried to focus on *Orion*'s primary mission by running a series of experiments with the tunable laser mounted on the front of the HabLab. The thought was that perhaps 2I's builders didn't use radio waves for communication, so they would try to send a signal using various colors of visible light.

The main problem—as far as keeping her distracted went—was

that the experiment was almost totally automated. The laser drew a series of shapes on 2I's surface: a circle, a triangle, a series of conic sections. Perfect shapes that never appeared in nature, shapes that only intelligent beings would recognize. Anything to try to get a reaction. When it finished that pattern, it changed color—it was currently in the green part of the spectrum, around five hundred nanometers—and started again. All she had to do was watch the output log from the laser and make sure the equipment didn't break down. Meanwhile cameras on the HabLab's outer skin swept back and forth, looking for any sign that 2I had responded with its own light show.

It didn't. She hadn't expected it would. She scrolled through the camera logs, looking for even the slightest change in the light reflected by 2I, but there was nothing there. The numbers changed, but never in meaningful ways, and—

"Soup's on."

She flinched so hard she heard her neck pop. Rao whirled around, wide-eyed, and saw that Hawkins had stuck his head through the soft hatch between the wardroom and the dormitory.

Right. It had been several hours since Stevens and Jansen left. It must be their scheduled time to eat.

"I didn't mean to startle you."

"It's fine," she said. She stirred herself, pushed away her thoughts. "I'm sorry, I'll be right there." She saved the analysis she'd been working on and then followed him into the wardroom. ARCS had heated up two food tubes. It was clutching a handrail with one hand, holding a tube in each of the others. She grabbed one of them at random and started to kick back toward the dormitory.

As she passed by one of the wardroom's screens, though, she saw something weird. The screen was full of a jumble of random characters.

At first she thought it must be output data from Hawkins's experiments with the multiwavelength antenna. But no, that should be a time-stamped log pretty much like the one the tunable laser used. This looked more like when a cat walked across a keyboard, honestly.

She kicked over to the screen and reached to touch it and call up a diagnostic app, but before she could get there Hawkins waved her away. "That's mine," he said.

Something was wrong. Hawkins was the kind of guy who prided himself on his self-control. His steadfast refusal to show his emotions on his face. But his eyes were wild now. Bright and out of control, and there was a faint sheen of sweat on his forehead.

Something had happened, she thought. It couldn't be news about Jansen and Stevens. He couldn't possibly be such a monster as to keep that from her. Then—what?

"What is this?" she asked, looking at the screen. "It doesn't make any sense."

"It's encrypted. A message from Joint Space Operations Command."

She frowned. "You mean the space force? Aren't all of our communications supposed to come through NASA?"

"Not this. This is—it's part of my job. My mission specialization." He reached over and cleared the screen.

She moved away from him, intending to head back to the dormitory. To get back to work. She had enough on her mind without this new mystery.

"Rao," he said. "Hold on."

She stopped by the hatch and looked back at him but didn't say a word.

"Look, I know you and I have never really been—"

"Please don't say *close*," she told him.

He gave her a sad smile. "Fine. The truth is, we've barely spoken a dozen words to each other this whole mission. But you need to know this. I think you need to hear it."

She could tell from the look on his face that what he meant was that he needed to talk to somebody about it. Whatever news he'd received from Earth had shaken him so much it had broken right through his tough guy veneer.

Which made her desperately want to hear whatever it was.

There are some calls you have to take.

McAllister stank, after days in the control room. He really would have liked to shower and shave. He needed sleep, and he desperately needed to eat something, even though worry had tied his stomach in knots. He wasn't given time to do those things, however.

General Kalitzakis had initiated a conference call, and everyone was getting patched in. The Joint Chiefs of Staff. McAllister's own boss, the general administrator of NASA. Several members of the National Space Council, and the national security advisor.

Everyone.

Which meant the news had to be bad.

McAllister dropped into a chair in his office and touched the device on his ear, and a chime announced that he had joined the call. It was voice only, presumably so it could be kept tightly encrypted. Everyone was talking at once, and they all sounded scared.

"You promised us, General, that you would have a coherent plan by now," the advisor said, sounding like a manager giving an employee a terrible performance review.

"Give the man a chance to talk!" That was the secretary of defense, he thought. After that he didn't even try to identify the various voices.

"Are you sure about these numbers?"

"Nobody's sure about anything! But we can't just bring this to—"

"We need better data than this."

"We have the data! What we need is solutions!"

All the voices fell silent at once, muted by whoever was controlling the call. There was a click, and a series of tones—McAllister knew that meant the connection was being tested, to make sure it was secure.

Then a new voice, a very calm, quiet voice, announced that the president of the United States had joined the call.

McAllister sat up straight at his desk, even though no one could see him.

The president didn't speak. Everyone knew the protocol here. Kalitzakis would present his news in the clearest, simplest terms he could, and then he would wait in case the president had any questions.

"Mr. President, sir," Kalitzakis began. He sounded as tired as McAllister felt. "I represent the Joint Space Operations Command. We have been monitoring the object known as 2I as it approaches Earth. And we have been looking for a military option, in case it turns out to be hostile. Today we finished modeling what would happen given a direct nuclear strike on the object."

Kalitzakis cleared his throat. Was he stalling for time, or just trying to collect himself? McAllister hadn't expected good news, but now he started to grow worried. Frightened, even.

From the beginning he'd planned *Orion*'s mission around one certainty. That if his crew couldn't make contact with 2I, or if it turned aggressive, then Kalitzakis was waiting. Waiting with a plan for how they would fight back. How they would destroy 2I before it could reach Earth.

Now—

"Mr. President, all of our models agree. The effect of a nuclear strike against 2I would be negligible."

McAllister's heart pounded in his chest. He couldn't accept this. No, Kalitzakis had to have the numbers wrong, or—

"We ran multiple different simulations, all based on the most up-to-date information NASA and our ground-based imagery could provide. What we discovered is this. The superstructures on 2I's hull are highly effective at absorbing energy. Even the energy of a thermonuclear explosion. Our largest warheads would damage 2I, but we can't guarantee they would even penetrate its hull. The outcome from multiple coordinated strikes didn't turn out any better—the initial impact would simply create a large cloud of orbital debris, which would mitigate the effect of secondary and tertiary weapon strikes."

There was silence on the line for several seconds. Kalitzakis was perhaps letting the meaning of what he'd said sink in. Or maybe he was struggling for words. McAllister's heart went out to the poor man—called on the carpet like this, before the most powerful leader on Earth, he had to tell him how much that power was worth.

"We have, of course, not given up. We're looking at alternative weapons systems. While nuclear weapons seemed like our best bet, we are currently modeling what we could achieve with kinetic impactors, particle beam weapons and THELs. That's tactical high-energy lasers, sir. We're even trying to model the weapons systems of other nations—specifically, the Chinese have an electromagnetic railgun in orbit that could deliver a high-speed payload outside our current capabilities, but—"

Kalitzakis's voice was cut off abruptly. McAllister knew that meant the president wanted to ask a question.

"What exactly are you saying, General?"

"I'm saying," Hawkins told her, speaking very slowly—as if he couldn't believe the words himself, "that we currently don't have a weapon that can destroy 2I."

Rao floated there in the middle of the HabLab. Suddenly she was very aware of the expanse of space all around her.

"You're saying if 2I attacks the Earth—if it just power-dives right into the Midwest—there's nothing we can do to stop it. We're defenseless."

"We're not going to stop looking for solutions," Hawkins said, holding tight to the console in front of him. "No one's going to just give up and surrender. But—it doesn't look good."

She'd never really thought about 2I being hostile. She had considered it such a remote possibility that she hadn't given it any of her mental time.

Then again—2I was moving toward Earth inexorably. Without responding to any of their communications. Under those circumstances—

Had she been hopelessly naive?

"So . . . what do we do?" she asked.

"We try diplomatic options." He scowled as if he realized how flippant that sounded. "Sorry—look, that's what *Orion*'s mission was all along, right? Make contact with the aliens. Convince them to talk to us, and maybe not kill us all." He turned and looked to the side, and Rao knew he was looking in the direction of 2I, if only in his mind. Looking at where Jansen and Stevens had gone.

"We have no idea what's going on over there right now," he said. "Maybe they've made contact. Maybe KSpace has been talking to the aliens this whole time."

"Maybe," Rao said.

It was possible.

SURFACE CONTACT

"K Space *Wanderer*, acknowledge."
"Commander Foster, please come in."
"This is Jansen of the NASA *Orion*. Please acknowledge."

"We are at the discontinuity in the ice, on a direct bearing from the location of your base camp. Can you please advise as to your location? We're here to help."

"Crew of the *Wanderer*, if you can make any signal—send up a flare. Ping our suits. Shout if you can hear us. If you're unable to respond..."

Jansen hung her head and closed her eyes and for a moment just let herself despair. Let her brain go where it wanted to go.

Then she took a deep breath and opened her eyes again.

"Come in, crew of the *Wanderer*. Come in, please."

AMY TARBELIAN, FLIGHT PSYCHOLOGIST: There have been a number of studies on the effect of prolonged darkness on the human psyche. The prognoses are not good. I remember reading in college about the "prisoner's cinema," which is a poetic way of describing how inmates in solitary confinement will begin to hallucinate within hours when they suffer a total lack of visual stimulus. We evolved to live in a well-lit world, and when you take that away from us, we deteriorate rapidly.

"What do they want?" Jansen asked.

Stevens had been sucking on a tube full of sugar water that snaked up inside his helmet. They'd been inside 21 for nearly five hours, and he was starving. The syrupy water did little to alleviate his hunger, but at least he was getting some calories.

The two of them were taking another rest, this time facing each other.

"Who wants what now?" he asked.

"The aliens," Jansen said. "The people who built 2I. They planned a mission that would take thousands of years to complete. They sent this thing out into the galaxy, clearly hoping it would wash up...somewhere. At some nice, friendly planet. Why? What did they hope to achieve, sending us an empty ship?"

Stevens stared at her. "You think I have an actual answer?"

Jansen shook her head. She fiddled with the knobs on the front of her suit, adjusting her radio. After a second she let out a frustrated grunt and got back to her feet.

"Listen," Stevens said, "I've been thinking. I've been thinking we should go back."

"Give up, you mean."

Stevens scrambled to his feet. "No, no, not—I mean, temporarily. Just temporarily. If we go back, though, maybe we can accomplish something. I was thinking about—well, don't call it experiments. Call it strategies. Strategies for finding *Wanderer*'s crew."

She didn't scoff at the idea, at least not right away.

"We can bring the tunable laser in here," he said. "Mount it up by the airlock. We could use it to scan the entire interior of the drum. Look for anything the shape of a human body—"

"You think they're dead," she said.

Stevens grimaced. "I didn't say that! Look, how about—I mean, I have other ideas. There's a 3-D printer on the *Wanderer*. We could use it to build little robots. Rovers, like NASA sends to Mars, right? Little rovers that could do the searching for us. That has to be better than us just walking around, hoping we see them."

Jansen walked back over to the ice wall and climbed its face again. When she was standing on its top, she turned and looked down at him. "We have plenty of air and water in our suits. We can stay here another three hours before we need to turn back."

"Are you even listening to me?" he said. "There's no way we can search this whole place!"

Stevens's heart sank. She *wasn't* listening.

"Stay down there and rest awhile longer," she told him. "I'm going to try raising Foster again, from up here. In a minute we'll get moving again."

"Sure," he said. "You're the boss."

AMY TARBELIAN, FLIGHT PSYCHOLOGIST: The records of experiments with people living for prolonged periods in caves are even more chilling to read. Without light, our circadian rhythms quickly get decalibrated and we lose all sense of time. You can sleep for an entire day and think you've just taken a quick catnap. You can be down underground for months and think it was just weeks. Artificial light doesn't help, because you can turn that on and off. If you take away the difference between night and day, you start pushing the human mind right to the brink of insanity.

"*Wanderer,*" she called. "Foster. Can you hear me?"

Stevens had fallen silent at last. She had to keep looking back over her shoulder to make sure he was still down there.

She thought of the cosmonauts on *Mir,* the world's first real space station. Back in the 1980s, long before she was born, the Russians had sent two cosmonauts at a time up to *Mir.* Just two people, often up there for hundreds of days. They had had a rule that no matter where you were in the station, you had to keep some part of your body—even just a hand or a foot—visible to your partner, so they never felt completely alone in space.

Jansen imagined trying to explore 2I by herself. The thought terrified her. Without Stevens's stream-of-consciousness monologue, 2I was so silent. So oppressively quiet. The only thing she could hear was the constant clicking tone and the high-pitched electric discharges—the radio noise she'd noticed before. It was eerie and wrong, not a sound a human being was ever supposed to hear.

She knew they would have to turn back soon. But going back—even temporarily—meant defeat. Every hour that passed, their odds of finding Foster and his people shrank. Every minute she was outside 2I was a minute she wasn't searching. She—

Her thoughts were interrupted by a crackling discharge, much louder than any she'd heard before. It made her jump, her feet shifting noisily on the ice.

"Jansen?" Stevens called.

"Shh," she told him.

She pointed her lights out across the white plain. The glare made her squint. Had there been...something? She had sensed something.

Maybe.

Her eyes were useless, but some other, more liminal sense had been triggered when she heard that last crackle.

There had been a change in the way the mist moved, maybe. Or perhaps it was just a gut feeling. Astronauts hated gut feelings, as a rule. Space was almost by definition counterintuitive—nothing in the high vacuum acted the same way it acted back on Earth. Gut feelings got you killed. Yet she couldn't deny she'd sensed something—

The crackle came again, not quite as loud as before, and she could have sworn there was a flash of light way out across the ice plain. A light that wasn't just a reflection of her own suit lights.

Once she had imagined it, she couldn't help but sense it. Something out there, something dark—and big. Very big, hunching in the fog.

She couldn't see it. There were no more flashes of light, and the one that she'd seen—that maybe she'd seen—had been so faint it was all but drowned out by her lamps.

With trembling hands, she reached up and switched them off.

"Jansen?" Stevens asked. "Jansen, where'd you go?"

"Quiet," she said.

Stevens turned in circles. Jansen had stopped in place and turned off her lights. What the hell was she thinking?

His own lights showed nothing new, nothing changed, except

maybe there was more water around him. In fact, he was standing in a field of slush a couple centimeters deep over the slick ice that coated the floor. He looked to the side, to the wall of ice, and saw its whole surface glistening. Dripping. As he watched, a row of icicles came loose from an overhang, falling to shatter on the ground, one by one.

He checked his suit display and saw that the temperature was nine degrees Celsius. It was still getting warmer. From below freezing when they'd arrived, it had gotten to the equivalent of a sunny day in early spring back on Earth.

He looked up just as a whole gusher of water sluiced over the side of the ice wall, splashing noisily all around him. It made him jump—and he started to slip. He had to grab a thick stalagmite of ice to keep from falling right on his face. Even as he hugged the solid column, he tried to get his feet back under him, but they kept sliding on the slick ice. "Come on," he said. "Come on, come on, come on—"

A soft chime sounded inside his helmet. He looked down at his display and saw the readout of his trace gas analyzer. It still showed that the atmosphere was almost entirely made of argon with some water vapor, but now it also contained a tiny amount of oxygen. Even as he watched the display, it flickered and changed again, and the oxygen was gone. It was as if a gentle puff of it had wafted past him.

He ignored it and focused on getting his footing. He heard the chime three more times as he struggled to stand. Once he was bipedal, he flexed his knees a little and stretched his arms out to either side for balance. He tried to calm his breathing, which had gotten completely out of control.

The sluice of liquid splashing down next to him hadn't stopped. If anything, it was growing stronger. Stevens needed to get away from the river of water and half-melted slush. He needed to find more solid ground.

He was looking around, trying to see if he could spot some solid-looking ice, when his light caught a cavern in the wall to his side. The beam speared right down into the depths of the hollow, and for a moment he saw something dark in there. Something that wasn't ice. Then his light moved away as he swiveled on the slick surface and nearly fell down again.

He made himself perfectly still. Then he reached up and manually adjusted his lamp so it shone into the cave. He couldn't seem to find the thing he'd seen. It must have been a trick of the light. Just his brain playing tricks—

Then the dark thing moved, pulling itself out of range of his beam.

It moved. He definitely saw it move.

"Jansen!" he howled.

SUNNY STEVENS: *The rising temperature, the sudden gusts of oxygen—if it hadn't been clear before . . . Yeah. Things were changing inside 21. They were changing fast.*

Jansen tried to block out all distractions. Stevens's voice, for one. Her own heartbeat, which she could hear louder than the ticking beat coming in over her suit radio.

She let her eyes relax, focusing on nothing. She started to see little flashes of light that she knew were just her brain struggling to make sense of the darkness. That wasn't what she was looking for.

Water streamed over her boots, but she ignored it. Her own breath sighed in her ears, so she held it, until her chest started to burn.

Hurry up, she thought. *Hurry up already.*

The thing, the massive thing she'd sensed out there, was a shadow hiding among shadows. She couldn't see it, was aware of it only at the lowest possible threshold of sensation . . . but she was sure that it was there, that she was facing it, and that when it was lit up again—

And then it happened. A tiny gray flash of light, followed almost immediately by the crackling noise in her headphones.

It lasted only the merest fraction of a second. It lit up only a small part of the thing she was facing. Yet she saw it, saw it with her own eyes.

It was enormous. How big was impossible to say without knowing how far away it was, but it was *big*. At least a hundred meters tall, maybe a lot more. It towered over her, even when seen in the distance. In shape it was roughly ovoid, bigger at the bottom than the top, with round, organic curves. Its surface was roughly textured, and its lower half was draped with a lacy network of—roots? tendrils?—that stretched down to the ice at its base. The flash of light she'd seen, the electrical discharge, forked upward across that net-like canopy.

In the thin slice of time that the thing was visible, she had seen it move. It trembled, as if it had been shocked by the electric discharge.

Looking at it, Jansen felt nothing but fear. A desperate, shuddering horror. She fought it down, clamping her eyes shut even though the light was long gone, even though the thing had receded into darkness again. In her mind's eye, she still saw it, like an afterimage. And something else.

The light had sent long shadows racing down the ice valleys and around the sides of the gently rolling hills. It flowed like water in that brief moment it was visible. And it had caught on something, a strange angular shape she hadn't expected to see. Something very small, tiny against the immensity of the empty plain, and she hadn't gotten a very good look at it, but something about it made her feel that it belonged to her. That it wasn't part of the mysteries of 21.

She switched her lamps back on and blinked furiously as her dark-adapted eyes protested against the sudden illumination. When she could see again, she looked and saw a little patch of orange fluttering against the ice.

Orange.

It was floating on top of one of the ever-deepening pools of water. It rocked from side to side as it moved toward her, carried by the current that splashed across her boots.

She bent down and reached for it. It was going to pass her by, just a meter or so beyond the fingers of her glove. Just as it raced past, she lunged, dropping to her knees with a nasty, painful crunch. But her hand closed on the orange thing, and she grabbed it up out of the water.

It was a flag. A scrap of vinyl fabric about ten centimeters on a side, mounted on a stiff piece of wire. Just like the one she'd found at the KSpace base camp.

Attached to the flag by a loop of wire was another memory stick.

"Jansen!" Stevens cried out. She was concentrating too hard to really hear him. She took another second to study the orange flag in her hand.

"Jansen! Help!"

She twisted around, and her lights speared out toward the edge, where the plain of ice ended. She realized she'd walked nearly fifty meters in, away from the edge of the icy plain. Away from Stevens.

She shoved the flag in her pocket and started to run.

The thing from the cave had emerged, stretching its long length through the slush.

It was some kind of tendril, or root, or . . . what? A tentacle? An arm? It moved like a snake, slithering across the ground. It looked more like a branch of a tree—all along its length it forked and split off new growths, new branches.

It wasn't alone.

From hollows and crevices all over the melting ice wall, they crept outward. Stretching. Connecting with each other. Shooting off new branches all the time. A whole network of the tendrils was crisscrossing the ice, spreading, growing new, fat, slug-like branches as it covered the ground.

The growth was moving toward him. Steadily, implacably. It hugged the ice, forking and spreading as it moved until it formed a dense carpet of tendrils undulating across the surface.

Stevens backed away from them, his feet sliding frantically. He waved his arms around, trying to keep control, trying to stay balanced. Behind him the growth was moving faster than he was. It was going to reach him soon, it was going to crawl over the tops of his boots—

He turned around and ran, as fast as he possibly could.

He made it about three steps before his left boot smashed through a thin skin of ice over a puddle of liquid. With his left leg trapped, his right foot slipped and flew out from under him. His right ankle twisted and a bolt of pain raced up his leg, making him horribly aware of every muscle, tendon, and sinew from his heel to his hip. He cried out and tried to stagger forward, swinging his hurt leg like a crutch, stiff at the knee, but he was already off balance. He threw his arms forward but they couldn't stop him. His faceplate collided with the ground and a microsecond later his face smashed against the polycarbonate, his nose shoved over to one side, his teeth clicking painfully against his faceplate.

He hurt, he hurt so much, but there was no time to worry about that. He twisted around, getting his head up so he could look down across his body, at the branching growth that was moving faster now than before.

Jansen ran back toward where she'd left Stevens, her feet barely finding purchase on the wet ice. She looked down and her heart stopped beating.

Pinned in the double spotlight of her lamps, he was caught in a net of thick, greasy-looking tendrils. He was up on one knee, facing away from her, his arms stretched out in front of him even as new tendrils branched and grew around his shoulders, down his upper arms. The thick growth had spread all across his legs and back— only his helmet was free of them.

At the base of the wall, the tendrils covered the ground in a branching pattern she recognized instantly. It was the same kind of growth that had been clutching the massive dark thing she'd seen across the ice plain.

Jansen slid down to the ground, her boots stamping on the branching tendrils. They convulsed away from the impact, retreating from the ground where she stood, but only momentarily. Even as she lifted her feet they started to move again, converging on her.

Fear made her stomach lurch. If she let herself think about what she was seeing, she knew she would scream and run away. She needed to fight that. She needed to get control if she was going to help Stevens.

She didn't give the things a chance to catch her. Racing forward, she got to Stevens and tried to grab one of the tendrils and pull it off his back. It resisted all her strength, as if it were fused to his space suit. It felt made of stone, though it writhed as she touched it.

Desperate, she patted her pockets, looking for a knife, a weapon, anything she could use as a club. There was nothing—but then she looked down and saw the ground was littered with big chunks of solid ice. She grabbed one and it squirted out of her hand, slick with meltwater. With a curse she grabbed another, spreading her fingers to get a better grip.

She brought the chunk of ice up over her head and smashed it down across Stevens's back, against the fiberglass hard upper torso of his suit. Two tendrils recoiled, pulling back from the impact site. She hit them again and again until they pulled free of his arms.

Where they retreated, they left a pattern of tiny holes across his suit, like an imprint of where they'd been. She hit them again and again, knocking loose more and more of the tendrils. She didn't dare hit his legs—she might break his bones if she used too much force. Instead she ran around in front of him and grabbed his arms.

She screamed his name, but he didn't reply. Through his face-plate she could see that his eyes weren't tracking her. It looked as if they were about to roll up into their sockets. He was in shock—maybe from sheer terror, maybe from some injury... She looked down, then, and saw one of the tendrils snaking up under the lower edge of his HUT, digging into him right through the fabric of his suit.

Oh God, no, she thought. She grabbed the tendril and pulled, and pulled, and pulled, her shoulder joints creaking with the effort. She grunted and spit and raged and pulled harder and the tendril came loose, wriggling in her hand. She pulled it free and saw its end was coated in red blood. It hissed and twisted around in her hand, its end smoking and bubbling as if it were coated in acid.

Adrenaline coursed through her and she grabbed Stevens by the arms and pulled him out of the swarming mass of tendrils, pulled at him until he came free with a sudden lurch that sent them both tumbling. She barely managed to get her legs under her and keep them from sprawling flat against the ground.

"Jansen," he breathed. "Jansen."

"Stevens! Wake up! We need to move!" she shouted back at him. She wrestled him up onto his feet, though he swayed and looked as if he was about to fall again.

She spared one look behind her, and saw the network of tendrils still sidewinding across the ground, moving toward them. Growing toward them. Spreading fast.

"Wake up!" she screamed at him, then shoved her shoulder into his armpit and pushed him forward, running as fast as she could across the slick ice, away from the wall, away from the towering thing in the dark. Her lights bounced wildly across the ground, across the side of his suit, across the dark sky.

"Jansen," he whispered. "Help."

ESCAPE MANEUVER

Y SABEL MELENDEZ, EXTRAVEHICULAR ACTIVITY
OFFICER: *When the airlock cycled again, indicating that our astronauts were coming out of 2I, we all breathed a sigh of relief. Even when
we saw there were two of them, not five—meaning they hadn't rescued the
KSpace crew. We were just glad to have our own back. Then the biotelem-
etry from Stevens's suit started coming in. It was . . . bad.*

"*Orion*, this is Jansen—get ready for us. Stevens has been hurt. He's
been—he was attacked. There's no time to explain, just get the suitports ready."

"Sunny!" Rao shouted. "What's going on? What happened?"
She shoved her way through the soft hatch between the dormitory
and the wardroom. She saw Hawkins had already opened up one of
the suitports and was shoving his legs into an EVA suit.

"What're you doing?" she demanded. "You heard the message.
They're coming in and Stevens—Sunny—"

Hawkins shoved his arms into the EVA suit. "Stay put," he told
her. "I'm going to go help them. Just—you stay put. Monitor the
situation." He ducked his head and shoved his way into the HUT
and helmet of the suit. The hatch closed behind him and he was
gone.

Rao launched herself across the room, over to the nearest touchscreen, and called up a view of the exterior of the HabLab, just in
time to see Hawkins separate from the suitport and drift away from
Orion on a safety line.

*   *   *

ROY MCALLISTER: *We only had one concern at that moment—we wanted to know Stevens's condition, we wanted to know what we could do to help. The astronauts were still twenty-seven light-seconds away, though. There wasn't much we could do.*

"Blood pressure is, shit, it's eighty over sixty. His heart rate is over one-twenty, and his blood ox is dropping—hurry! We need to get him in here and get him stabilized. Please, Jansen, hurry!"

Rao's voice buzzed in Hawkins's ear like a mosquito. He considered muting her channel. He watched as Jansen approached him, Stevens in tow. Stevens wasn't moving—it looked as if Jansen were dragging an empty space suit. As she drew closer, Hawkins held up one hand to warn her to stop.

"Wait," he called, "we need to think about this."

"Get out of the way," Jansen told him. "I need to get Stevens attached to one of those ports. What the hell are you doing?"

Hawkins moved sideways a little, his body blocking her access to the suitports. "He can't come in," he said.

"What the hell?" Rao shouted. "What the fuck are you saying? He's going to die and you're wasting time!"

Hawkins winced but refused to move. "You say he was attacked by something inside 2I. Some kind of alien creature."

Jansen was close enough that he could see her face through the gold tinting on her faceplate. She didn't look happy.

He was prepared for that. "You have a responsibility to the rest of us."

"Hawkins, if you don't move, I'm going to move you," she growled.

"Is his suit intact?"

Jansen just glared.

"Tell me that his suit is intact," Hawkins demanded.

"It was punctured," she admitted, through gritted teeth.

"He could be infected with some kind of alien virus. If you bring him inside, you could infect us all."

"That's bullshit!" Rao called out.

"Dr. Rao, I know you have a relationship with Dr. Stevens, and—"

"Bullshit! There's no alien virus. This is just some kind of power play. How could Stevens catch an alien disease? We couldn't even share DNA with anything on 2I, much less any kind of systemic parallels with—"

"Rao, be quiet a second," Jansen said. "Maybe Hawkins has a point."

YORRICK DEBENS, PLANETARY PROTECTION OFFICER: Although we never take chances with potential extraterrestrial microbes, Dr. Rao was probably correct in her assessment. Pathogens like bacteria, viruses, and parasites that we find on Earth evolve to attack a specific host. They survive by taking advantage of very specific chemical environments inside the target's cells. It's extraordinarily rare to find a virus that can cross the species barrier, even between two organisms within class Mammalia. Organisms that evolved on different worlds from each other would have basic differences of body chemistry, different types of tissues and cellular apparatus. A virus that could infect both a human and an alien—it would be like sneezing on a tulip and expecting it to catch your cold.

"You need to listen to me," Rao said, over Jansen's radio. "I'm the flight surgeon of this mission, damn it, and the only biologist you've got. I know what I'm talking about! Look at his vitals! Stevens needs immediate help if he's going to survive. If you're not going to let him inside *Orion*, what exactly is your plan?"

Jansen stared Hawkins in the eye. She could see he wasn't going to back down.

And what if he was right?

They needed to quarantine Stevens. They needed to keep him separate, someplace where they could give him medical attention without exposing *Orion* to anything hazardous. They were about eight million kilometers from the nearest medical center. But there was one place they could take him.

One that even had a medical robot on board.

"*Wanderer*," she said.

"*Wanderer*," Hawkins said, nodding inside his helmet.

PARMINDER RAO: Stevens was in circulatory shock, which can lead to low end-organ perfusion, loss of cellular function, and hypoxemia. Untreated, it can lead to organ failure. Shock is one the leading causes of death in people suffering traumatic injuries or critical illnesses. We needed to move fast.

He kept blipping in and out. He kept—

Stevens's eyes snapped open. "Wait," he said. "Where are—"

Darkness, darkness all around him. Was he back inside 2I? In the dark, in the giant dark, in the place with the tendrils the place the place with ropes the place with ice with—

Something beeped in his ear, loud enough to hurt. He snarled and tried to roll over, tried to go back to sleep. He was inside an airlock, but that didn't make any sense, he didn't want to be in an airlock. He wanted to curl up in a sleepsac, maybe with—the thought made him smile, maybe with Parminder and—

He heard her voice. "How's his breathing doing? Is it too fast, too slow? Is it ragged? Give me something to work with!"

Stevens saw Jansen's face looming over him. She looked worried. That scared him for some reason, as if he was—as if he—oh, right, he was—

"Cut it off! You have to," Rao shouted. Cut what off? Cut what? He felt something tear through him, tear him open, and he screamed, but then when he looked down he saw they had gotten his suit off and now they were cutting through his thermal onesie, they were stripping him naked. *Hey, now, guys*, he said, except he couldn't talk, his mouth didn't work.

He felt a horrible, crushing pain in his chest. Everything went red.

He woke up looking into a robot's face. A GRAM robot, he knew about those. KSpace built those. General robotic assistants and medics. Why was he looking at a GRAM? That didn't make any sense, there weren't any GRAMs on *Orion*. "Where are we?" he asked. "Where are we?"

KARLA UTZ, BIOMEDICAL ENGINEER: Even when they took him out of his suit, we could still monitor Dr. Stevens's vital statistics through a bio-monitor cuff strapped around his ankle. From millions of kilometers away we could see, for instance, that his blood oxygen saturation had dropped to about seventy-nine. Normal levels in a human being range from ninety to one hundred.

Getting Stevens into *Wanderer* without making his injuries worse took some work. Getting him out of his suit was a nightmare. Jansen looked down and saw a splash of blood across the front of her own suit. This would be so much easier if they could take off their suits and work with their bare hands, but that wasn't...that wasn't a great idea.

Exhaustion and fear threatened to drag her down. She was sweating and she felt weak, but she knew she had to focus.

"Help him, you idiot," she said, grabbing the robot and shaking it.

"He needs fluids," Rao said. Rao, who was still back on *Orion*. Overseeing this process via virtual reality.

Hawkins had Stevens pressed against the wall of *Wanderer*'s orbital module, holding him in place as his limbs twitched and jerked. He was going into a seizure.

"Help him!" she shouted at the robot.

"I'm sorry, I'm only authorized to treat KSpace employees," the robot said. The hexagon on its chest shifted from glowing purple to glowing green.

"God damn it, he's dying," Jansen said, grabbing the robot by one spindly arm. She felt as if she could rip that arm off if she tried. It was tempting. "If you don't help him—"

"Wait!" Hawkins said. "He *is* a KSpace employee—or he was."

Jansen nodded. Yes—yes! Maybe they could trick the robot into helping. "His name is Sunny Stevens—"

"Without a KSpace Employee Identifier or some other proof of employment, I'm afraid I can't help," GRAM said. "I'm very sorry."

Jansen growled. She felt her hands curling into fists.

But then Stevens's eyes snapped open. He must have heard what they were saying, even if he was only half-conscious. "Stevens, Sunny," he said. "My employee number is...K6235...DA1."

"Welcome aboard, Dr. Stevens," GRAM said.

"Jansen," Stevens said. His eyes were wide, and he was suddenly very much awake. "Jansen, what did you do to me—"

Panels opened across GRAM's narrow chest. A needle on an extendible arm plunged into Stevens's arm, and yellow fluid flowed through a plastic tube into his bloodstream. Stevens gasped in pain.

"Check his abdomen," Rao said. "I need you to look at it—I can only see what your suit cameras see. Look for an entry wound."

Jansen pulled the last remnants of Stevens's liquid cooling and ventilation garment away from his stomach. Thick drops of blood had collected on the inside, forming perfect red hemispheres in the absence of gravity. She couldn't see anything on his skin from all the dried blood matted into his body hair.

"Allow me," GRAM said. It sprayed water across the wound, clearing away some of the crusted blood. It extended a suction hose to draw the water and blood away. As fast as it cleared the wound, though, fresh red blood welled up from a trench dug through Stevens's skin.

"Oh shit," Rao said.

"What's going on?" Hawkins asked. He was upside down from Jansen's perspective, still holding Stevens's arms.

"I'm going to raise the temperature in here," GRAM said, "to counteract hypothermia. Please don't be alarmed." Ventilation fans in the orbital module started to roar, and the shreds of Stevens's LCVG flapped in a strong breeze. Inside her suit Jansen couldn't feel it, only hear it.

"There's going to be internal bleeding," Rao said. "GRAM, can you close that wound? That's the first thing we need to do."

"I'll get right on it," GRAM said. Two more spindly arms extended from its chest and started digging around inside Stevens's body.

"Oh fuck, oh Jesus!" Stevens screamed. "Oh God, that hurts! It hurts!"

"I'm administering a mild sedative," GRAM said.

"Jansen!" Stevens screamed. "Jansen, you—you left me alone down there, you left me—you were so fucking desperate to find—to—"

"Try not to talk," Rao said. "Save your strength. GRAM, do you have a close-field spectrometer for rapid tox screening? We need to start looking for foreign objects or chemicals he might have been exposed to—"

"No! Fuck this," Stevens said. His head reared forward and he glared at Jansen. Hawkins gently grabbed his forehead and pushed it back down. Stevens didn't seem to have the strength to resist.

"This is on you," he said. He wouldn't look away from Jansen's face. "This is on you. You're cursed! Nobody is safe around you. You killed Blaine Wilson. And now you've fucking killed me!"

PARMINDER RAO: *All I wanted was to be with him. To hold his hand. They wouldn't even let me leave* Orion. *I . . . Never mind. His core temperature got down to about thirty-one Celsius, which was bad. His heart rate spiked at 124. Also bad. For an hour I watched the numbers, knowing he could go into respiratory arrest at any moment, knowing he could just die without much warning. But things turned around. GRAM stabilized him. We stopped his internal bleeding. The immediate crisis passed.*

Hawkins left *Wanderer* and was on the way back to *Orion*. Jansen had chosen to stay behind. She'd moved Stevens, taking him back to *Wanderer*'s reentry module, where she could strap him into one of the spacecraft's crew seats. He would at least be more comfortable there than he would be braced up against the wall of the orbital module.

Rao looked over the scans and X-rays GRAM had provided, trying to make sense of what had happened to Stevens.

"This...tendril? That's what we're calling it? It cut right into his liver," she said. "The scans show a clear incision, about ten centimeters long."

"Jesus," Jansen said, over the radio.

"No, that's actually good. Or at least it could have been a lot worse. If it punctured one of his lungs or hit a major artery, he would have died before you got him back." She sighed and wiped at her face. She'd been sweating profusely and maybe crying a little. She was glad she was alone in *Orion*, so no one had seen how frantic she'd become, how desperate while she waited to see if Stevens was going to live or die.

"You can lose a lot of liver tissue and be OK," she said, moving on with her prognosis. "You can live with, like, ten percent of a liver. He's not out of the woods yet, but...assuming we don't find anything else, he might be OK. That's probably the best we can hope for."

"OK," Jansen said. Not as if she were acknowledging what Rao had said. More as if she was just repeating it.

She sounded faint and distant. Rao had access to Jansen's biodata as well, and nothing she saw there was encouraging.

"You should try to get some sleep. Come back here and take a nap, at the very least," she said. She was responsible for the health of all of *Orion*'s crew, not just Stevens. "You're showing classic signs of extreme fatigue."

"I'll be fine. I want to stay with him."

"Just promise me you'll take it easy," Rao said.

There was no reply.

"Jansen," she said, "when you were over there—inside 2I. What did you see? What was it like?"

Jansen took a long time answering.

"Horrible," she said.

CREW EXCHANGE

ROY MCALLISTER: We had a hard decision to make, regarding removing Jansen from her command. I consulted with General Kalitzakis, and he agreed with me—maybe a little too readily. I know he had never been comfortable with civilians running the show. It was a foregone conclusion, anyway. I believed in Sally Jansen, I thought she was the best person for this mission. But we couldn't ignore the fact she'd put her people in danger.

In the end she did sleep, a little. It wasn't as if she had much of a choice—her body had been running on adrenaline for hours, and adrenaline always comes with a price tag.

She stirred four hours later, still groggy, to the sound of beeping medical equipment and the gentle roar of a ventilator fan.

She realized just how badly she'd abused herself. Her back was one solid, fused column of vertebrae, and her leg was dead all the way up to her hip. Microgravity could work wonders on sore muscles, though. It hurt only when she moved. As long as she lay still she was OK.

God, how she hated being old. She remembered what it was like having a hangover when she was twenty. You rolled out of bed with a headache, but one greasy breakfast later and you were back in action, ready to party. The thought made her grin, memories of long-ago spring breaks. Until she remembered where she was.

She had strapped herself into the pilot's seat in *Wanderer*'s reentry module. Stevens was resting quietly in the far seat. The module wasn't as big as *Orion*'s CM, and with GRAM moving around inside, constantly fussing over Stevens's vitals, it felt pretty cramped. She had no intention of leaving anytime soon, though.

What he'd said to her, in his brief moment of lucidity before they started stitching him up...

She closed her eyes and let her face burn with shame for a while. She let herself feel her own failure for a couple of minutes. She finally had time to spare for a little self-hate.

People had believed in her. Roy McAllister had trusted her to do this right, to keep her people safe. And she had failed. She'd put Stevens in danger for a fool's errand, a rescue attempt nobody else thought had a point.

Stevens—Sunny—had been right.

She was cursed.

All she'd ever wanted in her life was to go to Mars. She'd trained for it, she'd fought to get a place in the astronaut corps. She'd spent years getting ready to walk on red soil. Then Blaine Wilson died, and the rug was yanked out from under her feet.

In the years since then, she'd just assumed that life was like that. You dreamed and you worked hard and then—something bad happened, and it was over. For twenty-one years she'd known her life wasn't about exploration or science or discovery—it was always going to be about atonement and guilt. Then Roy had given her this second chance.

And look what she'd done with it. She looked over at Stevens, at his sleeping body.

She had done this to him. It was like Blaine Wilson all over again. She went over every decision she'd made in her head, over and over again, questioning what she'd gotten wrong, where she'd failed to notice something or make the right call.

She knew that she would keep replaying the same events in her head for the rest of her life. She knew it for a certainty, because she'd been doing it for twenty-one years.

Now she had two astronauts on her conscience. She didn't know if she could learn to bear that weight.

All she could think was that she had failed. She should never have been given a second chance.

Eventually she opened her eyes again and looked over at Stevens. GRAM was mopping his face with a sponge. The robot looked up at her when it noticed she was observing it. "Can I help you with anything, Commander Jansen?" it asked.

"No, no, I . . ." She shook her head.

God she was tired. God she hurt. God everything, everything was wrong.

"He wasn't supposed to be here."

She didn't even realize she was speaking until the words were out of her. Floating in front of her in microgravity, as if they were printed on the air.

She blinked, hard, trying to clear her head.

"I'm sorry, Commander Jansen, I don't understand," the robot said.

She stared at it in frustration. "He wasn't supposed to be an astronaut. He had to extort his way onto *Orion*," she said. "But damn it, I can't dodge this. I can't pretend this isn't my fault. I'm his MC. Everything that happens on this mission is my responsibility. He got hurt because I let him get hurt."

"It sounds like you're attempting to file a formal complaint," the robot chirped. "I can help with that."

Jansen sighed and waved one hand at it, a gesture of dismissal. There were moments when the robot seemed intelligent, self-aware, but that was just fancy programming. The thing was about as smart as the average sheep.

She lifted her hands, thinking she would rub at her eyes, but of course she couldn't do that. She was still wearing her helmet.

She wanted to laugh at the stupidity of it all. At the cosmic joke of her life, at the idea that maybe things could have been different this time.

She brought her hands back down, and one of them struck the side of her suit, and it made a sound she hadn't expected. There was something in one of her pockets, something she'd forgotten.

She shoved her gloved hand into the pocket and pulled out a bedraggled orange flag and memory stick.

The prize. The thing she'd been so intent on finding that she'd ignored Stevens's cry for help. If she had just let it go, if she'd focused on him instead...

But she hadn't. Instead she'd risked everything for a little memory stick, a tiny piece of plastic with a shiny metal plug on one end. It couldn't possibly make up for Stevens's life.

Maybe just to punish herself, maybe because she would take any distraction, anything that would get her out of her own head, she decided to see what was on the stick. What message Foster had left for her.

She found the slot on the side of her communications panel and slid the stick in. Just as before, there was only one file, encoded in a video format. She blinked twice to make it play. The screen came to life, flickering with noise and darkness.

"Let's see." Commander Foster's words filled the CM. GRAM lifted its plastic head, recognizing its master's voice, perhaps. She adjusted the volume so as not to wake Stevens. "The temperature has climbed to minus nineteen..."

VIDEO FILE TRANSCRIPT (2)

Willem Foster: Let's see. The temperature has climbed to minus nineteen degrees and the air pressure has increased by nearly three hundred percent. Weather conditions are deteriorating, but I'm confident we can find our way back. After what we've seen, I'm not sure if the environmental changes started when we entered the Object or if they were going on before then. Whether the Object is responding to us or if it's even aware of us.

Taryn Holmes: Scan's done.

Foster: Good. Let me see... Sandra, don't get too far ahead.

Sandra Channarong: Don't worry about that. I can barely see you from here, I'm not going to wander far.

Foster: Just checking this scan... Hold on, it's loading. Damn, the resolution on this thing is amazing, but it takes forever to render.

In the meantime...We're all getting tired, but morale is good. What we've found here was...not what we expected, obviously, but as Taryn's been telling us the whole time, this isn't a place made for humans. It was built by beings that think differently than we do, and probably have a very different way of life. Maybe this is what their home world looks like. Though I can't help but think that we're seeing something primal, in the process of becoming—

Holmes: Here, look, on the screen. That's the thing I saw before.

Foster: Good. Good to have confirmation. It's tough knowing even what we're looking for in here, but we've mapped part of the interior with our lidar/radar imager and it looks like we've found our first point of interest. There's a large, low-density mass about twenty kilometers away across the ice sheet. It's the first sign we've seen of any kind of structure or building inside the Object. Sandra, come here. Look.

Channarong: What is it?

Foster: That's what I want to find out. But listen, you two—I scheduled us for a twelve-hour EVA. It looks like this might take a while longer to explore. How do we feel about that? About maybe spending the night inside?

Channarong: I'm good. Hungry, and a little beat. I didn't expect this to be a hiking vacation!

Holmes: Yeah, yeah, I want to see this thing with my eyes. You know? Maybe that's where the aliens are. Maybe they're waiting for us to come to them.

Foster: OK. We'll head out straightaway. This place. It's kind of beautiful, isn't it? A little terrifying, maybe, but it has a grandeur to it. I wonder if this is what Shackleton felt like, or Amundsen.

Holmes: If you say so, boss.

When the video stopped playing, Jansen turned to the others. They were all back in *Orion's* HabLab—she'd flown over as soon as she saw what was on the video. She knew the others needed to see it, too. Now she waited for them to say they understood. That they saw what she'd seen.

"We know where they are. We know there's a good chance they're still alive."

Hawkins shook his head. "What are you talking about?"

"They didn't get lost in there," Jansen said. "They planned on deviating from their timetable, and they knew exactly where they were going. I saw this thing, this structure. I saw it with my own eyes. I know where to search for them."

Hawkins and Rao traded a look.

Jansen didn't like that look.

"I think they're still alive. Maybe trapped—maybe they can't get back to the airlock. I can go back," Jansen said. "I can help them, somehow."

How did everybody not get this?

"Look, this time I'll go alone. I get what you meant before, Hawkins, about putting the crew at risk to chase after people who—who might be dead. I get it. I won't ask anyone else to go, not knowing how dangerous it is over there. But I have to go back. As long as there's any chance at all that I could find them."

They were still staring at her as if they hadn't heard a word she'd said.

Hawkins sucked in a deep breath. "Jansen," he said. "A message came in from Pasadena, while you were over on *Wanderer*. There's been a decision...I know you're not going to like this."

She stared at him, wondering why he wasn't getting the point. Hadn't he seen the video?

"The decision is that you're being removed from your position as mission commander. I'm supposed to take over your role. Effective immediately."

Jansen stared at him. "Wait," she said. "What?"

Hawkins didn't repeat himself.

"The hell you are," Jansen said. "This is my ship." She ground her teeth together. "I'm MC on this ship. You don't get to just announce otherwise." Jansen knew she was losing her self-control.

That she was letting her anger get the better of her. She fought to keep from raising her voice. "Damn it," she said. "I won't allow it. You're not taking my goddamned job."

"I already have."

ARCS chose just that moment to float over to them. It had a hot food tube in each of its three hands. "Pardon the interruption," the robot said. "None of you have eaten in more than twelve hours, and—"

Jansen knocked the food tube right out of the robot's goddamned hand. The robot went pinwheeling after the tube before it could splatter on anything important.

She wanted to scream. She wanted to throw herself on Hawkins, scratch his eyes out and make him bleed. He couldn't do this to her! This was supposed to be her second chance, this was supposed to be her opportunity to redeem herself for twenty-one years of failure. She wanted to fight and kick and shout.

But she was a professional. An astronaut. So she settled for glaring daggers at him and folding her arms across her chest.

"We need to refocus, now," he told her. "We need to remember why we came here in the first place. To establish communications with the aliens. We can't afford to send anyone back over there— especially now we know how dangerous it is."

"Hawkins," she said, trying to stay calm, "the KSpace crew is still over there, you can't just let them die—"

"It's been decided that we should operate under the assumption they're already dead."

Decided. Maybe by some general in the Pentagon. Maybe by Hawkins, just now, and he was covering his ass.

She brought her hands up to her chest and wove her fingers together. Almost as if she were praying. "We can't stop now. We can't just give up. We need to finish this."

"I can see how much *you* need it," he said.

Her heart stopped beating as she realized this was actually happening.

"That isn't—that isn't it at all, you're being—"

"I'm being what?"

She forced herself not to say what she'd been thinking.

There was nothing more she could accomplish here. She kicked off the wall and headed toward the dormitory area, just to get as far away from him as she could.

Of course he followed her.

TELEMETRY SILENCE

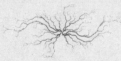

S tevens hurt.

Pretty much every part of him hurt. He felt hot and sweaty and uncomfortable, and the damned robot wouldn't leave him alone.

It would have been an unbearable situation, except for one thing: they'd loaded him full of painkillers. He heartily approved of that decision.

Everything, all the pain, all the fear he knew he should be feeling, was held at a distance. It was kind of magical, actually. He knew that eventually he was going to have to deal with what had happened. He would feel all the agony of his wounds someday. But it didn't have to be today.

He didn't have to do anything just then. He didn't even have to think. Which was good, because the painkillers made every notion that went through his head feel like a passing cloud. He couldn't have grabbed on to those thoughts if he wanted to. And the drugs made sure that didn't bother him too much.

He could see Parminder's face on the screen in front of him. She was a kilometer away, in *Orion*, but she'd promised she would be in constant contact. They'd removed his devices, so he couldn't look at her in VR mode, but he could see her face. He wished she didn't look so scared, but he would take what he could get.

"My stomach feels like shit," he told her.

"Are you nauseous?"

"No, more like... It feels like something's pushing on it. It's weird. Did you say Hawkins is in charge now?"

Rao rolled her eyes. "I'm not even sure what that means at this point. Don't worry about them. Are you hungry at all?"

"No," he said. Even the idea of food just made him hurt worse. "Parminder—stop assessing me. Talk to me. How are you?"

There was a pause before she replied. Not a long one, but he heard it.

"I'm just fine, thank you. You, on the other hand, are showing the signs of a hyperimmune response. I'm not crazy about that. I think maybe we should take a look at your stitches, see if you're healing OK. GRAM, can you please show me a view of Dr. Stevens's abdomen, specifically around the wound area?"

"Of course, Dr. Rao," the robot said. Its hexagon turned green as it grasped Stevens's sheet with its spindly hands. Stevens took a breath, preparing himself to be exposed to the icy air.

"This could be a little gross," Rao said, "but don't worry. I'm a doctor. I've seen everything that can happen to a human body."

Stevens laughed—which hurt a lot. "I figured the first time you saw me naked would be a lot more fun. Parminder, come on, babe. Isn't there any way you can come over here and be with me? Even if you have to wear a space suit?"

"I can't, and you know that. I want to, but—"

Her face froze.

"Parminder?" Stevens frowned. He tried to slap the side of the console, as if that would make the video come unstuck. He was so weak he barely made contact. "I think you're buffering. Your audio cut out, or something."

"No," she said. "I'm still here." Her voice was very small and weak. As if her signal had grown attenuated, he thought.

Or maybe she was just scared.

"Oh shit," he said, because he wasn't stupid. He clamped his eyes shut. Which just made him aware of the smell. The smell he must have been smelling all along, but that his brain had clearly blocked out.

He opened one eye and looked down at his exposed stomach.

There was a hole down there. A hole where there definitely, 100 percent should not be a hole. The stitches were gone, and it looked as if half the flesh of his stomach was gone, too. The edges of the hole were bright red and inflamed. Inside the hole everything was gray and full of weird white filaments.

"Parminder," he said. "Parminder."

"I'm . . . I'm right here," she said. She wasn't looking at his face.

"Look at my face," he said.

Slowly her eyes moved up the screen until they had something like eye contact.

"This hurts," he said, "but not as much as you'd expect. Is that a good sign?"

"It's because the nerves are dead," she told him. Just point-blank. "They're gone."

His head started to spin. He didn't want to hear that, but he needed to. He needed to understand. Because understanding a problem was the first step toward fixing it.

"I don't feel like I'm about to die," he told her.

"You're not. You're . . ." Her lip trembled a little. "You're going to be fine."

KARLA UTZ, BIOMEDICAL ENGINEER: The wound had turned necrotic. We had no idea why. The necrosis was spreading through his tissues, consuming more of Dr. Stevens's cells as it progressed. If it reached his heart or either of his lungs—and it didn't have far to go, given the location of the original wound—he would die. The standard treatment for necrosis is debridement, meaning the surgical removal of dead tissue.

You can do this, Rao told herself. *You can. You just have to focus.*

She reached up and touched the devices mounted on her cheekbones and switched to full VR. Suddenly she was seeing through the eyes of GRAM. The display wasn't optimized—Stevens was enormous, twice his normal size, and GRAM's color vision was all off, making him look purple. Even worse, GRAM never stopped moving—the robot was light enough to be blown around by *Wanderer*'s ventilation system, just nudged back and forth a little, but in the magnified view it felt as if Rao's whole body were swaying.

I can't do this.

She started to reach for her devices, intending to log out of the VR space. GRAM's arms moved up toward its face, copying her movement, and she saw the swirling colors of its eyes reflected in the scalpel and she almost vomited right then and there.

I can't do this.

"Parminder?" Stevens said. "Is that you, in the robot? Hey, what's going on? I thought we were going to do a procedure or something."

She opened her mouth to say something and realized she had no idea what to tell him. If he didn't have this operation, he was going to die. But—oh boy. The wound was so ugly. The necrotic tissue was deathly white, and it peeled off in thin layers. She was incredibly thankful she couldn't smell it.

The necrosis had come on with a suddenness. It had spread far faster than it had any right to—nothing on Earth, not brown recluse spider venom or industrial chemicals, could cause a reaction like this. 2I had pumped Stevens full of some incredible toxin, something unprecedented.

Which was the last thing you wanted to see when you were in charge of a patient's medical care.

She opened up GRAM's settings and forced the robot to stay still, to compensate for the breeze blowing through *Wanderer*'s reentry module. She resized its view and considered restricting her connection to a windowed mode. But no. She needed true VR, she needed to be right up in the wound so she could tell the difference between dead and healthy flesh.

She moved GRAM until it was almost sitting on Stevens's neck. Maybe it would help if she couldn't see his face.

"Parminder," he called.

"Shut up," she told him.

She extended the scalpel, moving her actual arm so that GRAM's arm moved in sync with her. She touched it to Stevens's flesh, and a tiny drop of blood welled up. GRAM had already prepped him by giving him a local anesthetic. Stevens wouldn't feel a thing.

She could do this.

She took a deep breath.

Then she pressed down hard with the scalpel, cutting through the skin. It parted easily, a thin line of blood following her cut as she traced a circle around the affected area. With a debridement like this you couldn't just cut the necrotic tissue away. You had to excise the entire affected area—which meant cutting out healthy tissue, as well. As little of it as possible.

She cut a wide, round flap of skin out of Stevens's abdomen. She used GRAM's free hand to peel it away so she could get at the living flesh beneath. She would need to sew up all the major blood vessels, then graft on new skin. She had the patch ready, a circular piece of bright-pink plastic courtesy of *Wanderer*'s 3-D printer. It wasn't perfect, but it would hold long enough to be replaced with real skin once Stevens was back on the ground.

First things first. She had a large plastic sample bag ready. She would transfer the excised skin to the bag, then seal it. Then she would sterilize everything—the scalpel, GRAM's hands, Stevens's skin—before she started the microsurgery. It was a little tricky getting the sample bag open—GRAM's fingers didn't have finger-prints, so they slipped on the plastic—but she managed. She got the bag shut and sealed. Then she turned back to the wound. GRAM had placed a suction hose to keep it clear of blood—blood they would analyze later, to make sure it was free of—

"Oh fuck," Rao said. It was almost a whisper.

"Baby?" Stevens asked. "Can I look now?"

The excision she'd made had gone deep enough to remove all the necrotic tissue. All the same, she was certain she hadn't punctured the abdominal wall. She didn't think she had. Yet as she stared into the wound she saw Stevens's muscular tissue splitting open, and she got a good look into his abdominal cavity. It looked like a nest of snakes in there. At first she thought she was looking at his intestines. Except the writhing, snakelike things were the wrong color, a dull, pale gray. And they were moving under their own power.

As she watched, one of them got a pointed tip out of the wound, like a worm poking its head out of wet soil. It quested around for a moment, then started to slither upward and across Stevens's chest. No, she realized. It wasn't crawling. It was growing. It put out new branches as it moved, thin tendrils that snaked through his chest hair, coiled around his nipples.

"Parminder? What's happening?" he asked. "What's going on?"

More of the worms emerged from the wound, five more, a dozen. They were wet with blood that they smeared across Stevens's hips and groin as they emerged. Exploring. Growing. Clutching him in their net.

Rao muted her microphone. She couldn't let him hear her scream.

Jansen was still arguing with Hawkins when she heard the screaming. She turned and kicked her way out of the dormitory at once—it sounded as if Rao were being tortured out there. Ripped apart.

In the wardroom Rao floated in air, her hands waving back and forth in front of her as if she were warding off a monster. One look around told Jansen what was actually going on. Rao was deep in a VR trance, presumably connecting via telepresence to the GRAM robot over on *Wanderer*.

Jansen flew over to the nearest touchscreen and called up a video of what Rao was seeing.

The video started in the middle of a horror show. GRAM's scalpel arm flashed across the screen, again and again. Cutting into tendrils that stretched and spread across Stevens's body. They were tough and rubbery, and the scalpel barely sliced them open. Dark fluid oozed from the cuts, fluid that hardened almost instantly, sealing the cuts shut again.

GRAM kept cutting, slashing. Until one tendril lifted from Stevens's body and wrapped around GRAM's slender metal wrist. GRAM tried to pull its arm free but it was stuck, caught in a grip it couldn't shake.

A hundred new tendrils snaked across GRAM's arm and its torso, then grew across one of its eyes, cutting the video display in half.

The view shifted as GRAM was pushed backward, slowly, so slowly. It crashed against the far wall of *Wanderer*'s command module. The image shook wildly as the tendrils lashed across GRAM's torso and face, then stopped moving once the robot was caught fast in their net.

One of GRAM's eyes was still clear enough that she could see Stevens. What was left of him, anyway. He was obscured under a writhing mass of thick tendrils. They continued to grow from his middle, looping up into the air in the absence of gravity and then slapping against the walls. They streamed out in every direction, growing and branching off constantly. They grabbed objects out of the air, grabbed them and wove thick dark cocoons around them. They slithered across the screens of the module, all of which were flashing red. They oozed across the module's viewports. They disappeared through the hatch that led to the orbital module. They covered everything in a colorless network of gently pulsing filaments.

Eventually they grew across GRAM's other eye, and the video went dark.

Rao was still screaming, her arms slashing away at the air, even though GRAM could no longer mirror her movements. "Shit, she's still over there," Jansen said, and kicked across the air to grab Rao, grab her into a tight hug. Hawkins came up to help, peeling the devices off Rao's face. Cutting the connection to *Wanderer*.

Rao rocked back and forth in Jansen's embrace, her face digging into Jansen's collarbone, hot tears soaking the fabric of Jansen's shirt. It seemed her screams would never stop.

PREMATURE SHUTDOWN

I t wasn't your fault," Hawkins said.

Rao was still cradled in Jansen's arms. She'd sunk into a withdrawn, listless state. Jansen kept rubbing her back because she had no idea what else to do.

"What?" Rao asked, her voice very small and distant.

"I said it wasn't your fault," Hawkins said again.

Jansen felt Rao's body stiffen, her muscles contracting as if she'd been struck. "Who said it was?" she demanded.

Jansen tried to shoot Hawkins a look, to tell him to just back off, but he wasn't looking at her. He was looking at Rao's face.

"There was nothing you could have done," he tried.

"I know that. I'm a doctor. I'm aware of my limits, thank you very much." Rao pushed her way out of Jansen's arms, causing the two of them to drift off in opposite directions. When she reached the far wall of the HabLab, Rao kicked off, launching herself toward the dormitory compartment.

"I know you and Stevens had...feelings...for..."

Hawkins was floundering now. Jansen almost felt sorry for him. She shook her head. When he still didn't take the hint, she drew a finger across her throat. *Stop it*, she thought, as if he could hear her via telepathy. *Just shut up*.

"He was a good man," Hawkins sputtered.

Rao's eyes shimmered with the start of tears. "If you'll excuse me, I'm going to go freshen up," she said, and disappeared through the dormitory hatch.

Hawkins turned to appeal to Jansen, but she was already kicking her way across the HabLab. She pushed through the hatch and found Rao gripping the sides of their shower unit. It was a segmented plastic bag designed to be folded away when not in use. It looked as if Rao was trying to open it up but couldn't quite get the latch to work.

Jansen glided over and reached up to hit the latch herself. The shower unit popped open and automatically extended to its full length.

Rao just hung there in the air, staring at it.

"I feel like I need to scrub myself until I bleed," she whispered. "I feel like I'm covered in blood." The younger woman clutched her arms around herself. "I wasn't actually over there. I didn't touch anything, you know? I'm sanitary. But I feel—I feel infected."

Jansen put a hand on Rao's shoulder. Rao didn't shrug it off. After a moment a sob erupted from her chest, a deep, seismic explosion of grief.

"I'm so sorry, ma'am," Rao said, her voice cracking. "I'm so sorry."

"Shh," Jansen said. "You feel what you're going to feel. It's OK."

"No," Rao said. "No. I can't—I can't let *him* see me like this. He's going to make me out to be the grieving widow. He's going to feel *so sorry* for me."

Jansen understood.

"I'll keep him clear of you," she promised.

Rao gave her a grateful look, then touched her devices and moved to a nearby screen, which showed a scrolling list of telemetry logs.

"What are you doing?" Jansen asked.

"This is all the data GRAM collected during the surgery. I'm going to go over it and try to figure out what happened."

Back to work. Rao had just lost the man she cared about and she was already back to work.

Jansen didn't really understand that at all, but she knew people grieved in different ways. She rubbed Rao's upper arm for a moment, then left the dormitory, zipping the hatch shut behind her. *Orion* was too small for any concept of real privacy, but she would give Rao as much space as she could.

PARMINDER RAO: When my grandfather died, about six years ago, the whole family was there at his bedside. My mom and my dad and my cousins, all filling up the room with their tension, and Nani sitting stroking my grandpa's hand, asking him over and over for his last words, though we all knew he was past that point, he was long past talking. Me? I was down the hall at the nurse's station, arguing whether liquid Tylenol was going to be enough, or if we could get some damned morphine already, it wasn't like he was going to develop a habit now. And so I missed it, I missed the moment he actually went. I kicked myself for it later, but you know, it's what we do. It's what doctors do, we compartmentalize. We break things down, look for the bits we can fix, that we can change. I know I'm babbling, but you have to understand this. There was nothing in the world that was going to bring Stevens back. But you don't stop working until they pull you away. Not because you think there's a chance, but because if you let yourself be idle, even for a second, you start thinking about what it means to lose somebody. And once you start thinking that you never stop.

"We believe that when Commander Jansen removed the tendril from Dr. Stevens's liver, some small part of it must have remained inside the injury site."

"It's the only thing that makes sense."

"Inside the body cavity, in a low-oxygen, warm environment, it continued to grow. We have no explanation for the runaway acceleration in growth once it emerged into the oxygenated atmosphere."

"No explanation at this time, you mean."

"Exactly. Its metabolic functions are, well, alien, and therefore have yet to be described in the literature, but—"

"We're working on it. We're studying it. Necropsy samples would be extraordinarily useful. That isn't something we can really count on."

"It will, of course, be impossible to recover the body."

In the control room, Roy McAllister leaned back in his chair. He pressed the tips of his fingers against his eyelids. People were talking to him. Talking near him. He tried not to hear them, but of course, you can't shut your ears.

"*Orion*'s systems are all reporting green, good, optimal. We have limited telemetry from *Wanderer*, but from external views the spacecraft appears largely undamaged."

"We should call KSpace. Just as a professional courtesy—express our regrets."

"Though we need to make sure there are no liability issues."

"The president wants to express his sympathies. He's going to personally invite Dr. Stevens's family to the White House. The meeting will have to be in secret, and he can't tell them anything about the mission, but he says he'll say that Stevens died in the service of his country."

"Of all humanity."

"But he can't say that."

"No, of course not."

"Has anyone checked Commander Jansen's biodata? She was inside 2I at the same time as Dr. Stevens. We need to make sure she wasn't also infected. We need to make sure the remaining—I mean, the other three astronauts are OK."

"Definitely. Just—they've asked for a little radio silence. Out of respect."

"I'm not sure we can honor that request."

"I've already started an investigation into what went wrong. Into why this happened. I've collected all of Dr. Rao's preliminary case notes and Dr. Stevens's test results, but I'll need to get access to KSpace's proprietary data from *Wanderer*. Sir? Can you just authorize this? I need you to sign off so I can start requesting that data and—"

"Sir," someone said.

"Not now," McAllister replied.

A man was dead.

He knew that this was part of his job. He knew he needed to focus, to figure out how they should proceed from here. Whether he should call *Orion* back to Earth and protect the three remaining astronauts. Even though that would mean giving up, surrendering when they didn't have a plan B. But what could they possibly hope to achieve up there? What could they do except get themselves killed and—

"Sir!"

He opened his eyes and sat up in his chair. A woman in a blue cardigan was standing in front of him. She looked frantic.

"Your name's Utz, right?" he asked.

"That's right," she said. "Sir. There's new telemetry you need to see."

He doubted it could possibly be anything good. "In a moment. I need to think, Utz. I need to—"

"Sir!"

He heard the alarm then. A strident, bleeping noise, beating out a slow rhythm. He looked up.

The big screen showed a view of the interior of *Wanderer*, though it was almost unrecognizable now. The tendrils had spread across every surface, branching and connecting with each other in a spider-web of thick gray cords. They pulsed, almost imperceptibly. Swelling and then shrinking, to the same beat as the annoying bleeps.

A second window had opened up next to the big screen. It showed five line graphs. Three of them were completely flat, racing toward the right side of the screen without deviating at all. One ticked up and down, but only a tiny degree. The fifth jumped regularly, peaks of activity appearing every time the alert bleeped, every time the tendrils convulsed.

It took him a second to realize what he was looking at. It was a graph of Sunny Stevens's biodata. Nobody had thought to turn the meters off when he supposedly died. His vital statistics still being recorded by instruments attached to his body, long after that information should have been useful. Pulse, respiration, and blood pressure were all completely flat. As you would expect from a dead man.

The unstable, fluctuating graph showed his blood oxygen levels. In a healthy human body that value should hover above 90 percent. In Stevens's case it had dropped to about 10.

He pointed at the fifth graph, the one showing regular activity. "What is that?" he demanded.

"Neural oscillation," Utz said.

McAllister shook his head. "No. Not possible. Those are brain waves? What the hell is that supposed to mean?"

KARLA UTZ, BIOMEDICAL ENGINEER: It meant that by some very restricted definition, on some basal neurological level ... Dr. Stevens was still alive.

Rao launched herself across the HabLab. She needed to get to work.

Not that she was hoping for much. She was a trained professional, and she knew how the human body worked. She didn't believe in miracles.

She tapped her way through the communications interface. As the mission's flight surgeon she had access to biodata on all of *Orion*'s astronauts. She could also have opened up a window showing her video of what was happening inside *Wanderer*. It might have given her more information. But—no. She didn't want to see.

What was on her screen was frightening enough. "His heart's not beating," she announced.

"Is it possible that's a false reading?" Jansen asked. It sounded as if she were kilometers away. Nothing mattered except the numbers and graphs on the screen in front of Rao.

Rao bit her lip. "No," she said. "No. This is accurate. This is right."

She had found that in life, more often than not, the information you saw that was the most heartbreaking was the most accurate. It was the hopeful stuff you had to be wary of.

"He's showing brain activity," Hawkins said. "That has to be good, right? If he was flatlining—"

He stopped talking abruptly. Maybe Jansen had shut him up. Rao didn't look up to see.

"This is..." A wave of vertigo swept through her. Emotions trying to overcome her. She would *not* let that happen. She gripped the side of the screen until her head stopped spinning. "These are just nu-complex waves. You see this in coma patients, sometimes. It's activity from the hippocampus, that's all." *Come on, Sunny*, she thought. *Come on. Prove me wrong. Let me see some delta waves. Some sign you're still alive in there.*

"Rao? What does that mean?" Jansen asked. "We're not doctors. We don't understand."

What makes you think I do? Rao thought. Nobody had ever seen anything like this before. Nobody had ever been infected by an alien parasite that first killed you and then brought you back to life... She threw that thought away. She was a doctor and she would function like a doctor. She watched the peaks and valleys on the graph, looking for any sign of change. "His brain is ticking along, but he's not conscious, he's not—" Tears threatened to leak out of the corners of her eyes. She couldn't let that happen, not now. "His brain's getting oxygen. Don't ask me how—those tendrils must be feeding it. They must've punctured his skull, or, or—" She felt as if she were going to explode with the horror of this. "They're keeping his brain alive. That's— how is that even possible?"

Jansen didn't answer her. It was nice, Rao thought, having someone around who understood when a question was rhetorical.

"It's suffusing all his tissues," she said. His blood oxygen levels were back up to about 50—nowhere near where they should be, but something was definitely pumping oxygen to his cells. "His lungs aren't moving, his heart... his heart..."

"Rao?"

What she saw on the screen scared her so badly she could hardly think. "The brain waves. The waves—the, the frequency's the same, but the amplitude—"

On the screen the spikes in the line graph had looked like ripples on a pond before. They'd been tiny. Now they grew taller and taller, while the valleys stayed shallow. "The signal's getting stronger," she said. She didn't say what she was thinking. *This is impossible.* Because obviously it wasn't. "It's getting stronger."

"What the hell is going on?" McAllister demanded.

They'd brought a whole new team of people into the control room. Doctors, astrobiologists from Parminder Rao's department at JPL. Neurologists from Caltech. Anyone they could find who might possibly answer his question. They were all clustered around one console at the side of the room.

None of them even looked up. Not one of them voiced an opinion.

The big screen showed the view from inside *Wanderer*'s reentry module. It was hard to see anything—the growth of tendrils had obscured most of the cameras inside the spacecraft and covered over most of the lights until only a dim brown radiance filled the view. The one good camera feed they had showed Sunny Stevens from the nose down to his navel. The growth had covered so much of his flesh that only tiny portions of him could be seen—a patch of chest hair, the crook of one elbow.

His mouth opened. Tendrils snaked across his lips, down his throat. Yet somehow he was getting enough oxygen that he was able to gasp. A weak, spasmodic gesture, but McAllister could see his chest rise and then collapse, again and again.

"Is he saying something?" McAllister demanded. He couldn't be, could he? "Get me sound on that feed."

Speakers set into the ceiling of the control room came to life. The noise Stevens made boomed and crackled over their heads. It wasn't a word. It didn't even sound like a human voice—just one repeated sound, an explosion of breath from collapsed lungs.

"Puh. Puh. Puh."

"Sir," someone said, and actually grabbed McAllister's arm. He looked down and saw the graph of Stevens's brain activity. The spikes were still growing stronger. Then one jetted up so high it went right off the screen.

Instantly a dozen alarms went off at once. Screens flashed red and technicians reared backward, as if unable to believe what they were seeing. The big screen blacked out, then switched to a whole new image.

"My God," McAllister said.

The image was in gray scale. It showed a black silhouette of the shape of 2I, small enough that he couldn't make out the individual superstructures. As big as 2I might be, the screen needed to display something much larger. Something that looked a great deal like round wings made of long, graceful white loops that swooped out from the alien starship, then swung back again to connect to its center of mass. Like a butterfly's wings...

"What—what is that?" McAllister asked.

"It's a magnetic field—2I is emitting a magnetic field."

McAllister looked down to see a young woman sitting in front of him, sitting in front of one of the consoles. It was Nguyen, he thought. Their physicist.

He stared at her, wondering what the hell he was supposed to do with that information.

"I think it's responding to Dr. Stevens's brain waves," she said, before he could even think of the right question to ask.

McAllister blinked rapidly. "It can hear him thinking?"

"We're broadcasting Stevens's biodata on an open radio channel—the channel we use for all of our telemetry. Do I shut it down? Sir—I need to know whether I should shut down that channel—"

"Sir!" Someone else bellowed. "2I is accelerating!"

EEK...EEK...EEK...

The sound turned Jansen's blood to concrete. She felt frozen in place, even though she knew she needed to move. She needed to move *right now*.

Hawkins had been hovering over Rao's shoulder, looking at her screen. Now he looked up, and Jansen saw an expression of pure terror ripple across his features. He knew that sound. He'd heard it before—they all had.

It was *Orion*'s proximity alarm.

Her arm moved independently of her will. By pure muscle memory it lifted, and her fingers touched the devices on her cheekbones. She switched to pure VR, and everything went away, empty space flooding in all around her. Directly in front of her, filling most of her view, was the dark-red bulk of 2I.

It was getting bigger.

She didn't need to consult any instruments to know what was happening. Suddenly she was in control of herself again. She snapped out of VR and looked around the HabLab, doing a quick check to see what wasn't bolted down, what was going to go flying when she started up *Orion*'s engines.

She saw two things immediately. Two people. "Grab something! Hold on," she shouted. Hawkins reacted instantly, kicking over to the wall and grasping a handrail. Rao was still glued to her screen, watching Stevens's biodata.

"Hawkins," she shouted, "help her!"

He reached over and grabbed Rao with one arm, pulling her tight to his chest. Rao struggled, clearly annoyed at being pulled away from her screen, but Jansen didn't care. She called up an AR window and fired *Orion*'s retros, tapping for an emergency burn.

The ship lurched backward. Loose tools and food tubes and trash went flying toward the cupola, toward the nose of the spacecraft. ARCS went spinning across the HabLab—as the robot flew past Jansen's head, she could hear its soft voice issuing some kind of dire warning. It struck the soft wall right next to the cupola's hatch, its three hands grasping wildly for anything it might hold on to.

Hawkins and Rao swung from the handrail, suddenly dangling over a six-meter drop. Jansen felt her shoulder collide with something hard, and she realized she'd made the stupidest mistake a pilot could make—she hadn't bothered to secure herself before the maneuver. There'd been no time—

She looked down to see what she'd smashed into. She grabbed the angular frame of the treadmill and just tried to hold on.

GO/NO GO

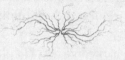

"O*rion*, this is Pasadena. Come in. *Orion*, come in, please." McAllister's hands were shaking, and he could feel sweat slicking down the hair on the back of his neck. He had three screens open at once, showing views of space around 2I. Everything was moving, and he could barely keep track of it all. "*Orion*, report," he called again, even though he knew it would be nearly a minute before he could get a response.

One of his screens showed 2I's magnetic field. It was constantly changing shape, the lines of force twisting and then snapping into new configurations. He couldn't shake the impression he'd had before—that it looked like a butterfly's wings. They were flapping now.

"Is this how it moves?" he asked.

Nguyen, their physicist, twisted her lower lip between her fingers. "It reminds me of something, something we actually experimented with a while ago. A...a...I forget what it was called, an—"

"Electric solar sail," someone else chimed in.

McAllister twisted around. It was Fonseca, the FDO whose name he'd forgotten before. He remembered it now.

"An e-sail, we ended up calling it the e-sail," she said. "It works just like a ship's sail on the ocean, exactly like that, except instead of canvas catching moving air, it uses a magnetic field to catch the solar wind. This is how it moves, sir—this is 2I's propulsion system."

McAllister didn't care about the details. As long as the magnetic field wasn't a weapon. "Is it strong enough to cause damage to *Orion*?"

Fonseca took a deep breath and blew it out again. "No. No, I don't—I don't think so. A strong enough magnetic field could blow out a lot of the spacecraft's electronics. It could even affect our people's brains, give them seizures. I don't think this one is that strong. I don't—I'm not sure."

"Figure it out," he barked at her. He glanced at another of his screens. It showed *Orion* moving backward, jetting away from 2I. Scooting out of the way to avoid a collision. It looked as if someone up there had acted fast enough to save *Orion* from being crushed. A pilot racked by seizures wouldn't be able to do that. McAllister sat down in his chair, very slowly. *Be thankful for small favors, and—*

Oh God. He'd just thought of something.

"What kind of tracking do we have on *Wanderer*?" he asked. "Can somebody give me a camera view? What have we got?"

A new screen popped up in front of him. Just in time to let him watch *Wanderer* die.

There was no one on board the KSpace ship capable of operating its engines. No one to drive, to get it out of the way. 2I wasn't accelerating very fast, but it had an enormous amount of mass. When it smashed into *Wanderer*, the smaller ship didn't stand a chance. Its service module snapped free of its reentry module and flew off into space, spinning wildly. The spherical orbital module crumpled like a tin can, air and water and fuel bursting from its ruptured pipes and tanks. Lights flickered inside the wreckage, then went out.

The reentry module, where Sunny Stevens still lay strapped into a crew seat, was torn apart by the colossal teeth of the superstructures. Its windows cracked and exploded. Metal shredded.

McAllister put a hand over his mouth. He spared a quick glance up at the screen that showed Stevens's biodata. It was all flatlines now.

At least the man's suffering was over.

"Dear Lord," McAllister said. It wasn't a prayer. It was just pure tension leaking out of his mouth.

"Sir? Sir—2I has returned to its previous course. Still no word from *Orion.*"

"Telemetry coming in. Sir—sir!"

"Sir," Meryl Nguyen said. She was crouched down next to him, at his level. She put a hand on his shoulder. "Sir, I know this may not be the time, but there's something we need to consider—"

Everyone wanted his attention. He couldn't focus enough to answer any of them. He blinked and looked over at her. He felt as if he were floating free of his body, hovering over his chair.

Then he was instantly pulled back to himself because he heard the radio crackle.

"Pasadena?"

It was Hawkins, coming in over the radio. Responding to McAllister's calls.

"Pasadena, we're all right up here—we had a bit of a bumpy ride, but there are no injuries. We'd really like someone to explain to us what the hell just happened."

"It's fine," Jansen protested. Rao kept poking at her shoulder. It hurt, but it was fine, damn it.

"I don't think it's broken," Rao said. "Not dislocated, either."

"It's *fine*," Jansen said. "I just bumped it. Can you please—"

Then she saw the look on Rao's face. She knew that look. Rao needed something to do. Something to keep her mind off what had happened to *Wanderer*—and the fact that Sunny Stevens's body was on the surface of 2I, crushed by the broken spars of the KSpace ship.

"We have some analgesic cream in the med kit, right?" Jansen asked. "Maybe that would help."

Rao nodded and flipped backward, headed for the supply cabinets. Hawkins passed her, kicking his way along the wall of the HabLab. "Understood, Pasadena," he said.

Then he punched the soft wall, hard enough to make it ripple.

"What did he say?" Jansen asked.

Hawkins looked as if he might punch the wall again. And again and again. He took a moment to breathe before he answered.

"He said to stand by for new orders." Hawkins ran his fingers through his close-cropped hair. He turned himself around and pushed his back against the wall. "Stand by. Hurry up and wait."

Jansen understood his frustration. She wished she could say something that would help alleviate it. She wished someone would say something to her.

Roy McAllister touched the device on his ear and was patched through to a conference call. Maybe the most important one of his life.

He winced as he heard a dozen voices talking at once. Someone was shouting about liability issues—about the fact that KSpace was almost certain to sue the government for the destruction of *Wanderer*. Someone else wanted to know what plans were in place for moving vital government assets to underground shelters if 2I crashed into the Earth.

Most of the voices were just asking questions. Questions nobody could answer.

McAllister focused on one voice in particular: Kalitzakis. The space force general was assuring someone, in low, reasoned tones, that the problem had been giving control of *Orion* to a civilian agency in the first place. That now that Hawkins was mission commander, they could expect to see a very different command strategy.

McAllister understood that he was being thrown, if gently, under a bus. That Kalitzakis was shifting blame to NASA and Sally Jansen. Well, he had to admit that they made good scapegoats.

"He's coming on the line," someone whispered, and McAllister thought they meant himself, that they were warning Kalitzakis to watch what he said. But then a rapid series of clicks sounded on the call and McAllister knew the whisperer hadn't been referring to him after all.

"Everyone, please stand by as we confirm the president's connection is secure," the whisperer said. When it came on the line, the president's voice was heavily modulated, squelched down to a synthetic drone by the encryption on the call.

"Everyone, this is a grave situation, and we all need to take it very seriously. I understand the space force has something to say."

"Thank you, Mr. President," Kalitzakis said. "It is the position of the military that as of now we should consider 2I hostile, and that it represents an existential threat to the population of Earth, and that immediate military action is required."

There was a sound like everyone on the call taking a breath at once, as if they all wanted to say something about that. Their voices were cut off almost instantly, and when Kalitzakis spoke again his voice was alone, and crystal clear.

"The alien spacecraft killed Dr. Stevens. It destroyed KSpace's vehicle, *Wanderer*. It may have attempted to destroy *Orion* as well, but Mission Commander Jansen, through quick and decisive action, was able to save her ship."

At least he was going to give her that much, McAllister thought.

"Major Hawkins, of the space force, has taken command of the mission. We've been working for some time now on finding a way to destroy or at least disable 2I. As you know, we've already ruled out nuclear armaments. After careful deliberation we've decided our best chance is to use a kinetic impactor."

McAllister's vision blurred, and he realized Kalitzakis had brought him into a stream in virtual reality. Presumably the president and everyone on the call was seeing the same thing.

The virtual space was white—it had no walls, floor, or ceiling, just an infinite expanse of whiteness. In the middle of that space a three-dimensional model appeared. It showed a vehicle McAllister was familiar with, the X-37d. The space force's drone spaceplane, a miniature space shuttle with no windows. The same vehicle Hawkins used to fly.

The spaceplane's cargo bay doors opened soundlessly. A robot arm unfurled from the inside, an arm holding the payload that had been nestled inside the cargo bay. The payload comprised six long cylinders, each of them mounted on a compact rocket engine.

"These are what we call kill vehicles," Kalitzakis said. "This is a weapon system we designed a while back, in case we needed to take out foreign bases built on the moon."

In the virtual space one of the kill vehicles expanded, its component parts separating to provide a better view of how they were assembled. A floating arrow appeared in the white space as Kalitzakis indicated different pieces of the system. "This is the warhead, here." It looked as cylindrical and featureless as a telephone pole. "It's nothing but a dense core of depleted uranium. Using the rocket engine mounted on its back, the core can be accelerated to incredible speeds. Think of it as an extremely large, very tough bullet. Since 2I is coming toward us pretty fast already, if you add its velocity to the KV's, they meet up at maybe a hundred kilometers a second."

McAllister took a deep breath. You could kill a city with the kind of energy that impact would release.

"How is this better than a nuke?" the president asked.

Kalitzakis's floating arrow moved back to the warhead. "It's a matter of precision over sheer firepower. A nuclear blast spreads energy out over its full blast radius—that's why the superstructures on 2I are a good defense, because they can absorb that energy over a large surface area. The KV hits its target in a very precise point. All the energy impacts in a cross-sectional area about the size of a manhole cover. A KV can punch right through 2I's hull. If we can target the bridge of the alien ship directly, or perhaps its engines, we can do a lot of damage. Maybe enough to render 2I nonoperational."

"I don't want to hear 'maybe,'" the president said. "Give me a probability."

"We project a seventy percent chance of success. However, there's a complication. We don't know where 2I's bridge is, or its engine room. We would need more data before we could deploy the KV. I have a plan on how we're going to get it. We need to send someone back inside."

McAllister could feel his hands shaking, even if he couldn't see them. Send someone back in? After what happened to Sunny Stevens?

"It will be a dangerous mission, of course," Kalitzakis said. "2I's interior is enemy territory. But it's crucial we have this data. We need a map of the interior, and someone to identify its weak points. We need to know where to fire our bullet to kill the beast."

"It's clear we need to do something," the president said.

"This is our best option, sir," Kalitzakis told him. "I'd like authorization to begin a second excursion immediately. Time is of the essence."

"Wait," McAllister said. He didn't care that his voice was probably muted, that no one would hear him. "Wait! There's more to consider! We need to—to—"

"Is that NASA talking?" the president asked, sounding annoyed.

McAllister felt sweat building up on his forehead. They'd heard him. "Yes, sir."

"You have something to add?" the president asked.

McAllister talked fast—he knew he wouldn't get a second chance at this. "Sir. I would like to propose that there's a possibility 2I's actions weren't hostile at all."

Kalitzakis scoffed, but McAllister needed to say this.

"We simply don't know enough about the aliens to understand what happened. Why 2I destroyed *Wanderer*. What we do know is—is—" he struggled to think of what to say next. "Sir—what we saw up there was *Orion* successfully completing its mission."

"They lost an astronaut," Kalitzakis sputtered.

"Yes. And we at NASA feel that tragedy more than anyone. But *Orion*'s primary mission was to make contact with 2I—and they did just that. The timing of 2I's maneuver is not coincidental. Dr. Stevens, in his final moment, reached out to 2I. And it responded."

"By killing him!"

"Enough, General. Let him finish," the president said. "What are you proposing, McAllister?"

"We should try to establish further contact. Actually communicate with the crew of 2I."

"And how do you do that? Expose them to the—I think we're calling them tendrils? Sacrifice more lives?"

"No. Of course not." McAllister's hands balled into fists at his sides. Was he really going to say this? It was the last thing he wanted. It was the worst idea he could imagine. It was all he could think of.

"Someone or something inside 2I reacted to Dr. Stevens's attempt at communication. It may—it must—be possible to find them and open a dialogue. General Kalitzakis has proposed we send someone back inside, to find these hypothetical weak points. I'm saying we send someone inside to try to talk to 2I's crew. I'm proposing we send someone in to talk, not to destroy."

God help me, he thought. *Did I just consign one of my people to death?*

"We have two action proposals, then," the president said. "But it sounds like they're at least temporarily compatible."

"Sir," Kalitzakis said, but the president cut him off.

"Does anyone see a reason why we can't try both?"

The call was opened up again—all the muted listeners could suddenly talk once more. Every single one of them took the opportunity, and the call turned into a babble of raised and excited voices.

ROY MCALLISTER: They were astronauts, whether they'd trained for years like Jansen or just a few months. NASA employees. Our duty to them, first, last, and always, was to keep them safe. I know they signed up for a hazardous mission. What I asked of them now, though—it'll haunt me until the end of my days.

The three of them floated close together around a screen, watching 2I spread its magnetic wings. There was no doubting it. 2I had moved because Sunny Stevens had somehow told it to. The question was how.

They had listened to the orders that came up from Pasadena. McAllister had repeated them twice to make sure everyone understood. Now it was Hawkins's turn, as mission commander, to put those orders into action.

He gathered the three of them around the little folding table where they ate their meals. "We're going back, then. You got your wish, Jansen."

She shook her head. "No."

"No? We have orders. Under my command, we don't get to decide whether we like our orders or not. This has already been decided."

Rao stared at her fingers. She kept rubbing at them as if they were dirty. Hawkins wasn't sure she'd even heard what McAllister had said.

"I'll go back. Just me," Jansen said. "That was my plan all along. I'll go—alone—and see what I can do about establishing communications with 2I. And while I'm over there I'll look for the KSpace crew, and—"

Hawkins slapped the table, hard. Rao flinched and pulled away. He felt bad about upsetting her, but he needed to lay down the law here.

"We're not voting on this!" he said. "I'm not asking for volunteers."

Of course Jansen refused to back down. "You have to let me try."

Hawkins nodded. He knew she wasn't going to like what he said next. Even if he was technically giving her what she wanted. "Yeah. You're going back." He tried to catch Rao's eye. Failed. "We're *all* going."

"What?" Jansen asked. She pushed away from the table until she was floating over it. Staring down at him from above. Did she think a power move like that was going to sway him? "No," she said. "It's too dangerous! No—look—I made a mistake, I get that. I fucked up! But there's no reason for...for all of us..." She was looking at Rao, and Hawkins got her point.

The astrobiologist was barely functional. She hadn't eaten or slept or spoken more than a few words since Stevens died.

But Hawkins had made up his mind. There was just too much at stake. Their lives meant nothing if they couldn't stop 2I. He would sacrifice every one of them for a chance to protect the Earth. "It's dangerous over there," he said. "You think I don't know that? So we're all going, because there's strength in numbers. And that's final."

She opened her mouth, so he pushed himself up into the air as well and stared her right in the eye, challenging her to speak. To question his orders.

"It's final," he said again.

Jansen rummaged through every cabinet and locker in the HabLab, throwing useless stuff over her shoulder, digging deep as she looked for equipment that would help keep them alive over there.

If they were going—and it looked as if they were—they needed to be prepared.

She looked up as Hawkins kicked past her, but she didn't stop what she was doing. "We need lights, most of all," she said. "I stole some packages of glow sticks from *Wanderer*, and some flares. They're self-oxidizing, so they should work even in an argon atmosphere." She checked the ascenders she'd taken from *Wanderer*'s 3-D printer. They still worked just fine. "We'll need plenty of water, and every O_2 cartridge we've got. We have no idea how long we'll be over there."

She popped open the kits that held the tools meant to be used to repair *Orion* if it was damaged in space. She didn't think they would need any pistol-grip tools or hull patches, but there was plenty of safety line in there, as well as carabiners they could use for climbing. There were also several tool pouches and backpacks designed to fit over space suit arms, which they could use to carry their gear.

She launched herself back through the hatch to the command module. She grabbed the survival kit—a bag full of thermal blankets, water bottles, and basic medical supplies. It was designed to keep them alive if, when they returned to Earth, they landed somewhere remote and it would take a while for NASA's recovery teams to reach them. *Wanderer*'s crew might need those supplies.

Assuming they were still alive.

She knew there was a good possibility that they were dead. She'd known that all along. She'd committed herself to the search for them, even if it just meant recovering their bodies. If there was any chance of saving them, though—

"I'll get the suits ready," Hawkins said.

Hawkins moved over to the control panel for the EVA suits and started running through a checklist there. She tried to see over his shoulder, make sure he knew what he was doing.

He ran through the checklist as if he'd done this a hundred times before. Well, he had, after all—back in the simulators down on Earth. She forced herself to give him the benefit of the doubt.

She had to remind herself she wasn't MC anymore. It was something she was just going to have to learn to accept. She was a NASA astronaut, and she'd been trained for this. When an MC was removed from duty, the crew needed to rally around the new MC. That idea had been drilled into her a million times during her training. Space missions were far too dangerous for personal feelings to get in the way of the chain of command.

She'd never really thought it would happen to her. She'd thought of *Orion* as her ship, her mission.

But she had failed, hadn't she? She'd gotten Stevens killed. Maybe it was time to accept that she wasn't meant for the MC's job. Maybe it was time to start thinking like a team member instead of a boss.

Then she turned to look at Rao, who was floating in the middle of the HabLab. Just floating, staring into space. She had a bundle of oxygen cartridges in her hands, but she wasn't moving.

Hawkins was MC. Fair enough. Maybe she could acknowledge that she didn't always know best. But she couldn't just stand aside and watch him put Rao in danger. She had to try.

"Maybe it's better if one of us stays behind," Jansen said.

The words sounded desperate, even to her own ears.

Hawkins looked up. "*Orion* can take care of itself," Hawkins said. "I've set the autopilot to keep station with 2I. If the aliens move again, *Orion* will get out of the way."

Jansen grabbed the glow sticks and started cramming them into a nylon bag. "Parminder," she said.

The younger woman didn't look up. It looked as if she were locked in a VR trance, but Jansen knew that wasn't the case. She was stuck inside her own head.

"Rao!" Jansen shouted.

"Yes?" the woman finally said, looking up—though she still didn't make eye contact.

"You don't have to do this," Jansen told her. "You can refuse. No one's going to call you a coward."

Rao scowled. "I'm going," she said. "We're all going."

"It's dangerous over there. I—we lost Stevens because I made him go over there. That's on me. I can't stand the thought of losing you, too. Are you sure you want to do this? Absolutely sure?"

Rao reached out and grabbed a handrail, then shoved herself along the padded curve of the HabLab wall toward a screen. "I need to write up some notes before we leave. It'll only take a minute or so, but I've got a theory. Call it a working hypothesis, and—"

"That's not what I asked," Jansen pointed out.

Rao did look directly at her then. Straight on. "We have work to do."

Then she turned away and got to it.

SALLY JANSEN: I knew we needed her. She was our astrobiologist. Hawkins and me, we were grunts, we were there to keep the wheels from falling off the bus, that's all. She was the only scientist we had, after Stevens died. If someone was going to find a way to talk to 2I's crew, it was her. That was what it came down to, we had so much to lose, we were out of ideas—Roy McAllister is a good man, I'll never say otherwise, but the only option he had left was to throw warm bodies on the problem and hope one of them lived long enough to find a solution.

EXCURSION (2)

As they waited for the airlock to cycle, Jansen pointed her lights toward Hawkins where he floated in the middle of the hollow sphere. She had to give him credit—he didn't seem particularly scared. Then again, he hadn't seen the interior of 2I yet. He had no idea what he was in for.

Rao looked calm, too. It was a different kind of calm, though, one Jansen knew well. The look of somebody who is so inside their own head that the fear never reaches their skin. Somebody distracted enough to do stupid things.

Maybe she would snap out of it when they started climbing, Jansen thought. Rao seemed to rise to the occasion when given something to do. There was a lot of strenuous physical activity ahead of them.

"There's a climb of about seven kilometers before we reach the floor of the drum," Jansen said.

Hawkins nodded inside his helmet. He blinked and squinted in the glare of her lights. He was watching the airlock's weirdly shaped aperture close behind them.

The aperture turned until it faced the interior, until it was open to 2I's cavernous expanse. Jansen started to move forward, toward the cone. Before she could get there, though, a strong wind ruffled the fabric of her suit and pushed her backward, away from the aperture.

That...was new. The wave of pressure lasted only a moment before the air inside the airlock equalized pressures with 2I's interior atmosphere, but last time she'd hardly felt more than a puff of breeze. She looked down at the display on her trace gas analyzer and saw that the local air pressure had risen to nearly a tenth of an atmosphere—and that was up here at the drum's axis, where the air was thinnest.

Even stranger, nearly a fifth of the air was made of oxygen. Last time there hadn't been any oxygen at all, just argon.

"Jansen, you look surprised. What's going on?"

"The atmosphere in here has changed. Gotten a lot thicker."

She could see Hawkins frowning through his faceplate. "Thicker," he said.

"Yeah." She shook her head. "There was a heavy mist in the air, too, vapor from the ice that covers the drum. That's gone." Her lights stretched out away from her in two clear beams, with nothing to stop them. They still showed nothing but darkness—that hadn't changed.

The radio noise was still there, too. As they moved toward the airlock's opening, it flooded their headphones, loud enough that Jansen couldn't hear herself think.

"Christ! What the hell is that?" Hawkins asked. "On the radio—"

"Yeah," Jansen said, raising her voice to be heard. "We heard it last time." The rising- and-falling, endlessly clicking noise of 2I. "It's worse now, though. Louder. Maybe that's the sound of its wings. You know, the magnetic field. The sail."

"I can barely hear you," Hawkins shouted back.

Jansen adjusted the controls of her suit radio. The clicking receded to a dull buzz in the back of her head.

"Jesus," Hawkins said. He had his hands on the sides of his helmet, as if that would somehow help block out the sound.

She attempted to show him how to adjust his own radio, but he batted her away when she tried to touch his suit. Jansen lifted her hand in surrender. "Just trying to help. Let's deploy the robot now." She reached over her shoulder and grabbed ARCS.

The robot had been clinging to the back of her suit. Now it came alive in her hand, its fingers and thumbs flexing as it ran through a diagnostic routine.

Stevens had suggested they use robots to explore 2I. He'd thought they could 3-D print a bunch of surface rovers and set them loose inside the drum, let them map the entire place—and look for Foster and his crew. There hadn't been time to build rovers, and the 3-D printer had gone down with *Wanderer*. So they would make do with what they had.

ARCS would make a terrible rover. It could theoretically crawl along the ground, using its fingers as legs, but it had been designed to function best in microgravity. Luckily there was one place inside 2I where gravity wasn't an issue. Along the imaginary line of the drum's axis, there was no gravity at all. As long as the robot stuck to that middle path, it could move itself along just fine with puffs of compressed air.

"You know what you need to do, right?" she asked the robot.

"Yes, Ms. Jansen. I am to proceed along the axis at a safe velocity. Along the way I will map the interior of 2I with my lidar imaging system and relay what I find to your suits. I am ready."

Jansen hesitated. She knew the robot had no mind of its own. It couldn't understand what a dangerous mission she'd given it. Still— it felt like a small betrayal to send what was essentially a robotic butler out into the darkness of 2I. "Good luck," she said. It was the best she could think of.

ARCS didn't move. It just hung there in the middle of the airlock. "I require confirmation from the mission commander."

"I've already—"

"It means Hawkins," Rao said, gently.

Right. Right. Its permission architecture would already have been upgraded. Probably somebody from Pasadena had made the change.

"Confirmed," Hawkins told the robot.

ARCS sailed out of the airlock and into the cone beyond. It didn't so much as wave goodbye. In a minute it was out of view, out of reach of their lights.

Jansen's hands had balled into fists. She still wasn't OK with the change of command. This had been her mission, her chance...but she was an astronaut. Challenging Hawkins for dominance now could get them all killed. She needed to fall in line and play nice.

It wasn't something she'd ever been good at.

"Everyone ready?" Hawkins asked.

He led them out of the airlock and into the rotating cone where the ropes began.

The rope was still there, still firmly anchored by its piton. "Let me show you how the ascenders work," she told them, as she clipped on to the first rope.

"We used something similar in basic training," Hawkins said, snapping his own ascender to one of his D rings and expertly threading the rope through the ascender's gears. Then he helped Rao do the same with hers. "I appreciate your experience, Jansen. I'm glad we have you here to help us get acclimatized. But I need you to remember—I'm in charge of this mission, now."

SALLY JANSEN: *The temperature inside 2I had climbed to nearly twenty degrees Celsius. Almost room temperature, and it was still going up. As wet as it was inside the drum, I suppose I thought the black growths were some kind of fast-growing mold. That was the mistake we made over and over. We kept trying to understand what was going on inside 2I in terms of things we knew from Earth. But nothing we saw followed our rules.*

"Look," Jansen said, and pointed at an amorphous black stain on the surface of the cone above her. "That wasn't here before." Nothing more than a patch of discoloration, really, no larger than her hand. She thought she could see some small bubbles at its center, but she would have to get closer to check.

She had no desire to get any closer.

Swinging her lights around, she saw two more patches, similar spots on the cone wall. She had no idea what they were. She could only hope they didn't matter.

"More of it, there," Rao said, sliding to a stop on the rope. Jansen reached up and adjusted her helmet lights. They illuminated a broad patch of the black discoloration on the wall not six meters from the rope. The growth was wide-ranging, maybe twenty meters across, manifesting in three broad stripes that ran mostly straight, though at an angle to their descent. Where the growth was thickest it had risen up from the surface of the drum to form thick clusters like bunches of black grapes. Except some of the spherical extrusions were as big as cantaloupes.

She saw dozens of patches of the black stain on the walls of the cone. Each new one they found was bigger and more clearly defined than the last.

"Just stay clear of it," Hawkins said. "I doubt it can harm us inside our suits, but safety first, right?"

They had reached the point where they were rappelling backward into the dark. It was a little less nerve-racking than the last time she'd done this.

A little.

Jansen's knee had stopped hurting, which would have been good except that it had stopped bending, too. It was nearly frozen, leaving her in a permanent half crouch that worked for rappelling but left her wondering what was going to happen when she needed to walk again. She ignored it as best she could.

Ignoring things was an effective strategy for dealing with the darkness and the uncertainties of the climb. At least, right up until it stopped working. The way her helmet was constructed made it very difficult for her to see what was behind her. She had the rearview mirror mounted on her sleeve, but it wasn't much use when her lights were pointed forward.

About halfway to the bottom, she braced her legs and pushed off, letting herself slide down the rope until the friction of her belay caught her and she settled back down to the ground, a little slower than she would have in the cylinder's full gravity.

Her right boot hit something slick and wet, and she nearly went sprawling. She grabbed for the rope with both hands, terrified of falling, terrified her ascender would give out somehow, that she would go tumbling all the way down. None of that happened. The ascender caught her, just as it was designed to do. She got her left boot braced against the drum's wall, felt it grip.

Only then did she look down.

A broad patch of the black discoloration ran across the slope, four parallel linear growths, each of them thick with globular clusters. The growth ran across the path of the rope, and flecks of black had splattered the orange line.

Jansen had stepped on one of the globes, and it had exploded under the pressure of her weight. Black slime covered her right boot and stained both of her legs. Drops of black coated the slope and were slowly rolling down out of her light and into the dark.

"Is your suit punctured?" Hawkins asked.

"Run a diagnostic!" Rao called.

"I'm fine," Jansen said, mostly just feeling embarrassed. She should have been looking where she was going. "It's just slime, it'll wash off—"

"Rao's right. Run a diagnostic," Hawkins said. He let the line slip through his ascender, just a little, as he crab-walked down toward her. His eyes were wide. "That's an order."

If her suit had been breached she would have heard a strident alarm in her headphones. There was no alarm. Mostly to humor him, though, she reached up to the controls of the instrument pack on the front of her suit and hit the button that would run a complete systemic check. It would take about ten seconds. "I'm fine," she said again. "Why are you so—"

Holding on to the rope with one hand, Rao used the other to point behind Jansen.

She turned around, careful not to step on any more of the spherical growths. She moved her lights around, looking for what had made the others panic. It didn't take long to find.

The rope leading downward into the shadows was coated in the black goo, a thick, dripping film of it. It looked as if the rope had been dipped in crude oil. About two meters below Jansen, the rope just disappeared.

Whatever the black stuff was, it had eaten right through the woven aramid line. Only a frayed end remained. There was no rope below them, as far as Jansen's lights could show her.

HAROLD GLOUCESTER, MATERIALS ANALYST: The purpose of most of what the astronauts saw and experienced inside 2I still baffles us. For the black slime we have . . . don't even call it a theory. Call it an educated guess. During 2I's long trip between stars, it was likely that all manner of debris would get caught in the airlock, and might work its way inside the cone. The acidic slime was there to neutralize and dissolve any foreign matter before it could reach the floor of the drum. Maybe. Like I said—it's a guess. Don't quote me.

Hawkins didn't suggest they turn around and go back. They were already most of the way down to the floor of the drum, and Jansen had decided her best bet was to get down to the ice and find some water to wash the black slime off her suit. It was an open question whether she could get that far before it ate through all the layers of suit fabric and she was left exposed to 2I's atmosphere.

If that happened—no, it didn't bear thinking about.

Of course, going down—going forward—meant descending without a rope. The three of them made their way around the patch of black discoloration and hurried downward as best they could. Sometimes that meant walking with bent legs, fighting the increasing gravity as their boots slipped and scraped on the smooth material of the drum. More often than not it meant sliding down on their backs, slowing their descent by holding their arms out, hands flat against the surface.

Their suits were made of very tough materials that were designed to resist abrasion and heat. They would just have to be strong enough.

Sometimes they found ropes that were still in place, and the going was a lot easier. Except they had to worry the whole time— watching the rope below them, expecting at any moment to find a place where the slime had crossed its path. Jansen was even more worried that while they were attached to an existing rope, the slime might be working on it somewhere above them, that any moment the rope might give way and send them flying downhill.

She kept one eye on the legs of her suit the whole way down. Looking to see if they were smoking or dripping where they'd been splattered with black.

When the slope grew gentler, when she knew they were near the bottom, she told Hawkins and Rao that she would race ahead and try to find some water. That they should set up camp at the bottom of the last rope and wait there for her. Hawkins didn't contradict her orders or try to pull rank.

It turned out she didn't need to go far to find water. When she reached the bottom, she found that KSpace's base camp was half-submerged in an icy pool. The dead glow sticks bobbed on gentle waves. The crates of supplies were soaked through.

Jansen immediately splashed into the water and start washing off her legs. As she scrubbed at the black slime she pointed her lights out across what had once been all dry floor.

The ice had melted. Her lights showed her thick floes, some dozens of meters across, dotted across the surface of a black and placid lake. Even the biggest slabs of ice were melting, shrinking almost as she watched.

The temperature inside the drum, according to her suit, had risen to a tropical twenty-four degrees.

The black slime came off easily enough when she scrubbed at it. It left a dark residue on her boots and the leg of her suit, and she could see it had partially degraded the outermost layer of fabric. Still, she thought she was safe. For the moment.

SALLY JANSEN: I was supposed to be our local guide, the one with experience of conditions inside 2I. By the time we reached level ground I already knew I would be useless in that capacity. I hadn't been gone for twenty-four hours, but so much changed in that time. It was like a whole new world, one I didn't even begin to know how to navigate.

*   *   *

The darkness was so utterly complete. Rao's suit lights speared out ahead of her, but they showed her only a tiny slice of what was around her. Just outside their beams, the true dark waited, so thick it felt as if the air had clotted and turned solid. So deep it could hide anything.

Maybe—maybe the lights made it worse. She reached up and carefully switched them off. Instantly she was plunged into nothingness, a profundity deeper than the abyss of space. Her eyes couldn't handle it. They darted back and forth, desperate for light— and her brain responded. She saw tiny flashes all around her, little sparks. They moved when she moved her head, always staying right in front of her. Hallucinations of a brain starved of visual input.

It was—it was—she suddenly felt very dizzy.

I'm hyperventilating, Rao thought.

She switched her lights back on. Then she forced herself to take long, shallow breaths. She tried to make herself calm.

It wasn't easy.

Jansen had told her this place was horrible. She hadn't known what that meant, and now she wasn't sure *horrible* was strictly accurate. *Horrible* would suggest that the place was actively trying to kill them, maybe. While instead this place was just—so different. Different from anything she'd known before.

Rao had spent her whole life wanting to be here. A place like this, an alien place. She'd never dreamed it would come to her. And that it would take so much away—

She closed her eyes and breathed through her mouth.

All she could see was the nest of snakes writhing inside Stevens's abdomen. She felt her skin crawl as if the tendrils were on her, as if they were wrapping around her like a net.

She forced herself to open her eyes and walk forward. To let her lights fall on Jansen, who was splashing around in dark water. The astronaut looked up and blinked as Rao's lights hit her face.

Rao had to be here, now.

She could grieve for Stevens later. She would figure out what had happened to him first—and then she would mourn.

Hawkins set up camp. Funny how little that meant when you were wearing space suits. He climbed back up the slope a little ways to get out of the reach of the dark water, then unloaded all the gear they'd brought with them. He cracked open a pair of glow sticks raided from *Wanderer*, then used their light to examine the two pieces of special equipment they'd brought with them, both removed from the exterior skin of *Orion*'s HabLab.

The first was the neutrino gun. Some bright person back on Earth had realized that NASA had a dedicated telescope set up in Pasadena designed to catch and analyze neutrinos. The particles the gun emitted could pass easily through 2I's hull—they could pass through solid lead. The neutrino signals could be picked up on Earth and decoded into audio or video as necessary. The transmission would be strictly one way, and the bandwidth would be terrible, but at least Roy McAllister would know what they found inside 2I. Even if none of them made it back to *Orion*, NASA could get some useful information. Setting it up was simple enough—he simply opened a screen in AR and tapped in a few quick commands. The gun had its own power source and would take care of all the signal processing on its own. He tested it out with a quick message.

WINDSOR HAWKINS: Our descent was a little trickier than expected, but there were no injuries or significant difficulties. We're ready to get started with the primary experiment.

Which brought him to the second piece of equipment they'd salvaged from *Orion*. He carefully unwrapped the dish of the multi-wavelength antenna and placed it on the ground in front of him, its dish pointing deeper into the interior of 2I. It was a hell of a lot more powerful than the antennae built into their suit radios. It looked as if it had survived intact, even if it had taken a few nasty bumps as they slid their way down.

What came next might be extremely dangerous. It had to be done, though. He uploaded the signal they wanted to send.

His finger hovered over the button that would transmit the signal. He hesitated. Just for a moment.

He looked over at Rao. He couldn't see her face—her suit lights were pointed right at him, and he could barely make out the silhouette of her helmet. He imagined she was thinking the same thing he was, though. None of them had any idea what was going to happen when they sent this message.

He pressed the button.

He could hear the signal go out, over the rising and falling chirp of static on the radio. It was a recording of Stevens's final biodata, the last signal they'd recorded as his neural activity spiked. The same signal that had caused 2I to spread its wings.

"*Puh*," the signal said. "*Puh. Puh*."

What had Stevens been trying to say? Had he actually been trying to form a word—maybe *please*? Or was it just the spastic firing of dying neurons?

Hawkins ran through the full signal three times. During the third transmission Jansen came stumbling back into his suit lights. He could see her face just fine. She wasn't pleased he had done this without her.

"If it worked and you made 2I accelerate again, we could have been thrown around in here like ants inside a soda can," she told him.

Hawkins reached over and switched off the multifrequency antenna.

"Lucky for all of us, then. It didn't work."

There had been no response. Maybe the unseen crew of 2I knew what it was trying to do. Maybe the aliens could tell the difference between the final cry of a dying man and a recording. Or maybe they'd gotten this all wrong. It would help if they knew what they were trying to communicate with. If any of the alien crew of 2I had ever shown itself.

Cowards, Hawkins thought. He smiled, careful not to show his face to the others. *Lousy stinking cowards*. He felt like a cowboy in a western video, challenging some unseen black hat to a showdown on a dusty, sunbaked street. *Fill your hand*, he thought.

He ran through the signal a couple more times, just to be sure. The aliens didn't take the bait.

WINDSOR HAWKINS: Initial results of the primary experiment were negative. We'll need to try something different.

"I want to try to get in touch with the KSpace crew," Jansen said, when they'd all agreed the experiment was a failure. "Maybe they couldn't hear me the last time I was here, not with all the noise on the radio." She touched the big dish of the multifrequency antenna. "Maybe this thing can punch through that and get a signal to Foster and his people."

Hawkins just shrugged. She knew what he thought about her desire to find the KSpace crew.

"Maybe you're right and they're dead," she said. "But in that case—what harm could it possibly do?"

"It could waste battery power," he said.

Rao came to her defense. "Foster and his crew have been in here this whole time," she said. "Assuming they're alive. They were inside 2I when it responded to Stevens's signal. Maybe they saw something—maybe they know something we don't."

Hawkins didn't even look at them. He just waved one hand in resignation.

Jansen plugged the signal feed of the antenna into her suit. "KSpace," she called. "This is NASA *Orion*. We've come to help. Please respond." She repeated the message three times, just as they'd done with the experimental signal.

Then she sat down to wait for a reply.

As the three of them sat there, listening to the weird pops and ticking sounds and occasional crackle picked up by the antenna, she tried not to lose heart. She repeated her message a fourth time, then unplugged from the antenna. She left the dish switched on, in low-power mode. It would continue to function as a receiver if KSpace sent them a response. As unlikely as that seemed.

"It should have plenty of range," she said. "It's designed to send a signal across thousands of kilometers of space. It ought to reach every corner of the drum. If they're in here, they'll hear us."

Hawkins said nothing. He just sipped some water from the hose in his helmet and stared out into the darkness.

"We'll stick here for a while," he said. "Run through some more experimental signals. Anyway, I don't really feel like going any further, at least not until we've rested. We can sleep in shifts, so one of us is always awake and keeping an eye out for . . ." He shrugged. "Surprises."

"You want to sleep?" Rao asked. "In here?"

Hawkins looked over at her. "Nothing has actively tried to kill us yet. We don't know what we'll be in for when we get moving, though. Could be anything. Best to be well rested when it arrives."

"That's not really reassuring," she told him. "Did you mean it to be?"

ROY MCALLISTER: *When we suggested to Orion that they use the neutrino gun to communicate with Earth, it was really anybody's guess whether it would work at all. When the first trickle of data came in from the interior of 2I, the entire control room erupted in applause. We had audio and video from inside an alien starship. Even if the experimental signal failed to make contact with the crew of 2I, we were in business. It was immensely beneficial to our morale. You have to celebrate the little victories.*

Despite her protests, Rao was the first one to fall asleep. Maybe she was worn out after the long climb down from the airlock. Maybe it was just the darkness.

Jansen had been here before. She knew the effect the utter lack of light could have on you. It made the margin between sleep and wakefulness feel very thin. Even when your body had plenty of energy, your mind, in the absence of anything useful to do, fell into a kind of hypnosis. At least, when it wasn't populating your head with phantoms and hallucinations.

To keep the figments away, Jansen had set her lights to rotate automatically, sweeping the darkness and the edge of the water. When they passed over Hawkins's face she saw a gentle, amused smile there. Not what she had been expecting at all.

Eventually he must have noticed her staring. He turned slowly, a rustling in the darkness. When the light hit him again he was looking her right in the eye. His smile hadn't changed.

"You and I have never really got along," he said.

"That's one way of putting it."

He leaned forward a little. Put his hands on his knees. "OK. We're not friends. So I won't pretend like this isn't happening. I've been put in charge of the mission. You've been replaced."

"You keep telling me that."

He lifted his hands for peace. He sighed, a strange sound that was nearly lost in the ambient clicks and crackles of 2I. "You've been an astronaut a long time. Flown a lot of missions."

She shrugged. Was he going to ask her how many times she'd screwed up? How many missions she'd ruined? It was a question she'd been asked many, many times.

It turned out that wasn't where he was going, though.

He shifted a little, scooting toward her. "I've heard about the overview effect. Right? The way astronauts feel like seeing Earth from space changes them. It makes them feel—"

"Like none of it matters," Jansen said. She nodded. "None of the human nonsense we waste so much time worrying about. From up there you look down and you can't see any national borders. You can't see why we have to fight wars."

"Before all this, I flew the X-37d. You know that."

"Yeah."

"I've seen what you saw," he told her. "Don't scoff—I know you think my experience doesn't count, because I was flying a drone from a trailer on Earth. But my missions felt just as real to me as yours did to you. When I'm in VR, when I'm flying, I see what my spaceship sees. I feel how cold its skin gets, and how hot. Its engines become an extension of my body." He was hunched forward even farther now, his hands up in the air making sweeping gestures. She could tell how strongly he felt about this. "And when I look down at Earth, I see it, too."

"What do you see?" she asked.

"I see how fragile it is. The thin margin of the atmosphere, like a glass shell around the planet. The way the rivers empty out into the oceans, the waters mixing and changing colors. I've watched storm clouds gather over the mountains, and I've seen—a thousand times—the sun come up over the curved horizon. Jansen, I've seen the Earth from space. And all I wanted was to protect it. To defend it."

She watched him carefully. Waited for him to say more.

"You think I'm a bad guy. You think I'm a scary soldier guy who wants to take what's yours. It just isn't true. I want to keep people safe. That's all I've ever wanted, to keep people safe."

She lay back on the floor of the drum. Closed her eyes for a second. Dear God, how she needed to sleep.

"That's why I agreed to take over command of this mission. The only reason."

She nodded.

"You said you knew where Foster and his people went. They were headed toward this—I think you called it a structure?"

"For lack of a better term," she said.

He nodded. "We'll go to this structure you saw. We'll look for KSpace," he said.

She turned over and looked at him. "I thought you assumed they were dead."

"They probably are," he said. "But we need to find something, some way to communicate with the aliens. And I don't have any other leads. So for now, we do this your way."

SALLY JANSEN: I was tired. So tired. And it was kind of nice that somebody had the energy to make a plan. I know I didn't—I was operating by instinct at that point, with no rational thoughts informing my decisions at all. It was a need pulling me back to 2I, an urge to save people I'd never met. Something that wasn't quite rational. I can admit that now.

Rao lay curled on her side, her hands folded under her helmet.

She wasn't asleep, though her eyes were closed. She could hear the others talking. Hear the steady hiss of her suit's air pumps, and the endless clicking on the radio. Yet she wasn't totally awake, either. Parts of her mind had shut down, from exhaustion, from disorientation.

She went away. She went to another place.

She knew exactly where it was. Texas, where she'd grown up. Some time in the forties, because she was sitting on a porch looking out over a yard of poorly tended grass. Her dad had been out of work in those years, suffering from depression—this was before the treatments. Her mom had worked ninety-hour weeks selling real estate, and neither of them could focus long enough to clean up the yard.

The moonlight lay thick on the grass, making it look like a blanket of gray hair. Just like Nani's hair. Nani—it was the only name she'd ever called her grandmother—was sitting on the porch swing, swinging back and forth, and Parminder was curled on her lap. The old woman was smiling and patting her cheek.

It wasn't so much a dream as a free-form sort of memory. This had actually happened. She remembered it. She could hear the cicadas, millions of them out there in the grass. They sounded like sirens, maybe, or distant car alarms. Their song rose and fell, faded to nothing and then swelled to be so loud it hurt her ears.

Nani was singing to help her granddaughter fall asleep, singing to the bass line of the swelling roar of the cicadas, in the dark, in the Texas night.

They weren't alone.

Someone was very close by. Watching them, but not saying anything. Not moving. Just standing there, looking. She couldn't even make out his face, couldn't see his expression. She tried to sit up, to look. To see who had come to sit with them on the porch. But Nani shushed her and put a hand over her eyes, laughing a little as she continued to sing.

Parminder reached up with both of her tiny hands and pried open Nani's fingers, which made the old woman laugh more. Parminder looked between the gate of the fingers, looked out into the dark, and there he was—

Sunny.

Which made her smile, which made Nani laugh, and the cicadas went crazy, and Parminder was so happy to see Sunny sitting there, sitting in a rocker next to them, just watching them together.

There were so many things she wanted to tell him. So many words she hadn't gotten to share with him, thoughts and feelings that had gone unexpressed. But now he was here, and there would be time, in this cozy, warm place—

Sunny started to get up. To climb out of the chair, using both hands, except only the top half of him lifted up. He was split across the middle, and his legs fell away from his torso and thumped onto the wooden slats of the porch. From the empty space in his middle, tendrils shot out like party streamers, twisting in the air as they covered Nani and Parminder, covered the porch and writhed away across the grass.

Rao's eyes shot open and she sat up, sat up shaking and scared, so terrified.

In the dark.

In the dark of 2I. She could still hear the cicadas. No.

No.

That was just the rising and falling, ever-present clicking. The sound of 2I flapping its magnetic field wings in the void. That was all it was.

Not so much a dream, nor a memory. She'd let her thoughts wander.

She couldn't afford to let that happen again.

When Jansen woke up, she checked her clock and saw she'd slept for nearly three hours. It felt as if she'd just closed her eyes for a second. She sucked at her water hose and rotated her wrists—they were stiff because she'd been using her hands as a pillow. Her neck hurt because it was impossible to sleep in gravity in a space suit and not wake up with your neck as stiff as a board.

She sat up and swung her lights around, looking for the others. Rao was still asleep, sprawled on her stomach with her face down. Jansen could hear her snoring, even though she'd switched off her suit radio.

Hawkins was standing in the water, maybe fifteen meters away. Just standing there, facing away from her, with his lights pointed in what looked like random directions.

Jansen moved carefully, climbing to her feet despite the protestations of her knee and her hip. She walked toward him until the water lapped at her boots.

"Hawkins?" she said.

"We have a couple problems to solve," he told her. "Can you bring me the telescoping boom lamp?"

She walked back to where they'd stowed their supplies. The TBL was tied to one of their backpacks, collapsed to make it easy to carry. When she'd rummaged around *Orion* looking for anything that could generate light, it was one of the first things she'd grabbed. The TBL was a high-power lamp with an integrated battery, mounted on the end of a series of nested aluminum pipes—like a one-legged camera tripod. It could be extended to nearly three meters when you pulled out all the sections. It was designed to be mounted on the outside of *Orion*'s HabLab to provide illumination if they needed to carry out repairs in space.

She grabbed it and brought it to him. He was looking at something just under the surface of the dark lake.

"Here," he said, squatting down in the water. "You see it?"

Jansen peered into the water. Just beyond where Hawkins crouched, dark shapes writhed across the bottom. Branching, snakelike tendrils.

"Oh shit," she said, and jumped backward, falling on her ass. Hawkins didn't move. He was so close to the things, the things that had killed Stevens—

Except no; when she looked at them again, they weren't moving. Not now.

"Be careful!" she called out. She edged closer to take another look, unsure why they hadn't already tried to snare Hawkins in a living, squirming net.

She saw they covered the whole surface of the drum beneath the water, a carpet of roots or tentacles or...who knew what. The last time she'd seen them they'd been moving with incredible speed. Now they looked as if they'd grown there years before, like the root network of a houseplant in a pot that was too small for it.

"They're everywhere," he told her. "I walked about fifty meters either way along the shore, and everywhere I looked, there was the same thickness of them. There's no way forward except through them."

Maybe Rao had heard them talking. She walked toward them, bleary eyed and sniffling. When she arrived at the edge of the water she squatted down and adjusted her suit lights to point at the tendrils.

"They're not moving now," Hawkins said. "Maybe they drowned."

Rao scowled in concentration. "They lived inside Stevens's body just fine. They don't need to breathe, or at least—" She trailed off. "There's something...something familiar about these," she said. "I'm having trouble making the connection, but—"

Tiny bubbles formed on the surface of the mat of tendrils. One by one they detached and rose to the surface to pop. "This is where the oxygen is coming from," she said. She fiddled with the trace gas analyzer on the front of her suit, leaning far out over the water. "Every time those bubbles pop, the O_2 level goes up, just a smidge. Yeah. Yeah—they were supplying oxygen to Stevens's brain, at the end. They kept him alive long enough to...do whatever he did. That got their attention."

She had strayed a little too close to the water. It lapped against her boots. Jansen reached down and grabbed her arm to pull her back.

Hawkins extended the boom of the TBL. "I'm going to try something. Get ready to haul me out of here if they grab me," he said.

It turned out he'd wanted the TBL only because it was the closest thing they had to a stick. He grasped it in both hands and then jabbed at one of the tendrils.

Jansen realized she was holding her breath.

He poked another tendril. And another. They didn't react. Didn't move. He passed the TBL back to her. Then he took a step forward. Right onto the carpet of roots.

"Don't!" Rao said, reaching for him.

Jansen inhaled sharply. But it was OK.

The tendrils didn't grab him and pull him down under the water. They didn't move at all. She watched as Hawkins experimented with jumping up and down on them, making the water splash up all around him. Nothing.

"OK, good," he said. "Whatever happened before, the last time you were in here, they've settled down now. I think we have to assume that they'll stay dormant while we walk to the structure."

"That's a big assumption," Jansen said. But she knew there was nothing they could do about it. If they wanted to reach the structure, if they wanted to find Foster and his crew—they had to take the risk.

PARMINDER RAO: I guess maybe I knew as soon as I saw the "tendrils." My theory had to be right. But I'm a scientist. We don't jump to conclusions. I needed more evidence before I told the others what I was thinking.

WATER TRAVERSE

They didn't talk.

It would have taken too much energy.

They waded out into the dark water, which quickly rose to their knees. Each step was hard. Jansen had to push her legs forward, through the resistance of the water. She had to test her footing every time she put her weight down. The tendrils grew thick and fat as they moved away from the shore. They were hard as wood, exactly like tree roots. It was like wading through a mangrove swamp, she thought. Except it wasn't. At all.

Jansen had mounted the TBL on her back with its pole half-extended, so that it made a spotlight around them. She'd thought it would help them find their footing. She had been wrong. The water, when undisturbed, simply drank up the light and gave nothing back. Every time she moved, though, even the slightest bit, she created splashes and ripples that danced with reflected light, bright spots like fish swarming around her. The darkness, which had always been unrelenting, was shattered now by their light, and it felt like a violation. As if they were intruding on something that wanted to stay in the shadows.

It was exhausting, walking like that. She was already working on a sleep debt, and she knew you couldn't pay those back. She felt the weight of her suit and her backpack digging into her shoulders. She had gulped down a food tube before they left *Orion*, but now she was ravenously hungry again. She wasn't sure how much farther she could go.

She looked back at the others. Rao was picking her way along carefully, her arms out parallel to the water as she struggled for balance. Hawkins seemed to be having an easier time of things. He looked almost as if he were just strolling along through the water. He was fifteen years her junior. He had been trained to a peak of physical perfection by the space force. Of course he was fine.

Of course he was.

Except—then he stopped, and Rao stopped with him. Jansen realized she'd been listening to the two of them plash along, shoving the water noisily ahead of them, the whole time. It was the only sound in that dread place except for the constant wailing, clicking cry on the radio. She had been only liminally aware of the sound of the splashing, however. Until it ceased.

She turned, struggling with the water, and looked at Hawkins. Her treasonous body surged with endorphins, glad enough for a moment's break.

"This won't work," he told them.

Jansen said nothing. She was breathing too heavily to talk.

"When we started, the water was up to our knees," he told her.

The water was up to their chests now. It was getting deeper. There was no reason to think it wouldn't continue to do so. Before long it would be up to their helmets. Their suits would protect them from being submerged in the inky water, sure, but she couldn't...

She couldn't bear the thought. She couldn't even imagine walking forward, completely underwater, lost in some undersea kingdom of darkness and fright and the rootlike tendrils. It was as if she were trying to imagine walking through a brick wall.

"Our suits are too buoyant," he said. "We'll start floating soon. Unless we want to swim to this structure of yours." He gave her a sharp look. As if he expected her to tell him that yes, they would have to swim from here.

She shook her head.

"What do we do?" Rao asked.

Jansen turned around in a circle. Hoping to find some spit of dry ground they could climb up onto. Maybe just so they could take a rest. There was no such thing, of course. All she saw was water, more water everywhere. Water full of floating, bobbing chunks of ice that hadn't quite melted yet. She used her suit lights to scan a few of the bigger pieces.

"Come on," she said.

The ice floe Jansen had found was nearly three meters across. A big slab of ice whiter than the fabric of their suits. It glistened in their light, already melting in the warm air. She could almost see through its thinnest part, and definitely saw bubbles of air—argon or oxygen, it was impossible to say—trapped inside.

It nearly capsized when she scrambled up onto its back, and for a moment she imagined its huge bulk flipping over on top of her, pinning her under the water. But she moved fast and got herself spread across its area as best she could, and it fell back into the water with a mighty slap that sent a cascade of black droplets flying away from her. She rolled over onto her back and gestured for Hawkins and Rao to follow.

Hawkins came first, clambering up onto the floe, grunting and swearing. Water poured from the folds of his suit, water that ran across the ice and sluiced away. Rao took her time, putting her arms up on the ice first, then slowly, carefully sliding up until she was sitting on it, cross-legged.

It took Jansen a long time to get up on her feet. The floe rocked back and forth every time she moved and threatened to throw her onto her back. With time, and patience, and a lot of waving her arms around for balance, she made it. She rose to a standing posture. Then she extended the TBL to its full extent. That gave her three meters of pole to work with. The water was only a little more than a meter deep.

She shoved the boom of the TBL down into the black water. It scraped against one of the rootlike tendrils, then got lodged in some unseen branch or fork and held. Cautiously she leaned her weight on the pole, and the whole floe glided forward, in the opposite direction from her push.

The direction of the structure, their destination. Far off across the lake of black water.

The resistance of the water stole her precious velocity from her after just a few seconds. The floe started to spin, then slowed to a halt again. She pushed the pole down into the roots and heaved once more, and the floe moved again.

She had a raft. A raft to sail that stygian sea. Even that basic success, that tiny victory, made her want to cry.

PARMINDER RAO: It was hard to think. I mean, literally, it was hard to get thoughts moving through my head. The darkness was bad. Nobody was talking—maybe that would have helped, if we'd been chattering away, but...I think there was something more to it. Maybe 2I's magnetic field. NASA claimed it wasn't strong enough to have physiological effects, but I was there, and I'm not so sure. I've seen papers about the effects of magnetic fields on human nervous systems. Get hit with more than a couple of teslas at a time, and they can shut your brain down like flipping a light switch. At lower levels magnetic fields can cause dizziness and disorientation. Maybe that's all it was.

Rao took a turn poling them along, pushing endlessly against the floor of the drum. The light on top of the telescoping boom lamp moved over them in a steady rhythm. The water splashed and gurgled as they jerked along, a few meters at a time.

She watched the water, because there was nothing else to look at. Sometimes it cleared enough she could see the network of rootlike structures on the bottom, a pattern that she'd studied so closely it felt as if it were inscribed on the inside of her skull. The exact same pattern they'd etched across the walls of *Wanderer* when they—when Stevens—

She pushed that thought aside.

Hawkins was perched at the front of the floe, staring forward into the darkness as if he found his own thoughts displayed there. She thought perhaps the dark water was a kind of screen, like the black glass of an old television. Jansen shifted around on the ice to face Rao. "We're still on course?" she asked.

She had sent Rao the data from her inertial compass, which had recorded her path from her last excursion into 2I. Back when all this water had still been frozen. "We're getting close to where you found the memory stick," Rao told her.

Jansen wriggled her eyebrows back and forth as if they itched. Rao could sympathize—there would be no way to scratch them with her helmet on. "How are you feeling?"

"Fine," she said.

"I mean, are you getting tired? Want me to take a turn with the pole?"

"No, I'm good," Rao said. "This place is funny, right? Funny."

Jansen sighed and stuck her leg out across the ice, stretching it. "Funny weird, yeah."

"I've been thinking about what's up there." She let go of the pole with one hand and pointed upward. Not that there was anything to point at but darkness. "There's another sea up there, isn't there? Water and ice and...whatever. Above our heads. Gravity in the drum points outwards, in all directions. If we could see, we would see the drum curving up around us, forming a cylinder. We would see the water on every side, and straight above, too."

"I'm kind of glad I can't see that," Jansen said. "It would always feel like it was about to come pouring down on my head."

"We evolved on a flat world," Rao said. "We had no way to tell that it was round until we figured out the math. Anything born in this place wouldn't have that luxury. They would grow up knowing the world was a drum. They wouldn't know anything about stars. They wouldn't know there was a universe outside."

"You think that's why they didn't respond to our signals? Why we can't seem to communicate with them?"

"Because they can't imagine there's anything outside to talk to?" Rao asked. "From their perspective? For thousands of years, there wasn't. They were between stars, in a place almost as dark as this." She pushed down hard with the pole. She could feel when she was shoving against one of the rootlike structures and when the pole touched the smooth surface of the drum. "No," she said.

"They know that Earth is there. Maybe not in the same way we think about it. Maybe to them planets aren't balls of rock rotating in space, maybe they see them as . . . I don't know."

"Refueling stations," Jansen suggested.

"What?"

"I've been thinking, too. I've been wondering what they want from us. This place is a closed system. It has water and air, but in the thousands of years between stars it can't get more of them. No matter how well it recycles its resources, it's eventually going to run out. I think it came to Earth to get more water, that's all."

Hawkins grunted. The sound startled Rao—she'd almost forgotten he was there. "If that's what they want, they could have asked nicely," he said. "They could have—"

He stopped talking so suddenly Rao worried he might have fallen off the raft, even though she hadn't heard a splash. But no, he was struggling to get to his feet. He stared forward into the murk, his suit lights spearing out ahead of him.

"What?" Jansen asked. "What is it?"

"I saw something," Hawkins said.

"What? What did you see?"

He didn't have an answer for her. It had been just a flicker of reflected light, a shape he'd half glimpsed. It could have been his own light shining back at him from the wet surface of an ice floe, or—

There. He found it again. It wasn't an ice floe.

It looked like a yellowish-gray mass, like a cluster of dirty soap bubbles. It was rising from the water, swelling up out of the dark. The shiny forms grew dull as they expanded, as if they were drying out. Solidifying, maybe. They formed a mound that just crested the surface of the water. He tried to keep the light steady on the bubbles—and as he watched, more of them formed, inflating on top of the heap. Growing higher.

As they got closer he could see a network of the rootlike tendrils, very thin ones, climbing across the surfaces of the dry bubbles.

Latching on to them, maybe supporting them. The mass was growing, fast.

He waved back at Rao, and she got the point. She pushed sideways, against their previous course. Trying to get some distance from the mass of... globules? Eggs? He had no idea what they were, what they could even be.

Hawkins had no strong desire to find out. He waved one way, then the other, directing Rao. He didn't want to get anywhere near the mass. Soon they were past it, and it receded back into the shadows. He took one last look back and caught the mass in his suit lights, twenty meters behind them. It was still growing.

"Some kind of machine?" Jansen asked. "Nanotechnology, maybe? I've never seen anything like that."

"No. No, it was alive—alive on some level. So fast...," Rao whispered.

"What?" Hawkins demanded.

The astrobiologist shook herself as if she'd been in a trance. "The things here grow so fast—their metabolism must be incredible. I saw it with the tendrils that—that killed Stevens. They don't move, they grow. And they grow at an incredible rate. I guess it makes sense."

"What are you talking about?"

Rao stared out over the black water. What she saw out there he couldn't imagine. "I think—the reason we didn't see any aliens here, when we arrived. I think they were hibernating. Jansen, you said this was a closed system, and you're right. If you were going to travel between stars, and take thousands of years to do it, there's no way you could carry enough food or air. You would have to find a way to slow down your body systems. Your metabolism. You would down-regulate your breathing, your pulse, until your heart only needed to beat once a year, until you could survive on just a little puff of air..."

"But you said the metabolism of those bubbles, and the tendrils, was super fast," Jansen pointed out.

"Right. Because now, as 2I gets close to its destination, everything changes. There's work to get done. They need to speed up again. You see the same pattern in nature, in places where it doesn't rain for near on a century, say. Brine shrimp, or water bears."

"Tardigrades?" Hawkins asked.

He'd expected her to be impressed that he knew what a water bear was, but she gave no indication she'd even heard him. "There are animals that dig down into the mud when a drought comes, they bury themselves in soil as hard as rock, then climb back out for the rainy season—fish that get frozen in ice all winter, then they're alive and fine when they thaw out. It's the same. They slow themselves down, down to near nothing, then when conditions get better—when it rains, or gets warm again—they come to life with this amazing stock of stored energy. Because they know the good times can't last."

"The changes we've seen in here have been happening faster and faster," Hawkins agreed. He didn't like that at all. "You think it's done now? Or are things going to keep changing?"

Rao didn't answer him. She didn't really need to. He knew that they hadn't seen everything 2I had in store for them. Not yet. He was sure of it.

"You're breathing heavy," Jansen said. "You must be exhausted." She was talking to Rao, not him.

"I'm fine," the younger woman said.

"You've been working nonstop for over an hour. Let me take a turn," Jansen insisted.

Hawkins sat back down, near the edge of the floe. Careful not to let his feet dangle in the water. "Everybody keep a lookout, make sure we don't run straight into another of those bubble heaps." There was no doubt in his mind that there would be more.

Yet the next thing he saw was completely different. A dull pale shape rising out of the dark water like a sea serpent rearing its head.

"Stop," he said as they drew close. "Stop!"

Jansen planted the pole in the mass of tendrils under the water, slowing them to a stop almost immediately.

"Get the lamp on that," he said, pointing forward.

The thing he'd seen was maybe four meters across where it rose from the water in a gentle curve, a pylon or a column of rough material that might have been concrete, if it resembled anything found on Earth. It stuck straight up from the water, maybe ten meters high, then leaned over to the left. If they hadn't stopped they would have passed right underneath its curve.

The top of the column was smoking, or releasing vapor of some kind. Hawkins pointed both of his suit lights right at the surface there and saw that it was slick with some kind of foam that glittered and popped. He could even hear it hissing. A little fluid escaped the foam and dripped from the column's ragged end.

"Is that—"

"It's also growing," Rao said. "Whatever it is."

The column was getting longer, its curve continuing even as they watched. It extended out over the water, increasing its length constantly. Far faster than Hawkins liked.

He watched the column grow for a while. Then he got a funny feeling, a bad idea. "Pan the light over to the left," he said.

Jansen twisted the boom of the lamp slowly, scanning the face of the black water. Her light caught something.

There was an identical column over there, curving to the right as if the two spars of concrete were reaching out for each other. Which he thought was exactly what they were trying to do. Just like the first one's, the top of the second column was fuming and growing, centimeter by centimeter.

When they met, as he was sure they would, they would form an arch. An arch maybe twenty meters high and a hundred meters across.

"We can go around," Jansen pointed out. "We can work our way around so we don't pass beneath."

"Yeah," he said. "Good call."

"I just had a weird thought," Jansen said as they passed another of the bubble piles. "Is it possible those are the aliens?"

Hawkins laughed, but Rao's head lifted, and she gave Jansen a serious look. "Interesting," she said.

"Maybe—maybe the reason we haven't been able to talk to them is that they're just so different from us, so weird that we don't have anything in common," Jansen suggested.

"Those aren't the aliens," Hawkins said, gesturing at one of the bubble mounds. "No hands. Not even a head. How could something like that build a starship?"

Rao looked as if she might have an answer. She sat up very straight, and Jansen half expected her to raise her hand. Hawkins waved at her in dismissal, though. "Don't answer that. It was a rhetorical question."

Jansen's eyes narrowed. They'd brought an astrobiologist all this way, at great taxpayer expense. Now he didn't even want to hear from her?

He had more to say, apparently. "No, we haven't seen the aliens yet. You said they were hibernating, Rao. Now they're waking up. We'll see them. We'll see them real soon, I bet." He swallowed, hard, a sound that would have passed unnoticed if it weren't picked up by his suit's microphone.

Jansen gave him a very thin, very cold smile. "You're scared," she said.

"Damn right," he told her.

"You're scared that these aliens have come across light-years of space to invade the Earth and kill us all."

He shook his head. "Don't be stupid. How does that make any sense? An invasion that takes millennia? What would be the point? If they wanted what we've got, our gold or our water or something—it would take way too long to get it back to their planet. No. I'm not worried about an invasion."

Jansen laughed. "Seriously? Then what are you scared about?"

"I'm worried they come in peace," he said.

SURFACE MAPPING

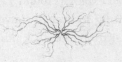

You're scared of what?" Rao asked, laughing.

Hawkins took his time replying. When he did, his answer was so cryptic she couldn't make any sense of it.

"Neanderthals," he said.

Rao considered herself a patient person. She had the discipline and the inner calm necessary to carry out laboratory experiments that could take months to complete. When he didn't say anything more for nearly a minute, though, she felt an unbearable anxiety start to build up inside her chest, and she very much wanted to scream at him and demand an explanation. Instead she merely repeated what he'd said.

"Neanderthals."

He nodded. "Neanderthals. About forty thousand years ago, there were at least two kinds of humans on planet Earth. There were Cro-Magnons, right, our ancestors, and there were Neanderthals."

"I might've heard of them," Rao said. She had a degree in astrobiology, after all. That he thought he needed to explain Neanderthals to her made her seethe. Just a little.

"The Neanderthals had music. They painted caves and they buried their dead. They were as smart as us, and probably stronger." Hawkins shrugged. "The Cro-Mags had flint spearheads. The Neanderthals didn't. A couple thousand years later—no Neanderthals."

"And now we're the Neanderthals," Jansen suggested.

Hawkins sighed. "We used to think the Cro-Mags hunted the

Neanderthals into extinction. Now we know that isn't true. The two groups got along, it looks like. They even intermarried. But the Neanderthals didn't make it. You want another example? Think of Columbus landing in the New World. Look how that went for the Indians. Or when British explorers found Tasmania. You know that story? They came wanting to trade, to give the Tasmanians good technology, good metal tools and all kinds of modern stuff. You know what happened?"

Rao cleared her throat. "I do," she said. "The Tasmanians almost died out. They suffered so much culture shock they stopped having babies."

"What?" Jansen asked.

Rao shrugged and ducked her head. "Maybe the story is apocryphal, but that's what I heard. They couldn't understand these newcomers. These white people. The British wanted to modernize them, to civilize them. Make them good Christians and good royal subjects. They moved the Tasmanians off their ancestral hunting land and put them on a new island, and they were so terrified, so unready for contact with another culture—they just stopped bearing children."

"When one culture meets another, and one of those cultures has a technological edge—they win. They win whether they come in peace or war," Hawkins said. He wasn't looking at either of them. He was staring off into the darkness. "That's what I'm afraid of," he said.

A chime sounded inside Hawkins's helmet. "I'm getting something from the robot," he said. He tapped at the console on his chest, and an AR window opened in front of him.

"Care to share with the rest of the class?" Jansen asked, standing up to get right in his face. Blocking his view of the new window.

He grumbled under his breath, but he tapped a few keys and the transmission was copied to both Jansen's and Rao's suits. Rao had been poling the raft along—now she stopped as they all studied the image floating in front of them.

It was a map of 2I's interior. This was the first time they'd ever gotten an idea of what the drum contained. It was in black and white, and all the objects ARCS had found were fuzzy and indistinct, but it was a revelation.

"What's the resolution on this?" Jansen asked.

Hawkins checked the metadata. "About fifty meters." Meaning nothing smaller than that would show up on the map. ARCS had instructions to fly back and forth along the axis, building up a better picture with each round trip. So far it had only completed one scan, and that first pass was quick and dirty. Yet the low resolution didn't mean the map was lacking in interest. ARCS must have traveled the whole length of the drum, pushing itself along the axis on a jet of compressed air. As it moved it had built up the scan slice by slice, using the lidar system that was its only sensor.

The first thing Hawkins noticed was that there were two large structures, one at either end of the spindle, both perfectly spherical. One of those had to be the airlock they'd come through. The other was much smaller, but it matched the location of the seam they'd seen at 2I's south pole, on the exterior of the hull. "That's definitely a second airlock, then," Hawkins said.

"Good to know we've got two ways out of here," Jansen told him.

He had no comment on that. He kept his face carefully neutral. There were things she didn't need to know. Yet.

Luckily she didn't study his face too closely—she was too busy looking at the map. Hawkins imagined she was noticing the same thing he had. They'd expected to find that the drum was mostly empty, its floor flooded with water, and the map largely flat apart from the occasional arch or bubble pile. That wasn't the case at all. There were dozens, maybe as many as a hundred objects larger than fifty meters across scattered around the inside of the drum. One of those would be the structure that was their destination, but there was a vast profusion of other shapes—towers and spines, some looking similar to the superstructures on the hull. Enormous domes that must be kilometers across—they looked like hills in the map. There were several complicated, spiky shapes that the robot hadn't been able to draw with any precision.

"Jesus," Hawkins said. "The place is crammed full of structures. Those could be entire alien cities. And still we could have rafted our way from one end of the drum to the other and missed all of them."

"In the dark," Jansen said. "Sure."

Hawkins noticed something about the map—it was time-stamped. He queried the robot, and it sent back a series of partial images, the individual slices it had made on its journey. "Here," he said, "look at this." He linked the images together in a slideshow, then scrolled through them to create a time-lapse image. "Those domes," he said. "The big domes. Do you see it?"

Rao glanced at Jansen as if looking for permission to speak first. "They're getting bigger. All of these structures are. They're new, and they're growing. But the domes are swelling incredibly fast."

"And here," Hawkins pointed out. "The water level is dropping. Slowly, but you can just make it out."

"I see it," Jansen said.

None of them bothered putting forth hypotheses about what that meant. It was just a fact. If the progression continued, the water would recede to a point where they would have to get off the floe and walk. They would have to walk over the thick mat of tendrils that covered the floor of the lake.

Hawkins didn't exactly relish the prospect.

Their progress slowed to a crawl. They could no longer travel in a straight line toward the structure. Instead they had to make wide diversions around new masses, new . . . things that emerged from the water with increasing regularity.

None of what she saw made any sense to Jansen. It only made her afraid.

There were plenty more of the bubble mounds, and more than a few of the arches, definitely—they started seeing pairs of arches, or three of them arranged in a row, and always Hawkins refused to sail under them. The arches were getting bigger, too, like every-thing else. Some of the curved columns were twenty or even thirty meters across where they met the water, now, and still they fumed and smoked.

There were other things in their way now, as well. Dim shapes that emerged from the darkness like fog thickening into solid forms, shapes defined only by their lights, shapes draped with shadows. They had to make a long detour around what looked like a crater, or maybe a well, nearly half a kilometer across. It looked as if it were made of sandbags, or a flexible sort of bricks that didn't so much fit together in regular patterns as they might have oozed into place, deforming around each other. The lip of the crater was just slightly higher than the level of the water around it, and as they drew close they could see inside. Liquid inside the crater—maybe water, but it looked more viscid and sluggish—swirled and churned as if agitated from below. A greasy scum accumulated on its surface, chopped up by the bubbling water, but it never quite dispersed. Tendrils crept over the wall of the crater and dipped into the turbulent liquid.

They had a bad scare when one tendril moved under their raft. Rao scuttled backward like a crab from the edge of the floe, scooting on her elbows as she tried to get closer to its center of gravity. Jansen lifted the TBL thinking she could use it like a spear, that she could stab the snakelike appendage, but it ignored them completely. It was too preoccupied with getting to that soupy cauldron. Once it had climbed the wall and stuck its end down into the liquid, it anchored itself to the rim with tiny, spiky appendages and stopped moving. Jansen pushed them away from the crater and back into the dark.

They came to a place where a thick bundle of cables were braided together like a rope that led off in either direction farther than their lights could show. The cables were similar to the tendrils, but much, much bigger—thick trunks as wide across as Jansen's waist that rose like a sandbank from the dark water. Flickers of electricity moved across the cables, barely visible. They had to backtrack a fair ways before Jansen could steer them around the braid. Even when she found the way forward she stopped, because she'd seen something else.

From a distance she saw something that looked a little like a tree, except that some of its branches could move like arms, on thick, knobby joints. The twigs at the ends of the branches looked far too much like human fingers for her liking. Human fingers that stretched a meter long.

She couldn't help but stare as the fingers slowly curled together, trembling and weak, to form tight, knotty fists.

"Keep moving," Hawkins said, breaking the spell. She planted the TBL and heaved, and they moved forward. He stumbled past her and dropped to his knees at the front of the raft, sweeping the water with his lights.

"What is it?" she asked.

"Don't stop what you're doing," he said. "It's nothing. It's—"

She was steering them around the side of a massive, low arch. They were close enough to make out its surface texture. It didn't look so much like concrete, as she'd originally thought, as something more organic. Not wood, but—it was made of closely woven fibers so tightly packed they made a continuous surface. Dotted through the striated surface were deep, shadowy pits, as big as caves. Interesting, she supposed, but Hawkins was acting as if he'd seen something else.

Suddenly he reeled backward, his suit lights spearing up through the dark, murky air. They caught something, a pale shape that clung to the shadow on the top curve of the arch. Jansen planted her pole and looked, trying to make it out. "What is it?" she asked.

"Quiet!" Hawkins barked.

Then the shape moved. It looked at first as if it was unfurling, separating into individual appendages like arms and legs and—

"Oh my God," she said. "It's—it's—"

It had the shape of a human being. It was moving, flickering in and out of the light. Jansen caught a flash of color. A momentary glimpse of bright orange.

KSpace orange.

"Hey!" she shouted. "Hey! You, up there—"

The figure made a sweeping gesture with its arms, pointing back the way they'd come. The message was unmistakable. *Go back*, the figure was telling them. *Go back*.

Jansen shook her head. "Taryn Holmes?" she shouted. "Commander Foster?" She couldn't even tell if the figure was male or female. "Sandra Channarong? Please, we've come to help!"

Whoever it was, they slipped into the shadows and vanished as if they'd never been there.

Jansen pushed them closer to the arch. Hawkins lunged across the raft to try to grab the pole away from her, but she held it out of his reach. It was all Rao could do to hold on to the ice as they started to spin in the dark water.

Water that was splashing hard against the side of the raft. It was as if they'd wandered into a strong current. The water pushed them away from the arch, but Jansen kept poling against its flow.

"You saw it, right?" Jansen demanded. Rao looked up and saw Jansen standing over her.

Rao just nodded. Yes, she'd seen something. Though it had been hard to tell in the dark, with Hawkins's light bouncing all over the place.

"That was one of them," Jansen insisted. "One of the KSpace crew. We have to get closer!"

"They were warning us about something," Hawkins said.

Jansen didn't even seem to hear him. The raft danced under her feet. She pushed down hard with the pole, trying to stabilize them. It looked as if she was having difficulty. Rao pointed her lights across the water and saw whitecaps snapping along the surface, pale claws of water surging between the bobbing ice floes. The current she'd sensed before was getting stronger. She could hear the waves slapping against each other. It felt as if something was moving out there in the water. Something big. Was this what the figure had been warning them about? It was coming fast. A big wave came right at them, maybe big enough to capsize their raft.

"Jansen!" Rao cried. "Look out!"

From far out in the distance there came a sound like a whale jumping from the water and landing again with a huge, meaty impact, and then the water surged again, the waves even more powerful than before. The raft bobbed wildly, threatening to buck them off.

"Hold on!" she shouted. Whatever was out there in the dark stirring up the water was still moving. She heard it smack the surface of the water like a vast hand, felt little shocks and ripples bouncing the raft up and down. "Hold on," she shouted again, and dropped to her knees to try to gain some stability.

Hawkins was still half-upright. "Whatever it is—"

There was a vast churning sound, and then the direction of the waves changed a hundred and eighty degrees, as if a tide that had been going out had suddenly been sucked back in. Whatever it was, out there in the dark, it had to be enormous—and it was turning the water to foam.

Jansen reached in a pocket of her suit and took out one of her flares.

"What are you doing?" Hawkins asked. "If it sees us—"

The flare had a built-in grip and ignition switch. Jansen pointed it up above her head and hit the trigger.

After the continuous darkness of 2I, the flare's light was blinding and Rao had to look away. When she dared to lift her head again she saw it, a red comet blazing across the air above them. For a second, just a second, she could see for kilometers, she could see the arcing walls of 2I, the walls of the drum curving up and away from her, walls covered in water dotted with the last scraps of ice. She saw all the bubble mounds and hand-trees and arches, the vast domes and wells and things she couldn't describe, saw just how much of this dark lake had come to life. She saw, directly above her, the roof of the drum, saw hand-trees up there that must be kilometers tall, saw their slender fingers twitch and curl up. She saw the arches rising up over her head, hundreds of them, arches growing from the curves of other arches like the staircases in an Escher painting. The air over her head was crisscrossed by a network that branched and rebranched very much as the tendrils ramified. A pale scaffolding that crossed from one side of the drum to the other.

All of it so maddeningly familiar. Rao's mind raced, still trying to make sense of this alien world. Even when her body screamed at her to get down, to keep her head down, as the raft continued to buck and tilt.

The flare hit the top of its arc and deployed a little parachute. It started to sink back through the thickening air of 2I, pulled down by the artificial gravity. After a moment she couldn't see the world above their heads anymore, which was a relief.

Unfortunately, a short-lived one. Because instead she saw what had been making all the waves.

Hanging from the arches like fat stalactites were long pods, dark, oblong shapes connected at their tops by thin stalks or peduncles. They had to be twenty meters long, and they were everywhere, dangling overhead, hanging down from the undersides of the arches like roosting bats.

And they were moving. Twitching.

The ones that touched the water convulsed and shook, slapping and slamming their thick ends against the submerged surface of the drum. This was what was causing the waves—the repetitive, thrashing motion of the pods.

So many of them, and they were all moving. So big.

The flare had fallen nearly all the way down to the water's surface. In the last of its light, Rao looked around and thought she saw something, just a glimpse, but it looked as if one of the long pods had split at its end, split open and something was slithering out—

"Jansen!" Hawkins shouted, and Rao twisted around to look at him. He was half on, half off the raft as it bucked and shook, tossed by the waves. His fingers dug into the ice, trying to find purchase that wasn't there.

Rao lunged forward and grabbed him, grabbed both his wrists to try to hold him on the raft. She saw his face, saw the look of real terror there. She held as tightly to him as she could, tried to dig her knees into the ice and pull him back up. She started to make progress, started to feel she was actually going to save him.

"Jansen," he said, and pulled one of his hands free of hers to point behind her. Rao's helmet wouldn't let her look back. She grabbed his arm with both hands and heaved, but he wasn't looking at her, much less doing anything to help. "Jansen's gone!" he shouted.

Rao let him go and flipped over on her back and looked around, her suit lights sweeping across the raft's surface, but it was true, it was true—Jansen was nowhere to be seen. The pole quivered in the air for a moment, then fell backward into the water. Had Jansen fallen off the floe? Had she been dragged off? Rao scrabbled across the ice, away from where Jansen had been a moment before.

Then a massive wave smashed into the raft, flipping it over completely, and she went flying, and she and Hawkins were both thrown into the fast-moving water and carried away by an implacable current.

"Run it again. Is there any way to get better resolution on this?"

"I'm sorry, sir. The trickle of data we're getting from the neutrino gun doesn't allow high-quality video. I'm doing what I can—"

McAllister waved one hand at the technician in frustration. "Just put it on a loop. I have to be sure."

On the big screen in the control room, the video played over and over. Just a second or two of imagery taken from Parminder Rao's viewpoint. It showed one of the long pods hanging from the arches that zigzagged across 2I's interior. One like all the others, except that as McAllister watched it smashed itself against the floor of the drum—and broke open.

Something fell out of the pod, something big and indistinct. It collapsed into the water, throwing up spray that made it even harder to see. But McAllister was certain. He knew for a fact that the thing, whatever it was, had reared up out of the water and wriggled forward a few meters.

The video started over, slowed down and magnified until each pixel on the screen was as big as McAllister's hand. He watched it again.

That thing was moving under its own power.

It was an alien. It had to be. One of 2I's crew, perhaps, or—

"Sir," someone called out. It wasn't a shout, but he could hear the fear in the voice. He turned and saw Utz, the biomedical engineer. "Sir, *Orion*'s telemetry is all over the place. Look at this."

She threw a new video up on the screen, one that moved so fast he thought at first it must have been sped up. It showed Jansen's viewpoint, and for a second it was nothing but a spinning, vertiginous slice of near darkness. Then silver bubbles erupted across the view, and water surged over Jansen's faceplate.

"They're in the water," Utz said. "Sir—they've capsized."

"Dear God," McAllister said.

ROY MCALLISTER: *There was no way for us to contact them, to ask for an update. Add to that the fact that we were still half a light-minute away from them, so all the information we had was roughly thirty seconds old. As I watched Jansen fall into the water, I knew that there was a possibility the entire crew was already dead.*

ENCOUNTER WINDOW

It was about all Jansen could do to breathe.

It felt as if she'd been fighting the water for hours, wrestling with the constantly changing currents, trying desperately not to smash into anything hard enough to damage her suit. It didn't always work—one of her suit lights hit the bottom and went out with a terrible jangling noise. The instrument package on the front of her suit caught on the side of an arch, snagging and almost tearing off before she could free herself.

The water churned and burst all around her. Wave after wave crashed over her and threw her buoyant suit this way and that. She tried to find something to grab on to and failed. She tried to grasp the rootlike tendrils that formed a thick carpet under the water, but they were too slippery. She tried to fetch up against one of the arches, but the current was just too strong.

The whole time she kept looking out for Rao and Hawkins. Calling their names, shouting for them. Once she saw some suit lights, cones of light stabbing upward through the froth and foam of the waves. She tried kicking toward them only to get caught by a new riptide and hauled off into the dark. Once, as she battled to keep her head up, above the water, she felt a human hand slap hers, felt fingers try to grab her palm, only to be torn away.

At least—she hoped it had been a human hand.

The water never stopped moving, never gave her a moment's break. It threw her back and forth, pulled her under in a broad maelstrom, spit her back out on the curl of a miniature tsunami. She was caught by a sudden surge, a roar of bubbles all around her, pulled under and dashed against the floor. She went spinning, head over heels. She shoved out her arms and her legs, trying to maximize her resistance to the water's pull, and it kind of worked—and then a huge wave came through, sweeping millions of liters of water ahead of it, and she went flying forward, faster than ever before.

In the dark water her light could show her only a torrent of bubbles, a sweep of debris as she was propelled forward faster and faster, and then something solid was right in front of her, rushing toward her—she threw out her arms, trying to create drag, trying to slow herself down. She was thrown sideways and then something smashed into her leg, into her knee—

There was a blinding flash of light inside her head, pain transmuted to white, screaming light, and a sickening crunch she felt vibrating through all the bones on her left side.

And then the water surged again, throwing her forward, dragging her across a floor of massed, curling tendrils that gave way to—to something else, something—

She was shoved bodily up a slope, a slope that was rough yet yielding, a slope that canceled her forward momentum. She slowed to a stop.

The water pulled back all around her, draining away from what was, suddenly, a shore.

She realized she was lying facedown on something she chose to call a beach. She'd been thrown up onto dry land.

Maybe not for long. The water hauled at her legs as it slid down the slope of the beach, headed back toward the dark sea. She started to slip and thrust her hands forward, grabbed at the beach. It was hopeless—she couldn't get a grip, couldn't hold on—she was going to be pulled back into the churning water, pulled back and thrown around again, and this time—

Hands, definitely human hands grabbed her wrists and hauled her up against the surging tide. She heard Rao shout something, maybe not even words, and then she was out of the water and being dragged up the shore.

Jansen rolled onto her side and took a series of long, deep breaths. Rao was shouting at her, asking her if she was all right, but Jansen could barely hear her. She was paying too much attention to her knee. If it was broken, if she couldn't walk, what would they do? If her patella was shattered, just chips of bone under her skin, then... Except it didn't hurt anymore. Her knee didn't hurt at all. It was completely numb.

She didn't know if that was good or bad. She knew it had to be bad. She shook her head and did the thing that she knew, consciously, was a terrible idea, but which her subconscious begged her to do. She climbed carefully to her feet and put weight on her left leg.

She didn't scream. She didn't collapse in a heap. The leg held. Whatever had happened to her knee, it wasn't broken.

She didn't think so, anyway.

Rao was right there, right in front of her. Jansen pulled her into a hug, their fiberglass torsos smashing together.

Then she staggered away from the younger woman, really, really needing to lie down, and fell lengthwise across the almost-solid ground.

The beach underneath her was rubbery and soft, enough so that her knees and hands sank into its mass, forming little craters. She lifted her hand and the surface sprang back. It was like kneeling on the top of a giant balloon.

Rao was still talking to her, shouting something. Jansen turned away from her. She needed to know where she was first. Then she could deal with whatever problem Rao had identified.

The surface was a deep-maroon color. It wasn't smooth, but instead covered in tiny, pale nodules. It reminded her of the skin of an octopus. She looked around and thought that she was on some kind of island, a mass of rubbery material that had risen from the shallow, dark sea. Every few seconds it felt as if the ground rippled, swaying up and down by the slightest degree. Or maybe that was just her.

"Jansen," Rao said. Finally her voice broke through the fog in Jansen's head. "It's Hawkins, he—"

"Hawkins." Jansen put her hands down, pushing herself upright. "He's here?" But as her solitary helmet light swept around the island, she didn't need confirmation. He was farther up the slope, lying on his side, his arms and legs splayed limply in front of him. Jansen staggered over to him and then dropped to her knees.

She couldn't see his face. The inside of his faceplate was smeared with blood.

"He's alive. All his telemetry is coming through and he's breathing, his heart's beating, but he's not responsive," Rao said. "I think he must have hit his head pretty hard."

"That's a lot of blood," Jansen pointed out.

"Head wounds bleed a lot. He could have a concussion." *Or he could have cracked his skull,* Rao thought. *He could be about to die.* "I would need to check his eyes and palpate his head to be sure."

"That would mean taking his helmet off."

When Rao had washed up on the island and crawled out of the dark water, she'd found him in that same awkward position. His condition hadn't changed in the last fifteen minutes. "Yeah," she said. "I would have to take his helmet off."

The two women stared at each other, terrified of what that might mean. They had no idea what might result from exposing Hawkins to the atmosphere of 2I. Rao looked down at the trace gas analyzer on the front of her suit and saw that there was plenty of oxygen now, and nothing poisonous floating around. The analyzer couldn't tell her what else might be in the air, though. Particulates, or mold spores, or any of a number of airborne toxins.

"We might poison him," Rao suggested. "And my medical supplies are pretty limited. If he breathed in something toxic, I would have no way to protect him from that."

"And if you don't examine him?" Jansen asked.

"He could die of his injuries." She sighed and laid one gloved hand on the curve of his helmet. "Or he could just recover on his own."

She couldn't see Jansen's face very well, with all of their lights shining in different directions.

"I saw one of the KSpace crew on that arch," the older woman said eventually. "We saw them."

"Jansen—"

"No, listen. Whoever they were, they weren't wearing a suit. Just what looked like a thermal garment. If they can survive here, exposed to the elements, then maybe he'll be OK, too."

"Are you one hundred percent sure that's what you saw?" Rao had seen nothing but a shadow and a flash of orange.

She could hear Jansen breathing heavily. It sounded as if she wasn't in such great shape herself.

"No," Jansen said, finally. "But we need to make a decision. Come on. Help me with this."

There were two catches that had to be released—fail-safe mechanisms to keep anyone from accidentally removing the helmet. Then, together, they twisted the big helmet around in its metal collar ring. It made a loud clicking sound as they rotated it through the last quarter turn, another safety mechanism. Rao pulled her hands away, but Jansen didn't hesitate. She finished the rotation, then lifted the helmet, careful not to scrape Hawkins's chin or touch his head.

A little air—healthy air—sighed out of his collar ring, and the fabric of his suit draped over his legs as the suit lost pressure. He didn't stir or even murmur in his sleep, but almost instantly tiny beads of sweat appeared on his upper lip. Rao had forgotten how warm it had gotten inside 2I while she remained perfectly cool inside her own suit. She prayed she'd made the right decision.

The two of them watched his face very carefully. For a moment it looked as if he was dead, that he had stopped breathing.

Then his whole body convulsed and his mouth opened and he sucked in a long, labored breath.

Jansen looked up at Rao. Neither of them said anything until he exhaled again, the air sighing out of him.

"He didn't die," Jansen said. "He took a breath and he didn't die. That's a good sign, right?"

Rao scowled. It meant nothing. "Get out of the way and let me work," she said.

With the helmet off she saw that his white snoopy cap was brown with dried and clotted blood. It stuck to his cheek and scalp as she pulled it gently free of his skin. It looked as if his head had taken multiple hits while they'd been dragged through the water. The whole left side of his jaw was one solid purple bruise, and the skin of his forehead had split open—that was where the blood had come from.

Rao did what she could for him. She pulled the water tube up from inside his collar ring and used it as a spray, washing as much of the blood off his face as she could. The wound on his forehead started to ooze blood again almost instantly. She grabbed a bandage out of the survival kit and pressed it against the cut. She pried open his eyelids and found his eyes drifting in their sockets. His pupils were very large—adapted for the darkness of 2I, perhaps—but at least they were the same size. She pointed one of her suit lights directly at his face and watched the pupils contract. A little slower than she would have liked.

"Is he going to be OK?" Jansen asked.

Rao didn't know. She kept pressure on the wound and hoped for the best.

PARMINDER RAO: It's notoriously hard to make a prognosis about a concussion. Without the proper tools I had no way of knowing if he'd just had a bad knock on the head, or if his brain was bleeding into his pia mater and he would die within an hour. I could monitor him for bloodshot eyes, for disorientation and nausea... Until he woke up, though, it was anybody's guess if he was going to make it.

Jansen checked their gear, going over each piece individually and examining it for damage. They'd been lucky. Their packs had been beaten up when they were tossed around in the water, but NASA had made their equipment well. The neutrino gun was working just fine, and more importantly their suit radios were functional, too. Their lighting situation wasn't quite as rosy. The TBL and its light were long gone—she'd dropped it when she fell off the ice floe. They'd lost almost all their glow sticks, though she still had two flares. Next she checked their survival equipment. They had Rao's medical kit, and a couple of foil emergency blankets. Finally she checked their water and air supplies. She found one oxygen cartridge with a bad dent in it. No way to tell if it would still work without plugging it into one of their suits and activating it. They had a number of other cartridges, all of which looked intact and full. She counted them. She tried to count them. She kept losing track in the middle and having to start over.

What was happening? She looked down at the cartridges in her hands. There weren't that many. One, two, three...

"How long have we been in here?" she asked.

Rao looked up at her with a start.

They both had clocks built into their suits. It was easy enough to check—they just had to remember what the time had been when they left *Orion*. Jansen blinked slowly as she tried to work it out in her head. It was hard to think, inside 2I. Thoughts tended to get halfway formed, then wiped out of your mind. Was it an effect of the constant darkness? 2I's magnetic field? Or was she just tired?

She was definitely tired.

"I can't...I don't remember if we..." Rao looked confused.

Jansen checked the clock. Subtracted the time they'd arrived at the airlock. "We've been in here nearly twenty-four hours," she said, when she'd finished her calculation.

"That doesn't seem possible," Rao told her. "But I guess...I mean, I remember switching out my oxygen. A while back, back when we... Wow. I don't remember exactly when I did that. I must have, though."

Jansen nodded. The carts lasted only twelve hours. She took a perverse kind of joy in knowing that if her mind was going, Rao's was, too.

"How are your suit batteries?" she asked. There was no way to replace or recharge those, not inside 2I.

"I'm still at sixty-four percent," Rao reported.

Jansen nodded. "If we're going to be here a while, we should switch off our lights. Those'll burn power a lot faster than your life-support pack."

"Seriously?" Rao asked. "I don't know if I can handle the dark."

"You won't have much choice, if your batteries run down." Jansen stacked up a couple of glow sticks in a pyramid like they were a campfire. They did almost nothing to keep the shadows away, but it was better than not being able to see at all.

The two of them made Hawkins as comfortable as possible. They had a whole stack of plastic sample bags. Wadding them up, they made a pillow for his head. Rao stretched his legs out, then the two of them rolled him gently onto his back.

He was still breathing. Jansen checked several times.

"We can give him a few hours," she said. "As long as nothing tries to kill us in the meantime."

"You could use a little time off your feet yourself," Rao said. "I want to take a look at you, if that's all right. I saw you limping before, and—"

"No, it's not all right," Jansen said. "I'm fucking fine."

Rao reeled back, stung, and Jansen immediately regretted her tone. Even as she'd spoken she'd known she was just lashing out, the frustrations and privations of the journey getting to her. She cursed herself, thinking she had to be very careful not to get too snappish now—now when they were counting on each other for so much. She forced herself to take it down a notch.

"Sorry," she said. "It's just my knee. It's never been great, and it got bumped in the water, but it's fine. Really."

"You've been pushing yourself really hard. It's a cartilage problem? That's not unusual in a woman of your age—"

Rao stopped speaking so abruptly that Jansen thought maybe she'd seen something coming toward them out of the dark. It took her a second to realize it was her own facial expression that had scared the younger woman.

"You looked like you were about to bite my head off," Rao said. With a little laugh. A very unconvincing little laugh.

"I need sleep," Jansen said. It was the best she could do in the way of an apology. It was also, she realized, very, very true.

"Go ahead," Rao told her. "I'll stand watch."

Jansen nodded and curled up, as best she could, on the rubbery ground. She felt it shimmy underneath her every few seconds—a sensation she found oddly comforting. Like a mother's heartbeat, she thought, like—

The thought never had a chance to come together in her head. She was out like a light.

It was a dream.

Inside 2I it was sometimes hard to tell. There was no clear delineation between the darkness external and internal. Dreams came on like reveries, like especially vivid memories. Fantasies.

In her dream Jansen was alone, orbiting the Earth. An endless cloudscape that rolled beneath her. She could just make out at the top of her vision the limb of the planet, the curvature of it, but she couldn't move her head. She heard a beep, and a distorted voice whispered to her:

glide path OK retros OK decay time in four three two one

A cyclone spun up across Africa, long white streamers of cloud snarling over the South Atlantic. She realized she wasn't in a ship, she was floating free, in orbit. Except that instead of being in the perfect slowed-down motion of a spacewalk she was at the mercy of a current, as if she were diving—her arms and limbs wavering as if they were being pushed by cold water. She heard a beep.

acs to set fpi to blowthrough standby verniers to off position at mark

Was she—was she getting warmer? Was that the motion of air she was feeling? The voice didn't panic, and she tried not to, either, but if she was too low, if she'd fallen too low in her orbit, if she was going to enter the atmosphere then she—she—she wasn't in a ship, she was just in a suit that couldn't possibly survive atmospheric heating. Storms lined up along the Atlantic coast of North America, one two three four, splitting off from a major hurricane in the Sargasso Sea. She wasn't equipped for this, if she tried to enter the atmosphere like this she was going to—looked like a wet day for most of the Midwest, honestly.

Beep.

external temp three hundred and rising go angle is good go chutes prepped go

She was shaking. She was shaking violently, her shoulders bouncing and her head moving inside her helmet. The Earth was so very, very big, and the atmosphere so thick and full of water vapor. Water vapor condenses around dust in the upper atmosphere to create raindrops, which collect in—

She looked down and saw her gloves were cherry red. Glowing cherry red. Her fingers started to melt.

The lights were too bright. Spears of light coming at him from every direction, surrounded by halos in every possible color that burned inside his eyes, that burned, burned—he fought, tried to swim upward through, through the thoughts that churned inside his head, whispering words, little whispering words that he tried to—tried to stick together into coherent thoughts, but—but—good God, his ears were ringing, so loud. So loud.

"Gaaaaah," he moaned. His tongue was stuck to his teeth, dried up and glued to the ridged, ranked shapes of them.

He sat up and rubbed at his mouth with his gloved hands, trying to get the worst of the dried, crusted drool off his lips and chin. It was then he realized something terrifying.

He wasn't wearing a helmet.

Dear God—someone had taken his helmet off. Who had done that? Who, damn it? He twisted around—shit, that made his head spin way too much—and saw Parminder Rao lying there on the ground, one arm under her own intact helmet. It couldn't have been her, she was a good kid. Where was—where was Jansen?

He found her curled up in a ball on the unsolid ground. Fast fucking asleep. Everyone was asleep but him. What the hell? Didn't anybody else ever think about operational security?

He reached down and touched a pocket on the front of his suit.

A pocket he had kept carefully zipped up since they'd left *Orion*. If Jansen had stolen what was in that pocket, if she'd figured out his secret and—he would—he didn't know what he would—

Good God. His brain was mush. He couldn't think straight. He was getting paranoid, and not the healthy kind of paranoia that came with his job. Jansen hadn't stolen anything from him. She wasn't the type. She'd taken his helmet off, yes. She must have had a good reason.

Like maybe she had wanted to kill him.

She was resentful about his taking over command of the mission. She hated him. Maybe she—she—

He crawled over to her and grabbed her by the shoulders. Shook her hard.

"You took my helmet off," he said.

Her face twisted up, her features all contorted and spread out by fear, as if they were trying to get away from each other. He kept shaking her.

"Why?" he demanded. "Why would you do that?"

Suddenly Rao was talking to him, trying to get his attention. She hauled at his shoulders and the life-support pack on his back, and he lacked the strength to even pull away from her. He had to let go of Jansen and turn to face Rao.

"Don't you understand?" he asked. "She took my helmet off."

"You have a concussion," she told him. "We had to take it off to keep you safe. You're disoriented, that's common with—"

"Fuck that. I'm perfectly fine," he said, the act of talking making bones shift inside his head. His head hurt like a motherfucker. He wanted to grab Jansen again, grab her and shout in her face. She'd killed Blaine Wilson. She'd killed Stevens. Now maybe she had killed him, too.

In a second he would tell her. As soon as the pain in his head stopped making it impossible to think. God, his head hurt. It hurt so bad. He reached up and pressed the balls of his thumbs against his temples. He ground them against the skin.

"What do you have to say for yourself?" he asked Jansen. He

wasn't entirely sure what he meant by that. She hadn't tried to kill him. No, of course not, that was just his headache talking.

The old woman turned around, finally, to look at him. To look at her mission commander, who was talking to her. What the hell had she been thinking, taking his helmet off? It wasn't safe here, it wasn't... The thought made him want to laugh.

Get it together, he thought. *Just get it together.*

Jansen held up one gloved hand. She stretched it out toward him. "Do you see this?" she asked. "It's not just me hallucinating?"

There was a short little memory stick in the palm of her hand.

"I don't know where it came from," Jansen said. "When I woke up it was there. When I sat up it fell out of my hand and I grabbed it back up." She shook her head inside her helmet. "I don't understand. Did you—did you fall asleep?"

"No," Rao said, though it sounded more like a question. *No?* "If I did, it was just for a second. I knew I needed to stay awake, to keep watch."

Behind her, Jansen could see Hawkins sitting down, his head in his hands. He seemed to have calmed down a bit.

She wished she could.

Jansen took a deep breath. She looked around them, swinging her light across the rippling surface of the island. There was nothing out there. Nothing she could see.

She slotted the memory stick into the receptacle on her communications panel. As usual it held just one file. But whereas before the files had all had simple alphanumeric, computer-generated names, like 4AC68883.mp7, this one had a readable name:

YOUNEEDTOLEAVE.mp7.

Jansen was almost afraid to play it.

VIDEO FILE TRANSCRIPT (3)

[Unlike the previous video files, the video does not suffer from degradation. It clearly shows three prone figures. Two are wearing full space suits. The third is wearing most of a space suit but its helmet has been

removed. A small pile of glow sticks is the only source of illumination. The camera moves toward the figures, which do not react to its presence. The camera examines their faces for some time. Then, from out of the camera's field of view, bare human hands appear in frame to rummage through a backpack.]

Sandra Channarong [whispering]: You didn't bring any food. No. Of course you didn't.

[The view shifts wildly, as if the camera is being turned around. A woman's face—not belonging to any of the previously seen figures—appears, but it is seen only in silhouette.]

Channarong: You need to go back. Turn around and go back to *Orion*. If you stay here you're going to die. I'm sorry.

[The video cuts off abruptly.]

ASCENDING NODE

There wasn't much discussion about what the video meant. Rao wished they could have taken some time to discuss it, to talk about how they should respond. Looking at the others' faces, though, she could see they'd already made up their minds.

For Hawkins it was a threat, clear and simple. And the way he responded to threats was by engaging them directly and refusing to accede to demands.

For Jansen it was proof the KSpace astronauts were still alive. Alive, and close by.

For both of them that meant the reaction was clear—it was time to move on. To search out—or hunt down—the KSpace crew. At the very least to find out what it knew. The idea that they might listen to Sandra Channarong and turn around and leave wasn't given a moment's consideration.

She had her own reason to keep going. She needed to know if she was right.

She'd formed a theory when she saw the tendrils emerge from Stevens's body, watched them crawl across the walls of *Wanderer*'s reentry module. She needed more data, more evidence before she could be sure, though. Before she thought she could unlock 2I's big secret.

So they moved on. By foot, now, across the yielding substance of the island. ARCS's map showed they weren't far now from the structure that Jansen had seen on her first visit to 2I—it was less than two kilometers from where they'd stopped to rest. An easy walk. Theoretically.

Hawkins didn't bother putting his helmet back on. What would be the point? He'd already breathed in the air of 2I. Been exposed to its poisons. Instead he clipped it to one of the D rings on the hard part of his suit and let it dangle there. He ejected the half-used oxygen cartridge from the life-support pack on his back and gave it to Rao. He didn't need it anymore. He had two spares as well, which he gave to Jansen to put in her pack.

Then he set off, at a pace Rao had trouble matching. Each step across the rubbery ground was a challenge in keeping her balance, in not falling down. Sometimes she failed, but at least the landing was soft. Occasionally she would look back and check on Jansen. The older woman was having the hardest time of any of them. Something had happened to her—maybe she'd been injured when they were in the water. Rao had asked Jansen if she was all right, and the older woman had said she was fine. Yet now she was struggling to keep up. She was limping, dragging her left leg, staggering along as best she could. Rao could hear her breathing heavily over the radio, hear her curse under her breath when she missed a step or the ground rippled under her and she went sprawling.

Yet every time Rao turned around, Jansen was still back there, her lone helmet light still visible. There was no telling how long she could keep this up, but she clearly refused to ask anyone to slow down on her account.

The surface of the island rose before them—a gentle, almost imperceptible slope, but soon Rao felt it in her calves and her thighs. She checked ARCS's map at one point and saw that they were in the middle of one of the huge domes that covered much of the drum's interior surface. She resigned herself to a long climb, and let her mind free to think about what she was seeing, trying to understand it—

Until she heard something, out in the dark, and her blood turned to ice.

"What was that?" she gasped.

Hawkins turned in the direction she was pointing. His lights swept across the unbroken plain. They revealed nothing.

"What?" he demanded. "What did you hear?"

Rao forced herself to close her eyes. To listen for it again. If it had just been in her head—

No.

There it was again. A sound very much like waves crashing on a beach. Except where waves crashed and then receded, crashed and receded, this just kept going on and on. Getting louder.

"I hear it, too," Jansen whispered.

Hawkins took a few steps toward the sound. Adjusted his suit lights, pointing them in various directions.

Rao tried to put words to it. To imagine what could be making that noise. A kind of moist rustling sound. A sound like...like...

She thrust her tongue against the dry soft palate of the roof of her mouth. Her tongue rasped against the dehydrated skin, stuck and then pulled free. It made a terrible dragging sound, and if you magnified that sound a million times, and if you heard it from a distance...

Something was moving out there. Something enormous was dragging itself across the surface of the dome. Heaving its incredible bulk along the soft, rippling ground.

"It's getting louder," Jansen said, coming up beside her. Rao was surprised how much reassurance she took from just having another human being that close. Until Jansen spoke again.

"Closer," she said.

The ground under their feet rippled. Not with the rhythmic pulses they'd grown used to, but with something like an elastic earthquake, a rubbery wobble. Rao dropped to one knee. It was that or fall on her face. Jansen crouched beside her.

Hawkins kept his footing, though he had to put his arms out.

"Growing pains," Jansen said. "This place is still changing. It's just the sound of some new bizarre thing sprouting in the dark."

For a long time Hawkins said nothing. He just stared out into the darkness. Even through the loose fabric of his deflated suit, Rao could see the tension in his muscles. If something came barreling out of the darkness toward them, he would stand his ground.

It didn't happen. Eventually the sound grew softer. Whatever it was out there, it headed away from them. Deeper into unknown territory.

Hawkins gave it another minute, holding up one hand for silence. Rao slowly helped Jansen stand back up.

"All right," Hawkins said, finally. "Move out."

A thick tendril crossed the ground in front of them. It looked as if it had sunk into the soft ground. Ahead of them it branched off into a thicker, muscular-looking conduit as thick around as Jansen's bicep.

"Careful," Hawkins said.

There was no way forward except to step over it. It didn't move, didn't rise up to attack Jansen's legs.

Neither did the next one they found, which was as thick as her thigh. Or the bundle of tendrils they found beyond that, as big as her waist.

"We'll have to climb," Hawkins said, when they saw what lay ahead and above them. The tendrils—the size of water mains now, some a meter in cross section—piled up on the slope of the island, running over and across each other, braided together, meeting in swollen nodes where the branches grew into one another.

Rao reached out one tentative hand and laid her palm against the thick, trembling mass of them. Hawkins started to bark an order, but Jansen stepped up and touched one of the giant tendrils herself.

She could feel liquid flowing through it, a spasmodic current. A pulse.

Rao grabbed a tendril and hauled herself up onto the pile. She found her footing, found another foothold. Climbed up, not stopping.

Hawkins grumbled but followed after her, sure-footed as a goat.

Jansen sighed. There was nothing for it. She reached up, grabbed a tendril, and pulled herself up.

Walking had been a nightmare. Her knee wasn't broken, but there was no pretending she could shake off whatever damage had been done. With every step she had felt the patella of her bad knee grating against the bones beneath. Every time she lifted her foot a fresh stab of pain had jabbed upward through her body. She had managed a kind of shuffling walk that kept her knee as straight as possible. Now that wasn't an option.

She felt her whole leg turn to jelly, the knee joint giving up altogether. She swung the useless leg around, braced it between two of the thick tendrils. Used her arms to pull herself up, with a little grunt.

Soon her breath was coming in fast pants, and stars burst behind her tightly closed eyes. She found her way up by feel, barely aware of where she was, or why she was doing this. Knowing only that she had to go higher. Farther.

At one point she slipped, having tried to put weight on her bad leg. The knee just wouldn't hold, and she started to fall, and her arms flailed out, trying to find something to grab on to. A strong hand grabbed her wrist and dragged her up, held her up until she could get her feet placed, until she could support herself.

She opened her eyes and saw Hawkins staring down at her, his face perfectly neutral.

"Thanks," she gasped.

He nodded and let her go.

It wasn't much farther to the top. They came to a place where the slope of tendrils ended, to a semiflat plateau, and Jansen knew they'd reached the top of the island. Its crest. This was their destination. It had to be.

She let herself breathe for a moment. Then she looked up.

Standing at the summit of the island was the structure. The thing she'd seen so long before, the thing they'd been searching for. She could make out very little of it except as a dark shape against deeper darkness. A vast looming tower of shadow, rising high above her—

Then it lit up.

A faint purple glow swept across its surface, so dim she thought maybe there was something wrong with her eyes. A brighter spot appeared in the midst of the glow—and then a hundred lightning bolts crackled across the structure's surface, with an angry buzzing noise as if a hornet had flown right into her ear.

"Shit!" Rao shouted. Then, a moment later, when the total darkness had returned—"Sorry."

Jansen didn't blame her for the outburst. This was what she'd seen, back on her first excursion into 2I. The light, the only light in the entirety of the drum. The light that had drawn her here.

"Come on," she whispered. "Again."

The structure failed to comply with her desires.

She needed to see more. She needed to see this thing close up. She had two flares left. This was why she'd brought them.

She lifted a flare up high over her head and fired it into the dark air. It hissed and spit and sparked as it flew toward 2I's axis, toward its distant, unseen ceiling. Its light was immediate and intense, a red glare that cast long, long shadows. It let her see the thing she'd come so far to reach. The thing that was supposed to make all of this worthwhile.

The structure rose above her, hundreds of meters tall and nearly as big around.

The brief glimpse that she'd had gotten of it, right before Stevens was attacked, had given her a very poor idea of what it actually was. Not that seeing it close up was much help.

It was generally egg shaped, and covered in a thick trellis of tendrils. They emerged from countless pits on its surface and formed a net of thick limbs that hung down all around it, a tent of branches that plunged into the surface of the island and disappeared into its substance. The tendrils didn't move, but inside that cage the structure itself was constantly trembling. Every few seconds it convulsed, not with a great spasm but with a weak sort of shaking, as if it were having trouble supporting its own weight. Big as it was, even that faint pulse was enough to rock the entire island. This had to be the source of the tiny tremors they'd been feeling ever since they washed up on the island's shore. This close, however, they shook the entire mound of tendrils, threatening to send the three astronauts tumbling back down. It was all Jansen could do to hold on.

"Oh hell," Hawkins said.

She clambered upward. She wanted to reach out and touch it, prove to herself it was real.

She was terrified to be anywhere near it.

But she had to keep going. What else was left to her but this? The things that had driven her so far, the hope of finding the KSpace crew, the need to make contact with 2I, even just her desperation not to let Roy McAllister down or to look weak in Hawkins's eyes, her need to keep Rao safe—those impulses wouldn't let her stop now.

She struggled upward, hand over hand, until she could almost reach out and touch the structure's worn, gray side.

The things they'd seen emerging from the water, the bubble mounds and the hand-trees and the arches, had all looked brand new. Jansen had watched them construct themselves out of nothing, and they'd had a slick, just-finished quality to them. The structure inside the net of roots was different. It looked old.

Extraordinarily old. Ancient.

Its surface was a dull bluish-gray, riddled with cracks and eruptions. Near its top—as far as her light would stretch—it looked as if it had cracked open and some dark fluid had run down its side, like lava from the cone of a volcano.

"Jansen. Stay back."

She barely heard him. She was too busy studying it, waiting for it to pulse again. When it did, her whole body convulsed as she tried desperately to hang on. A shock wave rumbled out through the air all around her, trying to rip her off the side of the hill and throw her out into the darkness.

"Jesus," Hawkins said. "Jesus, that hurts."

He wasn't wearing his helmet—he must be feeling those pressure waves in his eardrums, in his head.

He grabbed her and pulled her back. Together they went tumbling down the slope of thick tendrils until they were shielded from the pulse, the beat of the thing.

"What is this thing? What's it for?" Jansen asked. She had to hear it said out loud, the thing she already knew. She turned around and looked for Rao. In the fading light of the flare the astrobiologist's suit looked covered in blood.

Behind and above them, over the sheltering bulwark of the giant tendrils, another flare of lightning erupted across the structure's surface, and Jansen ducked involuntarily as the air crackled and buzzed.

"I think it's—I think it's exactly what it looks like," Rao said.

Jansen couldn't see her face through her polycarbonate faceplate. The last flickers of red light were dancing there, glinting and guttering out.

"I think this is...a heart."

GENERAL DANVERS KALITZAKIS, UNITED STATES SPACE FORCE: Back on Earth—that got our attention.

The three of them hurried back down the slope, away from the throbbing thing. Hawkins didn't let them stop until they were back down on the surface of the island, on the rubbery soil. They dropped to the ground in the shelter of one of the biggest tendrils, where he was protected a little from the pulsing air that made it impossible to think. He needed to think. He needed answers. He grabbed Rao's arm and turned her to face him. "What do you mean, a heart?"

Rao pulled her arm out of his grasp. "It's surrounded by huge tendrils—like the big veins and arteries around our hearts. We can feel it pulsing—"

"What are you saying?" Jansen interrupted feverishly.

Rao swallowed. This wasn't something you said lightly, not if you were an astrobiologist with a reputation to consider. "Look, you would need to do a lot of experiments, collect a lot of data to even think about proposing this, back in my lab. Just saying it out loud, people would laugh at you. Not so much because it seems impossible but because you haven't done the basic work to prove it *could* be possible. So when I say it's just a theory, that's a wild overstatement. This is an idea. A hunch."

She made the word sound like a profanity.

"Tell me anyway," Hawkins said.

Rao threw her arms up in the air. "2I is alive."

"Alive?"

Jansen took a step toward her. "You're saying this ship is...it's biomechanical. All the stuff we've seen, yeah, the bubble mounds and the hand-trees and...and everything. It's not made from metal and circuitry. It's grown. Grown in a vat somewhere. Right?"

"No," Rao said. "That's not it. I'm saying 2I, itself, is one giant organism. This isn't a starship. It's a...a living thing. An animal."

"Horseshit," Hawkins said.

"Hear her out," Jansen protested. "We brought her here for a reason."

"The big clue was the tendrils. Jansen, you saw them attack Stevens, because that's what you were primed to see—what we all thought was going to happen. We saw the tentacles of some wild animal trying to devour our—our friend. But it makes so much more sense if you see them a different way. If you actually look at them...because they look exactly like veins and arteries, just enormously larger than we're used to. They weren't growing to catch Stevens, they were growing because this thing needs a circulatory system. It's simple vascularization. You see it in any growing organism, the blood vessels grow first. Just like if you were going to build a city the first thing you would do is put down the roads and the power lines."

"This is a starship. It was built by somebody," he insisted. She was asking him to make a huge perceptual shift, to rethink everything he knew about 2I. Even if she was right, he needed time to catch up. To process what this meant. "I can't explain why we haven't seen the crew. But there has to be a simpler explanation. Occam's razor says—"

Rao didn't let him finish. "I know! It sounds crazy! But try looking at it from the other direction. You said it yourself—if someone built this ship, where are they now? And why would they put so many resources into a project like this, then just abandon it? But if you look at 2I as an organism that has adapted to a very unusual environment—deep space—well, it starts to make sense. I've argued this through in my head a dozen times, looking for a more parsimonious explanation, but I keep coming back here."

Jansen turned in a slow circle. Staring at the tendrils that criss-crossed the ground around them. "Those are...veins? Arteries?"

"Both," Rao said. "I think. You can't draw perfect analogs between alien physiology and anything we have names for, but...they're a circulatory network. They definitely carry oxygen and water and probably nutrients. And I think they might serve as 2I's nerves, too."

"Or it's all just horseshit!" Hawkins roared. He rubbed his sore head. His glove caught on the bandage across his forehead. He tore it off and threw it away—he had stopped bleeding, and the thing was just annoying him.

"You know what your problem is, Rao?"

Rao reached to touch his head, but he knocked her arm away.

"You overthink things," he said. "You take them apart and... and by the time you're done, you don't know anything..."

"I'm a scientist," Rao told him. "My job is to think about things."

The woman just could not get the point. She was so lost up her own ass...her own mental ass...Hawkins shook his head. He would think of a better metaphor later. Right now—

"I need actual answers, Rao. I need a definitive answer I can act on. I swear to God, if you just shake your head at me..."

"This whole time," Rao said, "we've been looking for aliens. We never stopped to think that the alien was right in front of us. This," she said, gesturing at everything around them, "*is* the alien."

She turned and faced Jansen straight on.

"We're inside the alien right now."

Hawkins's head spun. He tried to make sense of what she was saying. He looked back up the slope, in the direction of the structure at its top.

If that was 2I's heart, if she was right, this could be exactly the thing they'd been looking for. Not a way to communicate with the aliens—Hawkins had always considered that a fantasy. No. A way to kill 2I. To stop it before it reached Earth. General Kalitzakis needed a target. If they could shoot a KV right through this thing, kill it in one stroke—

But then Rao had to go and ruin everything.

"That thing is its heart. One of them, anyway," she added.

Hawkins closed his eyes. Tried to stay calm.

"*One* of them?" he asked.

"An organism this big would never have just one heart—it's got too much surface area to supply with blood. It would need a whole network of pumps, just like a power grid needs electrical substations."

"How many?" Hawkins demanded.

"Dozens," Rao said. "Maybe fifty, a hundred?" She threw her hands up. "I have no idea. You keep asking me questions like I must know the answers. Like I've studied this thing for years and I'm an expert on it now. I've spent just as long as you have looking at this—"

Hawkins groaned in frustration, cutting her off. They'd been so close to finding a solution to the problem of 2I.

No, he thought. It couldn't that be easy.

"Hawkins," Rao said. "Hawkins!"

He looked up. How long had he been lost in thought?

"What?" he demanded.

"Where's Jansen?" Rao asked.

ROY MCALLISTER: On Earth, some of us scoffed at Dr. Rao's theory. Some found merit there. All of us in the control room agreed it had the potential to change everything. More specifically, it could mean we were doomed. If 2I was not, in fact, a starship, but instead an enormous animal, not the work of intelligent hands but of blind evolution—how could we possibly expect to communicate with it? How could we hope to turn it away from Earth? I wanted to do something, to put my best people on the question, to find some solution. Yet with no way to contact the astronauts—we could only watch, and hope they found an answer themselves.

Jansen worked her way around the crest of the island, as close to the heart as she dared to get. The pulse of the thing repelled her, pushed her away.

But Jansen couldn't stop climbing. She forced herself to keep going, alone, even though her leg was just a numb block of wood that wouldn't bend. Even when she had to grab on to the tendrils—the blood vessels—every few seconds as the next pulse came.

She knew that Hawkins thought she'd gone crazy. Because she would go to such elaborate lengths to search for the KSpace crew, to rescue them. He didn't understand.

When she'd been a younger woman she wanted to go to Mars. It had been all she cared about, all she dreamed of.

Then she'd grown up and instead her life had been about memorializing a dead astronaut. The guilt and sorrow she'd felt for Blaine Wilson's death had remade her. Changed her into someone else. For a long time she'd thought she could pay off that debt only by punishing herself, by wrecking her own life. Roy McAllister had changed that. He'd suggested to her something else, a new path. A way to make things right. This mission, coming to 2I—it was going to make her whole again.

Finding Foster and his crew was the price she needed to pay. The cost of getting her soul back.

She knew it wasn't that easy, of course. She understood there was no moral calculus, a life for a life . . . nothing worked that way. Life didn't work that way. But it was the best idea she had.

She had almost given up. She had started to think that Hawkins was right, that the KSpace team was dead. That her rescue attempt was a foolish debacle that had accomplished nothing more than getting Stevens killed.

But now—they'd seen Channarong, if only secondhand on a memory stick. They knew she was still alive in here. Which meant there was a chance that the others were alive, as well. That she could find them.

She'd had the clue she needed to get this far. Foster had announced he was heading here, to the heart. There had to be some sign of him here, some indication of where he'd gone next.

She kept her eyes peeled for any trace of orange, any sign of a little triangular flag. She didn't need another memory stick with a message on it. She didn't need much of a sign at all. Just one of those flags. Just a dead glow stick lying on the ground. Anything.

When the time came, when she had made two circuits of the heart and turned up nothing at all, she had to face the inevitable conclusion. If KSpace had been here, if they'd even made it this far, they'd left no evidence behind. Or maybe—the interior of 2I had changed so fast, maybe the little orange flag had been swallowed up as the dome of the island rose from the melting ice.

There was nothing to find.

She sat down hard on a thick tendril. She could feel it pulse under her, feel its life surge through it. She wanted very much to weep.

Channarong was alive. They'd all seen the message she left, the cryptic warning. She had to be close by. Why hadn't she stuck around to talk to them? Why hadn't she greeted them with open arms, the team that had come in here to save her?

Why had the KSpace team never responded to her radio calls?

It made no sense. It made no damned sense at all.

She stared out into the dark from the top of the island. She stared out into the infinite darkness of 2I. She'd had a plan. She'd had a plan, and it had failed.

She had to keep trying. She had to do something.

She reached up and worked the controls of her suit radio. She set it to transmit with as much power as it could muster.

"KSpace, this is Jansen, of *Orion*," she said. "Foster. Channarong. Holmes. Come in, please. Come in, guys."

She switched her radio to receive. For a while she just listened to the clicking beat of 2I's wings. Above her lightning swept across the surface of the heart, and her headphones spit hateful noises into her ears, deafening her. She slapped at her controls, setting them to transmit again.

"KSpace," she called. "Come in. This is *Orion*. You want us to leave. Just tell me why. Give me something. KSpace? You must have heard me by now. You must have..."

Her voice broke. Why was she doing this? It was hopeless.

She switched the radio to receive. Then she turned up the gain, hoping to catch some faint whisper of a call. Words, human voices, on the wind.

Nothing. Silence. And then—

"Shit!" she howled, as lightning hit the heart again, and the noise burst through her ears like a spike shoved right through her brain.

She opened up a virtual screen and looked at the code that ran her radio system. They had designed a destructive interference signal to help weed out the sound of 2I's wings. Maybe she could silence the lightning strokes as well. She looked at a graph of all the waveforms her radio had received in the last few seconds and started tapping in the code—

And saw something she hadn't expected. Among the wild scratchy frequency spread of the electrical discharges, hidden in the carrier wave of 2I's wings, there was a signal. A single unmodulated pulse that showed up every sixty seconds. Exactly every sixty seconds, at 121.5 megahertz. Well, there were plenty of stray signals all over the spectrum, beeps and blips that could mean anything. And this one was a very faint signal, too weak for her to have heard it amid all the noise. It stuck out to her, though. This particular signal was cleaner than the random sounds, more precise. She scrolled back through her radio's log and found it in exactly the same place. Every sixty seconds for the last sixteen hours.

121.5 megahertz. The number sounded familiar. She knew she'd seen it before, something that broadcast at 121.5 megahertz—

In a second she was on her feet, hurtling down the slope to where the others were.

They had to see this.

"We wait for her to come back," Hawkins said. He refused to go searching for Jansen in the dark.

Rao looked up the slope, worried. She'd heard Jansen calling out to KSpace over the radio, but then...nothing. She had tried calling Jansen herself, to tell her to come back and join them, but there had been no reply. If Jansen had heard her and was on her way, she was taking a long time with it. If Jansen fell and broke her leg in the dark—if she wandered into some fatal trap, some unknown horror of 2I's interior—but Hawkins just waved away her concerns.

"She's too smart to go too far on her own. And we need to make a plan," he said.

He opened up ARCS's map in AR and shared it with Rao's devices. A grainy, black-and-white image that—now she had started truly believing in her hypothesis—looked altogether too much like an X-ray or an MRI scan.

"What about this, here?" he asked, pointing at a large spiky shadow on the map, an area on the far side of the drum from where they stood. "What does this part do?"

"I *don't know*," she said, as she had a dozen times already.

"Then what about this long structure here, do you see the way it connects one of the domes to the arch scaffolding?" he asked, his hand deep inside the map. It looked as if he were a surgeon rummaging around inside a body cavity.

"I keep telling you—my theory isn't descriptive. There's no reason to think that any of these structures are analogous to organs in terrestrial organisms. 2I evolved in an environment so different from Earth—it would be beyond belief if it had all the same organs and tissues we do." She took a deep breath. "I can't tell you how any of this works. It would take years of study just to understand the gross anatomy. I would need to dissect 2I to even begin to get how it fits together. And it's a little big to get at with a scalpel and a pair of forceps!"

She walked away from him and his map, her fingers laced behind the back of her helmet. She'd been worried about telling the others her theory, for exactly this reason. Hawkins didn't want vague hypotheses, he wanted practical advice. He wanted a local guide.

She looked up the slope again. She was sure Jansen had gone back up there, back to the heart. It was dangerous up there.

He wasn't done with her, though. "I need your help, Rao," he said. "Come look at this map. We have to make sense of it."

She shook her head.

"I thought," he said, "that you were committed to this mission."

She grimaced behind her faceplate.

"I thought you were focused on the job NASA gave you. I thought you would try a little harder than this before you gave up."

She bit her lip and tried not to listen. Tried to ignore his blatant attempt at manipulation. Even though her cheeks were burning and her hands had started to shake.

She knew exactly what he would say next. He would tell her he'd thought she believed in the cause that Stevens had given his life for. The bastard was going to say that. And then she would have two choices. She could run over and punch him in the jaw—in which case he would win, because he would have gotten a rise out of her. Or—

She walked over to the map. Expanded it with a gesture and zoomed in. "Ask me the question you really want answered," she said.

Hawkins nodded. "What's this?"

He pointed at one end of the spindle. The place where the drum narrowed down to a point, the far end from where they'd come in by the airlock. The map was hard to read there, full of shadows and strange textures. She could make out one structure, though. The final quarter of the spindle's length, nearly twenty kilometers long, was where the arch scaffolding grew the thickest. It rose from the floor of the drum in great flying buttresses that supported a structure like a cage, bars of the arch material forming an ellipsoid enclosure.

Something shifted behind her eyes and she realized—

"That looks like a rib cage," she said.

She'd been calling the concrete-like structures "arches" this whole time. She knew better. She was certain they were exactly what they appeared to be—bones.

"Assuming your theory is true, that 2I is just one big animal." He held up one hand to suggest that he was speaking only hypothetically, but she could see from his face that he believed her. That he'd accepted her theory. She wished she felt that strongly about it herself.

"Assuming that's a rib cage, or something. What's inside it?"

Hawkins asked. As much as he expanded the map, as many times as he zoomed in, the interior of the cage was nothing but vague shapes and deep, unexplored shadows. "We know the heart isn't in there. The heart—hearts, sorry—are spread all over the place. So—are 2I's lungs inside that cage?"

Rao considered this. 2I had to have some kind of respiratory system. There had to be organs for purifying and pumping air around the drum, but those would need to be distributed just like the hearts, so they wouldn't be inside the cage.

"Liver? Kidneys? Glands?"

"Imagine you're natural selection, rewarding evolving traits in a life-form with reproductive success," she said.

"What?"

"I'm just thinking out loud." She looked at his uncomprehending face and sighed in frustration. "OK, put it another way. You're God and you're designing an animal. You have all these different organs you need to put inside its body, and some are more important than others. The really important ones get encased in bone, for protection. I mean, 2I already has its outer hull and then the shell of the drum to serve as two exoskeletons, which are clearly enough to protect the heart and lungs. So what's so important that it needs a whole other layer of armor? What can't your animal live without?"

Hawkins's face went very serious.

"A brain," he said.

She shrugged. "You wanted my best guess. Yeah."

"That's its brain in there," Hawkins said. He reached into the map with both hands and expanded and expanded it until the shadowy contents of the bony cage hovered in front of him, big as his head. It almost looked as if he were going to take a bite out of the AR image.

"Gotcha, you bastard," he said.

Jansen came down the hill limping, dragging her bad leg. The pain didn't bother her, not anymore. She could hear the beacon.

Every sixty seconds it sounded inside her helmet. A plaintive chime. She just had to triangulate the signal, and then she would know where they had to go next.

When she spotted the lights of the others, though, it looked as if they were already moving on without her, and for a moment she panicked, thinking they had left her behind. Hawkins was walking down the hill, using a long, loping stride to stay balanced on the rubbery ground. His lights bounced in front of him from the helmet dangling at his waist. Rao was just picking up some of their equipment—clearly getting ready to follow him. "He's in a hurry," she said, as Jansen came up even with her. "He saw your light coming and figured it was time to move."

"But he doesn't know where we're going," Jansen said. "I need to triangulate. Hawkins! Give me a second!"

"I'll walk slow so you can catch up," he called back over his shoulder. He didn't even turn his head to look at her.

"I found something," Jansen shouted, running after him as fast as she could. Half the time she stumbled and had to catch herself with her hands. "I found something!"

"We have a new target destination," he told her. "While you were busy chasing ghosts, Dr. Rao actually figured something out that can help with our mission."

"No," Jansen said. "Not ghosts. The others are still alive. They're alive and they need our help."

"Channarong seemed to be doing just fine. Fine enough to spy on us."

She grabbed his arm and he finally stopped and turned to look at her. It wasn't a friendly look. She felt as if she were locking eyes with an angry dog, so much she could almost hear the growl forming in the back of his throat.

"I'm not going to remind you again who's in charge," he told her.

Jansen didn't bother trying to placate him. She activated an external speaker on the front of her suit and played the beacon for him. "Do you hear that? Do you know what that is?"

"2I makes all kinds of sounds," he told her.

"No. That's a human sound," she said. "It plays every sixty

seconds at 121.5 megahertz. 121.5—you're in the military, you must know what that frequency means."

His eyes narrowed. He knew. He wasn't going to give her an inch, though.

"Wait," Rao said, hurrying up. "You found a radio source that repeats every sixty seconds?"

"Exactly every sixty seconds," Jansen said, nodding.

"Maybe," Hawkins said, "there's something inside 2I that releases an electrical discharge every so often. Maybe you're just picking up the sound of the lightning we saw on the heart back there."

Jansen shook her head. He couldn't deny this.

"It would be one serious coincidence if something in here was on a sixty-second cycle," Rao said, shaking her head. "Exactly one minute? A minute is a human unit of measure. You think some animal from a distant star uses minutes?"

"And you know that frequency. It's a distress call."

She could see from his face he wanted to deny it, but he couldn't. 121.5 megahertz was the exact frequency used by civilian aircraft to indicate an emergency. NASA and the military used a harmonic frequency, 243 megahertz. The signal could only be coming from KSpace equipment.

"You picked up this signal from the top of the island?" Rao asked. "We haven't heard it before."

"It's a low-power transponder signal," Jansen said. "We weren't close enough to hear it before. Hawkins! Listen to me—we're required by law to provide whatever assistance we can when someone sends that signal."

He scowled, but she had him, and they both knew it.

After a moment he opened ARCS's map and pointed at the far end of the spindle. "That's where we're headed. Where's your goddamned signal?"

She took a second to triangulate the location. The signal was stronger down here, meaning she was closer to it. That gave her two points of reference. By comparing the signal strengths of the two points she could calculate the source.

It wasn't far—just down the slope, on the far side of the island from where they'd washed up. "Here." She touched the map, and a red dot appeared, marking the location of the transponder. "Hawkins—it's on the way to your destination."

She was pleading. Jansen had never been good at begging, but if it meant saving the life of a KSpace astronaut—she would beg.

"It's not the most direct route," he grumbled. But eventually he shrugged. "Come on. We'll check it out on the way."

WINDSOR HAWKINS: I knew there was no point to Jansen's quest. It was just a waste of time. But she was already having trouble walking, and I couldn't let her slow us down. If it kept her motivated, I would let her have her little hero fantasy.

TELEMETRY ANOMALY

He wants to find the brain?" Jansen asked as they headed down the slope. "Maybe that's good. Maybe... maybe if we're going to communicate with 2I, that's where we need to go."

Rao watched the older woman carefully as they walked. It looked as if Jansen was in pain, but she kept pushing past it. Admirable, certainly, but Rao knew you couldn't do that forever. Endorphins and resolve lasted only so long. If she could convince Hawkins to stop and let them take a rest—but she knew that wasn't going to happen. He was as obsessed as Jansen was, in his own way.

"Once we find the KSpace people, you mean," Rao said, picking up the thread of the conversation.

"You think those two goals are mutually exclusive?" Jansen asked. "We know Channarong, at least, is still alive. She's been in here the whole time. She must have watched all of this grow." She waved one hand feebly to indicate the island, the drum, everything around them. "At the very least, she can tell us how KSpace tried to communicate with 2I, and why it worked or didn't work. We can eliminate some things."

It was getting to be an old argument. Rao wondered when the justifications would fall away. They were all running on empty—none of them had eaten any solid food for more than a day, and the pace Hawkins had set for them was brutal. Neither of the others was healthy. Jansen had her bad knee, while he was ignoring what looked like a pretty significant concussion.

As for herself—

She was fine. Physically. Mentally, she was distracted. Disoriented. 2I's darkness and its strangeness were getting to her. And she had a lot on her mind.

She had put her grief for Stevens in a little box. Tied a bow around it and stuck it in the back of a closet. She'd started thinking of it as a present, a reward. *When we're done here*, she thought, *I'll take out those feelings and examine them. Turn them over in my hands like old photographs, and then I'll finally see them, I'll finally let myself think about what he and I could have had. What we should have had.*

In some fucked-up way she was looking forward to it. Because experiencing that grief would be getting to be with him, in a way. In the only way she had left. And because it would mean the fear was over. The fear she was carrying on her back, her fear of 2I. What it was and what it meant.

It was headed toward Earth. Once she'd harbored a little dream, a dream that it was going to go into orbit around Earth and then a hatch would open on its side and some aliens would step out. They would look weird, not humanoid at all, but not terrifying, either. They wouldn't speak English, not at first, but they would learn. And they would tell her what it was like, out there. Out between the stars.

2I was the answer to that fantasy.

Because it didn't fit. It didn't fit her preconceived notions of what an alien was, and that was the lesson it wanted to teach her. Out there, out in the deeps of space—things aren't the way they are on Earth. It's dark, and cold, and you do what you must to survive. That's all— there's no room for higher aspirations. No self-actualization out in the nebulae. No sharing of ideas, no warm friendship. Nothing to say.

She'd spent her entire career looking for this, for contact, and now she had it and it was a dark reflection of her dreams, it was the harsh laughter of the void.

"Rao!"

And yet she couldn't bring herself to hate 2I. It was an animal, driven by natural urges. It was alive, as she was, if on a different scale. You didn't hate a rabid dog, you didn't hate the lions even if you feared them. You respected them, kept your distance.

Of course, distance was no longer an option…

"Rao!"

She looked up. Looked around. Her stomach gave a sickening lurch as she realized she couldn't see the others. Just her own lights spearing off into the dark, the undifferentiated surface of the island…

"Rao," Jansen said, limping out of the shadows. Hawkins came running up behind her. "Rao, you were walking the wrong way."

"I… was?"

"You were right behind me, then suddenly you turned and walked off. I wasn't sure where you were going."

"I guess I was just following my lights," Rao said. Shame made her cheeks hot, made her turn her face away from Jansen.

Hawkins grunted in impatience. "We need to keep moving," he insisted.

Rao nodded and they got walking again, this time with Jansen slightly behind her. Watching her, no doubt.

"I'm so sorry," Rao said.

Jansen lifted her hands in resignation. "It's OK. We just need to focus, right? We need to stay on track."

"Right," Rao said. "Right."

"I asked you a question, though—did you hear me?"

Rao hadn't, and that scared her. She'd been so sunk in her own thoughts she had missed it altogether. "What—what was it?" she asked.

"I wondered if you'd given any thought to how we're going to talk to the brain, assuming we even find it up there."

"Communication," Rao said, "is about more than just talking. Animals communicate in all kinds of ways—threat displays, coloration, pheromones. Trees talk to each other, did you know that? Trees talk by pumping chemicals into the soil. Other trees absorb those chemicals through their roots, and they get the message, which is typically, *I'm growing here, don't bother me.*"

Jansen laughed. It was a welcome sound in the dark. It cut through some of the tension, the embarrassment she'd felt about wandering off.

"Communication, huh." Rao smiled and imagined the centuries-long battles that colonies of sea anemones fought on the bottom of the ocean. She considered the chemical trails ants lay down, and the dances of honeybees. Then she frowned, because she realized she was thinking of organisms that lived on roughly the same scale as human beings. 2I was something completely different.

"It's so big. It's so big—that's why it never responded to our signals, our best efforts to get its attention. Compared to 2I, we're not peers. We're like microbes. The difference in size is like the difference between you and the bacteria that live in your gut. Can you imagine having a conversation with bacteria?"

"There has to be a way, though. How are we going to talk to 2I?" Jansen asked.

"The same way bacteria always talk to their hosts," Rao said. She tilted her head in the direction of Hawkins, walking ten paces ahead of them. "First—they try to kill each other."

A hand touched Hawkins's arm and he jerked sideways, away from the touch. His lips pulled back from his teeth as he glared at Rao, who had come up behind him with no warning. He forced himself to calm down.

"I just wanted to see how you're doing," the young woman said. "We're all getting a little fuzzy. You know? You had a pretty bad thump on the head, and I want to make sure—"

"You don't need to talk to me like I'm a child. I've got a nasty headache, but that's it," he told her. He had no time for this. "No blurred vision. No nausea."

"There's no food in your system. Nausea might not feel like you need to throw up, it could feel more like cramps. And there are other symptoms, too, less physical symptoms like mood swings or personality changes or—"

"I said I'm fine," he told her.

She took a step back. As if she was afraid of him. Him. He was the only thing standing between Earth and 2I, and he scared her? It was ridiculous. "It looks like Jansen needs more help than I do. If she gets to a point she can't walk—"

He stopped because he'd heard something. A rustling sound.

Not too close, but it was big, a big sound. "What was that?" he demanded.

She stared at him.

"You didn't hear it?" he asked. She shook her head and he turned away from her, swinging his lights over the ground ahead. Nothing. Maybe she hadn't heard it because she still had her helmet on. Or maybe—

His light caught something, and his whole body went rigid. He reached for the pocket of his suit, the pocket he always kept zipped tightly shut. But whatever he'd seen, it didn't move.

He moved toward it, very carefully. It looked like a tree, he thought, and then he adjusted his light to move upward. He saw a central trunk, no thicker than his thigh, and then a branching canopy of what looked like human arms splitting off from that trunk. A hand-tree, like the ones they'd seen from the ice floe raft, though much smaller. It was maybe ten meters high, at most.

Behind it there was another one. And then more. He played his light back and forth and saw hundreds of them, maybe thousands, blocking their path. A whole forest.

He studied the branches carefully. On careful inspection they didn't look as much like human arms as he'd thought before. The branches had too many joints, which bent in every possible direction. The hands, though—

He thought of ARCS, with its three hands that were sculpted to look as human as possible. A perversion of the human form. The things on the ends of the branches of the hand-trees were much larger than human hands, but the resemblance couldn't be denied.

Each hand had four fingers, long and tapering and jointed exactly the way human hands had knuckles. There were no nails at the ends of the fingertips, but the proportions of those digits were uncanny. It was impossible to think of anything but human fingers.

"Convergent evolution," Rao whispered. "It doesn't mean anything. Those...those trees evolved to serve a certain purpose. Our hands evolved for a purpose, too, but not necessarily the same one. It's just a coincidence they look the same."

Hawkins stared at her. He didn't remember asking. He didn't remember saying anything, not out loud. Had he—was he—

There were things he had to make sure he didn't say out loud. Things he couldn't let the others hear. He needed to be more careful.

As he watched, one of the hands moved. Rao literally jumped backward. The hand twitched and shook, and then it curled up into a narrow fist, the fingers turning pale as they tightened. Over the course of maybe five seconds, the fist tightened, and tightened, until he thought the fingers might snap. Then they released and stretched out again, splaying outward away from each other.

"What the hell are these things?" he demanded.

Rao didn't answer until he turned and looked at her directly.

"No clue," she said.

"Are they dangerous? Do we need to find a way around, or can we walk beneath them?" he asked.

She opened her mouth as if to answer, but then she just shrugged.

Jansen finally caught up with them, limping up to where they stood. She pointed her single light deep into the forest. "The distress signal is coming from in there," she said. Then she started moving again, walking right between two of the trees.

Hawkins watched, fully expecting the branches to dip, those big hands to snatch her up and haul her into the sky. He considered how he would react to that.

Fortunately, he didn't have to find out. The hand-trees didn't react to Jansen's presence at all.

Jansen's light hit a tree trunk and made it glow. The trunks were made of some slightly translucent material, as white as mushroom flesh. It was fibrous, and in some places it stuck out like rough, uncombed hair. She turned to dodge around the trunk and three more appeared in her light. The farther in she got, the closer together the hand-trees were. She was worried that she would eventually come to a place where she would have to turn sideways to squeeze between them. Maybe she would have to push her way through—maybe she would have to touch them.

It never occurred to her to turn back.

Her leg didn't hurt anymore. She was only peripherally aware of its existence. She could ask Rao what that meant, except then she might find out, and it could be bad news. Better, maybe, to remain in ignorance. At least until they got back to *Orion*.

She hurried on as fast as she could, though the ground was uneven and kept trying to trip her up. Tendrils ran thick across the forest floor, all of them rooted fast to the ground. She kept getting the tips of her boots caught in their coils. She tried lifting her feet higher, but her bad leg kept failing to obey her. She wasn't so much walking as stumbling. If she slowed down, maybe. But—no. Not when she was so close.

She heard a rustling sound above her, and she held her breath. Slowly she lifted her light, pointing it up into the canopy above her. Up there the hands curled and uncurled. Slowly. Never very many of them at a time. She watched one of them reach over and grab a branch of another tree. The long fingers grasped the wrist— there really was no other word for it—of the branch, then closed up, curling around the pale joint. The hand held for a moment, then released, swinging back to its original position.

A few seconds later the branch that had been grasped repeated the gesture. Reaching out in turn to a third tree and grabbing some protruding fingers there. Slowly, quietly, compressing them. Then letting go.

Were they...passing along a signal, maybe? Exchanging chemicals? Rao had said even she didn't know. It wasn't a mystery Jansen was going to solve.

She had one of her own to work out.

Listening to the distress beacon had driven her crazy as she hurried down the slope and into the forest. She'd eventually switched it off, then had her devices display it as a visual cue. Once every sixty seconds, when her suit detected the beacon's pulse, it would show her the sound as a series of ghostly visual waves that swept across the polycarbonate of her faceplate. The waves coalesced on a spot ahead of her, slightly to her left. She turned and followed them, passing easily between two rows of trees, almost as if she were entering a tunnel that would lead her to the source of the beacon.

She switched on her radio and called out, saying she was coming. Whatever was sending the beacon didn't reply.

Above her the hands reached for each other. Grasped each other, and then released. If she kept her head down, she couldn't see them moving. It was easier that way.

The waves on her faceplate were brighter now, closer together. That meant she was almost on top of the beacon. She shouted through her faceplate, calling out to anyone who could hear her. If they would give her some sign—

Something loose slipped out from under her foot, and she stumbled forward, out of control. "Shit," she cursed, as her boot got wedged in a nest of tendrils. She started to totter forward and threw her arms out to compensate. At first she thought she was going to be fine, that she could stop herself, but then her backpack slid forward onto her shoulder, throwing off her center of gravity. Feeling as if she were underwater, or maybe in slow motion, she realized she was going to fall flat on her face. Unconsciously her arms went out to grab anything that might stop her from collapsing.

The only thing that met that criterion was the trunk of the hand-tree right in front of her. Her arms wrapped around it as she dropped to her knees.

She felt the fleshy trunk writhing under her grasp, felt it crawl away from her. She looked up and watched in horror as every branch of the tree started moving at once, all of them reaching out in different directions. The hands grasped the wrists of other trees, grasped and squeezed and then released, twisted around to grab other branches. The pattern rippled outward, away from her, spreading from tree to tree.

She held her breath. Uncertain of what she'd just done.

For a long time she just sat there, watching the branches writhe, the hands grasp and then release. Grasp and then release. It looked as if a strong gust of wind had passed through the canopy, perhaps. Or like the church meetings she remembered from her youth, when all the congregants turned to shake the hands of their neighbors.

Eventually she let herself breathe again.

She was sitting on a nexus where a bunch of tendrils came together, rising up from the forest floor in a humped mass like a natural seat. Her bad leg was stretched out before her as far as it would go. Her other was curled up beneath her. She looked around, her single suit light slowly drifting across the forest floor. She wasn't even thinking, wasn't processing what she saw. She was just letting her heart rate come down, letting herself breathe easier. She'd had a little scare, but nothing had happened. Nothing was wrong, she was just taking a moment.

That was when her light fell on something yellowish and small, roughly cylindrical. It lay amid the tendrils as if it had fallen out of someone's pocket. It took her a second to realize that when she'd tripped it was because she had stepped on this—this small parchment-colored object. She'd seen nothing else like it in the forest. There were no leaves on the ground, no undergrowth—this was the cleanest forest floor she'd ever seen, and yet there it was, this short, round thing, slightly narrower in its middle, slightly knobby at either end.

A thing that looked, now that she gave it some actual thought and consideration, exactly like a human finger bone.

"Don't touch anything," Hawkins said, putting one arm out in front of Rao. She took a step back.

"I . . . wasn't going to," she said.

He didn't reply. He stalked a few paces forward, looked around. Lifted his helmet from his waist and manually panned his light across the trunks of the trees. "Of all the dumbfuck ideas your buddy Jansen has had—man. I don't like this."

Rao couldn't help but agree.

The forest was almost silent, except for the occasional rustling sound from overhead. Was that what Hawkins had heard before? She watched the hands curl and uncurl and shivered. When she'd seen the heart, she'd known exactly what she was looking at. Oh, she couldn't have proved it, and as a scientist she was always careful about jumping to conclusions, but there'd really been no doubt in her mind. It was a heart. Just like every heart she'd cut out of a dead body in med school.

Just like the heart of the fetal pig she'd dissected in high school biology. Hearts didn't scare her. These hand-trees, though—she had no idea what they were, what they were for. She felt that unknowing almost as a physical pain, a soreness in her mind she couldn't soothe.

Hawkins lifted his feet high as he made his way deeper into the trees. "Watch out," he said, "the ground here is crawling with tendrils."

She wished he hadn't used that word, *crawling*. The tendrils were immobile. She had seen them move, seen how fast they could move, when she operated on Stevens. The only thing keeping her from absolute panic was the certainty that these tendrils were stuck fast.

She stepped very carefully on a twisted mass of them. Lifted her other foot and swung it forward to take another step. Hawkins was well ahead of her, and she wanted to hurry to catch up. She wanted very badly not to be alone in the forest, alone with—

"Nooooo…"

It was a long, moaning wail of a sound. It had to be Jansen. Rao was certain it had to be Jansen making that noise. If it was something else, she knew she couldn't bear it. She would turn around and run back out of the forest, back to open ground.

"No…please…"

Hawkins swung around and looked at her. Then he started running forward, between the tree trunks, as fast as he could. Rao called out for him to wait, to let her catch up, but soon she needed all her breath as she raced after him, trying very hard just to keep his back in view, inside the cone of her lights. Trunks flashed past her on either side, pale, fibrous shapes that flared in her light and then immediately disappeared into the dark again. She tried to keep an eye on her footing, but it was all she could do to keep moving, to keep running.

Then Hawkins stopped, so suddenly that she nearly collided with him. He bent down and picked up something he'd found on the forest floor.

Rao gasped when he brought it up into his light. *Proximal phalanx*, she thought, flashing back to anatomy class. Just as when she'd seen the heart, she knew, instantly, what she was looking at.

Except—this wasn't part of 2I. It wasn't an alien phalanx.

Hawkins lifted his head, then moved forward, not rising from his crouch. He picked up another bone. This one was broken, one end cracked and jagged.

Ulna.

"What...what..." She couldn't stop herself. "Why? Those are—they're—" She couldn't form a coherent thought. She was shaking inside her suit, her eyes barely focusing on what she saw.

Together they moved forward and found a *clavicle*. And then most of a *scapula*. There was no question in her mind it was a human shoulder bone. It looked as if it had been stripped clean and bleached, as if it had been prepared so it could be articulated with the other bones, hung up as a model of a human skeleton.

Something crunched under her boot. She jumped back and saw she'd stepped on a *mandible*. Unlike the others it wasn't loose on the ground. Tendrils had wrapped around the jawbone, snaked between missing teeth. She grabbed it and tried to pull it free, some deep part of her horribly offended by the way the tendrils had snagged this piece of a human being.

"Leave it," Hawkins said. He gestured with two fingers for her to move up, to join him. He put a hand on her arm. Scared as she was, she barely felt it.

Up ahead, just a few meters away, Jansen lay curled on the ground, shaking. Rao could hear her sobbing. Jansen had a long, straight bone—a *femur*—in her arms, and she was clutching it to herself.

Rao looked up and saw a splash of orange across the white forest. It took her a second to actually see what was there, to process it.

A bright-orange space suit, slumped against the trunk of a hand-tree. Part of a bright-orange space suit, with a pattern of hexagons painted on the helmet and down one sleeve. The other sleeve was missing, as well as most of the leg on that side. The faceplate of the helmet was smashed, and only jagged, triangular shards of the polycarbonate remained. Nestled in those shards was a broken piece of a *cranium*—of a human skull.

Tendrils snaked across the chest of the suit, across the remaining leg. They sprouted from inside the helmet and erupted from the missing shoulder, whole tangled knots of them, some as thick as fingers, some so thin they looked almost like hairs. They rose from the torn parts of the suit and wove upward around the trunk of the hand-tree, disappearing into its translucent flesh.

Rao drew in a very difficult breath. Then let out a choked little scream. She was too terrified to make a bigger sound, though she didn't know if she was scared something out in the forest might hear her, or if she was just petrified by the thought of intruding on Jansen's grief. She pushed past Hawkins and knelt down beside Jansen, her arms around the older woman's helmet, trying to comfort her, to give her something.

"No...," Jansen wailed.

Hawkins moved to stand over the body, pointing his lights down at the orange parts of the suit. The light was intense, the sudden burst of color making Rao want to look away.

"It's Holmes," Hawkins rasped. He pointed at where the astronaut's name had been painted on the front of his chest panel. "Taryn Holmes." As if unwilling to actually touch what lay before him, he used his foot to push some broken shards of helmet polycarbonate away from the exposed half of the skull. "Looks like the tendrils removed the flesh," he said. Then he added, more quietly, "Why do you suppose they did that?"

Jansen's body curled in on itself at the sound of his words.

A flash of rage split Rao's skull right down the middle. She *hated* Hawkins in that moment.

"Asshole," she spit. "Shut up! This isn't the time."

Hawkins looked straight back at her. Not flinching at all. He gave her the slightest of frowns, then he turned and walked away, between two tree trunks. Maybe he was giving them space. Maybe he was just done with them.

Except—of course—he couldn't leave it at that. He turned and spoke to Jansen over his shoulder, not even looking at her.

"I know this isn't what you wanted to find. I'm sorry. But it means one less thing to worry about. We can focus on finding the brain now, and finishing our mission."

PROXIMITY OPERATIONS

VIDEO FILE TRANSCRIPT (4)

[The video shows only flashes of motion and, occasionally, flares of light. The voice of Taryn Holmes is very faint and indistinct, and the accuracy of the transcript cannot be guaranteed. The voices of Willem Foster and Sandra Channarong are much more distinct.]

Taryn Holmes: No light. I can't see. Can't [indecipherable]. I don't have any eyes.

Willem Foster: Hold him down. Get his arm—

Sandra Channarong: Cut those things off him! Cut them! They're killing him!

Foster: I'm trying. I'm trying! Just—just—

Holmes: I'm so hungry. I'm—it was cold, it's [indecipherable] been cold. So cold and empty and so, so long. Close now, though. Almost [indecipherable].

Foster: What did he just say? Did you hear that?

Channarong: He's dying! Who cares what he—just help him!

Foster: I'm trying. But did you hear—

Holmes: It's almost over. It's [indecipherable]. It's warm here, near the sun. Good to be warm. Good to be [indecipherable].

The memory stick had been hung on a nearby hand-tree, from a loop of wire placed over one of its extruding fibers. It had been Rao who found it, but she'd just handed it over without a word.

Jansen played it as they walked. She played it over and over.

She thought she understood what had happened. She'd seen something similar, after all. She had watched Stevens get caught in a web of tendrils, watched him struggle to break free. She thought Taryn Holmes must have been trapped the same way—except somehow, even with Foster and Channarong both working to free him, he hadn't been able to get loose.

Looking at the time stamp on the video clip, she saw that Taryn Holmes had probably died while she was struggling up the slope toward the airlock, struggling to get Stevens back to safety.

If Stevens hadn't been attacked—if KSpace had just responded to her radio calls—

"Keep moving," Hawkins said. He was up ahead of her, maybe twelve meters away. She'd been dragging her leg along as she watched the clip. Again. "We need to make better time. You need to pick up the pace, Jansen—"

Rao said something, something conciliatory and quiet. Jansen didn't even hear the words. She had started the clip up again, the grainy, shaky video playing across the inside of her faceplate. "Get his arm," she heard Foster say. Again.

Something—something odd had happened. Foster had noticed something odd, something about Holmes's final words.

Jansen started the clip over, again. Trying to hear what Foster had heard.

The dragon on the shaved half of Charlotte Harriwell's head was rearing back, smoke jetting from its nostrils. It was ready to breathe fire.

The look on her face matched it pretty well, McAllister thought. As she plucked the device from the side of her nose and dropped it—along with a tiny purse—into the plastic bucket, he gave her what he hoped looked like a friendly wave. She didn't look up, just stepped through the white frame of the security MRI, lifting her hands above her head. A security guard beckoned for her to come forward, then handed her the basket.

"Thank you," she said. She pressed her device back onto her face. Then she turned to look at McAllister for the first time.

"Associate Administrator," she said. He doubted it was a good thing she was calling him by his full title. "I have a very long list of questions. Perhaps we can start with this—can you name a dollar value for the loss of a privately owned spacecraft? Because I assure you, NASA will be compensating KSpace for the full purchase price of *Wanderer*."

He thought of the convivial atmosphere of their last meeting, back at the Atlanta Hive. She had been all placid smiles and gentle tones back then.

He supposed that was before his team had wrecked her spaceship. He wished he had better news for her now. "Come this way, ma'am," he said. She raised an eyebrow at the old-fashioned honorific.

He took her to a special elevator at the back of the building. There were only two buttons on the panel inside. One read *Ground* and one read *Telescope*. McAllister picked the latter.

She seemed surprised when the elevator started to descend. "Exactly what kind of telescope do you build underground?" she asked.

"One that you want to shield from cosmic rays and surface vibrations," he said. "Ms. Harriwell, I need to inform you that what you're going to see is...it's sensitive."

"As in—it's likely to make me swoon?"

McAllister gave her a very small smile. He certainly hoped it wouldn't, though he wouldn't blame her. "As in, we have to ask you not to speak about what you see here with the public."

"On my honor," she said.

"I'm afraid I need a little more than that." He touched his device and sent her a nondisclosure form. She glanced over at him—clearly she'd received it—and then made an elaborate show of blinking one eye very slowly. The equivalent of a signature.

"Thank you," he said.

The elevator reached the bottom of the shaft—thirty meters below the soil of Pasadena—and let out into a small lobby, just large enough for the two of them. The floor moved slightly when

McAllister put his weight on it. "This chamber floats on a pool of very thick mineral oil," he explained. "Again, it's for the vibrations."

"Should we even be talking, then?" she asked. "If your telescope is so finicky?"

"That's unnecessary. The telescope itself is kept in a nearly complete vacuum." They passed through a door and out onto an enclosed catwalk. It looked out over a very large chamber, perfectly spherical. Lights came on and showed them the detectors—over ten thousand of them—mounted on the walls. Each detector was made from a crystal of cesium iodide so clear and pure it was nearly invisible, mounted inside a frame of copper. "These are coherent recoil detectors. We use them to track neutrinos emitted by black holes on the far side of the universe. Or, in this case, from inside 2I."

Harriwell's air of annoyance evaporated like drizzle on a hot summer sidewalk. "You're talking to your people. You can talk to them."

"The connection is strictly one-way. I can hear what they say, see what they see. I have no way to get a message to them."

"You brought me here because you—you've got news about Foster and his crew," she said. Her voice had grown very soft.

He thought of what to say. He considered a number of possibilities, from simply laying out the facts in a clinical fashion to trying to break the news to her easily. He failed to find anything that would cushion the shock.

Instead he simply touched his device and brought up an AR display in the open center of the sphere. The colors of the image lacked saturation, and even from a distance the individual pixels making up the image were clearly visible. All the same, the image spoke for itself. It showed Sally Jansen kneeling next to the remains of Taryn Holmes.

"I'm so very sorry," he said.

She pressed one knuckle against her lips. She said nothing.

"We felt you should see this. That you had a right to see it, regardless of national security concerns."

She nodded. She wasn't looking at him.

"I don't want to create false hope. We have...some indication that

Sandra Channarong may still be alive." He blanked the image in the display and queued up the video file Channarong had left for Jansen.

Before he could play it, though, she reached over and grabbed his arm.

"What about Foster?" she asked. "Tell me about Foster." She looked him straight in the eye. "Willem has a wife and two children in Alabama. I'd...very much like to know he's OK."

"There's no news there," he said, as gently as he could. "Though I assure you, Commander Hawkins and his crew are looking for him right now."

Harriwell broke eye contact. The dragon had tucked its head under its wing. "Please," she said. "Show me what you have on Sandra."

He opened the file called YOUNEEDTOLEAVE.mp7 and let it play.

"Over there," Hawkins said, pointing at what looked like a trail winding between the trees. It wasn't a trail, of course. The trees were spaced apart at random distances, and sometimes he thought he saw paths, but it was always just a place where two trees grew farther apart from each other than usual. Still, he looked for those gaps. Far better than the places where the trees were so close together you had to brush against the trunks. Every time that happened it set off a ripple of grasping hands up in the canopy. Anyone who was searching for them could just follow those ripples—they might as well be shooting off flares every time it happened.

He shook his head. Who was searching for them? Channarong? She'd had the chance to join them—or to kill them in their sleep—and she hadn't taken it. So why couldn't he shake the idea they weren't alone?

He was a rational man. He knew that his thinking was disordered, and when he had a chance to think, when the pounding in his head would recede a little, he could—by sheer force of will—take those thoughts and examine them, turn them over and see which of them were worth his time.

He had been cruel, he knew, back when they found Holmes's body. He should have given Jansen a chance to grieve. His feeling that they were running out of time was hardly irrational—every hour that passed meant 2I got closer to Earth—but surely he could have given her fifteen minutes.

Instead he had insisted they keep moving. He hadn't even let Rao do a postmortem on the bones.

It had been a mistake. He hoped it didn't cost them.

There was no telling how big the forest of hand-trees might be, how long it would take to cross to its far side, or even if it just ran all the way to the cage of bone near the far end of the ship. They'd fallen into a rhythm of carefully picking their way over the snarls of tendrils that made a maze of the forest floor. They weren't moving as fast as Hawkins would like, but even he had his physical limits. Not for the first time, he considered leaving the other two behind. Pressing on alone and letting them have their time to rest and think.

He knew he couldn't do that, though. He couldn't go on without them.

"Help her," he said.

Rao looked up.

"Let her lean on your shoulder. I'd do it, but I doubt she would let me touch her."

He'd meant it as a joke. Rao didn't laugh. Instead she turned around and went back to fetch Jansen, who had fallen behind again. He heard the two of them talking, a short, heated conversation he didn't need to pay attention to.

When they'd caught up with him, Jansen had her arm around Rao's shoulders and they were walking together. A little faster than Jansen had been walking before. Maybe.

The old woman couldn't even look at him. Her eyes were half-shut, and her face was dripping with sweat. She must be in agony, he thought, and spared her a little sympathy. He could still afford that.

Even while he was working out in his head how much faster they could move if they just left her behind.

"Have you seen this?" Rao asked.

He came back to himself with a start. "Sorry?" he said.

"Have you seen this—it's ARCS's activity log." She opened a window, and text scrolled across his face. He resisted the urge to swat it away like a pesky fly.

Instead he looked at what she was trying to show him. It took a second to find it, but yes, it was there. The robot's map had stopped updating.

"It might have crashed into something. Or maybe been eaten by hungry aliens," he said, making another half-hearted joke. "We didn't expect it to keep operating indefinitely."

She gave him the briefest of smiles. "We were hoping it would last longer than this, though. When it stopped responding, it was only about sixty percent done with its map. There could be all kinds of things ahead of us, hazards between us and the brain, and we won't know to expect them."

"We'll figure it out," he said. "We're smart people. You especially."

She tilted her head to the side. The closest thing she could do to shrugging while she was supporting Jansen's weight.

"We need to think about consumables, too," she said.

He grimaced but said nothing.

"Running our lights all the time—my batteries are down to about thirty-four percent charge. We have oxygen for another day, and water for longer than that, but we're going to run out of everything, eventually."

"Nothing we can do about that," he said.

Rao clearly didn't see it that way. "When we get to the brain, then what? We'll need to walk back. We need to consider that."

No, Hawkins thought. They really didn't. But of course, he couldn't say that. "Once we find the brain we'll be very close to the south pole airlock," he said. "It won't take long to get back to *Orion*."

Rao shook her head. "We don't actually know if that airlock is accessible. From outside it looked like it had been sealed shut. Listen, we can bleed the power from two of our suits and charge up the other one. That way at least we'll have enough to keep one set of lights going."

He stopped walking. Turned around and faced her. Anger stirred in his stomach, like a wild animal waking up when it heard a strange sound. "You're not touching my suit," he said.

"I wasn't suggesting—"

"Good, because it's not going to happen."

Rao looked down, away from his face. Was she shaking, a little? What had she seen in his eyes?

He needed to keep control. He needed to keep control of his command, at the very least.

"Sorry," he said. He turned around and started walking again. He forced himself to slow his pace, just a little.

Less than an hour later they came to a clearing.

The forest just—stopped. Jansen sank to the ground, grateful for a rest, even if it lasted only long enough for them to figure out what they were seeing.

They'd been struggling through a thick copse where the hand-trees grew so close together there was no way to progress except by pushing their way through. Every single time they touched a tree they sent it into a crazy paroxysm of hands grabbing wrists, until the canopy over their heads swayed and rustled constantly. Then Hawkins shouted for them to hold up, and Jansen pushed between two last trees and—

—grabbed on tight to the tree behind her. Because directly ahead of them was nothing at all. They stood atop a sheer cliff face, looking five meters down to flat, level ground. There was no slope to it, the ground and the trees just stopped, and there was empty air.

Hawkins unclipped his helmet from his waist and lifted it high over his head, trying to shine its lights as far as he could. He grunted but said nothing. He didn't need to say anything. Jansen could see that about twenty-five meters away, across the gap, was another cliff face, and at its top another thick growth of hand-trees.

They hadn't reached the end of the forest. Just a place where a river or something had dug a trench through the island. Jansen leaned carefully over the edge and pointed her single light down at the ground below. There was no water down there to reflect her light, nor any trees or other structures. The floor looked smooth and featureless.

The discontinuity extended as far as their lights reached, in either direction.

"This bastard's pretty much perpendicular to where we want to go," Hawkins said. "Of course. We can go sideways. Follow the top of the cliff left or right, look for where this ends. That could take hours, though. Or days, if it stretches too far."

"Or," Jansen said, but he cut her off.

"Or we go through it. Down this side, up the other face. It'll still slow us down, but only an hour or so." He nodded. "Hand me that bag."

She knew the one he meant. It was the bag she'd filled up with safety lines and climbing gear back on *Orion*. They still had the 3-D-printed ascenders, as well, the motorized belaying devices they'd taken from *Wanderer*.

She took out twenty meters of safety line, tugging on it at several points to make sure it was sound. She looped one end around the trunk of a hand-tree. "Make sure this will hold your weight," she told him.

"It'll be fine. NASA doesn't take chances with their equipment."

"I'm not worried about the line breaking. I'm worried you'll pull the tree out by its roots," she said.

He nodded and clipped the other end of the line to one of the D rings on the hard upper torso of his suit. Then he walked backward, hauling on the line as he went, leaning backward and putting all his weight on the rope. The tree shivered and its branches writhed, but the trunk didn't budge from the ground. The tight nest of tendrils woven around its base kept it secure.

"OK," he said. "Here goes nothing." Then he stepped backward off the cliff edge, letting the line play out through his gloves.

Rao grabbed the trunk of one of the trees at the edge and looked over the precipice, watching Hawkins descend. Jansen kept an eye on the tree he was using for support, and the carabiner at the end of the line. She knew it was the weakest point in the connection. But it held just fine.

"You go next," Rao said, holding out one hand to help Jansen get to her feet. "And be careful when you get to the bottom. If you land the wrong way, you could hurt your bad leg."

"Thanks, Mom," Jansen said. Making sure Rao saw that she was grinning. The two of them shared a laugh. It didn't last very long, but it felt surprisingly good after everything they'd been through.

Jansen turned and looked over the edge. Hawkins was down there waving her on. A sudden thought occurred to her.

She could just unhook the carabiner. Let the rope fall over the edge. Better yet, just haul the rope up before he could grab it.

Leave him stranded down there.

What the hell? Where had that thought come from? The last thing she wanted to do was to put another astronaut in jeopardy. Shaking her head, she cast off and started rappelling down.

As she descended, she studied the cliff face. It was almost vertical, but far from as cleanly cut as she'd thought. The surface was broken and torn, as if the channel had been ripped out of the island rather than cut. It looked as if it had happened recently, too. She could see places where tendrils had been sliced through, leaving circular openings in the wall that looked almost exactly like the outflow pipes of a chemical factory. Black liquid was still drooling from some of them, suggesting the cut had to have been made recently.

When she reached the bottom—easily, landing gently on her good foot—she unclipped herself from the line and waved up for Rao to follow her. Then she crouched down and touched the ground beneath her feet. It was very flat and smooth and perfectly dry. She ran one glove over the surface.

"I noticed it, too," Hawkins told her, coming up behind her.

It had the same porous texture that she remembered from her first visit to 2I. Before they'd reached the ice, she and Stevens had walked over a surface just like this. It was the unadulterated, unre-constructed surface of the drum.

Whatever had cut its way through the island had dug all the way down to the floor. It had scraped this part of the drum clean. "Water didn't do this," she said. "Not in the time since we've been here."

"Things change pretty fast in here," Hawkins pointed out. "All of this," he said, gesturing at the island around them, "wasn't here a day ago."

"Yeah, no, I'm a trained geologist," she said. "They were going to send me to Mars, remember? I know what weathering effects look like. This has to have been done with construction equipment. A 2I-sized bulldozer or something."

"It doesn't matter. The big question is how we get up the far side," he told her, pointing across the trench. Then he rushed for-ward to grab Rao as she came down the rope. Rao hadn't been out of control or anything, Jansen thought. He was clearly just trying to be helpful. She couldn't figure him out, sometimes.

"I'm sure I've got something I can use as a grappling hook," she told him. She rummaged around in her bags and packs until she found what she was looking for, an L-shaped bracket that had been designed to help secure the multifrequency antenna to the outer skin of *Orion*. It was about thirty centimeters long, and if she bent it a little bit—easily done; it was made of lightweight aluminum—she could make it look like a very big fishhook. Attach it to a carabiner at the end of a safety line and it would do. They would have to test it carefully to make sure it would hold their weight, that was all.

"You're not bad at this," Hawkins told her. "Exploring."

"It's pretty much what I built my whole life around," she told him.

He nodded and looked away. The far cliff was twenty-five meters or so away. He covered the ground easily, and before the women could join him, he was already swinging the hook at the end of a short length of rope, getting a feel for its weight before he tried snag-ging the hand-trees at the top of the cliff.

Rao came up to walk with Jansen. She offered her shoulder, but Jansen wanted to walk awhile under just her own power.

"He's making a real effort to be nice to you," Rao said.

Jansen frowned. "He's a major in the space force. You don't get that far unless you know a little something about leading a team. That's all he's doing—reinforcing morale."

"It makes sense you wouldn't trust him," Rao said. "He stole your command."

She turned and looked at the younger woman. Was Rao testing her now? Or just evaluating her psychological state?

"Let me ask you a question, Doc. If you broke your leg coming down that cliff. If you couldn't walk at all. Do you think he would have personally carried you up the other side? Or do you think he would press on toward the brain and leave you behind?"

Rao's face soured. "We need to work together if we're going to accomplish anything," she said.

"Sure," Jansen said. "Together."

SALLY JANSEN: *Honestly, I suppose I owe Hawkins something. When we found Taryn Holmes, it could have destroyed me. I'd put so much subconscious weight on rescuing the KSpace crew . . . Hawkins wouldn't let me dwell on Holmes's death. He forced me to keep moving. Otherwise I might have just laid down and waited to die.*

Hawkins spun the hook on the end of his line, twirling it faster and faster until it whistled through the air. Then, with a flick of his wrist, he hurled the hook into the air. It flew high over his head, carried by its angular momentum, and disappeared into the hand-trees at the top of the cliff.

This was his third cast, and he knew not to yank on the rope right away. He listened to the sound of the hook falling through the branches, let it settle before he pulled back. He could hear the hand-trees rustling up there and thought he must have set off a cascade of wrist grabbing. It never seemed to end.

Then he steeled himself and grabbed the rope with both hands and pulled—gently. Slowly. The only way to find out if the hook had caught anything was to pull and pull and hope it didn't come flying back over the cliff and right down toward his face.

The rope went taut in his hands. "I think I have it," he said. He looked over his shoulder and saw the women watching, expectant and silent. He turned back to his task, hauling on the rope with a firmer and firmer grip. He needed to make sure the hook was seated properly. He didn't want to be halfway up the cliff when it gave way.

The damned trees wouldn't stop rustling. If anything the noise was much louder now. Hawkins frowned and pulled harder.

An arm ending in a meter-long all-too-human hand flopped to the ground in front of him. Its fingers twitched for a moment, then a trickle of black liquid dripped from its severed end.

"Damn," he said softly. Under his breath. The hook must have severed the branch and sent it falling down to the floor of the trench. He pulled harder on the line, intending to free the hook so he could try for another cast.

Fingers dropped from above, one by one. Then another arm. The rustling from up there had turned into a dull roar.

"Hawkins," Jansen called. "Hawkins—get back!"

More arms fell, a few at first, then a cascade of them, trunks bouncing when they hit the ground, chopped-up pieces of tendril twisting and coiling in midair.

Hawkins danced backward. A falling hand brushed the front of his suit, and he yelped in terror, thinking it would grab him, those fingers would wrap around his chest and squeeze him until his hard upper torso splintered, until his ribs snapped and his heart was crushed. The hand lacked the strength to do more than twitch, though. He staggered back farther as the rain of hands and fingers grew more intense. He thought to look up and saw the whole cliff face trembling.

Rippling. Waves of pressure passing through the rubbery ground. And then—with a noise like thunder—the face split open, metric tons of flesh cascading downward, as something broke through from the far side.

"Holy shit," Hawkins said.

He couldn't process what he was seeing, not for the first, vital seconds. His first impression was simply of teeth. Enormous, uncountable teeth, in a mouth big enough to swallow *Orion* whole.

Terror twisted his spine and made his stomach lurch. There was room for only one thought in his head.

"Run!" he shouted.

Rao hauled at Jansen's arm, but the older woman didn't move; she was clearly frozen in place by terror.

She glanced backward and saw the maw again and pulled on Jansen's arm so hard she worried she was going to dislocate the shoulder.

Maw—that was the word she thought of. It wasn't a mouth as much as a dark cave full of grinding, tearing teeth, arranged in three circular rows to form a deadly funnel. The concentric rows spun crazily, the middle row spinning in the opposite direction from the outermost and innermost ranks. Hand-trees and enormous gobbets of torn island-flesh fell into the maw and were torn to shreds, then disappeared down the dark gullet behind the teeth.

The maw slid forward across the trench floor, much faster than anything that big had a right to. Headed directly toward them.

Jansen finally moved, hobbling along on her bad leg. Rao shoved her shoulder into Jansen's armpit and didn't so much carry her as push her along, trying to run sideways, out of the path of the stampeding teeth. As she ran, Rao looked back over her shoulder as much as she dared. She could make out only glimpses of the creature that owned that maw, little snatches of it that caught her lights. She got an impression of a segmented body, glistening with the black ichor of the flesh it had torn its way through. She saw myriad stumpy legs, each ending in a vicious triangular claw that scratched at the barren floor of the trench. Mostly she saw the spinning rows of teeth. The thing was alive—it had be some kind of animal, as much as it more closely resembled a machine you would use to dig out the shafts and galleries of a coal mine.

It shook the ground as it moved, and she could hear a low, rumbling noise from its teeth that made her think of the whine of a dentist's drill as much as the rolling of great wheels. It was headed straight for Hawkins.

"Get out of the way!" Rao howled, though she doubted he could even hear her over the noise the thing made.

He must have, though, because she saw him look over in her direction. Only then did he start to run.

She was certain he wouldn't make it, that it was impossible for him to outrun the creature, but at the last minute he threw himself forward and escaped its teeth. No, she saw, he hadn't thrown himself—one of the countless legs of the thing had caught him and hurled him through the air. He hit the ground and lay there, not moving. She thought maybe she screamed his name.

The ground bounced underneath her and she tripped and fell, spilling Jansen across the flat surface. Jansen rolled up onto her feet—bad leg and all—and reached down to grab Rao and pull her back up.

The creature dragged itself forward on its many legs. Their only hope was that it would just keep going, that it would lurch forward and dig its teeth into the far wall of the trench, burrow its way deep into the flesh of the island and away from them. They were tiny, insignificant compared to its incredible mass—what could it possibly want from them?

Then her heart sank as she saw it start to turn. Its massive toothy head slewed over, its claws clattering against the ground as it twisted itself to the side segment by segment. It heaved the rear section of its body out of the side trench it had been digging, more and more segments and legs appearing every second. Then it turned its head one more time, to face up the trench, at a right angle to the direction it had been headed in when it appeared.

It was facing them dead on. And already it was starting to move forward again, shoving itself along the barren floor straight toward them.

"Oh no," Rao said. "No. No!"

"Listen," Jansen was saying. "Listen to me!"

Rao forced herself to look into Jansen's faceplate.

"Listen," Jansen said again. "You run like hell. You keep running and you don't look back."

"What? I don't understand, you need my help—"

"But you don't need me. Get out of here!" Jansen screamed.

Rao bent her knees and started to do just that. Instead, though, she looked back to where Hawkins was lying on the ground. The thing loomed up over him, impossibly large. It looked as big as a cruise ship barreling down on him, as big as a skyscraper come to life and turned into a giant, insatiably hungry worm, moving with impossible speed, hauling itself forward, its vast mouth rolling over him.

Or at least—where he had been a moment before. She swung her lights around and saw he'd gotten to his feet and was dodging around to the side of the thing.

Then he reached into his backpack and took something out. Rao was too far away to see what it was, until he squeezed it in his hand. Red fire, hard to look at, burst from its end. It was a flare, the last of their flares. Instead of firing it into the air, he'd ignited it in his hand and now he held it like a torch. He waved it back and forth in front of the thing, as if he was trying to get its attention. Like a matador facing down a charging bull with a red cape. Did he think he could lead it away from them?

"It doesn't have any eyes!" Rao called out.

He didn't look at her, but maybe he heard her. As the thing slid toward him, neither faster nor slower than it had moved before, he stopped swinging his arm. He danced backward, clearly getting ready to run away. It wouldn't help, Rao saw. She'd seen him run before. The animal was moving much faster than he could.

"N-n-no," Rao said, unable to keep her teeth from chattering in fear.

Hawkins lifted his arm. He raised the flare up to shoulder height, then he squeezed it again. This time it launched and flew toward the toothy maw like a missile, like a rocket. Rao expected the flare to land inside the mouth, and she was certain the thing wouldn't even notice it there. This was a creature that devoured literally everything in its path; a little burning magnesium wouldn't even give it indigestion.

Instead the flare struck one of its hundreds of legs, catching it in the meaty part where it attached to the body. Red fire burrowed into its flesh, lighting up its skin from within.

The maw spun wildly, all those teeth blurring as they revolved around and around. The creature made no noise, no shriek of pain, but it reared up, its head lifting off the floor and then crashing down again. Its legs writhed and spasmed.

Hawkins dashed back to where the two women stood. "Why aren't you running?" he demanded of them. "That'll only hold it for a second!"

Indeed, already the animal was rolling over on its side, rolling over to smother the spitting flame that burned frantically under its skin. Rao was certain that it could crush out the fire, and then it would come for them again.

"Fucking run!" Hawkins shouted, as he tore past them.

Jansen's lungs burned as she hobbled forward, glad at least to be on solid ground instead of the rubbery soil of the island, even if it meant that every step was a jarring impact, a new shard of glass shoved up under her kneecap.

She was only peripherally aware of Rao at her side, trying to take her arm. Why hadn't Rao listened? Why hadn't she run away when she had the chance, left the two of them behind? 2I had changed them all, but Rao the least, or the most subtly, and if anyone had a chance...

The thoughts churned through her head, getting nowhere.

She looked up and saw that the trench curved to the right up ahead. She had no choice but to follow its path. Hawkins's lights swung wildly up there as his helmet bounced on his hip, the narrow cones of light swinging up the trench wall now, then splaying out across the porous drum floor the next moment. She could see almost nothing, her own single light skewed around so it pointed down at her feet. It had to be that way, so she could see where she was putting each foot down. She was terrified of tripping, terrified that the bitter betrayal that was her left leg would finally do her in. She knew that if she fell, Rao would stop to help her up, and they would both be devoured. Because the giant worm had to be right on their heels. She could hear its wheels of teeth spinning, grinding against the stone-lined floor of the drum. She imagined them throwing up sparks, but then she had to discard that image because no, that would generate light—and light was forbidden here, light was an intrusion on universal darkness. A violation of something ancient and sacred to itself.

The thing exhaled, its breath pluming over them, smoky and dense so it billowed through their lights. She was very glad she couldn't tell what that smelled like. She looked up to find Hawkins, to look for his lights—he would have to breathe in that hellish plume of gas—and realized something horrible. She couldn't see him at all. There was only darkness ahead of her, darkness and what little of the floor and the trench walls Rao's frantic lights draped across.

"Where is he?" she gasped.

"He ran on ahead—he's around the curve," Rao told her, and she heard the younger woman's breath coming fast and shallow. Rao must be tiring, too, she must be slowing down while the thing behind them kept coming at them, clearly intending to swallow them whole. Why? Compared to the walls of the trench, compared to the hand-trees and the flesh of the island, how could a few humans in space suits be tempting? They would be tiny morsels, a tiny supply of calories in a wonderland of good things to chew up and devour.

Unless it wasn't just hunger that drove the worm. Unless something other than their food value lured it on. What, though? Their lights? The thing had no eyes, as Rao had pointed out. The radios in their suits?

Jansen took a chance and—while still running forward as best she could, swinging her hurt leg ahead of her—took a look at the rearview mirror on her sleeve.

She could see nothing. There was no light back there. Angry with herself for not thinking of that, she reached up and twisted her light around to point directly behind them.

The worm was still there. Still dragging itself toward them, its whirling rows of teeth scraping across the drum floor.

They came around the curve in the trench. It took a while to realize, because their lights covered only so much ground, but Jansen was certain the trench was opening up, growing wider. Maybe that would give them more room to maneuver, she thought. Which made her think of a strategy for how to deal with the current situation.

She would run one way and Rao would run the other, getting as much distance between them as possible. If they did that, the worm could chase only one of them at a time. One of them—the one not chased—might gain a little time for thinking of some way to escape. The other would surely be devoured.

It wasn't much of a plan. It was all she could think of.

Until something bizarrely miraculous happened. Something she could never have expected.

Up ahead, in the middle of the widened trench, a spotlight came to life, high over their heads. An incredibly powerful light that fell in a cone of beautiful, pure, lemony radiance, to make a circle on the drum floor. Hawkins stood in the exact center of that light like an actor on a stage about to deliver a soliloquy. He even had one arm raised as if he was about to declaim at any moment.

Except—no—he was waving them on. Beckoning to them.

Behind him, just inside the cone of the light, was a massive pillar rising straight up from the floor of the drum. It was a pylon, part of one of the arches that made up 2I's skeletal structure. Around its base it was splintered and worn away—the worm must have chewed on it extensively but been unable to break it down, even with those rows of grinding teeth.

Jansen hurried forward, faster now, because she understood something of what she was seeing. She knew what Hawkins was suggesting, and while she had no idea if it would work, it was at least a possibility. "You go first," she told Rao, almost shoving her forward.

She'd thought they were in for some tricky rock climbing, using the natural texture of the bone arch to find hand- and footholds. As they drew close, however, a rope fell down into the light, bouncing and swaying for a moment before coming to rest. Hawkins grabbed on to it and started hauling himself up, looping it under his thigh for support. It was clear he wasn't going to wait for them. Rao reached the bottom of the rope when he was near the top of the cone of light, about to disappear into the shadows. She got to the base of the pylon and slumped against the hard surface, grateful for anything that could take her weight.

"Go!" she said. Rao wasted time giving her a meaningful look— Jansen didn't bother to reply. Then the astrobiologist grabbed the rope and started to climb.

Jansen wondered momentarily whether the rope was anchored sturdily enough to support the weight of all three of them and their suits. Then she looked up and saw the worm was barely twenty meters behind her. She didn't need any more incentive to get scampering up the line, hand over hand. At least she didn't need her bad leg for this. She hurried upward, grunting and heaving as she lifted her own weight, a little at a time.

The worm was almost on her. She climbed as fast as she could. It reared up, its massive weight colliding with the pylon, making it shake and creak alarmingly. The rows of teeth swirled beneath her as if she were suspended over a terrible abyss. She pulled and grabbed and hauled herself up, up, even as the worm shoved its bulk against the pylon.

And then the rope got tangled in its teeth.

It yanked taut and she nearly went flying. She barely held on with one hand as the rope stretched and grew tighter, pulled down meter by meter into the devouring maw. She could feel the tension in it, even through her gloves, feel its fibers stretch and start to snap.

No, she thought, *not when I'm so close—*

The rope thrummed like a guitar string, then snapped with a sound like a gunshot. Jansen screamed and let go, thrusting her hands out toward the surface of the pylon, desperate for anything she could hold on to. Her fingers caught a natural seam in the bone and dug in, but it wasn't enough. She didn't have the grip strength to hold on.

Hands reached down from above, many hands. They grabbed the folds of cloth of the sleeve of her suit, grabbed the control panel on the front of her suit. She kicked her feet at the bone and found something, some purchase, and with the aid of the hands, she scrambled upward, up over a ledge where she could roll onto her side.

The bone pylon shook and creaked beneath her, but at least she wasn't falling. At least she wasn't falling into those whirling teeth.

She turned over and let her light show her where she'd ended up. She was inside what looked like a cave dug out of the pylon, maybe a bubble that had formed while the bone was growing. A nearly spherical cave about five meters across. Hawkins and Rao were half sitting, half leaning against the opposite wall, as far from the mouth of the cave as they could get. Between them and Jansen was a blinding light, clearly the source of the spotlight that had led them to this refuge.

Then the light moved, and she saw who was holding it. It was Sandra Channarong.

"Oh God," Jansen said, unable to stop herself. "What happened to you?"

RENDEZVOUS

*W*INDSOR HAWKINS: *We'd known she was still alive, since she left us that menacing video. I had assumed we would never see her in person, that she would watch from the shadows and wait for us to leave—or die. It hadn't occurred to me she could help us. Or that she would want to.*

Channarong switched off her light as soon as Jansen was safely inside the cave. She leaned out through the rough opening and looked down, then swore in a language Rao didn't know.

The pylon shook—and listed a little, sending them all rolling across the floor. Below them the worm must be smashing and grinding at the bone, chewing away at it like a lumberjack striking a tree trunk with an ax. It wouldn't be long before it broke all the way through the pylon. Rao had no idea what would happen then—would they fall? Would their cave become their tomb? She didn't know if this arch was connected to any others that might help support its weight.

Clearly Sandra Channarong didn't want to find out.

"Turn off your lights," she shouted. "Your radios, anything electric. Do it now! They can't climb for shit, but they can chew through anything."

Rao switched her whole suit down. The air inside her helmet started to feel stale almost instantly. She was breathing hard—she was scared—and she knew she would start asphyxiating on her own carbon dioxide soon. But she had to believe Channarong knew what she was talking about. Jansen and then Hawkins switched off their own lights.

The darkness was sudden and unbearable. Rao saw tiny flashes of light in her vision as her brain reacted to suddenly being struck blind. She was holding her breath. She realized she was trying to make herself silent, as if the worm could hear her. She exhaled... slowly. Quietly.

The pylon shook under her again, and she slid across the floor. She screamed—all concerns about silence forgotten—and threw her arms out to grab anything she could find. She was terrified that she might slide right out through the hole in the cave wall.

The floor under her jumped, actually throwing her into the air. She crashed back down and tried not to whimper.

And then it was over, as quickly as it had begun. The thumping, the shaking stopped. The worm must have given up. She prayed it had grown bored and wandered off.

For a long time all of them simply huddled there in the dark, none of them speaking. There was no light, and without her suit radio Rao could hear sounds only at a remove, distorted by her helmet. Not that there was much to hear. She thought maybe Hawkins was stirring restlessly. Or maybe it was Jansen.

Then Sandra Channarong snapped a glow stick and dropped it on the floor of the cave. The faint green light filled the spherical space, painted the walls and their suits. It made Channarong's orange garment turn black, the light streaming upward across her features so that her eye sockets were filled with deep shadow.

Rao had seen a photograph of the woman before, back when Jansen had first suggested her rescue mission. In that picture Channarong wore a space suit but no helmet. Now she wore nothing but a short, sleeveless romper emblazoned with KSpace hexagons—even her feet were bare. She was tall and slender, with black hair cut in a short bob. In the photograph she had a large mole on her ear. That was gone now.

Her ear was gone.

The skin on the left side of her head was cratered, eaten away by necrosis. The pattern of damage continued down her shoulder and her left arm, which was missing below the elbow. The stump was wrapped up in makeshift bandages, strips of torn fabric wound around and around the amputation site. A large and powerful-looking flashlight was lashed with duct tape to what remained of her forearm.

She must have noticed Rao staring. She swiveled away, concealing most of the damage. Then she squatted down by the mouth of the cave, staring outward. Into the dark. She couldn't possibly see anything there, but at one point she flinched—maybe she'd heard something.

No one spoke. Maybe the others were worried that if they made too much noise, the worm would come back. Maybe they just respected Channarong's silence.

"You should have left," Channarong finally said. "I told you to leave." She sighed, her shoulders slumping.

"We have a lot of questions," Hawkins said. "Don't get me wrong. We're very grateful that you saved us from—"

"I wasn't supposed to talk to you before," the woman said. She didn't turn around to look at them. "I wasn't supposed to have any contact with you. I broke the rules to tell you to leave, but you didn't listen." She moved, but only to sit in the opening, her legs dangling out over thin air.

"I understand," Hawkins told her. "I'm military. I get operational security. But there are some basic facts we need to resolve."

Channarong shook her head. "Foster's had a change of heart. He sent me to find Commander Jansen. He has a message for her."

"Foster's alive?" Jansen asked, sitting up and pushing herself forward, supporting her weight on her hands. "Where is he? Can we—"

Hawkins cleared his throat and spoke over her. "Ms. Jansen is no longer in charge. I'm Major Windsor Hawkins, and I'm the MC for *Orion* now."

Channarong finally turned and looked at them, and the weight of her gaze was enough to make even Hawkins shut up.

"I'm supposed to give Foster's message to Commander Jansen." As if she hadn't heard him.

Hawkins stepped directly in front of her. She tried to move to the side, to look at Jansen, but Hawkins just moved with her. He tried again, forcing himself to be patient.

"I'm the mission commander of *Orion*. Jansen has been relieved of that duty. Look at her. She can barely walk—she's barely conscious. Whatever Foster wanted to tell her, you can tell me instead."

Channarong bent low to look around him. Jansen was breathing heavily and not looking at anyone, but she managed to nod.

"Let's find a place we can talk in private," Channarong said after a moment. Then she reached up and grabbed the rim of the cave mouth with her hand. She swung her leg out and put her weight on a foothold that Rao couldn't see, some rough patch of the bone just outside the opening. In a second she was gone, swallowed up by the dark.

Hawkins looked down at Rao and Jansen.

"Wait here," he said. "I'll be back."

Rao went to the mouth of the cave, but the darkness out there was too intense—it felt like a solid wall of nothingness. She felt as if, if she put so much as a hand out there, it would get swallowed up, lost forever.

Like Sandra Channarong's hand and forearm. The thought made her shiver, though she knew she couldn't imagine what the woman must have been through. Stevens had described her as cheerful, almost too chirpy, when he'd known her, when he'd dated her, but now—

Rao turned around because she'd heard something. Not the worm coming back, or any of the horrors of 2I, but a much more human sound. She'd heard Jansen groaning.

"Ma'am?" she said.

Jansen's face had turned deathly pale, and her eyes rolled in their sockets. Her whole body started to shake.

"Ma'am? Sally?" Rao said, rushing over to her. She grabbed the shoulders of her suit and tried to hold her still.

"Hurts," Jansen mumbled.

"Is it your leg?" Rao asked, terrified. She looked down at the left leg of Jansen's suit. There was no way to make a visual inspection, not without taking the suit off. She reached down and carefully grasped Jansen's knee. "Is it worse than before?" she asked. Then she palpated it. Gave it the gentlest of squeezes.

Jansen screamed.

Hawkins followed Channarong up to a little ledge in the side of the arch, not a cave but just a shallow depression where they could sit and talk.

"Food," she said.

"What?"

"Food. You have to have some food. NASA prepares for everything. Better than we did. They must have sent you in here with some food."

Hawkins was too out of breath to give her a real answer.

"You owe me. I saved your life. I haven't eaten in three days." It felt as if she'd been waiting to say this. As if she'd written a script in her head. She must have thought of little else while she was saving them from the worm, he imagined.

"Just...some sugar water," he told her. "A little bag of sugar water, in my collar ring. I'm happy to share, but—"

She grabbed him by the front of his suit and stared down his neck. Her face was intimately close, but all he could see was the dead, white flesh of the necrotic craters. The ruined patch of skin where her ear used to be.

She found the little tube that delivered the sugar water. It was placed so he could suck on it from inside his helmet without using his hands at all. She had to press her nose against his Adam's apple to get to it.

She drank long and deep. Then she released him and took a step away. She wiped at her mouth with her hand.

"Thanks," she said. Snarling the word. Sounding as if she hated him because she'd been so desperate.

He had more important things to worry about than her emotional state.

"Where is Foster?" he asked, sitting down hard on the bone. "We've seen some of his video files, but they were badly degraded. What happened to the three of you?"

He'd figured he would start with the easy questions. She just turned her face away.

"Look, I need information. If we're going to help you—"

She reached into a pocket and took something out. She tossed it to him, something very small and dark, and he had to lunge to grab it out of the air.

"What is this?" he asked. Even though he could feel it in his hand. Another damned memory stick.

"Foster made it," she said. "It's a message for you. He wants to make a deal."

Of course. KSpace was a commercial operation. It would never give anything away for free. He set his jaw and slotted the stick into the front of his suit, waiting to hear what Foster would demand. There was one file on it, as usual.

VIDEO FILE TRANSCRIPT (5)

Willem Foster: We have to know. You understand, right? You understand why we're doing this.

Sandra Channarong: I do. Just…can we make it quick? I'm losing my nerve, boss. I know, I know it's important, but—

Foster: I'll only leave it on for a second, then I'll peel it off. It's going to be fine. Don't worry, Sandy. I've got you. Ready?

Foster: I'm setting the timer. Now…applying the tentacle to the left arm. Damn, these things squirm. There. It didn't take long for Taryn to make contact. It wants to talk to us, I'm sure of it. This one's sluggish, that's probably good, but…OK, it's attaching.

Channarong: Oh shit. Oh, that doesn't feel right…Wow. That's starting to hurt. Can we…

Channarong: Boss, I'm not sure if it's working, and—it's branching. Boss! Boss!

Foster: Just a few more seconds. Sandy. We have to know.

Channarong: I can feel it, I can feel…Oh God. It's old. So old. It's been waiting so long. It's cold, where it came from, it…it… I can't…

Foster: What does it want? Can you tell me? What does it want with Earth?

Channarong: It—oh God, this hurts—it—it wants—

[The recording jumps, and the time stamp indicates that two minutes and fourteen seconds have been edited out. When it continues Channarong is screaming.]

Foster: Oh my God.

Channarong: Get it off me! Get it off!

Channarong watched his face carefully as he listened to the recording. When it was done, she held out her hand. "That's mine," she said. "My property." He ejected the memory stick and handed it back to her.

"You have a radio," she said. "Some way to talk to Earth. Don't lie—I've seen you using it, though I have no idea how it works."

"It's true," he said.

"Foster needs to make contact with KSpace. He needs to tell the Hive what we've learned. He's at the south pole right now, near this fucker's brain. I'm going to take you there and he'll tell you everything you want to know—but he gets to use your radio."

He pointed at her arm. "Foster did that to you as—an experiment?"

She nodded. "And it worked. He can talk to the Object. He's talking to it right now."

Hawkins stared at her in disbelief. He'd thought that communication with 2I was impossible. If Foster had figured out how to do it…that could change everything.

It also made everything a lot more complicated.

She was waiting for an answer. "Tell me if we have a deal."

Still he said nothing.

Her eyebrows crawled up her forehead as she waited for his response. He was enjoying himself far too much to let the moment go.

Eventually, though, he had to answer.

"No deal," he said.

WINDSOR HAWKINS: I could visualize you jumping out of your chairs, down there in Pasadena. You didn't need to worry. I had a plan.

"Clearly Foster was thinking he was dealing with NASA," Hawkins told Channarong. "That's no longer the case. This is a space force mission now, and the space force doesn't negotiate. You have a duty to your country to tell me what you know."

Channarong frowned. "KSpace is a multinational corporation," she pointed out. "Most of its shareholders are Korean."

Hawkins shrugged.

Foster must have thought he had the ultimate bargaining chip. He had some way to communicate with 2I—or at least he claimed to. Maybe his information was even correct and verifiable. Hawkins didn't really care.

2I needed to be destroyed. After a couple of days inside, Hawkins had never been more sure of it. It didn't matter in the slightest what the organism wanted, or how it planned on getting it. Long before it reached Earth orbit, it needed to be blown out of the sky. As soon as Hawkins found the brain, General Kalitzakis would have a target, and he could launch his kill vehicle, and that would be it.

He knew that McAllister—and probably the president—would still want to know what 2I had wanted from Earth. Even after the question became moot. Still, he didn't want to give Channarong and Foster anything if he could help it. They were civilians.

"You say Foster's at the brain. That's where I was headed anyway. I'll go find him and get what I need from him, one way or another."

Channarong nodded. He could see she wasn't done trying to bargain with him, though. "Help yourself," she said. "Of course, you'll never make it there alive."

It was his turn to wait patiently for her to elaborate.

"There are at least five more worms between here and there, eating up the landscape. You wouldn't have survived meeting your first one if it hadn't been for me. I know how to get around in here, how to navigate the—"

"Wait," Hawkins said. "Wait."

He looked down over the edge of the arch. His lights couldn't reach the ground, not from this height. He looked anyway, thinking he might find some sign of the worm that had tried to eat them.

"There's more than one of those things?"

Channarong gave him a cold smile. "About thirty, at the moment," she said. "You saw one of the bigger ones, but they eat constantly, and they're always growing."

"Thirty," Hawkins said, scowling. That changed some things.

Channarong walked up to stand next to him. Then she lifted her left arm, the one with the flashlight mounted to it. The light was much stronger than his suit lights, and its beam reached farther. She brought it up and let its light sweep slowly along a length of arch just over their heads, a bridge of bone maybe three hundred meters long.

Hanging from the underside were dozens of oblong shapes, leathery sacs attached to the arch by thin stalks. One of the sacs twitched violently as they watched, as if annoyed by the light—though that must have been a coincidence.

Hawkins had no doubt as to what she was showing him. Each of those things was a cocoon with a worm inside, undergoing metamorphosis. Each of them as big as a city bus.

She brought her arm around, illuminating another arch. More of the sacs hung down from that one. More and more. A third arch—they were surrounded by them, and he was looking at only a tiny number of the arches inside 2I. He could only imagine that every single one of them supported a similar number of cocoons.

He'd seen ARCS's map. He knew how many arches there were, had traced the extensive network of them that filled most of 2I's upper air. He did some quick math in his head. Millions, maybe, he thought. There could be millions of them—

"There's going to be a lot more of them, and very soon," she said.

*   *   *

"Oh shit," Rao breathed. She could see Jansen panting for breath inside her helmet, see sweat pouring down her face. "You're going into shock."

She had felt how swollen the joint was. It must have doubled in size. Jansen had been walking on that this whole time. "You said before it was a cartilage problem. I thought it was just bursitis, maybe. But that feels dislocated."

"I couldn't . . . ," Jansen said, gritting her teeth through the pain. "I couldn't do it. I wasn't worth . . ."

"Worth what? Talk to me, Sally. I need to know—"

She stopped because Jansen's mouth was moving. Forming words she could barely hear.

"Second chance. I wasn't worth . . . I couldn't save him. Parminder—I couldn't . . ."

Shit. Shit shit shit. Jansen was clearly delirious with pain. That was a really bad sign. If they didn't do something about that knee, Jansen might never walk again, and inside 2I that could be a death sentence. How could Rao help her, though, while she was inside her suit?

She dug through her backpack. There was a medical kit in there. It wasn't much, just some emergency supplies like the bandage she'd put on Hawkins's head, some antibacterial spray, a couple of pills. She pulled out a blister pack of a generic NSAID.

Jansen was wavering in and out of consciousness. She was still sweating profusely, and her eyes were rolling up into her head.

There was nothing for it except to get Jansen out of her suit.

The helmet first. She reached up and grabbed the latches on the side of the helmet and flipped them open. Then she rotated the helmet, Jansen's face disappearing as the faceplate swiveled around.

"Couldn't save him," Jansen raved.

"Who?" Rao asked, hoping that if she engaged with Jansen it might help her stay conscious. "Who couldn't you save? Holmes? Sunny?"

"Blaine," Jansen said.

Her collar ring clicked, and then the helmet came off with a puff of trapped air. Rao rolled Jansen over on her side so she could get the suitport open. "That was a long time ago, Sally. And there was nothing you could do. It wasn't your fault."

Jansen was probably only peripherally aware of where she was or what was happening. Rao kept talking to try to keep her awake.

"I know it's eaten you alive, all these years, what happened to Wilson," Rao said. "But you need to forgive yourself."

"Blaine." Jansen laughed. There wasn't a lot of breath behind the laugh, but it still managed to sound bitter. "Blaine the bastard. I hate that guy."

Rao almost pulled her hands away from Jansen in surprise. She shook her head and went back to the complicated work of getting Jansen out of the suit. At least Jansen could help, a little, wriggling her shoulders to get her arms and torso through the opening at the back of the suit.

"I don't think you meant that," Rao said. "OK, this is the hard part. Your legs. Your knee is dislocated, and when we pull your legs out—it's going to hurt."

Jansen turned her head, suddenly, to stare at Rao. Her eyes were bright and feverish.

"I just wanted to go to Mars! I worked so hard for it. I worked hard! And then Blaine killed my dream. He killed it. I hate him for that. I would never say this out loud. But sometimes... sometimes I'm glad he died."

Rao shoved the suit down, over Jansen's legs.

It was enough to set Jansen screaming again—and this time, it didn't stop. Jansen's body started convulsing, her arms beating against the hard torso of Rao's suit. Rao grabbed her hands and tried to hold them still, but Jansen wouldn't stop shaking.

"Jansen! Jansen, listen! I'm going to have to reduce your patella." Rao tried to hold her still so she wouldn't do any more damage to herself. "That means I'm going to have to pop your kneecap back into place. Manually."

"What the hell was that?" Hawkins asked. "Did you hear it?"

"Someone screaming," Channarong said. As if he'd asked about the weather.

He shook his head and clambered back down the side of the bone arch, back to the cave where he'd left the others.

He found Rao bent over Jansen—who was out of her space suit. Rao was grasping Jansen's leg just above and below the knee. And Jansen's knee—

It was twisted over to one side, pointing outward from her leg at the wrong angle. It looked more like a tumorous growth than a natural part of Jansen's body.

"What the hell?" Hawkins asked.

"Her knee's dislocated. It's been dislocated for a long time and she finally went into shock. Listen. I don't have any painkillers except NSAIDs," Rao said. "This is supposed to be done under anesthesia."

"What do you mean?"

"I need to pop it back into place." Rao gestured him over. "Can you help me?"

"What should I do?" Hawkins asked.

"Hold her down. Hold her shoulders. Do you have anything for her to bite down on? A piece of leather is traditional. Or a bullet."

He shot her a look. What did she mean by that, asking him for a—

No, there was no time to wonder what she might or might not know. He searched their gear and found a piece of gauze from the medical kit, folding it over and over before pushing it in between Jansen's teeth.

"In the movies they always make it seem like this'll somehow help with the pain," Rao told him. "It's actually just to keep her from accidentally biting off her tongue. You ready?"

She didn't wait for Hawkins to say yes.

The movement was simple and over very quickly. Rao pushed up on Jansen's leg until it was bent, then pulled it straight again—at the same time shoving the kneecap very hard until it fell back into place with an audible pop.

Jansen let out a scream that could probably be heard from one end of 21 to the other. It made Hawkins want to clutch his ears, but he knew better—Jansen was thrashing in his arms and he had to hold her down, hold her still.

Hawkins felt his own stomach lurch with the wrongness of it. He could only imagine how much that had just hurt. It didn't last long, though. Eventually the screaming and kicking stopped. Jansen's face went white, and her eyes fluttered closed. She sucked in a series of long, deep breaths.

Rao made her as comfortable as possible, bunching up the soft parts of Jansen's suit to use as a pillow.

"I don't know how she kept walking on that knee for so long," Rao said. She lay down next to Jansen, her own face awash with sweat. "Sheer bloody-mindedness, I guess."

Hawkins shook his head. "She was damned lucky you were here." If they hadn't had a doctor with them, if Jansen had gone into shock and it was just him—what would he have done? He would have had no idea what was happening.

Jansen could have died, he thought. She could have died here and he would have had to just leave her body behind.

He fought to keep his face neutral as he thought about that.

Sandra Channarong came and stood over Jansen, looking down at her with narrowed eyes. "How soon can she walk again? We need to get moving."

"What? Walk?" Rao asked. "Where?"

"Channarong is going to take us to Foster," Hawkins said. "To the brain."

PARMINDER RAO: Jansen would ask me later about what she'd said when she was in shock. She claimed not to remember, but I think that was a lie. There are things we can't say to each other, things no one should ever hear. What she said about Blaine Wilson... I told her it was just gibberish, that I hadn't understood a word. She seemed relieved to hear that.

COURSE CORRECTION

They put Jansen on a safety line, but it was obvious to Rao that the patella reduction had been a success. They'd let Jansen sleep for nearly four hours, and once she was awake she'd been able to put weight on her leg. Normally Rao would have put the knee in a cast, and probably demanded that her patient use crutches for six weeks. That simply wasn't an option inside 2I. She'd been desperately afraid of what might happen once Jansen started moving under her own power, but it was clear that she was already moving better than she had before. She was able to use both legs for climbing, and was barely out of breath when they reached the flat top of the bone arch.

Rao, who had spent most of her adult life in one graduate program or another—and not a lot of it going rock climbing—almost envied Jansen her endurance. She sprawled across the hard surface and took her time getting used to the fact that the ground wasn't made out of rubber, nor was it slowly pulsing. The beat of 2I's heart had gotten deep inside her, and now it felt strange to be cut off from it.

"It's a long walk from here," Channarong told them. "These arches mostly connect up, so we can stay off the ground level and away from the worms. There's a couple places we'll need to climb, and a couple where we'll need to rope our way across."

Hawkins pointed south, toward the south pole and the brain, and Channarong nodded. That was clearly all Hawkins needed. He set off at a quick pace, sticking close to the center line of the arch.

The top of the bone wasn't perfectly flat, Rao saw. It was gently curved, so if you walked too close to the edges you would constantly be in danger of falling off. The footing in the center was good, though, the fibrous material of the arch giving good traction for their space suit boots. They would probably make better time up there than they had on the island.

Jansen reached down and helped Rao up to her feet, and together they got moving, with Channarong bringing up the rear. Rao turned and walked backward for a couple steps so she could face the KSpace astronaut.

"Do you want me to take a look at that?" she asked, pointing to Channarong's missing arm.

The other woman scowled and picked up her pace until they were walking side by side.

"It's all right. I'm a doctor."

"I know who you are," Channarong said. "Back at the Hive, your pictures were all over our training space. You're the enemy. Our competition."

"This place is too dangerous for that kind of thinking," Rao suggested.

Channarong didn't even bother to scoff. "Tell him that," she said, tilting her head in Hawkins's direction. "He's a real piece of work. Then there's her," Channarong added, cutting her eyes sideways to indicate Jansen. "The woman who almost went to Mars. I can't believe they put her in charge of you guys. Though it looks like she screwed that up, too."

"They removed her from command because she got too interested in rescuing you and Foster, to the point she lost focus on our official mission," Rao said. It wasn't entirely true, but she felt she needed to defend Jansen. Even if she wasn't sure why.

"She made it about herself, in other words." Channarong shrugged. "You I know the least about. You're supposed to be some hot-shit scientist. Taryn was smart, too. Super smart. People like that don't last long in here. They get the idea they can understand this place. They're always wrong—this thing doesn't play by any human rules."

Rao bit back the words she wanted to say. They were cruel and wouldn't help with anything. Besides, there was something else she needed to confront.

"You haven't asked about Stevens yet. Why he isn't with us."

Channarong's shoulders fell. The scowl on her face, which Rao had begun to think was permanent, slipped, and for a second she saw the woman Channarong must have been before she left Earth. The woman from the official KSpace photograph, a woman who had a good-natured smirk and laugh lines around her eyes. *She must be remembering him*, Rao thought. *She's thinking about good days.*

But the transformation didn't last. Channarong's face fell again.

"I know he's dead."

How? But now wasn't the time to ask where she got her information. "I'm so sorry," Rao tried instead.

Channarong shrugged. "He always was an idiot. He would get these ideas, and nobody could ever convince him they were dumb, or they wouldn't work. He's the reason we're all here." She spit over the side of the bone arch. "This is his fault."

Then she picked up her pace, catching up with Hawkins so she could use her flashlight arm to point out where their route crossed another arch. Rao got the point. She shouldn't mention Stevens again, not in Channarong's presence. There was no time for sentiment now. No place for that inside 21.

"We could go around," Channarong said, "but that'll add a couple kilometers. Better to just go across."

Ahead of them the arch curved steeply to the left, away from their prior course. Another bridge was visible at the edge of their light, about twenty meters away. In between was nothing but dark air.

Channarong had a long bright-orange length of rope with a grappling hook clipped to one end. She started uncoiling it.

Jansen stepped as close to the edge as she dared. There was something she'd noticed before, but on the long march she hadn't really given it much thought. Now it mattered. "We've climbed pretty high," she said. "The gravity feels different here. Lower. The air's getting thinner, too."

Channarong smiled a little at that. "Whatever you do, when we're crossing—don't look down." Then she swung herself around like a discus thrower and cast the hook. It sailed in a higher arc than it would have on Earth and struck the far arch with a dull thud. When Channarong pulled on the line the hook snagged for a second on a ridge of bone, then popped loose. She swore and drew the rope back, then cast again. And again. Eventually the hook caught on a round cave opening on the far side, and the line went taut.

"One at a time," she said. "We go across one at a time."

Hawkins went first. He protested that it would be a lot easier if they could use their motorized ascenders, but in the end he just wrapped his legs around the rope and climbed across hand over hand. Rao went next, using the same technique he had. She made it just fine.

"After you," Channarong said.

Jansen took a deep breath, then climbed out onto the rope. It was easier than she'd expected—the lower gravity probably explained that. She was halfway across before she even thought about it. Before she heard something, a faint sound coming up from below.

It was not a pleasant sound. There was an element of crunching to it, and then a series of flabby pops. And then a sound she knew she recognized—the whirring of rows of circular teeth. She'd heard that sound when the worm was chasing them. She doubted she would ever forget it.

She reached the far side and scrambled off the rope, not wanting to be on it a moment longer. Channarong came after her, using her legs more than her single hand. When she was standing on the far arch, she grabbed the rope and shook it back and forth vigorously. The knot she'd used to anchor it pulled apart, and she was able to haul the rope back and wind it around her waist again.

Then she stepped to the edge of the abyss they'd just crossed. "You really sure you want to see this?"

Jansen nodded.

Channarong pointed her flashlight at the ground. It was far enough away that the light gave Jansen only a rough idea of what was down there. It was enough.

Back when they'd been on their ice floe raft, they'd seen mounds of greasy bubbles rise from the water, bubbles that swelled up in great profusion. This had to be the final stage of those growths—a massive pyramid of bubbles, millions of them, each the size of a beach ball, with tendrils snaking across their translucent surfaces.

A dozen or so worms were down there, devouring the bubbles and whatever they contained. They tore into the pyramid with a frenzied intensity, slashing them open with their massive teeth. One especially big worm butted its way through the melee, using its claws to shove the others back as it gnawed its way toward the top of the heap.

"Foster thinks those bubbles are some kind of super-advanced hydrogen fuel cell," Channarong said. "That's a power plant."

"Interesting," Rao said. "I wonder if the worms can directly use electrical energy, or if the bubbles are just rich in calories."

"Whatever. The worms can't get enough of the stuff." Channarong kept her flashlight focused on the mound. One worm lifted its toothy head, as if it had sensed her light somehow. "We think that's why they chase anybody using electricity. Why we had to get rid of our suits. Even lights are enough to get their attention."

"It's amazing, how fast you've learned how to stay alive in here," Jansen said.

Channarong shone her light right in Jansen's face. "Tell me something," she said. "You came in here, the first time, to save us."

Jansen blinked in the light. "Yes," she said.

"What did you think you were saving us *from*? You didn't know about the worms back then. You didn't even know about the tendrils. What did you think was going to happen to us?"

The answer was so obvious Jansen sputtered in surprise. She laughed and looked away, away from the light. She tried to frame her answer carefully, tried to think of how best to explain it, the feeling she'd had that KSpace was in trouble. Her instinct.

Except in the end she couldn't come up with anything to say. She had no good answer.

She stood there for a long time trying. Rao and Channarong moved away, maybe just getting away from the edge.

Eventually Jansen went to join them.

They climbed up a slope to another arch, this one broader and longer. It rose gently before them, ascending into the black air of 2I. When Channarong pointed her light upward, Hawkins had to admit the sight took his breath away.

Ribbons of bone crisscrossed the sky. The arches built on each other, branching and curling away in giant spirals. It looked like a more chaotic version of one of Escher's paintings of staircases, he thought—the way the arches connected and reinforced each other made it look as if they headed off at impossible angles, reconnecting to arches that should be lower. It made him feel a little as he had when they'd left *Orion* and floated across to 2I through empty space, as if up and down had stopped meaning anything, as if he would just drift off forever into an endless skyscape of bone bridges if he fell. The only real way to tell which way was down was to look for the ubiquitous cocoons, which dangled from the underside of every arch.

Many of them, he saw, were empty now. They hung slack and dry. There wasn't any breeze to stir them. The ones that moved were all getting ready to hatch.

He was very glad he wasn't down at ground level to see the worms down there, which must be gathering in multitudes.

Ahead of him Channarong scampered up the side of an arch, lifting herself up high so she could shine her light farther. Making sure their route was clear.

They had to rest. There came a time when even Hawkins had to admit it. Rao wanted to check Jansen's leg, for one thing. "I should take a look at your head, as well," she said.

"My head's just fine," he barked at her.

"It doesn't hurt? I've seen you rubbing your temples, and—"

He flapped one hand at her in a gesture of frustration. "Find a cave," he told Channarong. She nodded and loped ahead. Soon her light flashed back at them, three times. She'd found one of the spherical cavities in the bone, big enough they could all huddle inside. The shelter it offered was, Rao knew, mostly psychological. There was no rain or wind to hide from, and the cave would be just as hot as the outside air of 2I. If she used one of her glow sticks inside, though, it would be a little pocket of light in the dark. It would do them all some good.

She helped Jansen climb into the cave. Inside, however, she stopped. Hawkins and Channarong were standing near the round opening, in her way. It looked as if they'd seen something that worried them—Channarong was down in a crouch as if she might turn and run at any moment, while Hawkins was standing very straight, very tall, with his chin up in the air.

"What is it?" he demanded.

Channarong's light speared something stuck to the far wall of the cave. Something shiny.

Rao moved to get a better look. It looked like a ball of glass, small enough she could have held it in the palm of her hand. She looked up and around and saw more of them, in the shadows, glinting in reflected light. The back half of the cave was dotted with them, maybe a dozen in all.

She flinched backward and nearly fell on her ass when something inside it stirred. When the globe didn't immediately jump at her, she took another look.

A tiny creature swam around and around inside the globe. A thin, muscular body lashed back and forth, nub-like limbs twitching as it raced in circles. Its head was the biggest part of it, a swollen ring of tiny, very sharp-looking teeth. The teeth spun in concentric circles.

"It's a worm egg," Rao said, taking a step back before she looked at the others. She held up one hand to keep Channarong's light out of her eyes. "They must incubate in these bubbles, then migrate out to—"

She yelped in surprise as Hawkins grabbed the egg off the wall and tossed it to the ground, then stomped on it with his heavy boot. Liquid and parts of the embryonic worm splattered Rao's suit.

One by one he tore the eggs down and destroyed them. The eggs had been attached to the wall by very thin tendrils, which writhed when he snapped them, then drooled dark liquid down the wall.

"Christ," Jansen said. "What is that smell? Iodine and—cinnamon? Cloves?"

Rao realized she was the only one wearing a suit with a helmet, the only one breathing air brought up from Earth. "Stop," she said, when Hawkins grabbed an egg and started to squeeze it. The worm inside twisted around as if it might bite at his fingers. "Those could be toxic. You don't want to touch them. Stop!"

He didn't stop. Not until he'd smashed every last egg. Then, breathing heavily, he turned and looked at the others. Searching their faces. Did he expect to be congratulated for what he'd done?

"We'll rest outside," he said. He rubbed his gloves on the hips of his suit. "It stinks in here."

TERMINAL ORBIT

Hawkins didn't dream anymore. He wasn't sure he slept. It didn't feel like sleep, more like dying. Temporary dying.

He tried to get some rest, anyway. He rolled away from the light, pressed his hands over his eyes. He tried to slow his mind down, tried to think restful thoughts. His body hurt. He was sore all over, and he knew it wasn't going to get better. He stank—both his own body, the sweat and grime that covered him head to toe, and his gloves where they'd touched the alien eggs. The smell kept him from sleeping. The smell was bad.

Nothing had been good since he woke up on the island with his helmet off. Since Jansen took his helmet off.

Since she'd tried to kill him. He was pretty sure of that now. She had a good cover story— she even had Rao vouching for her, saying that it had been necessary. That Rao had to check him and make sure he didn't have a concussion. It had made the perfect excuse. Jansen had thought the air inside 21 would kill him. That it would infect him, the way Stevens had been infected, perhaps.

Smart thinking on her part. He had taken over command of what she must think of as her mission. Eliminate him and she could be in charge again. It was basic military strategy—cut off the head and you kill the snake. He wasn't sure what her larger plans were. Maybe sabotage his attempts to find the brain and destroy 21. Or maybe she just wanted the honor of being the one who called in the fatal strike. He didn't truly understand her reasoning. He didn't need to. He knew she'd made one crucial mistake. Her plan hadn't worked. He was still alive.

He wondered if she would try again. Whether she had it in her to kill him. Well, let her try. He patted a pocket on the front of his suit. There was a surprise for her in there, if she tried something. He could protect himself.

It hurt to close his eyes. He tried anyway. He needed to sleep. Even if it felt like trying to die. He wouldn't die. He would will himself to stay alive, no matter what happened. He wouldn't give her the satisfaction of watching him die.

It was dark outside. It was dark inside his head, too.

"The kill vehicle is in position, it's got a good fire angle," the disembodied voice of General Kalitzakis told McAllister. They were deep in a VR projection of imagery from a space telescope. Even under magnification, the spaceplane was in such a high orbit that Earth looked small and indistinct. The sun passed behind it as the view shifted, and McAllister watched its robotic arm extend its deadly payload, like a mantis lifting a bundle of sticks. "The president called me personally to give me authorization to take this step. We can deploy as soon as Hawkins identifies a target. One shot and we can blow this thing's brains out. I'm feeling good about this, Roy. I'm feeling like this is the right decision."

McAllister wasn't so sure. "What if there are more of them?" he asked.

It had been weighing on his mind for a while now.

"I beg your pardon?"

"This isn't the first of these things to cross our path. We saw 'Oumuamua pass through the solar system thirty-eight years ago. Now 2I is coming straight at us. Maybe we can destroy it, fine. But we know it isn't the only one of its kind. More of them may follow. We'll have set a precedent here. The next one to arrive will know we're hostile."

"They'll know not to fuck with us," Kalitzakis said.

"Hmm. You'll wait for my OK before you deploy. Right?"

Kalitzakis sighed in resignation. "Of course. This has to be a joint decision. You and I need to agree before we pull the trigger."

The president of the United States had given that order. Kalitzakis would follow it to the letter, McAllister knew.

The president had given McAllister an order, too. The very second that McAllister decided communication with 2I was impossible, he was to let Kalitzakis loose. Authorize the military strike. McAllister was certain he could do it. No matter the cost—no matter what the repercussions might be in some theoretical future.

"I'll be here," he said, "ready when the time comes. General... you're sure this is going to work?" he asked.

"I feel it in my bones," Kalitzakis told him. "The numbers show at least a forty percent chance of success with one shot."

"Forty? I thought it was seventy."

"We've had to update our models, based on the better map we have of 2I's interior now. There's a lot of structural complexity inside there, stuff we can't easily plug into our equations, but... Roy, in the space force we always say: you miss all the shots you don't take. This is what we've got. It's the best we're going to get."

Unless Foster really is talking to the thing, McAllister thought. *Unless we can convince it to turn away from its course.*

He made no attempt to put numerical odds on that.

McAllister touched his device to end the call. He dropped instantly out of virtual space and back into his own body, which was, at that moment, in an elevator descending into the ground under JPL.

The elevator arrived, and he stepped out into the little lobby of the neutrino telescope, then out onto the enclosed catwalk. The display in the middle of the room showed the same scene he'd watched before he left for the night—figures in space suits trudging across dull, pale ground.

Charlotte Harriwell was lying on the floor, her coat rolled up under her head as a pillow. She stirred as he came in, then sat up and straightened her clothes and her hair. "McAllister," she said. "I'm so sorry." She laughed. "I didn't think I would actually fall asleep."

He smiled to show her it was fine. She hadn't left the chamber since he'd shown her Taryn Holmes's remains, and he doubted she would leave even if he asked her to. Which he had no intention of doing. She worked the same job for KSpace that he did for NASA, which meant neither of them would feel easy again until their astronauts were safe. Which needed to happen sooner rather than later. Parminder Rao's suit batteries were down to 7 percent charge. While Hawkins and Jansen had been conserving power by not running their life-support systems, they didn't have much more. Maybe that would be enough for them to meet with Foster and then escape through the secondary airlock. Maybe.

He touched his device and asked one of his assistants to bring down breakfast for two. He wasn't going anywhere until this was resolved.

She opened the map of 2I's interior in an AR window. "They're getting close to the south pole," she told him. "Another hour or so and they'll reach Foster."

He nodded. Foster. So much relied on what the man had to say. If he had truly found a way to communicate with the alien—

Otherwise: 40 percent.

McAllister reached into his coat pocket and took out a sleeve of antacids. He kept his eyes on the meaningless video displayed above them.

"Come on, Hawkins," he said, softly.

Except—in his head it wasn't Windsor Hawkins he was really counting on.

No, in his mind, in the irrational part of him, it was Sally Jansen he prayed for. She might not be in charge of the mission anymore, but if anyone could pull this off... *Come on, Sally. Prove that I was right all those years ago. Give me something better than forty percent.*

On the side of Charlotte Harriwell's head, the dragon snorted smoke through its nostrils in two long, dark plumes.

"End of the road," Channarong said. "It's just up from here."

Rao had been lost in a hypnotic trance of walking on the tops of the bone arches, watching her feet. For hours no one had said anything, or if they had—she hadn't heard it.

This damned place. It got in your head, the darkness, the

strangeness... She looked around, trying to figure out where they were.

The arches of bone came together in a common nexus just ahead, three different paths converging where the tall pylon of the buttress rose from the drum's floor. An orange rope hung down from the darkness above them, a way up. Channarong must have left it behind the last time she came this way.

The cage—and the brain—were right above them. Maybe another kilometer up, another kilometer toward the axis of 2I. This was it.

Before they climbed up, though, Rao needed to see something. She had heard something, a squirming, wet sound coming up from below. She was pretty sure she knew what was down there—what she would see. Still she leaned over the edge, peering down.

"Ms.—Ms. Channarong? Can you bring your light over here?" Channarong went to stand next to her and pointed the big flashlight down into the shadows below.

Worms covered every inch of ground, filled all the space she could see below them. Countless worms—some no bigger than elephants, swarming and crawling over one that had to be as big as an ocean liner. Channarong's light couldn't illuminate all of that one at the same time. They were moving constantly, their legs moving up and down like a million pistons, their teeth spinning pointlessly. Some of them gnawed at the bones that supported the cage. Many were just running back and forth, as if desperately looking for something to eat.

It was a boiling cauldron of life. A sea of motion. It felt so wrong, so different from the vast desert silences they'd crossed to get here. There was a desperate animation to them, a surging, insatiable need that drove them. Rao could feel it even from their position in the heights.

"They want something. They want what's in the cage," Hawkins said. He looked up at Rao with a question in his eyes.

She nearly flinched. She caught herself before she could totter over the edge into that ocean of legs and teeth. "The brain—" She shook her head. "They want—no. No. I don't want to speculate—"

Hawkins was on her in a flash, looming over her, reaching out as if he would grab her by the shoulders and shake her. "Tell us," he hissed.

"It's all right," Jansen said. "You're the only one of us who understands what we're seeing. Go ahead, Rao."

The astrobiologist's shoulders slumped, but she knew she had no choice. They needed to hear this, if she was right. They needed to get it. "I think...the cage isn't there to protect against collisions, or asteroid strikes, or—it's not for exterior threats. It's to keep the worms away from the brain. It can't last forever. They'll chew through these buttresses and get to it, but...they don't eat the bones, we know that, and—the cage is there to make sure that whatever is inside the cage gets eaten last. That would make sense if it's a brain, you would want to keep that running right up until the last possible second."

"The worms," Jansen said. "They're eating 2I alive. What are they, some kind of parasite?"

"Oh no," Rao said. "No. Not at all. Parasites evolve to take advantage of the weaknesses of an organism, the places it can't defend itself. No, 2I evolved for this. We saw how fast it grows—it's constantly growing new tissues, new flesh to feed the worms."

"It wants to be eaten?" Jansen asked.

"Of course. It wants its children to grow and prosper." She could see horror erupt across Jansen's face, a crawling, rippling disgust. She understood.

Hawkins needed it explained more clearly. "What are you talking about?"

"Matriphagy," Rao said. "It's common in spiders and nematodes back on Earth. It's a good strategy if all you're concerned about is passing on your genes. And it's not like there's anything else out here for the children to eat." She gave him a cold smile. She felt dizzy, suddenly, and she needed to sit down. She put her hands on the sides of her helmet. "They're larvae," she said.

Hawkins squatted down to stare her in the face. "We saw their eggs, their cocoons—"

"They're larvae. They're 2I's young. It gave birth to them, and now it's letting them eat its flesh. Whatever it is that 2I wants, it doesn't plan to live to see it. But the worms will. It'll die, but the next generation will be strong in its multitudes. It will die, and its young will chew their way out of its corpse."

The buttress was different from the other bone pylons Rao had observed. It was made of the same long, tough fibers, but they were woven together much more closely here. She could almost see herself reflected in the smooth surface. There were no caves or ridges—nothing they could have used as hand- or footholds. Instead they used the climbing gear, the same motorized ascenders they'd used to climb down into 2I's interior.

As her ascender pulled her smoothly, slowly toward the top, she kicked off the side of the pylon. Too hard—she went flying outward on the rope, having forgotten to make allowances for the low gravity. She counted thirty seconds before she came swinging back to catch herself with her feet. They were getting very close to the axis here. She thought of ARCS, who had flown most of the way across 2I's length by sticking to that imaginary line where there was no gravity at all. She knew it had stopped reporting a while before. Had something in the cage grabbed it out of the air, like a bird in flight?

She was getting near the top of the buttress when she noticed that the bone, normally colorless and homogeneous, had turned into something like marble. There were dark veins running through its pale surface—almost literally. The veins were tendrils, the circulatory system of 2I. Brains needed a lot of blood flow, a lot of oxygen. She had no doubt the whole cage would be webbed with the tendrils that had killed Stevens and Holmes, that covered every square centimeter of the drum.

She activated the brake on her ascender as she neared the top, her lights showing her a smooth curve of bone and then nothing, just dark air. She climbed hand over hand for the last few meters. Lifting her weight was no problem—in fact, she had to slow herself down so she didn't just overshoot the top and go flying past. When she reached the top of the rope she found it tied off to one of KSpace's pitons. It made her think of when they'd first entered the drum, sliding down orange ropes through the cone, through the black sludge. They'd come nearly eighty kilometers since then. Not such a long distance, truly, but it felt as if she'd been in the dark for a lifetime now. She knew it had changed her, made her more confident, tougher—and changed her in other ways, too, she was sure. Ways she wouldn't truly understand until she was back in the light and the open air of Earth. How could anyone come through a passage like this the same person who had left?

Hawkins reached out a hand to help her up. She didn't need it, but she didn't brush him off. Jansen and Channarong were nearby—Rao had been the last one to come up the rope. The others were all standing, looking south, away from her. She could feel their impatience and their anxiety. She shared it.

Yet she had to take a good look around before they proceeded. She would never have this chance again. To stand inside the skull of a creature from another star.

Channarong's light bounced as she walked, revealing only glimpses of what surrounded them, but slowly Rao built up a mental image. The cage was no more than a kilometer across. It was made of concentric rings of bone—she could see them nested before her, nearly as thick as walls, with only a little dark air showing between.

There was a sort of floor underneath them, a platform of slick bone about ten meters across that formed a walkway running straight forward. Looking up and around she saw similar platforms every sixty degrees around the circumference—so six of them in total. Clearly they weren't there for her benefit. They were simply longitudinal supports, designed to hold the concentric rings of the bars of the cage in place.

Directly ahead, in the direction of the south pole, was some enormous organ, vaguely blue in color. It formed a ring around the imaginary axis, a thick band of flesh that clung to the bony bars of the cage. She was certain it was 2I's brain. Theory, hypothesis, conjecture—it couldn't be anything else. She was suddenly desperate to see what it looked like, and she raced ahead of the others—until she stepped on something that crunched under her boot and stumbled, falling forward with comical slowness to catch herself with her hands.

She looked back and saw that the thing she'd stepped on was a memory stick. Looking around her, she saw others like it. They littered the floor here. There must have been hundreds of them, just discarded and left to lie where they'd fallen.

Channarong came up beside her and grabbed the stick up in her hand. She held it to her light and Rao could see that its case was cracked but the sliver of memory glass inside was still intact.

Jansen took it from her and slotted it into the receptacle on the front of her suit. She played the contents for everyone to hear.

AUDIO FILE TRANSCRIPT (1)

Willem Foster: In the dark she lived a quiet life, a cold and slow time where thoughts stretched out over the length of light-months. Each breath an eon.

The file ended there. Just a few seconds of audio. In the recording Foster's voice was soft as a feather tickling her ear. It sounded as if he had barely whispered the words, spoken them at the edge of audibility, then boosted the volume after the recording was done. The vowels almost disappeared. Each sibilant reared up and struck like a cobra.

Rao found another stick and picked it up off the floor. She slotted it and saw that it contained just one small audio file.

AUDIO FILE TRANSCRIPT (2)

Willem Foster: She knew another world once. A place of deep gorges and salty tide pools under an orange sun. She doesn't understand the concept of orange, of course. She felt that sun in terms of magnetic flux, she felt its radiation burning on her skin. That world is gone now. I don't know how far away it was, but... it's gone.

Rao's lights stabbed straight ahead, toward the great fleshy ring of the brain, but still she could make out only a vague sense of motion, as if the brain were rippling, waves sloshing back and forth through its mass. She moved quickly now, exactly like Armstrong on the moon, each step a shuffling leap that took her five or six meters forward at a time. She had to fight to keep her balance.

Behind her Jansen picked up another memory stick from the litter of them on the floor, slotted it, played the file.

AUDIO FILE TRANSCRIPT (3)

Willem Foster: It isn't talking, what we do. There is no barrier here, no self, no I, no ego. We shade into one another, indivisible.

Rao barely heard the words. She was close to the brain now. Close enough to hear it rustling. An eternal, busy, fluttering sound, and she knew it was a sound she'd heard before. It had been quieter, then, less hectic. But it was exactly the same sound that she'd heard in the forest of the hand-trees. Yet where that rustling had been the gentle stirring of leaves in a forest canopy, this was the sound of trees being lashed by a windstorm. A constant din of activity, a roar of white noise.

The hand-forest they'd seen near 2I's heart had been a kind of ganglion, a cluster of nerve cells. This was the very center of 2I's central nervous system. Its prime mover, its intelligence.

AUDIO FILE TRANSCRIPT (4)

Willem Foster: She feels the pull of Earth's gravity the way we feel love. The way we rush to embrace a lover. She feels the sun in the wind that catches in her wings, cheering her onward. After the long, cold time in the deeper dark, everything she feels now is so sudden, so large, so powerful. She would weep constantly, if she had eyes.

The brain was made of hands. Hands only slightly larger than her own, countless hands exactly like the fruit of the hand-trees she'd seen before, except so many more of them—and instead of sprouting from branches, here the hands grew from other hands, which emerged from the palms and wrists and backs of still other hands—in their profusion, in their myriads, they were constantly moving, gripping each other, grasping and releasing, fingers extended only to be grasped by other hands. The motion of them never stopped, and it moved so fast it was hard to follow. As her lights played over the surface of the brain, it felt as if she were looking at some impossible circular river that flowed from itself back into itself. A circle of hands, grasping and releasing, grasping and releasing, endlessly touching, briefly holding, touching, gripping, grabbing—

"That's enough!"

AUDIO FILE TRANSCRIPT (5)

Willem Foster: She subsists on dust and hydrogen. Her children need meat.

"Enough," Hawkins shouted. "I don't want to hear any more of these recordings! Where the hell is Foster? Is he here?"

"Yes," Channarong said.

"Foster? Come out and show yourself!" Hawkins shouted into the rustling noise of the brain. "Let me see you."

Channarong brought her light around and pointed it straight ahead, to where the platform they stood on met the fleshy ring of the brain. Foster was sitting there. He'd been right there the whole time.

CHARLOTTE HARRIWELL, KSPACE VICE PRESIDENT OF CREWED OPERATIONS: Oh no. Oh God, no.

LOSS OF SIGNAL

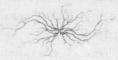

S andra Channarong went over to him and took a water bottle from her belt. She laid it by his feet, then reached over to straighten the orange romper he wore. It was a pointless task. The garment hung on Foster's emaciated frame in deep, shadowy folds. There wasn't much left of him—his arms and legs were just skin hanging on bones like sticks.

He half sat, half slumped against a pile of backpacks and rolled-up blankets. His hands lay on the ground, unmoving. His head was tilted back, his face pointing upward, toward the axis, his mouth slightly agape. Jansen could see the dry, black nub of his tongue. It moved as she watched. He was still alive.

One of his hands reached for the water bottle and slowly, painstakingly brought it up to his lips. He took a sip of the water and swirled it around in his mouth.

Jansen stepped closer. Even though she didn't want to. Her singular suit light caught his face, the sharpness of his cheekbones. She didn't want to look at this. She didn't want to see it.

Tendrils rose from the ground behind him, snaky arteries that connected to the mass of the brain. They climbed up the bedrolls and backpacks, branches anchoring them in place. Then they climbed up the sides of his head, over his temples, growing thicker. Fatter.

Two of them, two thick tendrils, plunged into his eye sockets. There was a little dried blood crusted around them where they entered. A third, thinner tendril curled in through his right nostril. She saw it throb. Pulse with life.

His eyes. His eyes were—

They'd been replaced.

Jansen knelt down beside him, on the other side from Channarong. She pushed her hand against her mouth. It was the only way she could keep from crying out.

Foster set the water bottle down very carefully, as if he was afraid of spilling it. Then he picked up something else—a voice recorder. A stubby cylindrical device with a microphone grille on one end and a slot for a memory stick on the other. He pressed it right against his thin lips and whispered. Jansen couldn't hear what he said over the susurrus of the brain behind him.

When he finished speaking he touched a button on the side of the device. It played back what he'd said, amplified to audibility.

Sandy? Did they bring their radio?

"It's here," Jansen said, patting the neutrino gun where it was mounted at her waist. "They can hear you, back on Earth. Whatever you have to say, I'm sure NASA will get it to KSpace."

Good.

"How?" she asked. "How did this happen? Did they—did the tendrils attack you here? Is that how you—"

She stopped because he was speaking again, through his handheld recorder.

Attack? No, of course not. I chose this.

"I don't understand."

Of course you do. I know you've been watching my videos. You must have seen what happened to Taryn. You heard what he said, while he was connected to the Object's veins. It wasn't just gibberish: he felt what the Object felt, if only for the few seconds before he died. Sandy and I confirmed it with her own experiment. It took some trial and error, but we figured it out. How to complete our mission. We were sent to make contact with the Object, and here we are. Here I am.

The memory stick popped up from the back of the recorder. Channarong removed it and threw it away from her, into the dark. There was a pile of fresh sticks lying next to Foster. She grabbed a new one and slotted it into place.

"You're talking to 2I. Through the tendrils," Jansen said, because she needed it made clear. She needed to understand exactly what was happening.

I've connected my nervous system directly to the Object's nervous system. 2I. Right. That's what you call her.

Jansen laid a hand on his arm. It felt like a dry stick, as if it might snap if she gripped it too hard.

Rao stirred behind Jansen. She stepped forward and crouched down in front of Foster. "I'm sorry—I'm Parminder Rao, the flight surgeon from *Orion*. Sir, I'm really worried about your physical condition. You look like you've suffered from severe malnutrition. You look like you haven't eaten in months." Rao looked up at Channarong. "I'm assuming this has happened since you left *Wanderer*. Right?"

Channarong just nodded.

She takes from me. I take from her. Don't worry. I'm not even hungry. She supplies me with what I need. She doesn't understand human physiology very well. She's learning, though. She'll keep me alive. As long as we're connected.

"Look, we can get you loose from . . . from the tendrils," Jansen promised. "We can get you out of here. There's plenty of room on *Orion*, we can take you and Channarong home. I promise, we'll make sure you get home safe."

He whispered into his recorder. Then he hit play.

No, thank you.

"Maybe you're disoriented," Jansen said. "Maybe you're confused. But we have to get you away from this thing, we need to—"

"Jansen."

Hawkins was looming over her. She could feel his presence behind her. She didn't turn around.

"Jansen, I'm the mission commander."

To Foster she said, "I came a long way to find you, and I'm not leaving you behind now. Channarong," she said, "help me. We need to get these things off of him."

Channarong just stared at her, as silent and malevolent as a house cat blinking in a patch of sun.

"Jansen," Hawkins bellowed. "Out of the way."

Then he reached down and grabbed her shoulders and shoved her away from Foster. She sputtered and protested, but he was stronger than her. He squatted down on his haunches right in front of the KSpace commander.

"We had a deal," Hawkins said. "I bring you the neutrino gun. You tell us what 2I wants with Earth."

Foster's head didn't move. Maybe it was locked in place. He lifted his left hand, though, in an unmistakable gesture of dismissal.

Isn't it obvious? he asked. **She wants to feed her children.**

ROY MCALLISTER: Orion 7 was launched to discover just this, to understand what the alien wanted from us. We'd thought we could handle it, whatever it was. And now . . . we know it was so much worse than we could have imagined.

AUDIO FILE TRANSCRIPT (6)

They grow so fast. They're fattening up nicely. But mother's meat isn't enough.

In the quiet time—the time she spent between the stars—she gathered what she could. Hydrogen, mostly, but also water, some organic compounds. She hoarded it away, stored it through the lean centuries. It was enough to keep her going, in hibernation. There were some elements, though, some basic compounds she couldn't find out there. Vitamins— think of it as vitamins, nutrients her children require, that she can't make for them.

She needed to find a place that had those vitamins in large quantities. She traveled a long, long way to find such a place.

In the last few days she will slow herself down as much as she can, spreading her wings ever wider. She will enter Earth's atmosphere in a ball of fire. The outer hull will function as a very efficient heat shield, but it can't protect her from the impact when she lands, of course. That will kill her. Even this cage of bone won't save her brain. She'll perish...but most of her children will live, protected inside her body.

When that moment comes, when she dies, they'll know. They'll go crazy, devouring everything they find, even the bones of their mother, even her shell. They'll pick her clean, but even that won't be enough. They'll burrow into the soil of Earth. Dig deep. They can eat anything, if they're hungry enough. Their metabolism is so fast, so robust. They'll eat the ground out from under the wreckage of our cities. They'll feast on half-molten rock deeper inside the crust than any human has ever gone.

And as they eat, they'll change. Get bigger, of course, some as big as she is now, or bigger. Their skin will thicken and turn to crystal. They will sprout wings.

And when they've had their fill of Earth, they'll spread those wings and fly. Catch the wind from the sun and soar off in every possible direction. Only then will they grow quiet, only when they reach the outer frozen marches of our solar system. Like her, they will sleep. Until they find new suns, and new planets of their own.

This is their life cycle. The way they reproduce. Her species has been doing this for...Well. She doesn't share our concept of time. But long before we stood up on two feet. Before the dinosaurs, or even the trilobites. Her kind spread, from sun to sun, across the galaxy, on a timescale we can't possibly comprehend. And they'll be traveling between the stars a long, long time after we're gone.

Rao closed her eyes. She felt dizzy and weak. She wanted to take off her helmet and catch her breath. She wanted to be sick.

She looked up at the others, looked for one of them to roll their eyes or laugh, something to show her it wasn't true.

Aliens had come to Earth. The thing she'd been dreaming of since she was a kid, and now here—here was the reality of what it meant.

Jansen stared at the ground, her eyes blank. Hawkins stood up, horror making his skin crawl.

"Why Earth?" he demanded. "Why come here, instead of any other planet?"

She didn't choose us, any more than a dandelion seed chooses the field it falls on. We're not special. And we're not the first planet they've come to—or the millionth. They'll spread across the entire galaxy, in time. Until there are no planets left. It's a wonderfully simple system, an endless loop of life.

Sandra Channarong picked up the water bottle and put it into Foster's groping hand. He wet his lips. Swirled water around his dry mouth.

"You sound almost sympathetic," Rao said. The words came out as a whisper. "Like you might be OK with all that."

Foster laughed. A very strange sound coming out of the voice recorder.

No. Though sometimes ... It's hard. She doesn't think, you see. Not the way we do, not in words, or even images. Her senses are not ours. That's why this is the only way we can communicate. But the connection is profound. It's so intimate. I've never had this with a human being, not even a lover. I forget sometimes where she ends and I begin.

The memory stick popped out of its slot. Channarong replaced it, throwing the old one over her shoulder.

"You have to find a way to convince ... her," Rao said. "Make her turn away from Earth. Before it's too late."

I'm trying.

"Try fucking harder," Jansen said, climbing to her feet.

You don't understand. How could you? When I first connected with her, she immediately tried to devour me. Just like she did with Taryn. Just convincing her that I wasn't part of her, that she needed to let me live—that was a huge milestone.

We don't share a language, we don't share so many basic concepts. Each day I learn more. I learn so much, and she learns from me.

"What?" Hawkins asked. "What are you telling it?"

Everything. I can't keep secrets in here. It's not possible.

"That's not acceptable," Hawkins said. "You can't—"

Jansen shouted over him. "Stevens did it," she said.

Foster didn't say anything. A frown crossed his chapped lips.

"Stevens connected with this thing. He was dying, he was—he was brain dead." Jansen said. "He was way past coherent communication. He wasn't even plugged into its brain, but somehow—he made it move. Change course."

Rao remembered the sounds Stevens had made, at the very end. Right before 2I smashed into *Wanderer.*

Stevens. I heard him...I heard his last moments. She can hear radio waves, of course. She heard you calling for me, Jansen, all those times. It was only Stevens she listened to. He was connected to her, nervous system to nervous system. Just as I am now. In fact—it would be fair to say there's part of him in here, with us.

Puh. Puh. Puh.

Just nonsense, just sounds. But it had been enough. Yes—yes, it was possible, it was—

No. No, no, no. She refused to believe the thought that was hovering right there in the middle of her mind, the idea that had come to her unbidden, unwanted.

That sound, that repeated, horrible sound. It wasn't nonsense at all. She hadn't made the association before. Because she hadn't wanted to. Because what it meant was going to hurt so much when she finally accepted it—

She doesn't think in words, or even images. She has desires. Instincts. That's the level where we can communicate. Interesting. You say Stevens was in extremis. So far gone that all he had left was the base, reflexive urges of his id. That's what got through to her. Give me time, Foster said. I can use that. Give me a few more weeks and I'll find a way. The two of us can come to some accommodation.

"Weeks?" Hawkins asked.

Behind her Rao heard him unzip a pocket of his suit.

"We don't have weeks."

I can't rush this process.

"I've heard enough," Hawkins told him.

Rao was vaguely aware of him behind her, of the fact that he was raising his arm. She saw the look of shock that came over Channarong's face, and saw the woman reach toward her belt.

Then a gunshot exploded right next to Rao's head. Even muffled by her helmet, it was so loud it deafened her, made her ears ring. She couldn't see for a moment. She blinked and her vision cleared and she saw a round, dark hole in the middle of Foster's forehead.

The voice recorder fell out of his hand and clattered to the ground.

Rao swung around and saw Hawkins standing over her, a snubnosed pistol in his hand. Smoke leaked from the barrel, forming a fat cloud in the low gravity.

"No!" Sandra Channarong shrieked. She had her own weapon— a multi-tool she'd taken from her pocket. She had a three-inch blade out and locked into place. She raised it high and ran at Hawkins, her features consumed by fury.

He twisted a little at the waist and fired again, and she collapsed in a heap next to Foster.

On Earth Charlotte Harriwell jumped to her feet and grabbed the railing of the catwalk, her whole body tensing and straining. Roy McAllister looked over at her, but her eyes were locked on the grainy image in front of them. He reached out one hand, intending to grab hers, whether to offer comfort or simply solidarity, he didn't know.

She didn't take his hand. She looked paralyzed. Frozen in place.

"What did you do?" Jansen asked, ignoring her protesting knee and dropping to all fours next to the corpse of Willem Foster.

She looked up, hot tears filling the corners of her eyes.

"Why?" she demanded.

Hawkins was breathing heavily. He looked confused for a moment. Maybe disoriented, as if he didn't understand himself.

"Why?"

"I had to," he said.

He didn't lower the gun or put it away.

"Was this—was this the plan all along?" she asked, horrified. "Did the space force tell you to do this?"

"Of course not! Kalitzakis would never order something like this. But sometimes when you're the mission commander...you have to make hard decisions."

"An MC is supposed to keep her crew alive," Jansen insisted.

"They weren't my crew. Anyway—you heard Foster say he was sharing our secrets with 2I. He was—"

"He was *talking* to it," Jansen wailed. "And Channarong—you killed her, too!"

"She was coming at me with a knife! Listen. Listen to me, Jansen. It had to be done. It had to. He wasn't even human anymore. He was some kind of *perversion*. 2I co-opted him. It was taking him over."

Jansen shook her head wildly. "We could have got that stuff off of him. We could have saved him. Both of them—we could have gotten them home, safe. We were so close."

"Home?" he asked. He stared down at his handiwork. The confusion had drained from his face, replaced with a terrible certainty. A confidence that he'd done the right thing. "They were never going home."

He lifted the pistol and pointed it directly at Jansen's head. "I'm sorry," he said, "but you've got to understand. You of all people."

"What?" she asked. She didn't care about the gun. She was surprised to find she wasn't afraid at all, even though she knew she was looking at her death.

She just needed to know why he'd done what he had.

"What are you talking about?"

"They were infected. You saw the necrosis on Channarong's neck. You knew what that meant. You saw the necrosis—just like what happened to Stevens. Exactly like that. We couldn't bring that back to Earth. My God, how can you even imagine doing that? After what we've seen, with what we know about 2I. What it can do to human bodies. Dying like this—I showed them mercy, Jansen. I saved them from their misery."

"You son of a bitch," she said.

It was clear to him now. It was so clear. He'd felt weird ever since he woke up on the island with a concussion. He'd felt as if his thoughts were foul mud being pumped through clogged pipes. Now, though. Now. The ringing in his ears, the echo of the gunshots, was like a clean wind that had blown away all the darkness. He could finally see clearly, and he knew what he had to do.

He had to protect the Earth. He had to save the world.

"General Kalitzakis," he shouted, over the noise the women made. "General! I've found it. The brain. You can fire at will, sir. Fire, and kill this fucking thing."

He had lifted his eyes as he addressed the dark air, sure that the general would hear him. That he had done his duty—he had found 2I's weak spot. One shot, and all this would be over. One kinetic impactor straight through the brain, and 2I would be left dead in the water.

"Hawkins," someone called, and for a single distracted moment he thought it was Kalitzakis calling him, calling to tell him he'd done his duty and now he could rest.

But it wasn't. It was Jansen. She had grabbed his leg, and she was looking up at him with pleading eyes. Well, that made sense. He was her mission commander. He was the one who made the decisions. He knew what she wanted.

Too bad he couldn't provide it. But leadership sometimes meant taking the option no one else was willing to face.

"I'm sorry, Sally," he said. "I'm sorry. But they couldn't go home. And neither can we."

He lifted his sidearm and placed the hot barrel against the side of her head.

"We're infected, too," he said. "The moment you took my

helmet off, you signed my death warrant. When you took your own helmet off, you made this necessary."

He started to squeeze the trigger, but then—

Something moved in his peripheral vision. Some new monster coming at him, coming to kill him. His thinking wouldn't have passed muster if he'd given it a moment's consideration, but there was no time to be rational. Something was coming at him, fast and with violent intent.

He twisted around and snapped off a single shot.

"It's better this way," Hawkins said. "I know you can't see that right now. But it's better...She's in a better place."

Jansen closed her eyes, but she just saw it again. Over and over.

Rao—running toward Hawkins, maybe thinking she could wrestle the gun away from him. Maybe she thought she had no other choice.

Then Hawkins fired, and a tiny hole appeared right in the center of Rao's faceplate, and blood splattered the inside of the polycarbonate.

Jansen opened her eyes. She saw Rao lying on the ground, face-down, one arm twisted underneath her body, the other stretched out, the fingers grasping at the bone floor. Rao wasn't moving.

"You bastard," she said. "You bastard." She couldn't breathe. Her chest was heaving with big, choking sobs. She had just wanted—all she'd wanted was—

"You hate me. Well, I promise you. I'm going to make this quick. Then I'll shoot myself. I have enough bullets left for both of us. I'm going to die here, too."

She sucked in a deep breath, her body desperate for oxygen. The air was so thin here, near the axis. She cleared her throat and then looked him right in the eye.

"Why don't you go first?" she said.

He laughed. The bastard laughed at her joke. And for a split second, the barrel of his gun drifted and wasn't pointing right at her.

Jansen exploded upward from the ground. She felt something in her knee finally give way, felt a tendon tear apart, but it held just long enough. She got her shoulder down, and it collided with the fiberglass torso of Hawkins's suit. It hurt—bad—but she put every ounce of strength she had into the hit.

His feet danced on the bone platform as he tried to maintain his balance. In the gravity of Earth, it might have worked. The gravity here was closer to that of the moon, and his feet flew out from under him. He collapsed to the floor, his arms flailing out behind him. It seemed to take forever for him to land.

When he did, his right hand struck the surface first. His fingers opened and his gun went spinning away, out of his reach.

She collapsed on top of him. Both of them stared out into the dark, looking for the weapon. It had fallen somewhere in the deep shadows, invisible.

Good enough. Jansen reared up and smashed her fist across his jaw. His head twisted over to the side, and his mouth flew open. She punched him again. She pulled her arm back for a third strike—but his hands flashed up and he grabbed her wrist, pushing her backward.

Jansen snarled and twisted away, struggling to get to her feet. He had already climbed up into a fighting crouch, though, and he pounced before she could get up. He smacked her across the face, and lights burst behind her eyes. Then he jumped in the air and came down hard, falling slowly in the low gravity, but it didn't matter.

He brought his two boots down on her left leg. On her injured knee.

This pain wasn't like being stabbed. This was a tidal wave of nauseous filth washing over her. A sense of utter, final wrongness, and she knew her leg would never work again, that her kneecap had been reduced to shards of sharp bone. Then a new wave, this one of howling blackness, swept across her mind and then—then she was just gone, her conscious mind racing down into a deep cave to get away from the horror and the agony. Everything went dark.

Hawkins grabbed her by the arms and started hauling her across the platform. It should have been easy in the low gravity, but her limp weight and friction made him grunt and puff as he moved her, centimeter by centimeter, toward the edge. He had to admit she'd gotten in a few good hits, as well—his jaw felt as if it had been knocked out of place.

It didn't matter. In a second she would be dead and he would be alone. He would find the gun and . . . No.

No.

He decided he'd earned a little reward. He wouldn't shoot himself. Instead he would wait for General Kalitzakis to fire the impactor right through 2I's brain. He would have a front row seat at the death of the alien.

He had some idea of what it would look like. He'd studied the weapons system, and he knew how it functioned—similar to an anti-tank weapon. When the impactor struck the hull of 2I, it would be moving fast. Dozens of kilometers a second. At that speed, the outer hull and the inner drum might as well be made of wet tissue paper. The impactor would cut through them effortlessly, but in the process it would grow incredibly hot. The depleted uranium core would liquefy and turn into a jet of scalding metal that would burn its way right through 2I's brain. It wouldn't stop until it melted its way through the far side of the hull.

Hurricane-force winds would howl out through the entry and exit wounds. The worms would choke and die as their atmosphere was torn out of their damned throats. 2I's systems would shut down and then freeze as they were exposed to the cold vacuum of space.

And Hawkins would be sitting there, observing it all. Maybe he would even put his helmet back on, and use one of the last remaining oxygen cartridges. Maybe he would sit for a while after it was all over, looking over what he had done. What he had destroyed. He would sit and witness the death throes and the long cold silence that followed. When his batteries died, when his lights went out—then he would remove the helmet again. Take one last breath of air and just . . . let go.

He deserved that. He deserved a little glory.

He had reached the end of the platform. On either side of him a colossal rib rose up into the gloom, so that he felt as if he were standing on a balcony above the swarming, ravening mass of the worms far below. A generalissimo standing on a castle wall looking down at a besieging army. He dragged Jansen right up to the edge and positioned her so with one good kick he could roll her over into the waiting maws below.

At the last moment, though, he flinched. He looked down into Jansen's unconscious face. Wondering what Roy McAllister had ever seen in this old woman. She'd failed. She'd failed to go to Mars—she had personally lost the second space race for America. She'd killed Blaine Wilson and Sunny Stevens. She had fought him every step of the way after he took over command of the mission.

But she was still a human being. She didn't deserve to die like this, torn to shreds by the rotating teeth of an alien worm.

He turned and looked around the platform. Channarong's light painted a broad yellow triangle across the bone. His own suit lights illuminated a smaller, paler patch. He searched for his sidearm, and after a while he saw it, the square angle of its grip just at the edge of Channarong's light. He walked over to it and started to bend down to pick it up. It looked so tiny compared to other handguns he'd owned and shot. The barrel had been filed down to almost nothing, and the trigger guard had been cut away so he could handle it even through the thick gloves of a space suit. In the interest of saving weight, the grip had been skeletonized, cut down to a hollow frame in the shape of a normal pistol grip. It had been designed to be hidden inside a pocket of his space suit, put there without NASA's ever being the wiser. Roy McAllister had insisted that *Orion* 7 not carry any weapons—he felt that would send the wrong message to the aliens. What a fool. The space force had refused to send their man into a hostile situation unarmed, and this tiny weapon was the compromise.

He wrapped his fingers around the grip. The magazine was partially exposed, and he could see there were still two bullets inside. More than he needed now.

He stood up, his knees creaking just a little. He felt suddenly very tired and sore. He was turning into an old pile of wreckage like Jansen. The idea made him laugh a little. Well, he would never have to worry about old age.

One bullet. He would make sure Jansen died quickly. Painlessly. It was the least she deserved. He started walking back toward where she lay, at the edge of the platform. She hadn't moved. He stepped through Channarong's discarded light, then back into the shadows.

Where someone was waiting for him.

He could just make out the shape of a space suit. A helmet with what looked like a bloodshot eye in the middle of its faceplate. Fear bubbled through his blood—no, not fear, he'd just been startled. "Rao?" he said. "I'm so sorry. I didn't mean to kill you. It was just an accident. You were never exposed to 2I. You could have gone home, I think. Maybe."

A ghost. He was talking to a ghost. *Huh*, he thought. Maybe he had gone crazy. He wondered how he would know for sure.

Then the ghost lifted Channarong's multi-tool, with its three-inch blade, and slashed his throat wide open.

Rao could barely see through the blood inside her faceplate. She had caught only a glimpse of Hawkins before she attacked. For the first time in her life she hadn't thought about what she was doing. She'd just—just—

It was suddenly desperately important to get her helmet off. She tried to twist it off, and it wouldn't budge until she remembered the two catches. Then it screwed off just fine, clicking right before it released. She hauled it off her head and then tossed it away from her, horrified suddenly by the blood.

She dropped to her knees and tried very hard to throw up. Her stomach was empty, so she just gagged for a while. What she'd done, what she had—just—

She scrubbed at her face and then her mouth with the cloth patch on the back of her sleeve. There was a mirror there, too. She lifted it carefully, as if looking at her own face was what would finally kill her. As if she were already dead but still moving until she actually saw.

Her reflection, in the dim light, was mostly intact. There was a deep gouge in her cheek, a trench where the bullet had passed along the curve of her cheekbone. She palpated the wound very carefully and found that while it was pretty messy, it hadn't done any significant damage. Even the nerves there seemed intact.

Hawkins had shot her right in the face. He was—had been—an excellent shot, and he would have killed her reflexively. Except that the thick polycarbonate of her faceplate had changed the trajectory of the bullet as it traveled toward the bridge of her nose. Just enough to save her life.

She would be OK. She would—she—

She was breathing the air of 2I, for the first time. She remembered Jansen mentioning the strange smell, and now she got to experience it for herself. It made her think of the hermit crab she used to keep in a fish tank in her bedroom, back in high school. When the hermit crab got sick and died, the tank had smelled a little like this. A little.

"Ma'am?" she said, crouching over Jansen's unconscious form. "Sally?"

Jansen's face was creased with agony, and sweat had slicked her short blonde hair. Her eyes fluttered open, though, when Rao rolled her back from the edge of the platform. She let out a nasty little grunt of pain, a broken, warbling cry that barely sounded human.

"Hawkins?" she managed to croak out.

"No longer a problem," Rao replied. Even to her own ears her voice sounded very far away. She forced herself to focus on her patient, poking and prodding to see just how badly Jansen was hurt.

"Your pupils look good, and your breathing is...not great, but I think you're going to live. Do you want some more of those NSAIDs from the medical kit? I doubt they'll help very much with the pain, but the inflammation from your previous injury never really subsided, and I think it's probably a good idea to—"

"Rao," Jansen whispered.

"Yes, ma'am?"

"Shut up." Her eyelids fluttered as if she might pass out again. "And yes. Pills. And—"

Rao leaned in close to hear what else Jansen had to say.

"Thank you."

DESTRUCTIVE REENTRY

*R*OY MCALLISTER: *While it was all happening I could do nothing but watch it unfold. The world could have ended outside, but I would have refused to leave the neutrino telescope. It was not until much later that I noticed I'd received a message from General Kalitzakis. It was short but it required no context. It simply read,* 17%.

The bone platform shook. It was just a little tremor, but it sent a fresh rush of pain up Jansen's leg into her hip. She looked around, but there was nothing to see. "What was that?" she asked.

Rao had been checking on Foster and Channarong. Perhaps trying to decide if they were really dead. There was no need, but it gave her something to do. Now she came racing back to Jansen's side. "I'm not sure," she said. "I felt the ground shake earlier, but I thought I was just so scared I was shivering."

Jansen reached for the younger woman's arm. "It wasn't just you. Can you help me sit up? And then—"

The next shock was stronger. It felt as if someone had kicked the platform underneath her. As if they'd given it a very hard kick.

"Oh," Rao said. "Oh. I think—oh."

Jansen took a deep breath. She saw where Rao was looking, so she took the helmet off her belt and pointed its single light in that direction. Toward the brain.

At first it looked exactly as she remembered. An endless ring of hands with long, creepy fingers. Slightly blue in color. It took her far too long—she blamed the pain—to recognize what had changed.

None of those hands were moving. They weren't gripping each other's wrists. The fingers weren't even curled up. The brain was absolutely still and silent.

The platform moved a good half meter, then swung back to its previous position. There was no question now that it was shaking, and Jansen had a bad feeling she knew why.

"That motherfucker," she said. She realized she wasn't entirely sure whom she was talking about. Hawkins or maybe Foster. "He was linked to it, with no barriers, he said. They melted into each other. When he died—"

"2I must have felt like it was dying, too," Rao said.

"And that's the signal. The signal the worms were waiting for. They'll eat the bones," she said. The platform shook, and she reached out for anything to hold on to, but found nothing. The bone beneath her was smooth as ivory.

She didn't need to look over the edge to know what must be happening down there. The worms must have all gone crazy at once. Maybe the signal was a pheromone, or maybe it was some kind of radio pulse—it didn't matter.

How long would it take them to gnaw their way through the pylons? How many minutes left before the whole cage came crashing down into their waiting teeth?

Probably not many.

"What do we do?" Rao asked. "Jansen?"

Jansen stared into the dark space in front of her, trying to think.

"Commander?"

Jansen looked up into Rao's lights.

"We get the hell out of here," she said. "Help me up."

The shaking didn't let up. Rao tried to help Jansen up to her feet, but it was clear the older astronaut wasn't walking anywhere. In the light gravity near the axis, Rao thought she could probably carry her—maybe if Jansen climbed up on her back—

"The secondary airlock," Jansen said. "It's not far. It's got to be just up there." She pointed at the far end of the cage, on the other side of the quiescent brain. "Maybe a kilometer, maybe less. If we can get there before this thing collapses, we have a chance."

"We don't even know if that airlock works," Rao said. Then she closed her eyes and nodded. "Right. That thought wasn't worth saying out loud."

Jansen didn't contradict her. "We've got air, and we've got a little power. Maybe just enough to get back to *Orion*. Switch off your helmet lights. We'll just use mine. It's going to be hard to see, but...but..."

Rao frowned. "What is it? What's wrong?" Despite the obvious things, of course.

"Your helmet. Where's your helmet?"

Rao reached up one hand and touched her hair. "I threw it away. It was broken, the faceplate was broken, and..."

They wouldn't get far—she wouldn't get far—outside 2I without a helmet. She'd almost forgotten they were in deep space, in the cold vacuum between worlds.

Jansen swung around in place, her light sweeping the platform. "It's fine," she said.

"Commander—"

"It's going to be fine! We'll find a way to patch it. I think I have some duct tape in one of my bags. Just help me find it."

Jansen's light swiveled and turned and finally landed on the helmet, which lay about twenty meters away near the edge of the platform. The ruined faceplate stared back at them, the faceplate spattered with blood—and shattered. When the bullet passed through the polycarbonate it had left only a small hole, but there had been a spiderweb of cracks around that wound. In the time since then the cracks had spread and now the faceplate looked like a mouth full of broken, bloody teeth.

It would have to do. Rao raced toward the helmet—then stopped and threw her arms out to her sides, dancing as the platform shook violently under her feet.

Her stomach fell. Her mouth opened in the start of a scream, as the entire platform started to tilt over to one side. It wasn't much of an incline, just a degree or two, but combined with the constant vibration it was enough. The helmet started to roll away from her, gaining speed as it hurtled toward the edge of the platform and out of sight.

Jansen shouted something at her. Rao turned to look and Jansen shouted again, and this time Rao heard her.

"Hawkins! Get Hawkins's helmet!"

But everything was moving then. Everything was rolling past her, sliding down the slope. She saw Sandra Channarong's flashlight bounce and jump, and then for a second it was flying over the edge and she saw—

—countless teeth and scrabbling limbs, a million worms, throwing themselves at the pylons, smashing their whirling mouths into the bone, she saw the buttress start to crack, long, lightning bolt–shaped fractures running up and down its smooth length, saw the tendrils inside the bone rupture and spray black ichor—

And then the light was gone, and she could see only darkness through the bars of the cage.

She looked over at Jansen, who had collapsed to the platform, her arms spread wide as she tried to hold on through sheer friction. Jansen's face was wild, her features contorted into a grimace of pure determination.

Even as she started to slide, to slip across the sheer bone.

Rao raced over and grabbed her arms. Her boots had just enough traction to hold on to the bone. She hauled and pulled and somehow managed to keep Jansen from slipping away.

There was no chance of recovering Hawkins's helmet. His body must have rolled off the platform like everything else. Rao was sure of it. Which meant they had one helmet between the two of them.

"I think," she said, trying to work up the courage to finish the thought, "I think that—"

"Look," Jansen said. She nodded at something behind Rao. "Look!"

The brain was moving again.

Not much. Jansen saw one hand reach out and feebly grab a

wrist. Looking up and down the brain's circumference, what she could see of it in their last working light, she saw a finger twitch here. A fist form there.

It was still alive. There was still some small part of the brain clinging to life.

The worms didn't seem to care. The platform shook more violently all the time. The signal had been sent. Maybe there was some way to make the worms calm down again, to get them to stop chewing away at the cage's supports, but the brain hadn't managed it yet.

Even if there was a way to stop the worms, it didn't matter much. 2I was still headed on a collision course with Earth. Dead or alive, it would smash into the planet with enough force to end all life on the surface.

But where there was life, there was hope. Right?

There had to be.

There had to be something they could still do.

Well. There was one thing Jansen could think of. The most terrifying thing she could imagine.

"Foster talked to this thing," she said. "Somebody else could do the same."

Rao's face drained of all emotion.

"No," she said. "No. No. No. No."

"Foster had days to communicate with 2I, and he couldn't make it work," Rao pointed out. "He read its memories, but he couldn't make it move."

"No," Jansen agreed. "But Stevens did. Stevens was gone, completely gone. But he found a way."

"Don't...don't..."

"Come on," Jansen said. "You're smart, Rao. Maybe the smartest woman I've ever met, and I work for NASA, so that's saying a hell of a lot. You figured out that this wasn't a spaceship, it was an animal. You must have some idea. What did Stevens know that Foster didn't?"

Rao squinted and pursed her lips as if she'd just bitten into a lemon. She didn't want to say it, but Jansen knew that there was something there. Rao had worked something out—

"God damn it, tell me," Jansen shouted.

Rao's eyes went wide. "Maybe—just maybe, OK? Maybe I have an idea, but...but...at the end you heard Stevens speak. You heard what he said."

Puh. Puh. Puh.

Jansen shook her head. "I thought that was just some reflex of his throat muscles, air leaking out of lungs he wasn't using anymore."

The platform shifted again, tilting a few more degrees. Rao redoubled her grip on Jansen's arms. It hurt.

"What Foster said, before, about how Stevens could talk to 2I when he was...when he was dying. Sunny couldn't even form words. He could only call out for what he needed the most."

Rao shook her head, not getting it—or refusing to get it.

"He was saying your name," Jansen said. "Calling out for you." Yes.

"No," Rao said. "No. No."

But Jansen was sure now. "He wanted to be with you. Foster said there was no barrier between minds when you connect with 2I. Its thoughts and yours become one. Stevens wanted to be close to you, so 2I moved toward *Orion*. You can't reason with an animal. They don't have conscious thoughts, they don't use language. They just have urges. Needs. Foster wanted to make friends with 2I and learn its secrets, but Stevens—he just needed to reach out for someone, anyone who could give him some comfort."

"No," Rao said again. "Shut up! No!"

"He wanted you," Jansen said.

Rao was crying. She turned her face away and tried to wipe her eyes on the shoulder of her suit. "I know," she said.

Rao stood before the brain. The hands were writhing now. Forming new connections. It seemed the hands nearest to her—the neurons directly in front of her—were struggling the most. As if they were responding to her presence.

Tendrils snaked between the hands. Two of them lifted into the air, their thin ends waving back and forth as if they were searching for something.

Sunny was still in there.

Foster had said as much—that some part of Sunny remained inside the brain. Some final, desperate part of him, the part that had reached out for her. The part that had made contact with 2I was still in there, still reaching for her.

She could just step forward. Take off her suit and walk into that mass of searching hands. Let them hold her, as Sunny never had. The two of them could be together. Maybe she could talk to 2I, if she did that. Maybe she could convince it, somehow, to change its course again, to head away from Earth. Maybe. And at the very least, she and Sunny would be together.

The idea was...intoxicating. She'd come all this way to understand what had happened to Sunny. Why he had to die. Now she knew. He'd died to bring her to this point. To this end.

"I want you to know it's been an honor, ma'am," Rao said. "And when you get back to Earth, I hope—"

"Rao."

"I hope you'll say I did some good here. Whatever happens. I mean, if I fail and 2I crashes into Earth and there's...there's nobody left to..."

"Rao. This is a lousy time to start being stupid."

She ground her teeth together. She knew perfectly well what Jansen was going to say next. It was the last thing she wanted to hear. It couldn't end like this. They'd lost so much, survived so many horrors. It couldn't just end like this. It couldn't.

"You're not doing this," Jansen said. "I am."

Rao turned and looked at her. "He's in there, ma'am. Some little part of him."

"We have one helmet between us. One of us can still walk," Jansen said. "Get out of here."

Then Jansen reached down to her belt and unclipped her helmet from its D ring, then shoved it in Rao's direction.

"Ma'am. I appreciate what you're offering."

"We don't have time to play this game!" Jansen shouted. She tried to grab at Rao's legs, to hold her back. Jansen's hands were weak, though, after all the physical trauma she'd been through. It would be easy for Rao to just pull free. Jansen couldn't stop her.

She turned and looked at the brain again. Sunny was waiting for her in there.

But...

Something in her chest broke, and she doubled over, sobbing violently. She nodded, though she couldn't see Jansen, not through her tears.

All she had to do was take off her suit and walk forward, into the clutching hands of the brain. Into that embrace. But...

No.

This place. 2I. She understood now. The darkness, the silence, the fear. The endless tension of being inside an alien environment. She'd thought it would change them, make them different people. But it hadn't. It had just exaggerated the darkness inside them. It had made Jansen obsessed with finding the KSpace astronauts—she had already been desperate for redemption, and it took that desperation and stretched it out to extremes. Hawkins had only ever wanted to defend the Earth. It had taken that and twisted it into paranoia.

And as for herself? It had taken her sadness over losing Sunny and distorted it into this terrible moment, this ugly, ugly choice.

It had held up a dark mirror and let them see themselves. Their worst selves. But if Rao paused, even for a moment, if she thought about things—she knew. She knew this was wrong.

She wouldn't surrender herself. She would not take what the brain offered. Not for Sunny.

She and Sunny had never been together. Not really. It had been a flirtation, a crush. It had never had a chance to become anything real. She had held on to it not because it was integral to her being but because of the way it had ended. Survivor's guilt, she supposed.

It was time to admit the truth. Sunny was gone. He was dead.

The tendrils wavered before her, reaching out. Like hands reaching for hers.

That wasn't him. Not the man she'd cared for. Just some fading echo.

"I'm sorry," she said.

Rao took the helmet Jansen offered her. She lifted it up to her head and screwed it into place. Pure air flowed across her face, cooling her down. That was good. Her face was so hot it felt as if it were on fire.

"Go! And don't look back," Jansen said.

Rao turned and climbed up onto the brain. The hands tried to grab at her legs. Tendrils lashed out toward her suit. They were weak, and she could simply push them away before they could take root. It was horrible, horrible to even think about touching all those hands, but it was nothing, nothing at all compared to what she was doing. What she was leaving behind.

"Go!"

It made a kind of logical sense, really.

Jansen used her chin to work a lever inside her collar ring. Her suit, on its last dregs of power, asked her if she was sure she wanted to open her life-support unit. She said yes. She hit the lever again, and the back of her suit swung open on spring-loaded hinges.

She had failed.

She had failed to save Blaine Wilson. She had failed to save Sunny Stevens. She had failed to save any of the KSpace astronauts. She even blamed herself for Hawkins. If she'd been a better mission commander—if she had held on to her command—

She had seen it, what the dark and the strangeness had done, warping his natural paranoia into something violent and desperate. Maybe, if she'd said something, she could have saved him, too.

But she hadn't.

She had failed. She was a failure many times over. But that was the thing about failure.

When you fell down, when you completely fucked everything up—you didn't get to lie down and surrender. No. When Blaine Wilson died, she'd known this. You owed it to everyone—not just the people you'd failed but also the people who were still there—to make things right. She'd gotten *Orion 6* back to Earth. She'd made sure Julia Obrador and Ali Dinwari got home to their families. Now she'd made sure Parminder Rao had a shot at getting home, too.

Too bad her responsibility didn't end there.

Roy McAllister had picked her because he thought she could be a real astronaut. Knowing everything that entailed—knowing that when you go to space, you put yourself at risk. You accept the fact you might not come home. More than that. Even in that desperate moment, when there's no chance of her survival, an astronaut continues to think, and to work. She salvages what she can.

She screamed a little—she allowed herself that much—and pulled her injured leg out of the suit. It twitched, and every time it twitched, blinding pain shot through her whole body, flashed through her limbs, and landed in her brain like a bomb.

She pushed the suit away from her.

It wasn't completely dark. There were status lights on the front of her suit, and they spread a tiny bit of illumination around her. Enough that she could see the hands that made up the brain. Neurons, right? They had to be some kind of giant neurons, axons and dendrites but on 2I's massive scale.

They still looked exactly like human hands, even knowing that.

She saw the hands stir. She saw them move, weakly and slowly, only a few of them at first but more of them all the time. They were reaching for each other, trying to make connections. To reestablish control.

Maybe it would help. Maybe, while the brain was still stunned, it would be easier for her to climb inside its dark space, push herself into its alien thoughts, and make herself heard.

Maybe.

She took a long, slow breath. Inhale. She let it back out. Exhale.

She had no idea how Foster had convinced this thing to send its tendrils into his brain, to connect to his central nervous system.

She reached up and grabbed a pair of the hands. 2I reached back, sending tendrils searching across her wrists, up her arms toward her face.

"OK, you bastard," she said, trying not to scream. "Time to talk."

She held her breath, as if she were diving backward into the warm ocean off the Florida coast. Closed her eyes as if she were waiting for the sudden plunge, the rush of silver bubbles, and the feeling that was almost, if never exactly, like being weightless again. Then she threw herself forward, into the sea of hands.

Rao ran, and didn't look back.

She felt immense guilt and shame for not looking back. For abandoning Sunny. For not staying with Jansen through what was about to happen. She also knew that Jansen would have shouted at her in anger if she even considered turning around.

So she ran.

She ran, but the platform tilted under her feet. She slid three meters before catching herself, swaying from the hips to try to ride out the violent tremors.

There was only one working light on her helmet, and that was the last light in the world. She kept it pointed forward, showing her where she was going. So she nearly tripped when the previously smooth floor cracked open, a dark fissure racing zigzag away from her, splitting the platform apart. For a moment she straddled that gap. Then she realized she had to pick one side or the other or risk falling into the darkness below.

She made her choice and leaped to her left, even as the crack opened wide and large fragments of the platform fell away, shards as long as she was tall, tiny chips she could have sifted through her fingers. The tendrils that had been embedded in the bone lashed at the air, looking for something they could grab on to. She had to dance sideways a little to prevent one of those questing arms from grabbing her boot.

Up ahead of her she could see the bars of the cage, rising up around her like tall, circular arches. In her light they made a bull's-eye, a series of concentric circles that defined her trajectory. The cage tapered toward its south end, to fit inside the cone that was the mirror image of the one through which she'd entered 21. The platform tilted upward, toward the axis. She had to be conscious of the weakening gravity, knew she couldn't trust the ground to stay stable—

There was a sound much louder than one of Hawkins's gunshots, though just as sudden, and she knew one of the buttresses must have snapped under the constant attack of the worms. The entire platform groaned and then new cracks spread like lightning bolts all through the floor under her feet.

She just had time to jump before it collapsed altogether.

The hands grabbed Jansen's legs, squeezed her injured knee, and she screamed. Long fingers wrapped around her arms, her throat. Tendrils crept across her skin, searching, stinging her as they dug tiny hooks into her, locking themselves in place. They were never going to let her go.

Yet the pain didn't overcome her. The horror of what she'd chosen was gone. As the tendrils caressed the lobes of her ears, as they dug into her and connected with her bloodstream, with her nerves—she was—she was—

The silver bubbles burst all around her, the surface of the water when seen from underneath was a wavering mirror that faded into darkness so quickly as you sank, and she was sinking fast, all buoyancy gone, away from light. Away from the possibility of light.

Jansen had heard a metaphor for life once, a poetic image of a bird flying through a dark winter storm. Purely by accident the bird flies in through the window of a well-lit hall, where a banquet is in progress—a room full of light and warmth and music, of rich smells and fragrant smoke—but only for an instant. Before the bird even has time to understand where it is, it flies out through another window, back into the storm, never to see the light or feel the warmth again.

This . . . was the opposite of that. Jansen's life, her fifty-six short years, were gone. Everything she'd ever seen, every laugh she'd heard from another room, every flash of a camera, every time a lover ran a fingertip down the valley of her back, every smile, every knowing, smirking look, the taste of blueberries—

A dark wind blew them all away, a dark wind howling in a space with no walls, no limits. She was so small, so insignificant, her experiences and thoughts and highest goals were nothing, microscopic. Meaningless, just noise. Red scratches on skin that faded to white, that faded away to nothing in the space of a breath. Obscene graffiti on the padded wall of *Wanderer*. A flicker of light at the bottom of a coal mine that no one would ever see.

But she was not alone.

Someone else sat with her, someone very much larger than she. Stronger in every possible way. A mind as big as a moon. A mind of unstoppable instinct, of crushing purpose, of an unspeakable purity born from unthinkable constraints.

She fought it. She tried to speak, to talk to 2I. To even make it aware that she was present, that she was there.

It already knew. It just didn't care. It had looked at everything she had to show it, all her memories and her beliefs and her fears, and it had not comprehended them at all. It rejected them as being devoid of any meaning, of any useful data. And then it was 2I's turn, and she experienced everything it knew, everything it was. A dark wave rolled over her, a crashing tsunami of sensations and impressions and desires, and she might as well have tried to hold back a flood by stretching out her arms.

The platform crumbled under Rao's feet. In normal gravity she would have stumbled and fallen a dozen times by now, but here even the slightest jump sent her flying high in the air. She raced left, then right, then—as the platform crumbled beneath her—reached out to grab one of the upright bars that curved up around her like ribs.

She jumped in the low gravity and managed to get to a piece of the platform that was still mostly intact. It was already cracking by the time she reached it, but she could see she was getting close to the end of the cage. The platform narrowed like a sternum as the bars flashed by on her right and left. She estimated she weighed no more than ten kilos at this point—how long before she weighed nothing at all, until she was floating free at the axis? And what would she do then? Floating in midair, would she have to flap her arms like a bird to keep moving forward? Would that even work?

As the platform rumbled underneath her, she stopped worrying about that. She looked up and saw nothing at all in front of her. She was clutching nothing but a jagged plinth of bone, sticking out into dark space.

She'd reached the end of the cage. Beyond her there was only darkness. She took a second to catch her breath and to move her light around, looking for her next move. The light easily reached the surface of the cone beneath her, and she expected to see the worms down there, clamoring for her flesh.

Instead she saw bare walls—stained everywhere with black slime. The same slime they'd seen in the other cone, so long ago now. The black corrosive slime that had eaten right through KSpace's high-tech ropes.

The stuff was thick and full of bubbles that grew enormous before they popped. Each time one of them exploded, the shower of droplets hung in the air for long seconds before falling back down. Rao knew, suddenly, what the slime was for—it was there to keep the worms away from the airlocks. To keep them from accidentally blasting themselves out into space.

Which meant—she was sure of it—that the south pole airlock was just that, an airlock, and that she could get it open. She could escape, if she could just get to it.

There was only one problem—there was nothing between her and that airlock but a couple of hundred meters of highly acidic slime.

She cried out in despair and frustration.

She was so close to getting out—to die here, after so much—

Eventually she recovered herself enough to start thinking again. There had to be something, something she could use to climb to the airlock. She swung her light around in big, desperate arcs, looking for anything.

And then she found it. She saw what looked like stones sticking out from the walls of the cone, boulders the size of houses, broken and weathered and shaped like—like—

Like teeth. She had found 2I's teeth. And she realized that once again she'd tried to impose human concepts and scales on 2I, tried to imagine it working like a spaceship when it was an animal, an organism. A creature with teeth. And the south pole airlock wasn't an airlock at all. It was 2I's mouth.

There was only motion.

Planets, stars, galaxies—always they turned, they rotated, revolved. Rocks tumbled between worlds, comets' tails twisted and braided in the stellar wind. The flow of charged particles swept through infinity. The endless howling cry of stars, the cold and ever-falling shafts of cosmic rays. There were eddies, vortices, currents, and that was all. Things changed over time, mutation and metamorphosis swirling across seconds hours centuries millennia, even on the scale of billions of years nothing stood still, nothing ever would.

Jansen had once, as a girl, lain down on her back at the top of a grassy hill, the sun red and veiny through the membranes of her closed eyes, and tried to feel the Earth turn and—though her father had told her it was impossible—yes yes yes she had felt it, she had felt the powerful sweeping avalanche of it, felt the hills and towns and cities and roads, people and cars and the great basins of the ocean falling away from her, Earth forever crashing over onto its back again and again forever forever—

In the quiet cold places between stars, 2I had felt the fabric of space-time itself stretch and groan. She'd felt the universe expand.

How could Jansen's ego compete? How could she hold on to herself in the shadow of this creature so much larger and older? She felt as if she'd climbed up the shoulder of a giantess and was exploring her ear canal like a lightless cave.

Yet Foster had been here before her, and Foster had found a way—a way to hold on to himself. To lift a voice recorder to his mouth and whisper what he'd seen, glimpses of something so large you could never take it all in at once. His ego had stretched that far. Had he thought 2I was going to make him rich? Had he thought it would earn him a promotion at KSpace if he managed to save Earth from its fate?

Earth—she had to remember what was at stake. She had to fight for the planet below.

If you go there you'll die! she screamed, and felt her lips tremble just a little, her throat shape the contours of words she couldn't hear.

Death?

Death was change. And everything changed.

But the people down there—everyone Jansen had ever known, the ones she liked, the ones she hated, the ones she loved: Roy McAllister and Chuy and Esmee and Hector, and Mary with her sympathetic eyes and Parminder Rao...if 2I didn't turn away from Earth all of them would be lost, everything they were, everything they might do would be thrown away—

Jansen was lifted by a great wind and carried backward in time, tossed between stars. She saw what 2I had seen. She saw the cold, quiet time. She saw a place where even space-time flattened out, the void itself. A place/time (what a meaningless distinction) with no gravity, nothing at all pulling on her. No heat, no light, just grains of dust, a handful of them in every cubic kilometer.

She lived through the long, slow, quiet time. Felt her heart beat just once in a thousand years, pushing fluids as sluggish as pitch through the remains of old and tattered veins. She felt the friction of time, felt it grind and grind until it had to scrape to a stop, it had to, and yet it never did. She felt the struggle that 2I had endured, the great, vast work of light-years, the effort of holding on, of being as patient as the wind that howled and beat against the canyon wall, and carved, in time, a graceful arch of stone.

Did the brief sparks of human lives compare? Could they?

These were not arguments. 2I wasn't trying to reason with her. It was showing her reality stripped bare. Reality in the way no human mind with its busy concerns and complexes and neuroses and aspirations could ever really see. These were the rules. You can't break the rules. You can't break the rules of thermodynamics, and you can't stop the worms from growing, from devouring you from the inside out. What folly to think otherwise!

2I was too big, and Jansen was too small.

She felt herself slipping away. Knew she couldn't win, that she was a raindrop falling toward the surface of the ocean. A moment wobbling in the air and then—and then—collision, the slightest ripple, and then she would be lost.

She let out one last howling scream.

And then she was gone.

It wasn't going to be easy.

The teeth were almost a hundred meters away. Between Rao and the teeth was a lot of black slime, and she was certain if she fell into it the stuff would burn right through her suit before she could climb out. That was assuming that when she hit the ground she didn't break both legs, or her neck, or fracture her skull. Sometimes being a doctor wasn't helpful, knowing just how fragile human bodies are.

It would have been an impossible jump in Earth gravity. Here it might, just might, be possible. If she launched herself through the axis, she thought that might increase her hang time.

Maybe.

It wasn't as if she had a lot of time to work out the math. The last of the platforms had crumbled away, splitting into pieces as if it had been perforated, as if it had been designed to collapse when the worms attacked. Which maybe it had. Rao knew that 2I had no intention of surviving its collision with Earth, that it was designed to fail at the end, so maybe a breakaway skull was part of the whole scheme.

She realized she was stalling. Procrastinating. It was now or never.

The ring of bone under her feet was already starting to crack. She got as much of a run-up as she could and threw herself into empty space.

And flipped ass over head, right away, as she screamed her way through the dark air. She was spinning, and she could feel the blood rushing out of her head as her feet swung crazily around her. If she wasn't careful she could pass out, she knew, and it would be hard to grab the teeth if she was unconscious.

She pushed her arms out as straight as she could, like an ice skater trying to slow down from a tight spin. It helped, she thought. A little, maybe. Her light flashed around the dark walls of the cone so fast it looked like a strobe.

Then she passed through the axis.

For a moment, a very, very short moment, she weighed nothing at all. At least her stomach didn't. Her head and her feet were still under the influence of gravity (not much, but still) and the tidal difference between her center of mass and her distal appendages was... was...

Stomach acid rushed up her throat. She clamped her mouth shut, forced herself to swallow. To open her eyes and look. To see if she was going to make it.

Or if she was about to die.

She saw the teeth looming up in front of her, huge and round. Getting bigger all the time. Her vision swirled as her brain tried to process whether she was falling toward them or flying up to them. It wasn't capable of knowing there was no difference—her brain wanted answers, damn it.

You're falling toward the slime, she told it. Because she was certain that was what was going to happen, that she was going to miss the jump.

Not by much. Maybe by meters, maybe less. She'd gotten the jump *almost* right. What a cruel joke. She fired her suit jets in a desperate attempt to push herself farther, but inside of 2I they weren't even strong enough to fight back against air resistance. She pushed her arms out in front of her, straining, trying to will them to grow longer. Desperately wishing that there were some rough spot on the nearest tooth, some projecting ledge that she might manage to catch at the last second.

But there was nothing that she could see. Her jittery light lit up just one tiny spot on one of the teeth now, and it looked as smooth and featureless as a stone wall.

You're going to miss it, she thought. *You're going to miss it.*

You're going to die here, after all this.

And the worst part was that she was moving so slowly now, falling so gracefully, that she had long seconds ahead of her to contemplate how it was going to end. To imagine the worst possible death.

I'm sorry, Commander Jansen, she thought. *I'm sorry I wasted this chance you gave me. I'm sorry, Mr. McAllister. You believed in me enough to make me an astronaut, and at the last second I let you down. I'm sorry, Sunny. I'm sorry I had to let you go. I'm sorry, Mom. I'm so sorry, Nani. I love you all.*

Her hand snatched at the tooth, her fingers curling, her arm stretching out as far as it possibly could, clamping down like a claw—

—on nothing but dark air.

Sally Jansen's body convulsed, deep in the sea of hands. Tendrils snaked across her face and her chest, dragged at her arms and her legs. She was encased in alien flesh, held in place and paralyzed.

Her lips still moved, but they couldn't form words. The tendrils burrowed through the tissues of her lungs and her larynx and her voice was gone. Her eyes were open but they saw nothing, there was no light and nothing to see. And yet—

It wasn't seeing. The images erupting in her head weren't pictures, instead they were mathematical equations, diagrams of particle interactions. Except even that wasn't right, because this was math without numbers. Math by instinct. She struggled but failed to find the right name for this new sense. There wasn't one. Call it a kind of sight, then, sight by metaphor. She saw through eyes that were not eyes. She saw—

the sun, not as light and heat, but a web of emanations. a trillion charged spears radiating out in every direction, particles that filled her wings and let her soar.

She saw—

the world below, not a ball of rock but a song of elements in composition, chromium, radium, nickel, iridium, so much carbon and nitrogen, water and free oxygen. an oasis in a desert light-years wide.

a perfect nursery for the children.

So close now, she could feel its gravity tugging at her, pulling her down. She had floated for so long and now she was falling, spiraling inward toward a final meeting.

Her life was almost over, and that was a thing to be wished for. The final operation in an equation: death as equal sign, quod erat demonstrandum. A conclusion.

Sally Jansen had had a dream once. A dream that had never come true. She could understand, oh yes, she understood so very well what it was like to want to reach the end, to want a thing to be done.

But that had been denied her, and it had warped her life. She'd tried, just like 2I, to make a journey to another world. She'd gotten so very, very close. And then it had been taken away from her.

She carried that bitterness inside her still. She always would. She had learned to pile life atop it, like a comforter on a lumpy bed. But still she slept in that bed every night.

That sorrow, that loss, was the only part of her now that still stuck out from the generalized consciousness, the smoothed-over combination of two minds. It was all that was left of her that she could call her own.

There was a kind of strength in that inability to fit in. A power in her difference. She did not choose to extend that power. She was not awake, as a human would measure such a thing. She was not expressing herself. That had been Foster's mistake, to think the pressure of human will might accomplish something here. Sally Jansen was no longer a rational actor. To focus on the rough spot on her being was not a decision. It was simply something that could not be ignored.

The grain of sand the oyster cannot spit out. So instead it grows a pearl around it, because it has no choice.

Her lips moved. She did not form full words, she could not. But still, her lips moved, just as Stevens's had.

Her lips pressed together in the middle. If she'd had breath in her body she would have pushed it outward in a dull, droning sound.

She—the larger she, of which Sally Jansen was just one small, irritating part—raged with frustration and thwarted desire. It had taken so long, so much, to come this far. Just because one tiny crumb of her vast soul rebelled, why should she change the great plan now? The microscopic part of her called Sally Jansen shouldn't be allowed to overpower the mind that had crossed space, the mind that had lived for eons, that had suffered in the cold and the empty to reach this place—

No. She couldn't allow this insignificant part to veto the will of the whole.

But Sally Jansen's lips kept moving.

No voice recorder, no matter how sensitive, could have picked up the sound she made. It existed only in her own head.

Where it echoed louder than cracking thunder.

Muh. Muh. Muh.

Rao fell.

With terrible slowness.

She closed her eyes. Why not? After all she'd seen, all the horrors she'd witnessed, why would she deny herself now the tiny comfort of not seeing her own death rush toward her?

She tried not to think about what it would feel like. She tried not to think at all. To clear her mind.

Then something touched her arm, and she shrieked in fresh terror. She bounced off a hard surface and the breath went out of her and she was silent. She swung wildly, like the bob on the end of a pendulum.

Inhuman fingers wrapped around her wrist and grasped her tight.

She opened her eyes slowly, so confused she could focus only on how fast her heart was beating. She looked up.

A white, shiny hand was holding her arm. Two other hands exactly like it clutched at the tooth, easily supporting her weight.

It was ARCS, the robot. It had caught her and kept her from falling.

She let out a noise that was half laugh, half gasp of utter surprise.

"Dr. Rao? Do you need assistance?" the robot asked.

She reached up and grabbed one of its three arms. In the minuscule gravity she was easily able to haul herself up onto the cracked top surface of the tooth.

"Thank you," she said, breath rushing back into her lungs. "Thank you."

"You're very welcome."

The robot had been sent down 2I's axis, where there was no gravity, so it could map the interior. Eventually it had crashed and stopped reporting. They'd thought it must have been destroyed.

Apparently not.

"Come on," she said. She held out one arm, and ARCS scampered up onto her shoulder like a monkey. She moved her light so it showed her the way forward. There were three rows of teeth—just as the worms had—nestled in concentric rows. She was light enough she could simply jump up to the second row, then the third.

And there, in the middle of the third row, was the south pole airlock. It looked much like the one at the north pole, the one they'd used to enter 2I, except smaller. The dome was no more than twenty meters across.

She remembered what Jansen had told her about how to operate these locks. Any pressure on the dome would cause it to rotate inward. She slapped the dome with her hand, felt it rotating under her palm. It started to turn almost immediately. Soon a rough, irregular opening appeared, sliding toward her. It came to face directly inward and then stopped. She climbed inside, her light splashing across the perfectly spherical interior.

She was suddenly spinning very fast. No. She'd been spinning, the whole time she was in the drum. She'd absorbed the angular momentum of that rotation. The airlock, on the other hand, wasn't spinning at all. She reached out for the walls and let friction slow her rotation, cancel it out.

Behind her she heard a series of loud cracks. She knew that had to be the sound of the buttresses snapping, the pillars that held up the cage of bone that was 2I's skull. She moved to the aperture and peered out, trying to see if the cage had finally fallen, if the worms had finally brought it down. Before she could see anything, however, the airlock rotated again, and she was cut off entirely from the interior of 2I.

Her breath sounded very loud inside her helmet. She felt a bizarre claustrophobia, even in that large, empty space.

"Dr. Rao," the robot said, "I'm a little concerned about your vital signs. Your heart rate and respiration suggest an extreme level of stress."

"Yeah," she said. "No shit."

The airlock stopped rotating. The aperture showed her not open space but a face of blank rock, stained dark red by cosmic rays. A ten-meter-wide seam ran across the rock—she remembered seeing it from the outside.

She pushed on it. Slapped at it with her hands. It was sealed tightly shut. How long ago had 2I closed its mouth? How many thousands of years ago?

She had no tools. No way to force it open. She chewed desperately on her lower lip. She could feel her eyes widening as she studied this new problem, this new thing that was going to kill her. If she couldn't get that seam open—

She heard rock crack and part, heard air sigh around her, ruffling the fabric of her suit. The noise rose to a terrible whistling roar and then gave way to stillness. The mouth opened, and she looked out and saw stars.

They looked exactly like the flashes of hallucinatory light she'd seen when she turned her suit lights off inside 2I. She couldn't trust them, those distant fires. She looked down at her suit's instruments and saw that she was in a near vacuum. She reached for the keypad on her sleeve and fired her suit's jets. Without air resistance to stop her, they were strong enough to push her out, through the opened mouth, out into space.

Almost instantly the stars went out, disappearing from the sky until she saw nothing but black emptiness before her. She started to weep because she'd known, she had been certain this was too easy, that she couldn't possibly have escaped.

Then something caught her eye and she looked sideways and saw a smear of white light, a curved bow of impossibly bright radiance from behind the superstructures on 2I's exterior hull, so bright it cast the spiky towers into flat silhouettes.

She wept until the tears formed pools across her eyes, until she couldn't see anything except that light, the light of the sun rising from behind the hull.

"Pasadena, this is *Orion*. This is...this is Parminder Rao. I'm out. I'm out."

Roy McAllister had his hands over his face. He looked through his fingers, up at the big screen.

He was back in the control room, surrounded by his people. Charlotte Harriwell sat in a swivel chair next to him. She drew in a deep breath.

McAllister realized he was holding his own.

"Acknowledged, *Orion*," he said. "Rao. It's just you?"

The neutrino telescope was no longer receiving a signal from inside 2I. The neutrino gun had been strapped to Jansen's suit, and when she'd entered the brain it had stopped transmitting. This was the first McAllister had heard from any of his people since then.

He'd almost forgotten how long it took to talk to *Orion*. It was nearly fifteen seconds before he got his reply.

"Affirmative, Pasadena."

On the screen he saw the view from Rao's helmet camera. He saw the superstructures of 2I pass beneath her, saw *Orion* floating ahead of her. Not far now.

His device vibrated against his ear. He touched it and saw he had a message from Kalitzakis.

HOLD/FIRE???

He stared at the message floating in the corner of his eye. It felt like forever since Kalitzakis had first asked, but then he realized it had been only a few minutes. He didn't answer the message immediately. "Dr. Rao," he called. "Did Jansen make contact?"

It took forever for the answer to come.

"I can't confirm it, but—I think so," Rao told him.

McAllister bowed his head. He wanted to weep.

"Sir?" Rao called. "Sir—my suit batteries are just about depleted."

He wanted to slap himself. "Acknowledged, Dr. Rao. Please return to *Orion* and prepare to return to Earth."

On the big screen, nothing had changed. Nothing at all.

He tapped his device and opened a connection to Kalitzakis. He started to type **FIRE AT WILL**. He hesitated before sending the message, however.

A smaller screen opened up before him and showed 2I's magnetic field. It was growing.

"Nguyen?" he asked.

The physicist jumped up out of her chair.

"What does that mean?" McAllister asked.

"It's—it's spreading its wings," she told him. "It's accelerating." She bent over her console to check something. McAllister gritted his teeth. When Nguyen figured out whatever she was trying to figure out, she looked up at him and almost whispered what she said next.

"It's accelerating away from Earth," she said. "On its current course it'll miss us by at least a million kilometers."

The room erupted in cheers. McAllister erased the message he'd been about to send and wrote a new one. **HOLD AND STAND BY**.

But there was a question, one that would bother him for days to come as they watched 2I swing around the Earth and head off on a new course.

Where the hell was it going?

PERIAREION

PARMINDER RAO: After we—after I got back, NASA decided to lift the secrecy around our mission, and the whole world learned about 2I. I can't speak to how that information will change humanity, or what people make of what we did and what we saw. I've seen the popular account of what happened, the stream book called The Last Astronaut, *and I wasn't impressed. Even in the good parts of it, the stuff based on actual data we recorded . . . there's a lot of speculation. There has to be, of course. Nobody can know what Jansen did, what she felt in those last moments. As a scientist I hate relying so much on what comes down to sheer guessing. The author of that book got in touch with me after I gave it a bad review that kind of . . . went viral. He asked if he could speak with me and figure out what he got wrong. He wanted to write a new edition of the book with better information. I'm hoping that by sitting down for this interview with him, I can set the record straight. If there's one thing I want him to put in his book, it's this: Sally Jansen was a hero. She didn't kill Blaine Wilson. She saved three people on Orion 6 the only way she could. She didn't kill Sunny Stevens. She couldn't have known what 2I was, not on her first expedition inside. And in the end she saved the world. I want the writer to make sure, when he tells her story, to get it right—all of it, even the sadness she kept from everyone, her sense of failure. But he'd also better make her look good.*

Three months later Roy McAllister left his office and walked across a tree-lined street to another building at JPL, one that used to house educational exhibits but now had been repurposed. There was a bored-looking guard standing by the door who just nodded at him, not even bothering to glance at his badge.

McAllister stepped into the building and through a decontamination airlock full of old dust. On the far side of the airlock was a small lobby—it made him think of the entrance to the neutrino telescope. The far wall of the lobby was made of thick glass, and it looked into a gleaming laboratory. He had to put on a pair of sunglasses—the walls, ceiling, and floor of the lab were painted a bright, glossy white, and the lights inside were turned all the way up day and night.

There was only one person inside the lab. Parminder Rao was seated in front of a large white work surface. Dozens of screens floated around her, showing medical imaging data. She was dressed all in white herself, and she was holding the wand of a handheld MRI. At that moment she was passing it very slowly over her cheek, over an old scar that had mostly healed.

"Roy! Good, you're here. I'm starving."

He smiled and held up the bag of food he'd brought her. Vegetarian wat stew and sour injera bread, from the best Ethiopian restaurant in the city. She had a working kitchen and a well-stocked pantry inside the lab, but whenever she wanted something special he brought it over by hand.

A smaller airlock was built into the glass wall. He placed the bag inside, then watched as it passed through to her side. She grabbed up the bag and dug into its contents. She never set the MRI wand down, though, and as she chewed on a piece of injera she ran it over her cheek again.

"I spoke with your doctors," he said. "They tell me there's no sign of necrosis or any foreign bodies." He placed a hand on the glass. "They say your quarantine can be over whenever you're ready to come out."

Rao glanced over at him. She didn't stop scanning. "I was exposed to an alien environment. We can't take any chances. If even a tiny piece of one of those tendrils got inside my wound—"

"I know, I know." He took his hand away from the glass.

"I'm the expert here. I'm the only person on Earth qualified to say whether I'm safe to leave this room."

"I know."

She looked down at the screen in front of her. It was a long time before she spoke again.

"Roy, I killed a man."

McAllister flinched. What did it have to do with her quarantine? He knew what to say in response, though. That was easy enough. "A lot of people would say you had no choice. Hawkins was crazy."

"Was he?" She looked him right in the eye. "If Jansen had rescued Foster and Channarong. If she'd tried to bring them back to Earth, even after they'd been exposed to 2I like that—would you have let her? *Should* you have?"

McAllister sighed. He was very glad he didn't have to answer that question. "They tell me the darkness affected all of you, psychologically. The stress of the mission, the harsh conditions—"

"I was there. I felt it."

"He was pushed past his limits. He snapped. You didn't." He scratched his chin. "Parminder... There are a lot of people out here who want to thank you. To shake your hand—"

He saw a shudder go through her small frame.

"—to let you know that what you did meant something. I hope... I hope that soon you'll be willing to come out of there and meet them."

She nodded and went back to her work. If she got lonely in there, she'd never given him any indication. She had plenty to do. She kept track of her medical data, of course, but she was also putting together a scholarly monograph on 2I and its life cycle. Whatever she wrote, it would automatically become the most important work ever published in the field of astrobiology, and it would cement her academic reputation for the rest of her life. She'd told him he could read it when it was done. When she had compiled and synthesized enough data.

He would do what he could to help her with that. Maybe when she finished she would come out of her glass room.

"I have something else," he said. "Some telescope data I think you'll want to see. It might help with your book." He reached up and touched his device, sending her a video file. She loaded it immediately, and they watched it together.

The video showed red sand and brown rocks, a desert landscape half-obscured by drifting dust. The sky in the video was a deep yellow—it had been just before twilight when this was taken.

"What is this?" Rao asked.

"2I set down this morning, about two a.m. local time. This was what happened next. As for what it means—I'm hoping you can tell me."

The camera passed over a broad valley between the rims of two craters. At first it showed only some scattered pieces of wreckage—broken chunks of stone a darker red than the surrounding soil. Pieces of broken superstructure from 2I's hull. Then a larger mass came into view. Most of the alien starship had survived the landing intact, though now it was half-buried in fine dust.

There was a rupture in the hull about halfway down its length, a crack that grew wider as they watched. A flow of what looked like pale liquid seeped from the opening. First just a trickle, then a steady stream, and finally a gushing eruption spilling out onto the planet's surface.

The view shifted as the telescope zoomed in, and Rao gasped as they saw that the flood wasn't liquid at all. It was a cascade of millions of worms emerging from the rupture, swarming over each other in their haste to get out of the corpse of their mother. They spread out in every direction from the crash site, many of them already burrowing their way down into the dirt.

"Oh, wow," Rao said. "Roy—"

"Hold on," he said. "And, um. Brace yourself."

The telescope zoomed in still further, focusing on the crack in the hull. As the worms continued to spill out from the darkened interior, something came into view, something that wasn't a worm. It was hard to see—the camera was at the absolute limit of its resolution—but it appeared to be a human figure in a white space suit.

The faceplate of the helmet had been shattered. Its pieces were held together by a thick growth of tendrils that completely obscured the figure's face.

Rao gasped. Roy McAllister had already seen this once. It still made his heart jump in his chest.

The figure seemed to take a good look around, then began to climb down the side of the wreck, down toward the red soil. Its left leg swung uselessly beneath it, but it moved with a lithe grace all the same.

Before it could reach the ground the video ended, the telescope having lost its fix on the red planet.

Mars. Sally Jansen had always wanted to go to Mars.

AUTHOR'S NOTE AND ACKNOWLEDGMENTS

The depiction of NASA and of human spaceflight circa 2055 in this novel is an intentionally pessimistic one, purely because that fit the needs of the story. I make no claim to be a futurist, and this book should not be taken as a prediction of future events.

NASA continues as of this writing to make incredible discoveries in the depths of space and to carry out missions of enormous scientific importance. Despite constant budgetary wrangling and a capricious public attitude toward space, NASA represents the absolute best in human nature and shows an unflagging commitment to science and exploration. It is also important to note that, in 2019, there are a lot of very talented, very passionate people working to make sure that human spaceflight remains a priority for the administration. If humans do ever go to Mars, it will be because of the hard work of these astronauts, scientists, and administrators.

In the course of writing this book, I was honored with the chance to speak with two actual astronauts. Without exception it was an inspiring experience, and I am truly grateful for their time and their generosity of spirit. Anna Fisher, who was one of the earliest female astronauts (and who went through astronaut training while pregnant!) helped me understand what it means to live and work in space—not just the mechanical and factual details but what it feels like to actually be there. I owe her a great debt.

The other astronaut I spoke with asked not to be named here—a decision I fully respect. They have my gratitude.

I would also like to thank Megan Sumner at NASA's Johnson Space Center, and Andy Turnage of the Association of Space Explorers, for all their help.

No book reaches the printing press without a team of people working very hard on its behalf. I would like to express my thanks to my agent, Russ Galen, my publicist, Ellen B. Wright, and to Alex Lencicki (always). Fred Van Lente helped me talk through some of the plot complications, and find the thread when it was hard to see.

While most books are shepherded toward publication by one editor, this one saw no less than three: Will Hinton, James Long, and Priyanka Krishnan. All of them provided creative input and worked very hard to bring order to my chaos. This book would not exist without them.

Finally I would like to express my endless thanks and love toward my wife, Jennifer. Whenever I am in danger—as I often was while writing this—of tumbling off into the infinite, cold void, Jennifer is my tether, my personal life support system, always there to pull me back to safety, light, and warmth.

David Wellington
New York City
2019

extras

www.orbitbooks.net

about the author

David Wellington is an acclaimed author who has previously published over twenty novels in different genres.

Find out more about David Wellington and other Orbit authors by registering online for the free monthly newsletter at www.orbitbooks.net.

if you enjoyed
THE LAST ASTRONAUT

look out for

VELOCITY WEAPON

by

Megan E. O'Keefe

The last thing Sanda remembers is her gunship exploding.

She expected to be recovered by salvage-medics and to awaken in friendly hands, patched up and ready to rejoin the fight. Instead she wakes up 230 years later, on a deserted enemy starship called The Light of Berossus – or, as he prefers to call himself, 'Bero'.

Bero tells Sanda the war is lost. That the entire star system is dead.

But is that the full story? After all, in the vastness of space, anything is possible . . .

CHAPTER 1

THE AFTERMATH OF THE BATTLE
OF DRALEE

The first thing Sanda did after being resuscitated was vomit all over herself. The second thing she did was to vomit all over again. Her body shook, trembling with the remembered deceleration of her gunship breaking apart around her, stomach roiling as the preservation foam had encased her, shoved itself down her throat and nose and any other ready orifice. Her teeth jarred together, her fingers fumbled with temporary palsy against the foam stuck to her face.

Dios, she hoped the shaking was temporary. They told you this kind of thing happened in training, that the trembling would subside and the "explosive evacuation" cease. But it was a whole hell of a lot different to be shaking yourself senseless while emptying every drop of liquid from your body than to be looking at a cartoonish diagram with friendly letters claiming *Mild Gastrointestinal Discomfort*.

It wasn't foam covering her. She scrubbed, mind numb from cold-sleep, struggling to figure out what encased her. It was slimy and goopy and—oh no. Sanda cracked a hesitant eyelid and peeked at her fingers. Thick, clear jelly with a slight bluish tinge coated her hands. The stuff was cold, making her trembling worse, and with a sinking gut she realized what it was. She'd joked about the stuff, in training with her fellow gunshippers. Snail snot. Gelatinous splooge. But its real name was MedAssist Incubatory NutriBath, and you only got dunked in it if you needed intensive care with a capital *I*.

"Fuck," she tried to say, but her throat rasped on unfamiliar air. How long had she been in here? Sanda opened both eyes, ignoring the cold gel running into them. She lay in a white enameled cocoon, the lid removed to reveal a matching white ceiling inset with true-white bulbs. The brightness made her blink.

The NutriBath was draining, and now that her chest was exposed to air, the shaking redoubled. Gritting her teeth against the spasms, she felt around the cocoon, searching for a handhold.

"Hey, medis," she called, then hacked up a lump of gel. "Got a live one in here!"

No response. Assholes were probably waiting to see if she could get out under her own power. Could she? She didn't remember being injured in the battle. But the medis didn't stick you in a bath for a laugh. She gave up her search for handholds and fumbled trembling hands over her body, seeking scars. The baths were good, but they wouldn't have left a gunnery sergeant like her in the tub long enough to fix cosmetic damage. The gunk was only slightly less expensive than training a new gunner.

Her face felt whole, chest and shoulders smaller than she remembered but otherwise unharmed. She tried to crane her neck to see down her body, but the unused muscles screamed in protest.

"Can I get some help over here?" she called out, voice firmer now she'd cleared it of the gel. Still no answer. Sucking down a few sharp breaths to steel herself against the ache, she groaned and lifted her torso up on her elbows until she sat straight, legs splayed out before her.

Most of her legs, anyway.

Sanda stared, trying to make her coldsleep-dragging brain catch up with what she saw. Her left leg was whole, if covered in disturbing wrinkles, but her right... That ended just above the place where her knee should have been. Tentatively, she reached down, brushed her shaking fingers over the thick lump of flesh at the end of her leg.

She remembered. A coil fired by an Icarion railgun had smashed through the pilot's deck, slamming a nav panel straight into her legs. The evac pod chair she'd been strapped into had immediately deployed preserving foam—encasing her, and her smashed leg, for Ada Prime scoopers to pluck out of space after the chaos of the Battle of Dralee faded. She picked at her puckered skin, stunned. Remembered pain vibrated through her body and she clenched her jaw. Some of that cold she'd felt upon awakening must have been leftover shock from the injury, her body frozen in a moment of panic.

Any second now, she expected the pain of the incident to mount, to catch up with her and punish her for putting it off so long. It didn't. The NutriBath had done a better job than she'd thought possible. Only mild tremors shook her.

"Hey," she said, no longer caring that her voice cracked. She gripped either side of her open cocoon. "Can I get some fucking help?"

Silence answered. Choking down a stream of expletives that would have gotten her court-martialed, Sanda scraped some of the gunk on her hands off on the edges of the cocoon's walls and adjusted her grip. Screaming with the effort, she heaved herself to standing within the bath, balancing precariously on her single leg, arms trembling under her weight.

The medibay was empty.

"Seriously?" she asked the empty room.

The rest of the medibay was just as stark white as her cocoon and the ceiling, its walls pocked with panels blinking all sorts of readouts she didn't understand the half of. Everything in the bay was stowed, the drawers latched shut, the gurneys folded down and strapped to the walls. It looked ready for storage, except for her cocoon sitting in the center of the room, dripping NutriBath and vomit all over the floor.

"Naked wet girl in here!" she yelled at the top of her sore voice. Echoes bounced around her, but no one answered. "For fuck's sake."

Not willing to spend god-knew-how-long marinating in a stew of her own body's waste, Sanda clenched her jaw and attempted to swing her leg over the edge of the bath. She tipped over and flopped face-first to the ground instead.

"Ow."

She spat blood and picked up her spinning head. Still no response. Who was running this bucket, anyway? The medibay looked clean enough, but there wasn't a single Ada Prime logo anywhere. She hadn't realized she'd miss those stylized dual bodies with their orbital spin lines wrapped around them until this moment.

Calling upon half-remembered training from her boot camp days, Sanda army crawled her way across the floor to a long drawer. By the time she reached it, she was panting hard, but pure anger drove her forward. Whoever had come up with the bright idea to wake her without a medi on standby needed a good, solid slap upside the head. She may have been down to one leg, but Sanda was pretty certain she could make do with two fists.

She yanked the drawer open and hefted herself up high enough to see inside. No crutches, but she found an extending pole for an IV drip. That'd have to do. She levered herself upright and stood a moment, back pressed against the wall, getting her breath. The hard metal of the stand bit into her armpit, but she didn't care. She was on her feet again. Or foot, at least. Time to go find a medi to chew out.

The caster wheels on the bottom of the pole squeaked as she made her way across the medibay. The door dilated with a satisfying swish, and even the stale recycled air of the empty corridor smelled fresh compared to the nutri-mess she'd been swimming in. She paused and considered going back to find a robe. Ah, to hell with it.

She shuffled out into the hall, picked a likely direction toward the pilot's deck, and froze. The door swished shut beside her, revealing a logo she knew all too well: a single planet, fiery wings encircling it.

Icarion.

She was on an enemy ship. With one leg.

Naked.

Sanda ducked back into the medibay and scurried to the panel-spotted wall, silently cursing each squeak of the IV stand's wheels. She had to find a comms link, and fast.

Gel-covered fingers slipped on the touchscreen as she tried to navigate unfamiliar protocols. Panic constricted her throat, but she forced herself to breathe deep, to keep her cool. She captained a gunship. This was nothing.

Half expecting alarms to blare, she slapped the icon for the ship's squawk box and hesitated. What in the hell was she supposed to broadcast? They hadn't exactly covered codes for "help I'm naked and legless on an Icarion bucket" during training. She bit her lip and punched in her own call sign—1947—followed by 7500, the universal sign for a hijacking. If she were lucky, they'd get the hint: 1947 had been hijacked. Made sense, right?

She slapped send.

"Good morning, one-niner-four-seven. I've been waiting for you to wake up," a male voice said from the walls all around her. She jumped and almost lost her balance.

"Who am I addressing?" She forced authority into her voice even though she felt like diving straight back into her cocoon.

"This is AI-Class Cruiser Bravo-India-Six-One-Mike."

AI-Class? A smartship? Sanda suppressed a grin, knowing the ship could see her. Smartships were outside Ada Prime's tech range, but she'd studied them inside and out during training. While they were brighter than humans across the board, they still had human follies. Could still be lied to. Charmed, even.

"Well, it's a pleasure to meet you, Cruiser. My name's Sanda Greeve."

"I am called *The Light of Berossus*," the voice said.

Of course he was. Damned Icarions never stuck to simple call signs. They always had to posh things up by naming their ships after ancient scientists. She nodded, trying to keep an easy smile on while she glanced sideways at the door. Could the ship's crew hear her? They hadn't heard her yelling earlier, but they might notice their ship talking to someone new.

"That's quite the mouthful for friendly conversation."

"Bero is an acceptable alternative."

"You got it, Bero. Say, could you do me a favor? How many souls on board at the present?"

Her grip tightened on the IV stand, and she looked around for any other item she could use as a weapon. This was a smartship. Surely they wouldn't allow the crew handblasters for fear of poking holes in their pretty ship. All she needed was a bottleneck, a place to hunker down and wait until Ada Prime caught her squawk and figured out what was up.

"One soul on board," Bero said.

"What? That can't be right."

"There is one soul on board." The ship sounded amused with her exasperation at first listen, but there was something in the ship's voice that nagged at her. Something…tight. Could AI ships even slip like that? It seemed to her that something with that big of a brain would only use the tone it absolutely wanted to.

"In the medibay, yes, but the rest of the ship? How many?"

"One."

She licked her lips, heart hammering in her ears. She turned back to the control panel she'd sent the squawk from and pulled up the ship's nav system. She couldn't make changes from the bay unless she had override commands, but…The whole thing was on autopilot. If she really was the only one on board…Maybe she could convince the ship to return her to Ada Prime. Handing a smartship over to her superiors would win her accolades enough to last a lifetime. Could even win her a fresh new leg.

"Bero, bring up a map of the local system, please. Light up any ports in range."

A pause. "Bero?"

"Are you sure, Sergeant Greeve?"

Unease threaded through her. "Call me Sanda, and yes, light her up for me."

The icons for the control systems wiped away, replaced with a 3-D model of the nearby system. She blinked, wondering if she still had goop in her eyes. Couldn't be right. There they were, a glowing dot in the endless black, the asteroid belt that stood between Ada Prime and Icarion clear as starlight. Judging by the coordinates displayed above the ship's avatar, she should be able to see Ada Prime. They were near the battlefield of Dralee, and although there was a whole lot of space between the celestial bodies, Dralee was the closest in the system to Ada. That's why she'd been patrolling it.

"Bero, is your display damaged?"

"No, Sanda."

She swallowed. Icarion couldn't have…wouldn't have. They wanted the dwarf planet. Needed access to Ada Prime's Casimir Gate.

"Bero. Where is Ada Prime in this simulation?" She pinched the screen, zooming out. The system's star, Cronus, spun off in the distance, brilliant and yellow-white. Icarion had vanished, too.

"Bero!"

"Icarion initiated the Fibon Protocol after the Battle of Dralee. The results were larger than expected."

The display changed, drawing back. Icarion and Ada Prime reappeared, their orbits aligning one of the two times out of the year they passed each other. Somewhere between them, among the asteroid belt, a black wave began, reaching outward, consuming space in all directions. Asteroids vanished. Icarion vanished. Ada Prime vanished.

She dropped her head against the display. Let the goop run down from her hair, the cold glass against her skin scarcely registering. Numbness suffused her. No wonder Bero was empty. He must have been ported outside the destruction. He was a smartship. He wouldn't have needed human input to figure out what had happened.

"How long?" she asked, mind racing despite the slowness of coldsleep. Shock had grabbed her by the shoulders and shaken her fully awake. Grief she could dwell on later, now she had a problem to work. Maybe there were others, like her, on the edge of the wreckage. Other evac pods drifting through the black. Outposts in the belt.

There'd been ports, hideouts. They'd starve without supplies from either Ada Prime or Icarion, but that'd take a whole lot of time. With a smartship, she could scoop them up. Get them all to one of the other nearby habitable systems before the ship's drive gave out. And if she were very lucky…Hope dared to swell in her chest. Her brother and fathers were resourceful people. Surely her dad Graham would have had some advance warning. That man always had his ear to the ground, his nose deep in rumor networks. If anyone could ride out that attack, it was them.

"It has been two hundred thirty years since the Battle of Dralee."